THE WINDHAVEN SAGA

The great Bouchard family legacy began with one man, Lucien Bouchard, a man of vision and courage. He made claim to this land and to his heritage with the building of the stately mansion, *Windhaven Plantation*.

Windhaven Plantation and the Bouchard dream are shaken to their very roots, their very existence threatened as the first tremors of the Civil War reverberate across the land. Fathers and sons, mothers and daughters will soon see their love and loyalties put to the test of fire as the *Storm Over Windhaven* rages.

But Windhaven survives the private battles of a proud family and the terrors of a vicious war. The Bouchards are forced to move West, to Texas, and, in this rugged, untamed country, battle for survival against Indians, border bandits, and cattle rustlers. The Bouchards meet the challenge in *The Legacy of Windhaven*.

★ ★ ★

And now Marie de Jourlet brings us another towering novel, a blazing saga of the South during the Reconstruction years. The Civil War is not yet forgotten—its bitter aftermath will wreak havoc for generations to come. Luke Bouchard, who entrusts Windhaven Range to his son, Lucien, emerges as a new and vigorous man after the loss of his wife, Lucy. Starting life over in New Orleans, he becomes involved in a passionate struggle to win a young woman's heart and to regain an old, but not forgotten, plantation, so that the Bouchard family can one day *Return to Windhaven*.

The Windhaven Saga:

Windhaven Plantation
Storm Over Windhaven
Legacy of Windhaven
Return to Windhaven

RETURN TO WINDHAVEN

Marie de Jourlet

PINNACLE BOOKS • **LOS ANGELES**

RETURN TO WINDHAVEN

Copyright © 1978 by Book Creations, Inc.

An original Pinnacle Books edition, published for the first time anywhere.

Produced by Lyle Kenyon Engel

First printing, December 1978

ISBN: 0-523-40348-8

Cover illustration by Bruce Minney

Printed in the United States of America

PINNACLE BOOKS, INC.
2029 Century Park East
Los Angeles, California 90067

Admiringly dedicated to Marla Engel,
a magnificently gifted editor and
wonderfully gracious human being.

Acknowledgments

I wish to express my grateful thanks to those
who provided vital documentary data for this
book so that the historical account could be strictly
accurate. Herewith, an expression of my sincere
appreciation to Roseanne McCaffrey, Assistant Cu-
rator/Research Coordinator, The Historic New Orleans Collection, New Orleans, Louisiana; Renee
Peck, Curatorial Assistant, The Historic New Orleans Collection; Rose Lambert, Librarian, Louisiana Historical Center, Louisiana State Museum,
New Orleans, Louisiana; Philip D. Rich, whose apt
and timely suggestions helped solidify the basic
plot; Mrs. Doris Samuels, typist-transcriber, who,
with her background as a schoolteacher, contributed many valuable suggestions and—unlike
most transcribers—eliminated tiny, bothersome mis-
takes before they could see manuscript print. Also,
my heartfelt thanks to Fay Bergstrom, whose help
in typing the last part of the manuscript proved a
Godsend.

—Marie de Jourlet

PROLOGUE

It was only thirteen months after the final drama of the Civil War at the Appomattox Courthouse. Yet to Luke Bouchard, that short span of time seemed a veritable lifetime.

In a little more than a year, the Bouchards had endured change and adversity, and had made courageous progress. This included Luke himself, the fifty-year-old grandson of that indomitable pioneer Lucien Bouchard, who had left Normandy at the time of the French Revolution to seek freedom and land on which to bring forth bounteous harvests.

Luke had suffered tragedy in the death of his gentle wife, Lucy, who had died during a raid by the bandit leader Diego Macaras, while trying to save Carla and Hugo, children of their son, Lucien Edmond, and his young, chestnut-haired wife, Maxine. Maxine, a Baltimore girl, had captured

Lucien Edmond's heart with her intelligence and femininity. Luke was proud of his son—a young man as serious and dedicated to purposeful work and personal integrity as Luke was himself.

Thirteen months. . . . In that short time Luke had seen Windhaven Plantation burned by vindictive Union troops. The majestic red-brick chateau with its twin towers, located on the Alabama River near Lowndesboro, Alabama, had seemed indestructible. Yet it had been ravaged. But the towering red bluff that framed it, where his grandfather and his Creek wife, Dimarte, lay side by side in their eternal sleep, had remained untouched.

After the fire, Luke had gathered together his family, with the help of his courageous stepmother, white-haired Sybella Forsden. They had been joined by Maybelle Bouchard (Lucy's younger sister, who had married Luke's greedy, unscrupulous half-brother, Mark), Lucien Edmond and his family, and Mara (Lucien Edmond's sister). Arabella, Luke's half-sister, had come with her family—her husband, James Hunter, and their children, Melinda and Andrew—as had Maybelle's daughter, Laurette, who was now married to Charles Douglas and had twin sons, Kenneth and Arthur.

Accompanied by Djamba, his wife, Prissy, and their son, Lucas, as well as by a half-dozen loyal black workers from Windhaven Plantation, the Bouchard clan had traveled to New Orleans. There Luke had visited his friend and banker John Brunton. Through John and his fiancée, Laure Prindiville, Luke had been able to obtain the transfer of the legacy in gold that his grandfather had wisely secured for him in an English bank. He bought wagons, arms, and ammunition, and then the family set out on the trek that would lead them to the land near Carrizo Springs, on the Nueces River in southeast Texas, which would become Windhaven Range.

But Laure, piqued by Luke's seemingly indomitable morality and his unswerving devotion to his family, had tempted him into a single act of infidelity, only a week before her marriage to John Brunton. The consequences of that one lapse would alter the entire destiny of the Bouchards.

Charles and Laurette Douglas left the entourage in New Orleans. They would go on to Chicago, where Charles would manage a department store. Arabella and James Hunter and their children accompanied the Bouchards as far as Galveston, where Arabella's husband would become a sales factor for his cousin's cotton mill. The others took a steamboat to Corpus Christi. There began an arduous, sometimes seemingly endless trek toward the verdant valley where the dream of Windhaven Range would become a reality.

Only one member of the Bouchard clan was missing in this postwar reunion: lovely, red-haired Fleurette had gone to Richmond to work as a volunteer nurse. There she had met and fallen in love with Ben Wilson, a Quaker who was then a corporal in the medical corps. They had married and returned to Ben's home in Pittsburgh, where he would become a doctor.

Luke, thanks to his grandfather's legacy, had been able to buy eight thousand acres of land near

Carrizo Springs. His workers built a ranchhouse, a bunkhouse, and a stockade that encircled this new Windhaven home and provided defense in case of attack. In New Orleans, Luke had met Andy Haskins and Joe Duvray, who accompanied the family on their long journey, along with Simata, a "redbone" scout, half Kiowa and half black. Simata had taught Luke the languages of the Kiowa and the Comanche, and Luke, by saving the life of Kitante, son of the powerful Comanche chief Sangrodo, had assured the safety of Windhaven Range.

Throughout all this, Luke had managed to maintain his somewhat mordant sense of humor. He was often wryly self-critical and therefore capable of holding up his own errors to the light and critically analyzing them. It was this ability, he realized, which had allowed him to alter his course when necessary, without succumbing to the dark and bitter despair that had gripped him when Windhaven Plantation had burned.

Thirteen months. . . . During that time Lucien Edmond had proved himself to be resourceful and responsible by leading the first Bouchard cattle drive to Santa Fe. Luke knew that his son could ably meet the challenges of this new frontier. Lucien Edmond was zealously dedicated to his father's and great-grandfather's precepts. His seriousness was tempered, however, by youthful impulsiveness. This, combined with an easygoing gregariousness, had at once endeared him to the vaqueros of Windhaven Range. It was even possible, Luke realized, that Lucien Edmond's outgoing temperament might make him better suited to the task of running Windhaven Range than Luke himself with his more reserved personality.

Because of his son's newly discovered maturity, Luke's long-held dream of regaining Windhaven Plantation had crystallized. He had begun to plan to return one day to the land where his grandfather had founded a dynasty so closely united in love and peace and ambitious toil that not even the separation of hundreds of miles could diminish their loyalty to one another.

Now, on this late May afternoon in 1867, Luke prepared to start on his journey. He had received a letter from Laure, telling him that John Brunton had died of yellow fever, and also informing him of the birth of a son, whom she and John had called Lucien in honor of Luke's grandfather. Luke knew that his course was clear. That child was assuredly his. Now that Lucy was dead and Laure was a widow, honor demanded that he marry her and give little Lucien the Bouchard name. One day, if God so willed, the child might fulfill the ultimate destiny of the Bouchards.

It would not be easy, Luke realized. He was twice Laure's age, and her capricious, independent nature would shun an approach on the grounds of condolence or the offer of a comfortable sinecure. He would have to woo her, overcome her initial impression of him as a careful, logical man who was dull and stodgy.

But he had burned his bridges behind him. He had told Sybella, Lucien Edmond, and Mara about Laure's letter, and had confessed to them that he and Laure had been lovers for one blind, unreasoning hour. He was sure that the child was his, he had told them, and he had resolved to go back to New Orleans and marry her, if she would have him, and ultimately return with his new family to Windhaven Plantation.

After that conversation he had gone to his room, dressed in buckskins, and taken his leave of his family and loyal workers. Having said his good-byes, he rode off toward the south.

In his mind's eye, he could see Windhaven Plantation as it had been before the fire. The portico over the doorway was an exact replica of the one at the chateau of Yves-sur-lac in far-off France—his grandfather's birthplace. He envisioned the spacious kitchen set in the rear of the chateau and separate from the house. He could almost taste the hot biscuits and honey that Mammy Clorinda had so often given him as a boyhood treat. Closing his eyes, he saw the meandering waters of Pintilalla Creek, which marked the northern boundary of old Lucien's land. A shed had housed the cotton gin, near the wharf where steamboats had docked, to carry the cotton down to the counting house in Mobile. Most of all, he remembered the splendid twin towers, and how he had often climbed the stone stairway of the southern tower, holding on to his grandfather's hand. Now, as he rode away from Windhaven Range, as he glanced back to catch a last glimpse of the stockade, which faded in the distance, it seemed he could hear once more his grandfather's voice, repeating the stories to which he had listened in awed silence as a young boy.

Luke dragged himself away from his reminiscences. All that, he told himself, had taken place long ago, even though it was as fresh and vivid in his mind as if it had happened yesterday. He told himself that one day—God grant it might not be too far off—he would take that same trail back to Windhaven Plantation. . . .

Luke Bouchard

Laure Prindeville Brunton

The Bouchard

Edwina Bouchard 1868~

Hugo Bouchard 1861~ III IV V

Kenneth Douglas 1865~ III IV V

Joy Hunter V 1869~

Andrew Hunter 1854~ III IV V

Arthur Douglas 1865~ III IV V

Howard Douglas 1867~ IV V

Melinda Hunter 1852~ III IV V

Charles Douglas 1835~ III IV V

Sybella Wilson 1868~ IV V

Jimmy Belcher 1853~ III IV V

Connie Belcher 1855~ III IV V

Laurette Bouchard 1837~ III IV V

James Hunter 1822~ III IV V

Arabella Bouchard 1824~

Millie (deceased) III

Maybelle Williamson 1820~ III IV V

Mark Bouchard 1819~1864 III

Henry Belcher 1821~ III IV V

I Windhaven Plantation
II Storm Over Windhaven
III Legacy of Windhaven
IV Return to Windhaven
V Windhaven's Peril

RON TOELKE 1978 Op.IX

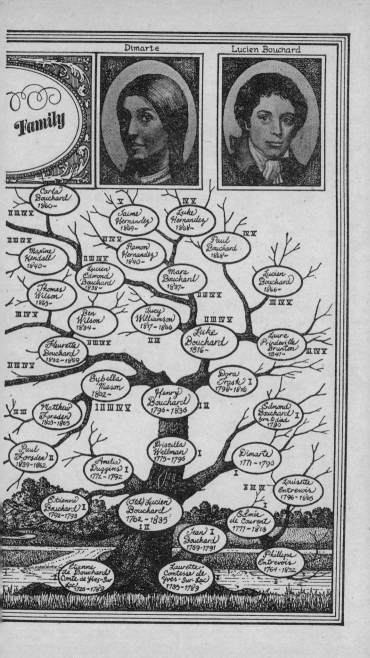

Dimarte   Lucien Bouchard

Family

Carla Bouchard 1860~
III IV V

Jaime Hernandez 1869~
V

Luke Hernandez 1868~
IV V

Maxine Kendall 1840~
III IV V

Ramon Hernandez 1840~
III IV V

Paul Bouchard 1868~
IV V

Lucien Edmond Bouchard 1938~
II III IV V

Mara Bouchard 1837~

Lucien Bouchard 1866~
III IV V

Thomas Wilson 1865~

Ben Wilson 1834~
II III IV V

Lucy Williamson 1817~1866
III

Luke Bouchard 1816~

Laure Prideville Brunton 1841~
III IV V

Fleurette Bouchard 1832~1869
II III IV V

Sybella Mason 1802~
III IV V

Henry Bouchard 1796~1836
II

Dora Trask I 1798~1816

Edmond Bouchard born & died 1790

Matthew Forsden 1803~1865
II III

Priscilla Wellman 1775~1795
I

Dimarte 1771~1790
I

Paul Forsden II 1839~1862
II

Amelia Duggins I 1772~1792

Louisette Entrevois 1796~1865
III IV

Etienne Bouchard I 1792~1793

(Old) Lucien Bouchard 1762~1835
I II

Edmée de Courent 1771~1816
I

Etienne de Bouchard Comte de Yves-Sur-Lac 1725~1789

Jean I Bouchard 1769~1791

Laurette Comtesse de Yves-Sur-Lac 1735~1789

Phillipe Entrevois 1764~1832

Return to Windhaven

CHAPTER ONE

Against the sullen blue of a cloudless sky, the setting sun hung like a bloody orange, dappling the sky with brooding tinges of purple and orange and red far in the west. Along the shallow bed of the Nueces River, a lone rider sat erect in his saddle, his pale blue eyes contemplative of the darkening horizon around him. A month past his fiftieth birthday, he was tall, wiry, his blond hair silvered in a wide streak down the middle, and there was a touch of gray as well to his short, pointed beard. He was dressed in the buckskin jacket and breeches that Catayuna herself had fashioned and given him as a parting gift before she had accompanied her husband, the Comanche chief Sangrodo, across the Rio Grande to sanctuary.

The reins in his left hand, his right touching the great jagged turquoise set in silver that Sangrodo's

1

war chief, Ipiltse, had hung around his neck as a talisman, Luke Bouchard rode slowly eastward. He was following the trail that he had taken barely a year ago from Corpus Christi.

Luke turned to look back a last time, but already the hacienda had disappeared in the distance. Darkness was falling swiftly this late May evening, and the only sounds were the soft splash of the gently flowing river and the querulous call of nightbirds seeking to settle in their roosts. There was no wind. It had been an oppressively hot day and there was an unearthly stillness all about him. Now that he was alone, his thoughts turned to the quest ahead of him. Was this trip really a desire to escape the anguish of the present, the despair of knowing that Lucy was dead and half his lifetime had ended with her passing? Or was it an unswerving urge borne of nostalgia and deepest love that turned his thoughts back toward the winding Alabama River and the towering red bluff where his grandfather and his family were buried?

There was all that and more, Luke Bouchard knew well. There was a debt of honor to be paid to Laure Brunton, and that must come first. John Brunton was dead of the yellow fever that perennially plagued the Queen City, and his own wife was buried near the hacienda he and his son and his workers had energetically constructed. Both duty and honor demanded that he see to the welfare of Laure and to the son he believed to be his own. This same code of honor had impelled his grandfather to repay the Creeks for their bounty long years ago.

Luke was leaving the valley. To his right was

2

the serpentine river that had been a guiding mark last year from Corpus Christi to the final site of the new Bouchard holdings. Even with the coming darkness he could make out the profusion of tall, yellowish reeds, as high as a man's head, and before him lay the rolling prairie, grotesquely ornamented with the shadowy outlines of pecan, elm, and oak trees, and huge clumps of mesquite with white hanging pods as large as rifle bullets. The soil near that winding river, which would be his constant marker until he reached the port of Corpus Christi, was a glossy black, but soon it would be sandy red. The hills and the canyons were far beyond him now, and there was nothing but isolation and silence and the elemental awareness of the earth and the sky.

The very immensity of the silence and gathering darkness made him reflective, as if he were entering a church, a stranger there, with no friend or neighbor in the other pews. Hearing only the sound of his horse's hooves against the sun-baked ground, he felt immersed in the timelessness of the land, which remained unsettled and was as starkly primitive as it had been since the beginning. On one side of his saddle, his Spencer repeating rifle was sheathed in a leather scabbard; in his saddlebags were provisions—a tinderbox, blankets, and a large leather canteen. He drew the roan stallion to a halt, dismounted, and took a long swig from his canteen to cool his parched throat, then led his horse toward the shallow bed of the river and let him quench his thirst. By following the river on his return to Corpus Christi, he would not lack for water. This knowledge reminded him of old Lucien's journey from Mobile to Econchate. His grandfather, a lonely wanderer like himself now, had followed a river also, to find his ultimate destiny.

The howl of a distant coyote broke the unearthly stillness of the night. Instinctively Luke Bouchard put his right hand to the belted sheath of his hunting knife, a blade of tempered steel, which Djamba had had the New Orleans blacksmith make for him along with spears and lances fabricated out of some of the old balcony ironwork that he and the Kiowa scout Simata had discovered in an abandoned mansion in the Queen City. As he touched the handle of the knife, he recalled his grandfather's story of how he had had to kill an enraged she-bear with just such a knife, because his musket had failed him. His pony had been disemboweled by the bear's viciously raking claws, and old Lucien had, despite the cruel wound he had sustained, removed those claws and brought them with him to the Creeks, to prove his courage.

How rich, how unending were these memories of the past! He gratefully allowed them to fill his mind now, since they furnished sustenance against the loneliness of his journey. To dwell upon them too lengthily, however, was too much the attitude of a man who has reached the end of his life and seeks comfort in retrospect. Instead, Luke felt himself on the threshold of a venturesome new life, to which he would devote all the resources of his finely honed mind and strong, vigorously disciplined body. Drawing a deep breath, he mounted and headed the stallion eastward once again.

A little after midnight he came to a row of steep

4

hills flanked with mesquite and topped with irregular crests of flowering cedar. The darkness hid the beauty of the flowers, but he remembered them from last year. He could just make out the outlines of abandoned Indian adobe huts, which years of sun had crumbled long after their dwellers had left the land.

His aching muscles told him it was time to make camp. Tethering the horse to one of the smaller cedar trees, Luke Bouchard unpacked his saddlebags, spread out a thick blanket on the hard ground near one of the adobe huts, and kept another for protection against the chill of the night. He made a small fire, cut off a sizable strip of dried salted beef, and roasted it on a stick; this and another swig of water comprised his meal. Then, after giving his horse several handfuls of oats, which he had packed in a small doeskin sack, he stretched out on the blanket, drew the other one over him, and fell into deep and instant sleep.

In the midst of that sleep, brought on both by physical exhaustion and by the emotional stress of having bidden farewell to his son and all those others dear to him, Luke Bouchard dreamed. He saw himself standing in front of the red-brick chateau, supervising a crew of well-paid white and black workers who were repairing the damages caused by the fire set by General Wilson's troops. In sleep, his lips curved in a smile of satisfaction as he saw himself walking out onto the rich land and instructing his foreman on the growing and harvesting of various crops. He would carry out all the experiments he and his grandfather had planned so many years ago. This time they would become reality and

5

bring a new meaning to the uneasy peace that had
followed the cessation of the Civil War. Golden-
haired Laure was there beside him, with little Lucien. He saw himself turning away from the
foreman to greet Laure, stooping to lift his son in
his arms, and gesturing to the rich land that
stretched beyond, the land of Windhaven, the land
of new promise and hope for the future, the life-
giving land that rewarded the devotion of unremit-
ting work, honesty, and love. . . .

The ten Kiowa braves and their chief, Setangya,
had hunted all day but found little to take back to
their lodges—only a very small deer and three wild
rabbits that were almost too lean for the cooking
fires. They had come forty miles from their no-
madic village in the north. Several of the younger
braves attempted to persuade their chief to ride
across the border and raid one of the drowsy little
Mexican villages. But Setangya, a stocky, taciturn
warrior of nearly sixty years, had shaken his head
and said gruffly, "The signs are not good, and there
are too few of us. Let us turn back to our village.
If the gods are good, we may find the buffalo or
fatter game."

The younger braves grumbled but did not dis-
sent; his leadership was acknowledged by all the
scattered Kiowa tribes. He was one of the chiefs
who, with the Comanche leaders, had signed a
treaty with the United States in 1865 reserving for
them the Texas Panhandle and sundry other lands.
In defiance of that treaty, Texans kept insisting on
the complete expulsion of all Indians, and Setangya had led many battles against raiding parties of

6

white settlers who sought to exterminate his people. In one of those raids his only son had been killed. He glanced back now from his gray mustang, his lips tightening and his dark eyes clouding with grief and anger as he saw the glow of a distant campfire.

"Ho, Setangya, some white-eyes makes a fire." Kugarto, the youngest and tallest of the braves, pointed toward the south. "Before the sunset, I saw the trail of one who rides tall in the saddle—it must be he. Before we turn back, shall we not kill the white-eyes? He may be one of those who brought death to your son."

"It is so," Setangya agreed. Lifting his feathered lance, he gestured toward the south. "We will follow the trail to where the fire burns. When it has gone out and when the white-eyes sleeps, we will make his sleep endless and take his horse and weapons. Perhaps it will make up for the bad luck we have had with game this day."

They rode swiftly till they came within a mile of Luke Bouchard's camp. By then the fire had gone out. A sudden wind stirred the clumps of mesquite as the Kiowas dismounted and crept toward the adobe hut in front of which Luke Bouchard lay.

The wind had driven heavy, ominous clouds over the full moon, and now there was no light. Unsheathing his hunting knife, Kugarto crept toward his intended victim. His teeth bared in a rictus of savage blood-lust, he waited breathlessly as he heard Luke Bouchard sigh in his sleep, then crept closer till he knelt beside him.

As he lifted his knife to strike, the moon came

7

from behind the clouds and its rays touched the jagged turquoise in its silver mounting.

"Stop! Hold your blade, Kugarto!" Setangya whispered urgently, extending his lance in a gesture of command. "He bears the talisman of Sangrodo, the mighty Comanche chief. Such a man is not our enemy but our friend, as we are friends to the tribe of Sangrodo!"

"But he is a white-eyes," Kugarto protested, still holding his knife over Luke Bouchard's heart.

"Rebellious son of a mongrel, have I not spoken? Am I not your chief? I will bring you death more swiftly with my lance than you can bestow it with your knife, and well you know it, Kugarto! No, he who wears the talisman must not die at our hands."

"But perhaps he has stolen it, Setangya," argued the obdurate young brave.

Dismounting, the elderly chief bent down and with a reverent gesture touched the turquoise and then the forehead of the sleeper. Luke Bouchard woke, sat up, and stared at the painted Kiowas surrounding him. Instinctively he raised his hand to the great turquoise and cupped it in his palm, then looked up at Setangya and said in Comanche, "It is the gift of Sangrodo, chief of the Comanches, who calls me Taiboo Nimiahkana."

"Kugarto, put down your knife and show respect for the talisman of a great chief," Setangya angrily commanded.

With a smile, the Kiowa chief again touched the turquoise and Luke's forehead, then said haltingly in the Comanche tongue, "Sleep now. Dream good dreams which the Great Spirit shall send to you.

No harm shall come to you. I and my warriors will guard you till you break your camp."

"The Kiowa chief is kind. I thank him," Luke Bouchard replied, again in the Comanche tongue.

Setangya gestured with his lance. The braves dismounted, tethering their mustangs to nearby cedar trees. Then, with two of them standing guard, the others joined Luke Bouchard in sleep. From afar, well beyond the deserted adobe huts, there came the soft hoot of a desert screech owl.

CHAPTER TWO

He woke to the fierce warmth of the noonday
sun, blinking his eyes to shield them from the sudden glare. Squatting before him was the old Kiowa
chief, his dour wrinkled face wreathed in an understanding smile. He saw now that Setangya's hair
was white, but the long braid that hung down his
back had been blackened with charcoal. Thrust
through the very top of the braid where it was
drawn away from the scalp was a black crow's
feather. Slowly Luke Bouchard placed his palms on
the blanket and forced himself upright, wincing at
the muscular twinges that reminded him that his
restorative powers were not what they once were.
Then he smiled wryly, admitting his age to himself,
and Setangya's answering smile deepened as he declared, "You, whom the Comanches call Taiboo
Nimiahkana are the first white-eyes in many a

moon whom I have not watched begin the sleep of death."

"I thank you for my life, then, Setangya, and for watching over me while I slept. And I ask your pardon for having kept you so long—"

"Ho, there is no need for that. When I was the age of the brave who sought to take your life last night, I had no patience with sleeping. Hunting and raids and the stealing of swift horses for my people kept my eyes from closing. Aiyee, though your weight of years is not so great as mine, nor can your sorrow touch mine, of that I am certain"—here the old Kiowa extended his left hand and touched the graying streak in Luke Bouchard's hair—"our bodies no longer leap to do our bidding."

"That is true, Setangya. You spoke of grief—no man on this earth, whether he be white or red, is ever free from it. I have mine. And yours?"

For a long moment Setangya studied Luke Bouchard's sensitive, inquisitive face. Then he said softly, still in the Comanche tongue, which he spoke with the thick and almost guttural accent of the true Kiowa, "Your eyes are shrewd to have known the meaning of the crow's death feather in my braid, oh Taiboo Nimiahkana. Many moons ago my young son and I went on a raid against the white-eyes who had driven away our buffalo and who killed even our most peaceful braves whenever they came upon them hunting in the brush. After the sun bleached my son's bones, I vowed to keep them with me always on a horse, so that my son's departed spirit could ride with me to bring

11

vengeance upon the white-eyes who drove us from our hunting ground."

He turned to gesture at the rows of crumbling adobe huts, and said with a bitter smile, "Once this was a village of my people when we were at peace upon the land. But the white-eyes could not bear to see us living in peace, and when they drove us from this ancient stronghold, the old shaman summoned a curse upon it so that no enemy white-eyes should remain alive once he had taken shelter here. The young braves do not remember such stories, but I heard them as a child from my father's lips when he sat at the council fire. But you, Taiboo Nimiahkana, you who have come to the land of the Kiowa and the Comanche, why do you now go back to where you came from?"

"Because, Setangya, a shaman of the Comanches said that it was decreed that I should go back to the land of my birth after the death of my squaw."

"Then you and I, Taiboo Nimiahkana, who have both known the deepest sorrow a man can bear, will go together on your journey."

"I would not ask my Kiowa brother to give up his hunting and make a journey that will take the rising and setting of at least seven suns." Luke Bouchard squatted now to face the Kiowa chief, extending his hands with the palms turned upward in a sign of friendship and truthfulness. It was Sangrodo, he remembered, who had taught him the universal sign language.

"You speak with a straight tongue, and the talisman of Sangrodo's tribe is not lightly given, least of all to a white-eyes. I would learn more of the man whom Sangrodo honors. It is new and strange for me to come upon a white-eyes who speaks so well the tongue of the proud people of the plains. I would know more of that shaman's prophecy, for my own medicine man has told me that we Kiowas shall not remain much longer upon our land. Already those who come with wagons and the long guns to settle here hate us and wish us destroyed. They seek to move us into what they call Indian Territory."

"That is so, my brother," Luke gently agreed. "It was so in the days of my grandfather, when the mighty Creeks of the distant south, who were then the rulers of the winding rivers and the forests, were forced from the land they had held long before the white man came across the seas."

Setangya nodded and uttered a deep sigh, then placed his hands, palms down, on Luke's. "Do you go back to the land of your birth because you feel pity that we are to be turned away from our homes?"

"I would not lie to my Kiowa brother. I came to that valley to the south, where your braves found my trail, and with my family and my workers I built a cattle ranch to provide meat for the other settlers as well as for the people of Sangrodo's village. It was he who protected me and mine from the border bandits and those whom they call comancheros, who are traitors to all men."

"This I have heard," Setangya replied solemnly. "But, a few moons past, around our campfire it was said that when the great Sangrodo left his stronghold with his braves to go hunting, the soldiers of the white-eyes came upon the stronghold and slaughtered his people."

13

"That is true."

"It is said also that Sangrodo avenged that treachery through the help of a white-eyes—"

"I did but little, Setangya. When I came to that valley I brought with me a Kiowa scout, Simata, whose own father was a chief among you."

"He was the son of a black woman whom the chief Pinamente—Great Hunter—made his squaw. He and his squaw were called by the Great Spirit before I lost my son."

"Before I came to the valley, Simata had told me much about the Kiowas and the Comanches, and thus it was that I vowed to become a friend to them, to thank them for letting me come upon their land. It was Simata who led the warriors of Sangrodo toward the *Cañón de Ugalde* so that the soldiers who murdered the women and children of Sangrodo's village would be forced to do battle with men, not the helpless and the aged."

"Hearing this from your lips, Taiboo Nimi-ahkana, brings a new joy and wonder to my old heart. I have not met many white-eyes like you. Perhaps if there were more, we Kiowas and the other tribes of the great plains could live in peace. In another summer or so more soldiers will come, so many that we cannot stand against them—except to die in courage and honor—and drive us like snarling mongrel dogs from the campfires they will build throughout this hunting land. But now let us share our food with you. Then I and Kiminato, the youngest son of my half-brother, who is almost as dear to me as was my own lost son, will go with you to the end of your journey. My other warriors

14

will return to our village with news of this meeting between us."

"I am honored by my brother's concern for me. But that journey will be no farther than Corpus Christi, where I will board the boat with paddle-wheels to take me to the city of New Orleans."

"Then it will be there that I shall say farewell. And when I return to my village, I will tell my people that the ranch in the valley far beyond belongs to your family and that no harm is to come to them." Setangya sighed again, then shook his head. "But even now the tribes of our people must move always to the north away from those who hunt us. And it is beyond my power to promise that there may not be some tribe, even among the Kiowas, who will feel only anger and hate for all white-eyes."

"I will gladly share food with you as a sign that there is friendship between us." Luke Bouchard, seeing the Kiowa chief rise to his feet, emulated him. With a hoarse cry, Setangya embraced the tall grandson of old Lucien Bouchard, and the two men stood united in a bond of almost mystic understanding and compassion.

By noon of the eighth day, Luke Bouchard, Setangya, and Kiminato had left the desolate level ground with sporadic clumps of mesquite and cottonwood scrubs, and come within sight of the range of low bluffs at the outskirts of the port of Corpus Christi.

"We go no farther, Taiboo Nimiahkana." Setangya held up one hand as he reined in his mustang with the other. "It would not be well for the white-eyes to see you ride with a Kiowa chief and his warrior. They would call you Indian-lover, and they might well try to kill you as they would us, without stopping to ask why the three of us ride together."

"There is sorrow in my heart, my brother. What you say is true. I pray to the Great Spirit that one day all men will live together and understand one another as you and I do, Setangya," Luke responded, his eyes fixing on the creased face of the old chief.

Setangya shook his head. "I have prayed for that since I was a young warrior and first learned the ways of the white-eyes, Taiboo Nimiahkana. But I do not think it will come to pass in my lifetime or yours. What I have learned is that good land makes men greedy. They take it, by battle or theft or lies, and it matters not at all to the takers whom they drive forth from what they seek to own, even if the women and children and the old and the sick are turned out of their homes."

"Yes, Setangya. You remember the stories I told you of my grandfather these past nights. When you and I made camp together. He and I saw the soldiers take the Creeks from their homes and drive them like cattle to the west."

"It will be so with us before many more summers have given way to the biting winds and the blinding snow, oh Taiboo Nimiahkana. I did not need the words of our shaman to tell me so. I have felt it since my son was taken from me." Setangya turned to look at the leather bundle strapped to the back of the black lead stallion. "Yet our meeting was good. I have learned that there is at least

16

one white-eyes who does not hate his red brothers."

"And for me it was good also, Setangya, and you and Kiminato have made my journey less of a burden. Now as we part ways, I ask you to take this small gift in remembrance of our friendship." Luke Bouchard unstrapped the sheathed hunting knife at his waist and offered it to Setangya.

The old chief smiled as he took it from Luke's hands. "I will keep this knife to remind me that a white-eyes has been blessed by the Great Spirit and can walk among us without hate or fear. And so that you will remember me when you are back in the land of your birth, I give you this in return."

Setangya removed from his own waist a wampum belt, ornate with shells and black, yellow, and red beads, and handed it to Luke. "It is the wampum of friendship, oh Taiboo Nimiahkana. We Kiowas use it also as your people use pieces of gold and silver. If ever you should return—and if the shaman's words do not come true and we are still upon this land—you have only to show it to a Kiowa, even if he is your enemy, and he will know that you are a friend. With this and the talisman of the great Sangrodo, your life will be protected always."

Luke Bouchard held the wampum belt in his hands and inclined his head in sign of grateful acceptance. "It is a priceless gift, Setangya. I will keep it with me always. And now a gift to Kiminato. He is a strong young warrior, and with this long rifle, which fires many times without reloading, he will become the mightiest hunter of all your people." He turned to the wide-eyed young

17

Kiowa who rode at his other side and handed him the Spencer.

"You do not fear to go without weapons back into that town and to the end of your journey, my brother?" Setangya asked.

Luke Bouchard shook his head. "I shall find no enemies in Corpus Christi. And once the boat with the paddlewheels takes me back to New Orleans, there I shall settle for a time, before I return to the red bluff that was once the domain of the *Mico* of Econchate. To you both, I wish good hunting, long years, and peace upon the land."

"Would that you were our shaman and your wish might come true," Setangya replied, his eyes suddenly brooding as he looked back along the trail. "Ho, *subeti, wisukaah!*" ("Now this is all, I am sad to say farewell.")

For a long moment he stared into Luke Bouchard's eyes; then, suddenly sidling his horse closer to Luke's, he extended his hand and touched the latter's cheek in a gesture of deep affection. Then, as if ashamed at so impulsive and sentimental a gesture, Setangya wheeled his horse toward the west, drawing the reins of the black stallion, which carried his son's bones, and rode off at a canter back along the trail followed by Kiminato.

Luke Bouchard turned in his saddle to watch them go. Already the thick dust of their horses' hooves began to obscure them, and the glare of the midday sun added its opaque haze.

As he rode down the dusty main street of the little town, Luke could see that the passing of a year had done little change to it. Perhaps there were more shacks, and several more false-front stores, none of which was over one story tall, but the harbor was still as desolate, and the grayish wood of the shacks was even drearier under the blazing sun, with no trees or other foliage to shade them. There were more loading docks, made of the same unpainted, sunbleached wood. Then his eyes brightened and he uttered a cry of joy, for at the main dock was the very same packet that had brought him from New Orleans just a year ago. Stevedores were loading cargo, supervised by the querulous, bearded little Scotsman who had been both guide and friend on that initial journey.

Spurring his horse to a canter, he reached the dock and dismounted. The steamboat captain, who had his back to him, cupped his palms to his mouth to bawl, "Avast, you stupid landlubbers! Careful with that crate now, it's worth more than the wages of all of you for a year!"

"Then it must contain a spinet piano or kegs of good rum, Captain," Luke Bouchard sallied.

Captain Jamie McMurtrie whirled, scowling, and said to the interloper, "Dammit, sir, it's none of your business. But the fact is, it's full of salted beef, bound for Galveston. And now if you don't mind, I'll get on with loading my ship."

"Could you be persuaded to take a passenger and his horse, Captain?" Luke asked, smiling.

Captain McMurtrie tugged at his beard, his bushy eyebrows arching as he scanned the buckskin-clad man before him. "Aye," he agreed at last, grudgingly, "if you've the money for passage for both of you. We pull up anchor tomorrow morning at the tide. Where are you bound for?"

19

"Where you found me a year ago, Captain. I see you've still the same fine packet, named after that hero of whom Robert Burns wrote so eloquently, 'Scots whi hae with Wallace bled,'" Luke prompted.

The captain again scanned Luke's smiling face. "By the eternal, I know you, but I can't place you—"

"It's the beard and the buckskins, Captain," Luke interposed. "Also, I had a few more horses with me when you brought us from New Orleans to this lonely port."

"Of course, of course—Mr. Luke Bouchard! Now you're leaving Texas, are you?"

"Just myself and my stallion, Captain McMurtrie. I'd like to book passage to New Orleans."

"Are you going back there for a visit?"

Luke shook his head. "No, Captain McMurtrie. My wife, Lucy, was killed in a bandit raid on our ranch, and I'm going to New Orleans to look after the wife and son of my best friend there, who died of yellow fever a few months ago."

Captain McMurtrie took off his braided cap and shook his head. "I am grieved to hear about your wife, Mr. Bouchard. I remember all of you, and I told myself when you went aboard that I'd never met a closer-knit family, nor more loyal workers to go along with you. I'm deeply sorry about your wife, Mr. Bouchard."

Luke Bouchard clasped the bearded Scotsman's hand and nodded understandingly. "We had a long, happy life together, and I'll always cherish the memory of her.

"But to tell you the truth, Captain, I've a notion

to go back to that chateau on the Alabama River where my grandfather first started, to see if I can make something of it now that the war is over. People will need food and clothing, and maybe I can help produce those things and we can all get back to serious work again and forget the hatreds of war."

"I'll say amen to that, Mr. Bouchard. Say now, what about that Mrs. Forsden—you see, my memory's coming back. The white-haired gracious lady who seemed to be such a comfort to the others on the trip from Galveston on here."

"Yes, my stepmother, Sybella Forsden. She's proved to be an intrepid pioneer woman in the best tradition. You know, we all learned to shoot rifles and pistols on the range back in New Orleans before we came out to this wild country. Well, she helped rout the leader of those bandits, putting a rifle ball in his shoulder."

"Damn my soul, she didn't! Why, that's wonderful, Mr. Bouchard! I wish I could tell her how much I admire her. I got to know her real well last year, and I told myself that here was a lady of real quality."

"Your judgment of people is as impeccable as your navigation, Captain McMurtrie," Luke declared.

Suddenly, as the thought struck him, Luke said, "You've cargo for Galveston—will you be stopping there long?"

"Two days."

Luke was pleased, for it meant that he would have a chance to visit Arabella and her family.

Opening his saddlebag, he took out a leather

pouch and from it several gold pieces, which he handed to the captain. "Will this cover passage for my horse and myself to New Orleans?"

"Of course it will, Mr. Bouchard. We haven't many passengers this trip back, to tell the truth. And I'd be mighty obliged if you'd honor me with your company at dinner in my cabin during our journey."

The two men shook hands, then Luke led his roan stallion up the gangplank and down into the hold of the *William Wallace*.

CHAPTER THREE

"Mama, Mama, come quick, there's an Indian here!" Melinda Hunter squealed. Having seen Luke Bouchard in buckskin garb, she had promptly slammed the door of the rambling two-story frame house.

"Melinda, whatever is the matter with you? The very idea—an Indian at our door indeed!"

Nonetheless, pretty, black-haired Melinda, dressed in white linen with tasseled belt, shrank behind her mother, her hazel eyes huge with apprehension, as Luke Bouchard's half-sister calmly opened the door. And then it was Arabella's turn to stare, at first not recognizing the tall, sinewy man before her.

"Oh, my goodness! Whom were you looking for—" she began.

"For you, Bella. Leastways, I was told that the

23

Hunters lived here on Darden Street, in one of the nicest houses. And unless my eyes deceive me, that's my cute little niece Melinda peering out at me from behind you."

"Uncle Luke! Oh golly, I never in the world would have known you, not with that beard and those clothes you got on!" Melinda scrambled around her mother and flung herself into Luke's arms, standing on tiptoe to give him a big hug. Stroking her head, he chuckled, then kissed her on the tip of her upturned nose.

"Now then, may I come in, or are you still afraid of an Indian raid on this house?"

"Oh, Luke dear, please do come in. You mustn't mind us—it's one of our usual domestic squabbles when James isn't home and I have to put up with everything. Andrew has managed to get the pony and won't give it up, and Melinda has been close to tears all morning."

"I have not, Mama," Melinda countered indignantly, her creamy cheeks flushing with embarrassment. "Young ladies like me don't cry, do they, Uncle Luke?"

"Not unless there's a very good reason, and I don't suppose having to wait your turn on the pony is really serious enough for that, honey."

Melinda promptly seized one of his hands, Arabella grabbed the other, and Luke allowed himself to be led into the attractively furnished living room. He leaned back on a thickly stuffed settee.

"I just made lunch for the children a little while ago," Arabella said, smoothing her blue cotton skirt as she carefully seated herself on a chair opposite Luke. "Would you like some cold chicken and coffee? I made some syllabub for their dessert, and there's plenty left."

"I'd welcome the chance to sample your culinary skill, Bella. I haven't had a chance to enjoy it since all of us left Alabama."

Arabella giggled, unfurling a lacquered fan and waving it briskly to hide her nervous excitement over her half-brother's unexpected visit. "I'm not really a fancy cook and you know it. James seems to be satisfied, though, and that's all that matters. But out here in Galveston we don't have the wonderful fruits and vegetables we had back at Windhaven."

"Well," Luke said, "maybe in a few years you'll be able to enjoy them again, when you and James and the children pay me a visit."

Arabella stared at him. "What do you mean by that, Luke? Are you going back to Alabama? I thought you and Lucy were settled on Windhaven Range by now."

"Lucien Edmond and Maxine are still there, with Carla and Hugo. And Maybelle's remarried to a widower with two children. Lucy was killed a few months ago, when bandits raided the ranch."

"Oh, Luke dear, I'm so terribly sorry!" Arabella declared, putting out her hand to him in a gesture of compassion. "Why, that's just dreadful!"

"She died saving little Carla, and she was spared pain. It was God's will, and I'll admit that was one of the reasons I thought seriously about going back to Alabama. The other—" He glanced at Melinda, who was sitting attentively on the edge of her stool beside her mother, hands folded in her lap, not wanting to miss a single word of the adult conversation. "Let's go have a looksee at how Andrew's doing on the pony. Then I'd like to see you ride, Melinda honey."

"Oh, thank you, Uncle Luke!" Melinda nearly squealed with joy as she sprang up from the stool.

"You go ahead out to the yard, Melinda. Uncle Luke and I will come out just a bit later."

Melinda hesitated, torn between her eagerness to replace Andrew on the pony and wanting to eavesdrop on the grownups' conversation. Arabella leaned over and applied a quick maternal spank. "You heard me, missy! Out to the yard with you. But don't get bossy with Andrew. Remember, you're older than he is, and you're supposed to be a young lady."

"Oh, very well." Melinda, affecting an adult tone, drew herself up solemnly, then gave Luke an enchanting little curtsy. "Don't be too long, please, Uncle Luke. I can hardly wait to have you see me ride!" Then, blowing him a kiss, she disappeared.

"What an irrepressible little minx that girl is becoming!" Arabella said with a sigh. "The novelty of Galveston is beginning to wear off for the children, I'm afraid. Cousin Jeremy and his wife and children have been wonderful friends and neighbors to us, but I think Melinda and Andrew are beginning to grow a bit restless.

"But you haven't finished telling me all your news, Luke. Are you really going back to Alabama for good?"

"That's the way I'm thinking now. You see, back in New Orleans, John Brunton arranged to have a black freedman buy the chateau and fifty acres of land. I had told him to try to get it back and keep it for me. The time isn't yet right to march in and take up where Grandfather and I left off. There's still too much hate between the North and the South, and this Reconstruction program, with the carpetbaggers using blacks as tools to humiliate the Southern whites, is going to keep sectional differences very heated for all of us.

"John Brunton married that blond young woman, Laure Prindeville—you remember I told you and James how I had to arrange to buy my weapons from that double-dealing Captain Soltis at the brothel that Laure ran for John?"

"Yes, of course I remember."

"Bella, I'd as soon you didn't tell James what I'm about to tell you. But you and I grew up together, you're my half-sister and very dear to me, so I can confide the secret to you."

"You know I'd never give away a secret of yours, Luke."

"John Brunton died of yellow fever soon after Laure gave birth to a son. I know the son to be mine—you see, Bella, just before John married Laure, she and I made love. I swear I was faithful to Lucy all the years of our marriage, till that one time. But—well, it happened. And now that I'm a widower, the honorable thing for me to do is to provide for her and the son I'm sure is mine."

"Luke, what you've just told me shows how very human you are. You've nothing to be ashamed of. I know that Lucy, God rest her soul, would never have held it against you."

"She never knew about it. I tried to put it out of my mind, and I think I could have, except that John died about the same time Lucy did, and then

I had this letter from Laure telling me about her son; she named him Lucien, after our grandfather."

Arabella grasped him by the shoulders and gave him a quick kiss. "You're very dear to me, Luke. And even though I loved Lucy as much as I love you, you and your Laure and little Lucien have my blessing in whatever you do."

"Thank you, Bella. As I said, I can't think of going back to Alabama right away. Once I get to New Orleans and see Laure and the baby, I'll have to decide how to bide my time till it's possible to rebuild the chateau and rework the land. Lucien Edmond did so well on the range, I've no fear at all for his future. He's already proved he can stand on his own, and it will be good for him to have that responsibility from now on. Out on the frontier, Bella, you grow up fast, believe me." With a rueful smile, he reached up and touched the streak of gray hair. "I'm fifty now, and I don't know how much time I have left, but I don't feel old at all, and this is my new challenge. Now, let's go see the children and the pony, shall we?"

The yard was spacious, with a small white gazebo at the very back. James Hunter had spaded up a kind of bridle path in a wide circle between the back porch and the low fence that partitioned off the last third of the yard, which was devoted to Arabella's lavish flower beds. There were even ivy vines entwining the white trellises of the gazebo. Luke stood entranced, remembering not only Sybella's floral cultivation back at Windhaven Plantation, but also Lucy's flowerbeds around the old Williamson house. A narrow gate in the middle of the white-planked fence permitted entry to this charmingly idyllic garden spot.

"It's like a breath of home, Bella," he said.

Melinda, impatiently awaiting their arrival, now ran toward her curly-haired brother, who was tugging on the reins, urging the placid beast to move faster.

"Now you just stop, Andrew, it's my turn now!" Melinda exclaimed. She reached out to seize the bridle and tried to bring the pony to a halt.

"Melinda, let go this instant!" Arabella stamped her foot, with a worried glance at Luke. "You might hurt yourself—the pony could bolt and throw your brother—"

"I don't care if it does! Mama, make him get off and let me ride!" Melinda quite forgot her sense of superiority at being fourteen to her brother's twelve, and stamped her foot in turn, her face flushed with anger.

Luke laughed as he came forward and eased the bridle from Melinda's grasp. "Let me take over, honey," he suggested. "Andrew, how'd you like to see a real Indian wampum belt?"

But the boy's attention was focused on the gleaming turquoise that hung about Luke's neck. "Gosh, Uncle Luke, what's that big blue rock?" He stretched a hand out toward it.

"I'll let you see it, and the belt too, if you'll get down and let your sister have a ride," Luke bargained.

"Sure I will!" The boy's light blue eyes glowed with delight as he vaulted from the saddle with all the expertise of a veteran equestrian. Luke took off the rawhide thong to which Sangrodo's talisman was fastened and looped it around the boy's neck. Fascinated, Andrew touched the silver-mounted stone, then glanced up at the tall man standing before him. "Where did you find that, Uncle Luke?"

Melinda, also momentarily spellbound by the magnificence of the jagged blue jewel, forgot the pony as she pushed up close against her brother to get a good look. "Oooh, it's beautiful, Uncle Luke! It must have cost lots 'n lots."

"Nothing so far as money is concerned," Luke answered gravely. "It was a gift of friendship from a Comanche chief. Each of us had done the other a service, and it was his way of wishing me good luck for the future. And the wampum belt was a gift from a Kiowa chief who rode with me on my journey from the ranch to the harbor of Corpus Christi."

"Can I try on the wampum belt now, Uncle Luke, can I?" Andrew persisted, taking off the turquoise and handing it back to Luke.

Luke allowed him to wear the wampum belt for a few minutes. Then, doubtless wanting to show his own generosity after having been permitted to hold these two extraordinary gifts, Andrew turned to his sister and declared, "I guess you can go ahead and ride Toby now, Melinda. I've had enough. I'd lots rather have Uncle Luke tell me stories about the Indians. Will you, Uncle Luke?"

"Melinda, you be very careful now, and don't you dare ride any other way except side-saddle," Arabella chided. "Andrew, if you want your uncle to tell you stories, come back into the house while I fix him a bite of lunch."

"Thank you, Arabella. But first let me help Melinda onto Toby. Andrew, bring me the side-saddle," Luke said as he came forward.

After changing the saddle and helping Melinda onto the pony, Luke followed Arabella and Andrew back toward the house. Arabella, however, did not go in without taking a last look back at her precocious daughter. Turning to Luke, she shook her head and declared, "If I'd let her, she'd act like a tomboy and ride that pony astride—would you believe it, Luke? I caught her once doing just that, and she had her skirt all the way up so that her pantalettes were in full view. It was a good thing the neighbors weren't out in the yard at the time. I declare, children can be such a botheration as they get older!"

"You know you don't mean that, Arabella, not really," Luke replied as he opened the kitchen door for her and gestured to Andrew to follow. "All the same, I think Sybella would be very proud of you, and as soon as I get to New Orleans I'm going to write her a nice long letter and tell her how I found you and the children."

"Oh yes, do remember me to Mama!" Arabella exclaimed, clasping his arm and squeezing it.

"She's been able to adapt herself very well to the new frontier in Texas," said Luke as he seated himself at the kitchen table, despite his half-sister's remonstration that as an honored guest he belonged at the formal dinner table. "You remember how expert she was with the rifle when we were practicing back in New Orleans? Well, she helped drive off some Mexican bandits who tried to bushwhack us as we were traveling from Corpus Christi to Carrizo Springs in the wagons. She wounded the

31

leader in the shoulder, and when he came back with stronger forces to attack the ranch, she set an example of courage for us all."

"My goodness, you mean Mama actually shot someone?" Arabella asked in amazement.

"With good aim, too. By the way, she told me to wish you and James and the children every happiness. I'm sure she'd welcome a letter from you."

"Oh yes, as soon as you've gone I'll start writing it, I promise!"

Although it was after five o'clock in the afternoon, the sun beat down relentlessly on the dusty streets of Galveston as Luke Bouchard made his way back to the dock where the *William Wallace* was anchored. He had wound a red calico bandanna around his forehead to protect him from the oppressive glare, tying it at the back of his head much as an Indian might. His contemplative walk through the town had shown him how it flourished in contrast to the bleakness of Corpus Christi. There was a theater, even a small opera house, and the stores showed a far greater variety of goods and services. Yet, once Texas cattle found a market by rail, as perhaps in Kansas or Nebraska—and he was convinced that this was imminent—Corpus Christi would certainly rise in prominence. He thought fondly of Lucien Edmond and made a mental note to write to him, as soon as he reached New Orleans, about the cargo Captain Jamie McMurtrie was carrying. Beef, brought in by a rancher near Corpus Christi; only two hundred and fifty head, but still it was a hopeful sign for the future. The people would always need food.

As he neared the dock he was halted by a sudden shout from behind him: "Hey there, you a damned comanchero or Injun, mister?"

Turning in surprise, Luke saw a bulky, bearded man in his mid-forties, leaning against the post of a saloon, a holstered pistol strapped at his left side, an angry scowl on his swarthy face.

"Neither one, sir, neither one," Luke called pleasantly, and made to turn back in the direction he intended.

"Not so fast, mister!" the bearded man snarled, lurching forward, his eyes squinting, his right fist clenched. "Come up closer. I got no truck with Injuns or them damned white traitors that sell guns and whiskey to the red devils. Hell, they killed my wife, Rachel, a year ago, and I ain't likely to forget."

"I'm sorry for your loss, sir, but I assure you I'm neither an Indian nor a comanchero. As a matter of fact, I've come from Carrizo Springs, where I fought off both kinds."

"So you say!" the bearded man sneered as he stumbled toward Luke Bouchard. "Then why the hell you wearin' what an Injun'd wear, answer me that! And that's a Kiowa wampum belt or my name ain't Dan Hogan, by God!"

"You're right, it is a Kiowa belt. Their chief rode with me from my range to Corpus Christi, and gave it to me as a sign of friendship."

"Then you're just a damned dirty Injun-lover, that's all you are, mister!" Dan Hogan bellowed. "If you've got any guts, you'll stand there and face my draw, hear me? If you don't, I'll make you dance and then I'll shoot you down."

33

The saloonkeeper hurried outside, wiping his hands on a dirty towel. "Dan, for God's sake, sober up! You don't even know who this fellow is!" he called anxiously.

"Hell, Morton, he talks so goddamn mealy-mouthed, I'm sure he's an Injun-lover. He might even've sold guns 'n whiskey to those murdering Comanches who scalped my Rachel!" His rage mounting, the bearded man dipped his left hand to the holstered pistol.

"For God's sake, I'm not armed!" Luke cried out, lifting his arms to show that he was weaponless.

But it was too late. Dan Hogan had already drawn, cocked his pistol, and fired. Luke uttered a startled cry as he felt the bullet tug at the jagged turquoise on his breast, and then looked down in wonder to find himself unhurt. There was a dent in the silver mounting; the bullet had been deflected by the metal. As Dan Hogan stared at him, open-mouthed, Luke swiftly unfastened the wampum belt and strode toward his assailant. Using it like a whip, he wound it around the man's left wrist and jerked, and the pistol flew to the ground. Then, letting go of the belt, he struck the man's jaw with all his strength. Dan Hogan stumbled, then fell full length on the ground, unconscious.

"I didn't want to hurt him," he explained to the saloonkeeper who was wringing his hands. "You saw that he tried to kill me, didn't you?"

"Oh please, mister, thank God you're still alive—sure I saw it—he's like a maniac when he's had too much and I kept telling him it was too hot a day to pour down all that likker," the bald little saloonkeeper babbled as he hurried to the unconscious man and began, with no effect, to rub his face with a towel.

Luke picked up the wampum belt and refastened it around his waist. Then he took a gold piece from the pouch in the pocket of his buckskin jacket and tossed it to the saloonkeeper. "When he comes to, tell him to use that money for prayers for his dead wife. Tell him also that there are plenty of decent white men who can get along with Indians without selling guns or whiskey to them."

"Yessir, I'll sure do that, mister. Ol' Dan was sure mistaken this time, I swear he was!"

Luke turned his back and walked on toward the dock. The aftermath of his danger came upon him suddenly, and he cupped the turquoise almost reving. The talisman had saved his life.

CHAPTER FOUR

Standing beside Captain McMurtrie on the quarterdeck of the *William Wallace*, Luke Bouchard felt a thrill of excitement at the sight of the New Orleans waterfront. This indeed must be the master street of the world, the five-mile levee bustling with ships, men, and goods. It was as if there had been no Civil War, Luke reflected, seeing how the line of vessels, curving with the river, lay two and three deep. A man might easily step from boat to boat without once touching shore along this entire stretch.

There were also some flatboats, keelboats, and smaller river craft, floating stores presided over by enterprising Kentuckians who would as soon fight ’urn a profit. There were tobacco, hemp, animal salted meat, kegs of pork, barrels packed ickled foods, rum, tar, and the rich, aromatic coffee of which the citizens of the Queen City were almost obsessively fond. One could see bales of cotton and tobacco towering on the open wharves, with no roofs to shelter them. The very lavishness of products proclaimed the cessation of hostilities, and the renewal of profitable trade. Still, Luke remembered his grandfather's remark that one day the impracticality of storing trade goods along the levee would lead to financial loss and the gradual lessening of the importance of this great Gulf port.

The *William Wallace* blew its whistle to announce its arrival. Into the Gulf came not only the white, elegant steam packets of which Luke Bouchard's vessel was one of the most famous, but oceangoing ships with their towering sails furled and their gangplanks already down to release their passengers. They were followed by sailors in the uniforms of foreign nations, from the French berets and striped jackets reminiscent of the Zouaves who had defended New Orleans at the outbreak of the Civil War, to the puffed, dark blue caps of the German and Dutch sailors who came down the gangplanks in carefully disciplined step. However, there were no flatboats or pirogues, in which Choctaw, Creek, and Cherokee squaws used to squat, displaying beaver and bear skins, bundles of herbs, and even kegs of crude and potent tafia. The Indians of the South had long since been banished to their reservations in the distant West. A new era had begun, in spite of the bitterness that the bloody, internecine war had created during its four dreadful years. Even to the casual eye, this crowded, bustling levee suggested a renaissance.

Now that peace had come, there must be time

for planning and working to build a solid future; and to the citizens of New Orleans, peace also meant a restoration of hedonism. Theater and opera were reestablished, elegant restaurants opened, and social life was renewed, along with the intrigues, the gossip, and the life after dark that flourished in the elegant *maisons de luxe*. The vitality and the unquenchable spirit of this city, which had been burned to the ground, then sobered and harassed by the occupation of General Benjamin Butler's vindictive troops, brought to Luke the same excitement he had known a scant year before, when he had come to New Orleans to begin his new venture.

"Busy place, isn't it, Mr. Bouchard?" Captain McMurtrie said, putting a hand on Luke's shoulder. "We'll be anchoring in about ten minutes, so you'll still have time for lunch at Antoine's, if you've a mind to."

"Not without a wash and shave first, Captain," Luke replied. "Maybe even a change of costume—I don't want to be taken for an Indian again, the way I was back in Galveston."

He touched Sangrodo's talisman. "I'm not by nature a superstitious man, Captain, but somehow I have the feeling that what happened in Galveston is a good sign, that I'm destined to be successful in my venture." He turned to stare again at the bustling levee. "I can see the signs of prosperity already."

The bearded Scotsman scowled. "Aye, it's better than wartime, for certain. Just the same, Mr. Bouchard, a lot of the folks coming to this port are Yankee carpetbaggers, eager to turn a quick profit and then head back for whatever mongrel's lair they were whelped in."

"You mean, this is part of Reconstruction."

"Aye, it's that and more, Mr. Bouchard. It wasn't bad enough that the Beast of New Orleans and his brother looted the city for all it was worth. They finally recalled him by the end of Sixty-two and General Nathaniel Banks was sent here in his place. Granted he was a good deal more easygoing, but he still wasn't popular—I suppose that was because the Creoles down here didn't take much of a fancy to having a Union officer set over them. Now they've got General G. F. Shepley, who was made military governor of Louisiana in May of last year. He's a fair man, so I've been told, but even he can't stop the scalawags and the scum traipsing down here to steal away all they can lay their hands on. And it's worse in other states, you may be sure of that."

"There's a lot of rebuilding to be done, Captain, and it's certainly going to take a few years before the South and North can act like friendly neighbors again. But I'm convinced it's going to happen, and I want to do my part in the Reconstruction as I see it."

"I wish you all the luck in the world, Mr. Bouchard. And by the eternal, I think you'll need it. Now if you'll come to my cabin, I'd like to toast you and your success and happiness in whatever you decide to do, Mr. Bouchard."

"I'm honored, Captain. You've been a good friend and I hope we'll meet again many a time."

"Amen to that, sir."

Shouldering his saddlebags, Luke Bouchard made his way down the gangplank, deafened by the unending din of the busy port. Along the passageways were tin-roofed shanties housing stores that sold trinkets for arriving sailors. There were grogshops almost every hundred feet, crowded with customers, while others waited impatiently in lines outside. He saw oyster stands, with freedmen scooping out the shells and dangling the fat mollusks to tempt the appetites of the jostling throng. There were blind men playing fiddles, little children dancing for pennies, and women with flower baskets, or carrying coffeepots, stopping to pour out cups of rich black chicory-flavored brew for those whose throats were parched from the blazing midday sun.

He made his way toward a line of drays at the back. They were heavy, clattering vehicles, hitched to two mules in tandem harness, and their drivers stood up to harangue the passersby as they sought their fares. Luke recognized some of the colorful New Orleans *patois*, each driver swearing that his price was the very lowest of all. Boarding the first dray in line, he told the diver, "The Saint Charles Hotel, if you please, *mon ami*," and settled back with a sign of satisfaction at being back on familiar ground. New Orleans might once again be his starting place. Luke felt only a twinge of regret for what he had left behind. The excitement of the thriving port and of the richly historic city made him feel as if he were a young man, anxious to begin a well-ordered, useful life.

The driver, a squat, middle-aged Creole, glanced

curiously back at his passenger. "This is your first time in New Orleans, m'sieu?" he queried.

"*Pas du tout.* I've been here often, the last time a year ago."

"Ah, m'sieu speaks French with a perfect accent," the driver beamed. "But this city has changed in the past year," he shook his head sadly.

"It is very bad, then?" Luke asked, with more than nominal interest.

The Creole nodded gloomily. "Just look to your left, m'sieu. There goes Joseph Brigaud, with two trollops from the best house on Basin Street. Truly, if his mother had changed the *u* to an *n*, she would have been right on the mark. He came here last fall from Ohio, lent a poor devil of a plantation owner some money, and foreclosed on the property last month. Then he turned around and sold it for three times its market price. The unfortunate owner was left penniless. He finally blew his brains out. That is the sort of man, m'sieu, who comes to New Orleans now and takes advantage of us."

"Then there is a great deal of land speculation?" Luke asked, leaning forward in his seat.

"A man who has money is king in New Orleans, m'sieu," the driver assured him.

They rode for a few minutes in silence. Then, the dray pulled up next to the hotel. "*Nous voici!* May I help you with your bags?" the driver inquired.

"No thank you, *mon vieux.* Here's for your trouble." Luke handed him a silver coin, then hoisted his heavy saddlebag over his shoulder.

The Creole squinted at the coin, bit it, then grinned and bobbed his head in grateful ac-

41

knowledgment. "Many thanks, it is a real pleasure to drive such a gentleman," he remarked, as Luke, turning briefly to bid him good-bye, strode into the hotel.

Half an hour later, seated in a lushly upholstered armchair, Luke Bouchard was wryly admitting to himself that the creature comforts of a city like New Orleans were welcome after an arduous year on the Texas range. With a fussy little barber deftly massaging his weatherbeaten cheeks through the damp, warm towel covering his face, he gave himself up to the luxury of being pampered for what seemed like the first time in his life. As he waited for the barber to finish his preparations for the shave, he lent an attentive ear to the latter's rambling discourse about what was taking place in the Queen City.

"I'll confess, sir, that when the desk clerk told me a Mr. Luke Bouchard wished my services, I was prepared for a fine Creole gentleman—no offense meant, you understand. Then when I saw you dressed like an Indian from the plains, I was almost glad I was carrying my razor with me—now, of course, it's plain to tell you're a gentleman of quality, Mr. Bouchard, sir."

Luke made a noncommittal sound under the towel, smiling at the effusive chatter from which he sought to glean some useful information.

"Is the towel too warm? I can have Josiah—that's my nigger-boy apprentice, sir—heat some more water."

"No, it's fine. Get on with it, Mr. Jespers."

The plump little barber chuckled with pleasure

42

at this. "Now you see, that's just what I was telling you, Mr. Bouchard, sir. Only a gentleman of quality would bother to remember a poor barber's name. Most of them here at the Saint Charles, they just say 'barber'—or worse on a morning when they've had a bad night at the faro tables or with one of Madame Queenie's fancy girls. Are you going to be with us awhile, sir?"

"Possibly. Remember to take off the beard, but not too close, and leave some of the sideburns."

"Ah, just leave it to me, Mr. Bouchard! I've always said it's like a tonic, a good dose of spring molasses to quicken a man's senses, no matter what the season that he visits our noble Queen City. Of course, in the next month or two, everyone who's anybody will be going upriver because of the yellow fever and malaria we can't seem to get rid of in the summer."

He whisked off the towel and began to rub in the lather of a finely scented French soap, then with great care began to shave his customer.

"Does the razor suit you, Mr. Bouchard? It doesn't tug?"

"No, it goes quite smoothly. Is it French steel?" Luke was thinking of his grandfather's hand-tooled razors and the gift of them that he made to Nanakota, the beloved man who had become *Mico* of Econchate.

"Not this one, Mr. Bouchard. It's from Solingen, the famous German steel-maker. A beautifully balanced blade, it'll split a hair with the lightest touch—there, the beard's gone and you didn't even wince, which is proof enough. Now a bit more

43

lather, and a little massaging. You've been out in the sun a good deal recently, haven't you, sir?"

"Quite a good deal for the past year, yes, Mr. Jespers," Luke agreed.

"Never you mind, a few weeks of regular treatment, and you'll look half your age, I promise. Would you like some macassar oil on your hair?"

When the barber was finished, he stepped back and uttered a softly approving gasp at his own handiwork, then gave Luke a hand mirror. Luke stared at his own reflection: without the beard, and with only the faintest trace of rice powder on his cleanly shaved cheeks and chin, he did look younger. Only the silver streak in his hair announced the true chronology of time. Yet the year of horseback riding, of working on the range, had given him a certain vitality.

"It's very good, Mr. Jespers. Now, when you began you were telling me about the land boom here, I believe," he remarked casually as he handed the mirror back to the beaming little barber.

"Oh yes, Mr. Bouchard. You've no idea how much speculation there is right now. And of course that's only natural; now that the troops are gone, the profiteers are making a beeline for New Orleans. If I had more capital myself, I'd buy some of the space in the American section, and out near the end of the city, too. New Orleans is going to grow, you mark my words, Mr. Bouchard. Of course, there are lots of splendid plantations upriver, but the gentlemen who owned them have been reduced to utter poverty. Believe me, sir, they're in such straits they're willing to sell at almost any price. Take Mr. Amberley's plantation forty miles upriver. Three Oaks, a really palatial mansion. Of course, all Mr. Amberley's slaves ran away when they were freed, and he and his ailing son tried to make a go of it, but now his son's dead and he's on his uppers, as you might say. Besides, he sold it, for two thousand dollars in gold, just last week to M'sieu Pierre Lourat's partner, Armand Cournier."

Luke straightened in the chair. "Armand Cournier? Lourat's partner?"

"Oh yes, Mr. Bouchard. Everybody knows M'sieu Cournier. He did a great business in slaves before all that was stopped, you know. He was really M'sieu Lourat's backer till that poor devil was murdered last year. And he still owns one or two of the fanciest pleasure houses in New Orleans, and of course his gambling rooms. Unfortunately, most of his patrons were Union officers who had real specie to gamble with. And now that most of them have left, he's had to cater to these wretched carpetbaggers, not a gentleman in the lot, with the most disgusting manners you've ever seen. Well, sir, it's been a pleasure—and I might tell you too that if you ever need a tooth extracted or leeches for bleeding, I'm your man in those little affairs."

"I'll remember that, Mr. Jespers. Good afternoon to you."

Luke Bouchard walked to the shuttered window and stared out into the street. With the full heat of early afternoon, it was nearly empty. He could see the rows of ornately decorated shops, whose displays of merchandise clearly indicated that peace

45

had come to New Orleans and with it, the eagerness to attract customers to make up for the losses and privations of the war.

He had thought of stopping at a tailor's shop to buy top hat, waistcoat, breeches, a pair of fine Italian-made leather shoes. But now, refreshed by the shave, and feeling himself so fit, he decided against it. Laure should see him exactly as he was. To adopt the fashions of a Creole dandy would be not only an affectation but a deception. At the thought of her he felt excited. A year's absence had sharpened, not lessened, the memory of her beauty.

But he could not be certain that he had first claim to her. Beautiful, in her mid-twenties, with the aura of widowhood and motherhood about her, as well as the security of John Brunton's fortune, Laure would have her choice of suitors. For all he knew, she might even be favoring one of those. He stood, nonplussed for a moment, frowning at the sudden, unpleasant thought. When he had read her letter back in San Antonio, he had made a sudden and determined resolve to regain Windhaven Plantation and share that new life with her; he had not even contemplated the prospect that she might refuse him. What he remembered of her, apart from that hour of forbidden passion, was her beauty, to be sure, but also her flirtatiousness and willful independence.

Leaving the hotel, Luke Bouchard stopped at a nearby restaurant for a bowl of Creole gumbo, redolent with Louisiana shrimp, oysters, crab, chicken, rice, and okra, and with it, a glass of fine French claret. He lifted it in silent toast to the golden-

46

haired young woman whose image already was vivid in his mind and drank with relish. Thus fortified, he went out into the street to hail a dray to take him to the Union House on Honorée Street.

CHAPTER FIVE

The only change that Luke Bouchard could see as he stood before the two-story, red brick house was that there was no doorman to greet him and open the heavy walnut door of the Union House. The windows were shuttered and there appeared to be no sign of life within. As he walked slowly toward the door he could see a black funeral wreath circling the brass handle, which was molded in the shape of a naked Venus—the symbol of a house of pleasure. Reverently making the sign of the cross, he tried the handle of the door; finding it locked, he knocked three times.

After a moment a little panel slid back and a young female voice indignantly remonstrated, "Does M'sieu not see that we are in mourning? If you have business with Madame Brunton, come back this evening, *s'il vous plaît!*"

"I have urgent business with Madame Brunton, *ma chérie*, and I have come to pay my respects as well as my condolences," Luke answered.

"*Mon Dieu, c'est un sauvage rouge!*" He heard her startled gasp.

"*Point du tout, ma petite. Je viens de* Texas, *pour voir* Madame Laure. *Je suis* Luke Bouchard."

There was another startled gasp, and then the voice eagerly exclaimed, "*C'est incroyable!* Please come round to the back, I will admit you. Oh, *quelle surprise heureuse!*"

Luke walked along the side of the house and found himself in an attractive courtyard with a colonnade of sandstone pillars supporting a sheltering roof. There were flower beds, comfortable benches with backrests, and in the center a marble birdbath where two swallows perched. As he looked at this idyllic retreat, the porch door opened and a petite, black-haired girl emerged. A lace cap topped her fluffy curls, and her surprisingly opulent figure was emphasized by the modest but very becoming black silk dress. "M'sieu Bouchard, *quel plaisir de vous revoir!* Please come with me. Madame Brunton is with *le petit bébé, vous savez.*"

"It's Mitzi, isn't it?" Luke smiled as he came forward and, bending like a courtier, kissed her soft hand.

Mitzi dimpled and blushed with pleasure and her large, dark brown eyes regarded him fondly. "You remembered! And I—I too remember how nice you were when you first visited M'sieu and Madame last year."

"You are very flattering, *ma belle poupée*, and

49

even lovelier than you were last year," Luke said, following her up the steps and into the house.

"You know, Madame is getting ready to close the house. It is open only certain evenings, and then only for esteemed clients. Like yourself, *n'est-ce pas?*" She gave him a coquettish look from under her long lashes.

"That's not quite true, *ma belle.* I wasn't a client then and I shan't be now."

"*Quel dommage,*" she replied, her voice a husky whisper of sensual promise. Then, turning, she led the way up the stairs to the second floor, lifting her skirts so that he could see her legs, sheathed in black net stockings.

She led him down the hall to the very last room at the right, knocked softly, and called, "It is M'sieu Luke, Madame." Then, dropping him a charming curtsy, she hurried back down the stairs.

Hesitantly Luke turned the knob and entered. Laure Brunton, wearing a simple black cotton dress with puffed sleeves, stood with her back to him, bending over a reed bassinet set on a wide, glass-covered coffee table.

At first glance he observed that her golden hair was cut unusually short, almost like a boy's, with her nape and dainty ears bare. As she suddenly turned, he saw that her face was drawn and pale.

"Luke—I didn't expect to see you so soon—did you come to New Orleans for supplies?" She came toward him, a faint smile on her lips.

He took her hand and kissed it, studying her as if for the first time. She seemed taller, thinner too, and her large green eyes were somber. For makeup she wore only the faintest patina of rice powder, and her perfume was a delicate lilac scent.

"I got your letter in San Antonio, Laure," he said after an awkward pause, flushing with self-consciousness as she stood before him, plainly aware of his intense scrutiny. "There wasn't time to write. So much happened. I wanted to tell you how much I mourn John. He was such a good friend to me and my family all these years."

"To me too, Luke. How are things with you in Texas?"

He told her about the ranch and Lucien Edmond's first cattle drive, then with pain in his voice he informed her of Lucy's death.

"Oh, how terrible for you!" she said softly, putting a hand on his shoulder. "You were married to her for so long, and so happily, weren't you, Luke?"

"Yes, Laure. Let me see the child."

"Lucien's a healthy baby, thank God. There was so much yellow fever this spring, I was terribly afraid he'd be taken from me as John was."

He walked over to the bassinet and stood, a tremulous smile on his lips, staring down at the tiny blond baby. Little Lucien opened his eyes and uttered a soft cry. Luke gently reached down to touch his hand, and the baby's fingers clung to his thumb for an instant. Deeply moved, he turned back to Laure. "I'll never forget your kindness in naming him after my grandfather, dear Laure." He could not control the trembling of his voice.

"It was as much John's idea as mine, Luke. He was a good, kindly man, almost as much a father to me as a husband, especially after my real father's death."

"What will you do now?"

"I'm trying to close the house. It's served its purpose, as you know. When John's bank was taken over by General Butler, he used this as a front so that he could continue serving his customers. And of course when high-ranking Union officers came here for diversion, the girls were able to get John a great deal of information regarding Reconstruction plans for the city."

"And what's to become of the bank, Laure?" He put his hand down again and once more Lucien took hold of his thumb. Luke Bouchard felt a strange, ineffable joy, turning to look at the young woman whom widowhood and motherhood had caused to mature so quickly.

"John wanted to continue the bank. Just before he died, he talked about applying to the provisional governor. Under the National Banking Act, passed three years ago, a banker has to have a set amount of capital, depending on the population of the city. There's also the state law that puts regulations on what private banks must do."

"But you're a woman—you can hardly expect to take over John's bank and run it yourself, Laure."

Her shoulders straightened and there was a flash of defiance in her green eyes. "I've already spoken to Gabriel Mercier, whose father ran a private bank that did some business with John's old house, and he seems interested in going into partnership with me."

A spasm of pain contracted Luke's weatherbeaten face. "But you haven't made a decision yet, I take it?"

Laure shook her head. "Not really. The first thing is to help the girls in this house find gainful employment, or, better still, decent husbands who won't hold it against them that they were once pleasure girls. Some of them have already left. Claudine, the redhead from Pensacola, and Aimee, the mulatto from Natchez—they were here when you first came to see John last year."

"I remember only you, Laure," he said in a low voice.

For a moment her eyes considered him, and then with a melancholy smile she retorted, "Don't say things you really don't mean, Luke. I know how much you loved your wife."

"That's true, Laure." He looked back down at little Lucien. "But I remember something more."

There was a flash of fire in her eyes as she drew herself up stiffly and responded, "You owe me nothing, Luke. I wrote you that John had provided for me, and he did, very handsomely. There's enough capital in the bank to carry it on as he would have wished, and in his name, though I'm not sure Mercier will agree to that."

"Laure, let's not fence with words. Admit that Lucien is mine, not John's."

"And what if he were?"

"Why, it's plain enough—I want to marry you and be father to my own son. Is that so strange?"

She lowered her eyes and bit her lips as a wave of color suffused her pale cheeks. "You're saying it because you're a decent, honorable man, but most of all because of your grief at having lost Lucy. It

53

would be much too convenient for me to say yes. But in spite of what's happened to me, in spite of that Yankee corporal who forced me to yield to him, the day after my father killed himself, John took charge of my life—he never told you, did he, that I wanted to kill myself after what had happened?"

Luke could not speak; he only shook his head, his eyes never leaving her exquisite, mournful face.

"He kept me from taking my life or going mad, Luke. He thought up the idea of my running this *maison de luxe* so that, in a way, we could both get back at the corrupt officers who had gouged and robbed and raped New Orleans. I loved and respected him—no, it wasn't a fierce young love, but then, I wasn't an innocent girl waiting for Prince Charming to teach me the ecstasies of romantic love."

"But—"

She put a hand to his lips to silence him. "You know I only supervised the Union House for John. Never once did I myself accept a patron."

"I know that, Laure. But it would make no difference to me if you had."

Again Laure touched his lips with her soft palm. Her face was grave. "I might have guessed you'd say that, honorable man that you've always been. But I remember that afternoon as well as you do. I led you on, teased you, because I looked upon you as an old sobersides whose manners came out of a book and who believed that right was right and wrong was evil. I respect those things in you, Luke, but you can't expect to come to me now and say suddenly that you want to marry me and have

Lucien as your child. Besides, what about your Texas ranch?"

"Laure, after Lucy's death, I told my stepmother, Sybella, that we had been lovers once and that you'd had a child and I was certain it was mine. As for the ranch, my son will run it, and all the loyal workers who followed us from Alabama are there to build it for the future. What I plan, what I hope for now, is to get back Windhaven Plantation."

"So you'd go back to the past." She shook her head. "But I live in the present, and each day I think of my son and his future."

"Why can't we share the future together?"

"Not your way, because I'm not sure it's the best one for me now. I made John a promise that I'd try to keep his bank alive, and I mean to do it."

"Then why not let me help you, Laure?"

Her eyes widened in surprise. "How could you help me?"

"You're forgetting that I often went with my grandfather to the houses in Mobile and New Orleans for the accounting. When I took charge of Windhaven Plantation I handled the accounts and dealt with the bankers and the factors. I'm familiar with the National Bank Act of 1863—even more than you are, Laure. For a city the size of New Orleans, your bank will have to have at least two hundred thousand dollars in capital, with deposits of not less than one-third of that capital in United States bonds if you're planning to open a new bank."

She frowned, considering his words. "I was thinking that Gabriel Mercier could merge his deposits with John's," she admitted at last.

"Mercier would insist that the bank bear his name if he put in his capital. I'll make you a better offer: I have about forty thousand dollars in gold, which originally came as my grandfather's legacy from the Bank of Liverpool; it's now in a San Antonio bank. I'll invest that in John's bank if you'll let me be a partner, and I won't even ask that you put my name on the sign."

"You'd do that? But I can't promise you anything—not what you're asking. I still have my grief, Luke, and you have yours, a grief that will last far longer than mine because you had so many happy years with Lucy."

"Laure, you must know that I had John negotiate for me to buy back Grandfather's chateau and the original fifty acres on which it was built. Phineas Atbury, a freed black factor, still occupies it with his wife."

"Yes, John told me that."

Luke nodded. "Back in Texas, when I decided to come here to see you and then to regain Windhaven, I knew they'd never let a former plantation owner take back his property, not with the hatred of the North for all Southerners. I knew it would be a matter of a few years. And that's exactly why I'm offering to go into partnership with you, to run the bank, under your husband's name, to preserve your interests and his and the trust left for little Lucien, just as I mean to preserve mine. You see, Grandfather first did business with old Jules Ronsart, who turned the bank over to his clerk Antoine Rigalle. And then when Rigalle died, John took over. It's a strong and solvent bank, and right now the banking system in this city is in a state of virtual ruin. The once-strong banks of this city sent most of their gold to the Confederate government, and all they have left is worthless paper and credits that will never be redeemed." He paused, watching her, then went on.

"The only money coming into New Orleans is brought by speculators, profiteers, and carpetbaggers. But I think that with my guidance, my knowledge of people and their business affairs, I can steer John's bank on a level course and help a great many people get back on their feet. And by then, God willing, it'll be time to go back to Windhaven and carry out Grandfather's dreams for diversified crops, even cattle—now that I've worked with them in Texas and can foresee the growing market for fresh meat throughout the country. Let me be your partner, Laure. I'll be honest in my accounting to you, I swear it."

"You don't have to swear. I shouldn't need even a signed agreement between us. But if I agree, it must be understood that it's strictly a business venture. I may keep the house, since it's paid for, but once the girls have left, don't count on moving in here and taking over. I don't love you, and if I do remarry, it must be for love. I don't need marriage for any other reason."

Once again Luke turned to the bassinet. He wrestled with his emotions as he fought back the impassioned speeches that came to his lips. When he turned back to Laure, his face was impassive, and his tone was impersonal as he said, "You have my word of honor. I'll say only that one day I'll try to persuade you to accept my love as well as my protection."

"No, Luke, don't even say it. Think it if you must, but the time isn't right for either of us. If you came to me, I'd want you to be very sure it wasn't just because of your loneliness and your dogged determination to start life over again where you began. I can't yet see myself as a plantation owner's wife." Then, with a flash of the same flirtatiousness that had captivated and ensnared him that one memorable afternoon, she teasingly added, "But I'm sure that you'll be able to find solace when you want it, Luke. Mitzi was just about beside herself when she saw you, and you know what a crush she had on you last year."

"I want no light of love, Laure. One day you'll know that it's you I want." And then, standing erect before her, his face expressionless, he added, "It's best to bind our agreement formally. With your permission, Madame Brunton, I'll bring an attorney here tomorrow afternoon to draw up our partnership."

CHAPTER SIX

That afternoon Luke sent a telegraph to the manager of the San Antonio bank, instructing him to prepare a draft for forty thousand dollars to be forwarded to him at the St. Charles Hotel in New Orleans. He added a secret code number so that the manager would have no doubt as to the authenticity of the request. He had arranged this convenience back in Texas just before receiving Laure's letter, and his intention then had been to allocate the rest of his legacy from his grandfather, along with his profits from the first year of Windhaven Range, to the eventual rehabilitation of the red-brick chateau on the Alabama River. This done, he sent off letters to Sybella and his son, in care of the same bank, for he had told them that he would communicate his plans as soon as they had crystallized.

The garrulous little barber had dropped much more than a single kernel of worthwhile news. Not only had he confirmed Luke's immediate impression that the profiteers had descended upon New Orleans like a swarm of hungry locusts, he had given Luke the name of a shrewd local entrepreneur in association with another name that Luke could never forget: that of the now-dead Pierre Lourat. As he enjoyed a solitary supper at Moreau's, he reflected on this news. Until now he had believed that his rebellious half-brother, Mark, had been Lourat's only partner in smuggling, buying, and selling slaves, and operating elegant bordellos. Now, it appeared, someone behind the scenes had taken over all of Lourat's holdings, since both Mark and the wily Creole were dead. Lourat had been a malevolent influence on the Bouchard family, corrupting young Mark and using him the way a master puppeteer pulls the strings on his disciplined dolls. But the name of Armand Cournier was unknown to him.

As he sipped his brandy and demi-tasse, another name, almost forgotten, came to him. It was that of Edouard Villiers, the suave Creole dandy who, twenty-three years before, had come to Windhaven and tried to win Arabella's hand in a speedy, ostentatious courtship. Villiers's romantic aspirations had quickly been crushed after Luke had received a letter from John Brunton, advising him that the Creole was in partnership with Pierre Lourat and Mark Bouchard. Villiers had returned posthaste to New Orleans, and in all this time not a word had been heard of him. It was curious indeed, and Luke found himself wondering whether Villiers

60

might be associated with Armand Cournier. He determined to make inquiries as soon as possible.

Now it all came back clearly. He recalled Lourat's attempt, over thirty years ago, to ensnare Mark when he was scarcely sixteen, by forcing him into a marriage with Louisette Entrevois. The marriage would have allowed the Creole to gain his own devious emprise from the thriving Windhaven Plantation. And Edouard Villiers's subsequent, sudden passion for Arabella had been only another cunning attempt to usurp the Bouchard holdings.

Luke had paid off Mark with a third of his own inheritance from old Lucien. Mark had been killed when a cannonball fired by a Union sergeant, a mulatto who had been Mark Bouchard's illegitimate son, had crashed into the cabin of the blockade-running steamer heading for safety in Barataria. Only death had ended Mark's implacable hatred of Luke, despite all Luke's attempts to be fair in the division of Lucien's legacy.

It had been like a spider's web, this entangling of the Bouchards with the inventive and spiteful Creole gambler. Even Pierre Lourat's death, at the hands of Louisette Entrevois, and her subsequent suicide, had been inextricably part of the destiny of the Bouchards. As he pondered the convolutions of fate, Luke wondered if this complicated scheme to wrest Windhaven Plantation from its rightful owners had truly ended with the death of Pierre Lourat.

Luke had placed Sangrodo's talisman in the hotel safe before visiting Laure, but he still wore the wampum belt. After breakfast the next morning, he visited a nearby tailor to acquire a wardrobe in keeping with his intended new role. After having spent a year outdoors where rugged garb was practicable, Luke was highly surprised to discover how much progress had been achieved in the manufacturing of men's clothes. The tailor, a middle-aged Englishman who had settled in Massachusetts before the war, coming to New Orleans at first to visit a relative, and then opening this progressive new shop, was delighted to acquaint his customer with the sweeping changes that had taken place in the clothing industry.

"You see, Mr. Bouchard, after the Howe and Singer sewing machines, they've developed a power-run machine. Now they'll be able to make a man's shirt or even trousers in a factory. Here, sir, is the latest fashion—a brown cloth, one-button sack coat, with smart gray cloth trousers in brown line plaid. The collar is turned down, and a modest black silk cravat sets it off. And of course you'll want a red velvet waistcoat and a black hard felt derby to go with your black shoes."

"A derby?" Luke echoed as the tailor held up the hat banded with a black ribbon.

"Oh yes, sir. In England they call it the bowler, because it was designed by a British hatter by the name of William Bowler about sixteen years ago. Here in the States we call it a derby because the Earl of Derby wore just such a hat to the races."

"It does have a certain style," Luke wryly admitted as he tried on the hat for size and contemplated himself in the full-length mirror at one side of the shop.

As the tailor took his measurements, Luke found

the prospect of wearing city attire quite pleasant. And after he had tried on what the tailor had recommended and surveyed himself in the mirror, he had to concede that it lent an air of authority to his appearance—one that, he hoped, might impress Laure.

"Why, Mr. Bouchard, it's as if it were made just for your proportions! You're luckier than most men at your age—tall but not too tall, and lean hips and a narrow waist. Why, sir, you'll be as fashionable as any Creole dandy, mark my words—especially with the ladies, if you'll forgive my saying so."

For more formal wear, Luke added a stylish Prince Albert frock coat and black silk top hat, a magenta-hued velvet waistcoat with multicolored embroidery, which fastened with jeweled buttons and buckles, several factory-made white shirts with colored neck cloths, as well as two black satin shirts, and a pair of black leather Wellington boots, which could be worn under the trousers. Finally, several pairs of silk socks, for the tailor explained that the vogue of ready-made trousers, instead of the time-honored breeches, called for these shorter accessories rather than the traditional long stockings.

After he had paid the tailor and arranged to have his purchases sent to the hotel, Luke went down the street to a little antique shop. He remembered going into a similar shop to buy a locket for Lucy, monogrammed w.r., the morning after his unexpected amorous encounter with Laure. As he entered the shop, he was struck by the abundance of exquisite statuary, bric-a-brac, golden candela-

63

bra, cherrywood taborets, and even fine oil paintings.

The proprietor, a portly German, immediately recognized Luke as a gentleman of quality, and proceeded to show him a French swordcane. "Of the finest ivory, *mein Herr*, it is both an elegant walking stick for a gentleman like yourself, *wirklich*, and, because one sometimes has to deal with ruffians these days, a weapon for self-defense, *selbstverständlich!*" Adroitly he twisted the knob of the cane and drew out a gleaming sword, about three feet long and just over an inch in width, with a viciously sharp tip.

"It's magnificent!" Luke exclaimed as the proprietor proffered him the sword by the knob-handle. Experimentally, he lifted it and leveled it out straight before him, testing the balance and weight. "Superb workmanship. And the price?"

The German shrugged. "It is as if it were made for you, *mein Herr*. And I am not too greedy. New Orleans has been good to me and my family. Say a hundred dollars—in gold, *natürlich*."

Prompted by sudden impulse, Luke sheathed the swordcane, took out his leather pouch, and dropped five twenty-dollar gold pieces into the German's outstretched palm.

"*Danke, mein Herr!*" The dealer's eyes glistened as he stared down at the shiny gold coins. "A real pleasure to deal with such a fine gentleman, *wirklich*. Are you new to New Orleans? I might suggest that if you think of settling down here, I, Heinrich Gruber, would be honored if you'd allow me to suggest a few items of decor for your new residence."

"I shall keep that in mind, *Herr* Gruber. By the way, can you recommend an honest lawyer of your acquaintance?"

"*Jawohl,* I know such a man. His name is Matthew Ernst, and he has his offices on Royal Street—you will be sure to see his sign over the door. He helped me purchase this store, you see. He was most honest and he did not charge too much. He has what you would call in my country much *Gemüt.*"

"I shall see him at once, and thank you for your recommendation. Good day to you, and perhaps I'll call on you again."

The shopkeeper hurried to the door and, beaming and bowing, he ushered out Luke Bouchard.

Using the swordcane as a walking stick, the tall man in buckskin walked slowly down the banquette, taking in the bustling activity around him. Drays were clattering through the street, elegantly dressed men and women paused at shop windows, or walked, conversing animatedly. A twinge of loneliness and a longing for Lucy came over him as he saw one young couple, the man black-haired and slim and in his late twenties, turning to smile fondly at a pretty chestnut-haired girl in white muslin beside him. For a moment Luke felt himself an alien, an intruder in a strange new world, an unpredictable plateau between the world he had just left and the other, which retained all the ardent memories of his youth. Then, with a sigh, he continued his stroll.

At very first meeting, Luke Bouchard shared Heinrich Gruber's estimation of the lawyer on

Royal Street. Matthew Ernst was stocky, of medium height, with a round, genial face set off by thick sideburns and a flowing gray beard. There was a pleasant twinkle in his myopic blue eyes as he shook hands with Luke and ushered him to a chair beside his desk. Briefly, after Luke had introduced himself, Matthew Ernst proffered his background in so straight-forward a manner that Luke was certain he need look no further for legal representation.

"I too am *Deutsch* like my friend Heinrich," he said as he adjusted the ribbon of his pince-nez, then thoughtfully stroked his beard. "*Aber, wissen Sie,* my father and mother and two *Schwestern* came to Pittsburgh in 1830 when I was still a *Jüngling* at the *Gymnasium.* There I studied the law, and then I received my license to practice, and married a sweet German girl, Rosa Wolheim, who had come with her parents from Frankfurt-Am-Rhein." He sighed, then went on, "When Rosa and the little one both died in childbirth, about ten years before this *teuflischen Krieg,* I came here to visit my cousin Hans. I fell in love with this beautiful city, *Herr* Bouchard, and also with a sweet *Mädchen* who did me the honor to become my wife and to give me two fine young boys. There was not much business for me during the war, *verstehen Sie.* But I believe in this city and its future. So *natürlich* I am eager to be of service to a man like you, who wishes to bring back prosperity to New Orleans."

"Your qualifications are impressive, *Herr* Ernst. What I have in mind is the opening of a new private bank. Actually, it is an extension of a bank that existed before General Butler closed all such banks and established his own."

Matthew Ernst's face clouded with anger. "That swindler left New Orleans with his pockets stuffed with *Geld*, he and his *verdammter Bruder*. You say the bank existed—under what name?"

"It was originally the bank of Jules Ronsart, then of Antoine Rigalle, and finally that of John Brunton."

The portly lawyer slapped his palm down on the surface of the desk and beamed. "He was my good *Freund, Herr* Bouchard. He appeared as a witness for me in a civil suit just six months before the war began, and helped me win a most difficult case." He frowned and lowered his eyes. "It was a great pity he had to die when he was still so young, *nicht wahr.*"

"Yes, *Herr* Ernst. He was my good friend too. My grandfather, my father and I had dealings with his bank for many years. Last year, when I came from Alabama with my family to make a fresh start in Texas, he was able to negotiate the transfer of a legacy in gold from the Bank of Liverpool and to help me acquire necessary supplies for the establishment of a ranch."

"Ach so! But I do not quite understand. You say you established a ranch in Texas, and now you consult me about the reopening of a private bank here in New Orleans?" The lawyer squinted at Luke through his pince-nez, again adjusting the ribbon and tugging at a wisp of his bushy beard.

"Yes, *Herr* Ernst. I turned the ranch over to my son, and I came back here because I want to be of assistance to John Brunton's wife, Laure. It was his last wish that the bank continue. Under the law, she could hardly operate it by herself. What I propose is a partnership in which the name will be Brunton and Associate—no reference to my name whatsoever, though I am prepared to put up about one-fourth of the capital."

"I do not see that this presents any difficulty. I am curious that you do not wish your name to appear, however."

"Shall we say I have a sentimental reason, *Herr* Ernst? You must know a great deal about the state of finances in this city, and I should be indebted to you if you could enlighten me on how to proceed in making the bank useful to the citizens of New Orleans."

Matthew Ernst leaned back in his chair and scowled. "We had great inflation here because of the worthlessness of Confederate currency. The Union soldiers brought in greenbacks, but the supply of goods was limited, so prices here for the necessities of life were beyond the means of most of the people. We still have some Federal troops in the state, so there is money in circulation, but what is most important of all is that Northern capital is coming here. Northern banks and businesses are making advances to our merchants and factors because they want to restore the cotton trade."

"I should have guessed that. As we worked it in Alabama before the war, cotton gradually became so cheap that it was hardly worthwhile to produce, when one considered the costs of shipping, commissions to brokers, and labor."

"Labor?" The lawyer squinted. "But you had a

plantation in Alabama, so you had no labor costs. I do not understand, *Herr* Bouchard."

"My grandfather, like myself, did not believe in slavery. He apportioned part of his profits for his workers. He saw to it that that money was put aside for them and used to buy the necessities. It wasn't possible to free them, because they would have been forced to leave the state, and would then have been caught by slave dealers and plunged back into slavery. Long before the war, *Herr* Ernst, I had been thinking of improved agricultural methods, of rotating crops, of raising cattle—such as I saw being done on Windhaven Ranch in Texas. And surely there are industrious merchants and planters still left in New Orleans who have learned a lesson from this war and will know how to pare their costs and make wise investments to build a sound financial future."

"You make it sound so simple. But it is a good thought all the same. *Wissen Sie,* we have eleven banks operating in this city. Few of them are in healthy condition. The value of their stock, which is set at a hundred dollars per share par value, now ranges from eight to seventy-six dollars, except for the First National Bank, whose stock goes at ninety-nine dollars. Interest rates are high because of this. Of course, before the war our banks were as good as any in the land, partly because the state of Louisiana had issued good bonds to provide capital for them."

"I don't propose to have exorbitant interest rates, *Herr* Ernst. I am also interested in acquiring land and holding it for future development, at a moderate profit for Madame Brunton and myself; the funds from this will be put back into the bank to strengthen it."

"I think I shall enjoy drawing up the articles of your partnership. You are a dreamer, but you are also a man of calculated action."

"Even calculated action carries with it considerable risk. Perhaps with your legal help, *Herr* Ernst, I shall avoid too much of the latter."

The lawyer's booming laugh resounded as he rose and extended his hand to Luke. "It will be my great pleasure to have you as my client, *Herr* Bouchard."

"Perhaps you would take supper with me this evening, and then accompany me to visit Madame Brunton and discuss the legality of our proposed partnership."

"I have a far better idea, *Herr* Bouchard. My Mathilda prepares sauerbraten like no one else. Do me the honor of being a guest at my *Haus* for dinner, and then we shall go to visit *Frau* Brunton."

CHAPTER SEVEN

Later that evening, after Matthew Ernst had read a rough draft of the articles of partnership for the proposed Brunton Bank, Laure pronounced herself satisfied with the lawyer's ability. "Draw up the papers, Mr. Ernst, and I'll sign them as soon as they're ready," she told him. "There remains now only the problem of finding a new location for John's bank. I don't suppose the old place on the Rue de Toulouse would be available now—"

Luke Bouchard himself answered that question: "No, my dear. I went by there this afternoon and it's still occupied by the Consolidated Bank of New Orleans."

"The American Quarter might be a good location. John always believed that the division of New Orleans into three districts was a very healthy state of affairs, and naturally, he favored the section above Canal Street. And don't forget that when the city was reconsolidated back in 1852, the new city hall was switched from Cabildo at Jackson Square to the American section."

"I'll see if there's a suitable empty store or warehouse in that area big enough to house the Brunton and Associate Bank," Luke promised.

"It was a great pleasure to meet you, *Frau* Brunton. You know, I was telling *Herr* Bouchard earlier today that your husband helped me win a very important civil case by his testimony, and I always admired him deeply. I give you my word that I shall try to handle the legal affairs of this new banking venture as I would a sacred trust." With this, Matthew Ernst took Laure's hand, bowed, and kissed it gallantly. Laure eyed Luke, her faint smile deepening, while Luke flushed self-consciously and could not suppress a twinge of annoyance. By that faintly mocking smile Laure was reminding him that she did not intend to succumb to his blandishments any more than she would to the lawyer's. And yet he could not but admire her almost defiant independence, her Spartan way of putting her grief behind her, and her determination to lead her own life. Until now he had thought of her merely as a very lovely and enticing young woman who had suffered tragedy and humiliation. Her flirtation with him had seemed to be her way of testing her restoration to the status of desirable female. Now he realized her strength of mind, character, and will, and with that realization came his growing awareness that she would be more than a fitting mate for him in his new life.

The next morning he strolled through the American Quarter in search of a suitable location for the bank. Crossing Greenley Street just below Canal, he came upon a small, dilapidated one-story warehouse. On one side of it was a bakery, on the other a flower shop—potential customers for the new bank. He entered the flower shop and, upon inquiry, learned that the Union Army had at one time occupied the warehouse but recently abandoned it. A visit to the city recorder of deeds revealed that the property was about to be offered at public sale, and Luke promptly made a formal bid.

Luke then went to meet Laure at Matthew Ernst's office, where both signed the articles of partnership. Luke took the documents back to the requisite official at the city hall and filed a declaration of intent to open a private bank. The capitalization was to be $200,000, and he agreed that he and his partner would invest one-third in United States bonds as a pledge of good faith. The officious clerk offered a highly useful piece of information: "If you're to be in the banking business, sir, you've doubtless heard that Congress passed an act last year to put a tax of ten percent on state banknotes, to drive them out of existence. I've heard they're going to start enforcing that act some time next month."

"Thank you for the information. However, if you'll examine our declaration, you'll find that we're using specie for capitalization. And we're quite happy to invest a third in government bonds—it's a unified country once again, and I for one am very glad of it."

"I'm sure there'll be no trouble then, Mr. Bouchard." The clerk's manner became ingratiating. "I'm from Illinois originally, sent down here at General Shepley's orders to help see that federal orders about Reconstruction are carried out. And just before you came in, sir, I had to shout down some damned Confederate—begging your pardon, Mr. Bouchard—but for a minute I thought he was going to try to fight the Civil War all over again. Good-day to you, and you'll have your license within a fortnight."

Three days later, Luke was pleased to find that the announcement of the public sale of the old warehouse on Greenley Street had drawn only a few mildly interested speculators. His bid of five thousand dollars for the land and the building as it stood was not contested. He paid the auctioneer in federal banknotes, having exchanged some of the gold he had brought with him from Texas. He could not know that this was the same warehouse into which Captain George Soltis and his cutthroats had broken over a year ago to steal arms and ammunition, to be resold to anyone who had the price. Nor could he know that the guns and ammunition he himself had bought to protect his family had been part of the pilfered materiel.

On June 16, the day on which the Fourteenth Amendment to the Constitution was sent to all the states for ratification, Luke received a telegraph from the Citizens' Bank of San Antonio, informing him that a draft for forty thousand dollars was en route to him. He had already hired a crew of white and black workers for the conversion of the old warehouse. There was far more space than the bank would need, so he instructed the crew to section off the back of the warehouse, leaving that portion of the building free for later construction. Very possibly several shops could be located there, the rentals accruing to the bank as an aid to paring down the operating costs for the first year. Or perhaps the area could be used for a small storehouse for a printer or drygoods merchant. During these weeks of preparation, he visited Laure several times to examine the folios of her late husband's accounts, and all this activity strengthened him against the growing impulse to convince her to marry him at once.

Laure maintained a cool demeanor throughout these visits. As she went over the accounts with him, he was pleasantly surprised to discover that she had an excellent grasp of monetary matters and in fact was acquainted with several of her late husband's accounts. Some of these had been arranged so that the funds would remain in the security of foreign banks until the owners required transference to New Orleans or other points of venue. Thus, the outlook for beginning the new bank with stable depositors was indeed heartening. Luke found all his energies being channeled into this intellectual activity, and it provided an enormous contrast with his former mode of life in the outdoors.

Back in the '30s, the merchants of New Orleans had determined to have their own connection with Lake Pontchartrain, and arranged a bank charter to cut a deep canal through the low swampy area. The project would have required thousands of slaves, and they were far too valuable to be risked under the killing sun. Accordingly, the appeal for labor was sent to famine-ridden Ireland, and ships brought sturdy Irish workers seeking a better life in the Queen City. Their descendants now populated the vital, dynamic American Quarter of New Orleans. Thus it was that Luke chose an Irish foreman, Paddy Quinlan, to supervise the labor gang hard at work turning the old warehouse into a resplendent new bank.

Paddy Quinlan's father had helped build the canal to Lake Pontchartrain and died of yellow fever contracted in that pestilential swamp. Paddy's two brothers, Matt and Devlin, had gone off to fight for the South and died at Chickamauga. Yet, curiously, Paddy, a brawny, tall and wiry man nearing fifty, shared Luke's belief that blacks and whites could work together for the same wage. "Mr. Bouchard, I'll not be sayin' you won't run into trouble, and lots of fine gentry will look down their noses and say you're a common nigger-lover. Now Matt and Devlin fought for the Confederate side, not to keep slavery, but simply because they didn't believe they should be dictated to about their lives. Devil take it, Mr. Bouchard, that's why my old father left Erin himself, what with the English landlords and the potato famine. But I'll get a good day's work out of any man in my crew; and it won't matter what color his skin happens to be if he's a lazy bugger—out he goes."

The work had gone forward energetically, prompted by Luke's then unheard-of wage of twenty-five dollars a week and a bonus of one hundred dollars for every man who stayed on to complete the job.

Farther west on the street where the new bank was being erected, Luke had found a small house with porte-cochere and inner garden, sadly neglected for more than a year. The previous owner had lost his sugarcane plantation through a combination of excessive gambling debts and confiscation by federal authorities. Consequently, Luke was able to buy the rundown property for less than a thousand dollars in gold. From a list of applicants whom Paddy Quinlan had interviewed and considered reliable, Luke engaged two men to clean up the house and garden and get it into livable condition. By the end of June he had moved from the St. Charles Hotel and retrieved his horse from the stable where he had quartered him.

On several occasions Laure accepted his invitation to dine, but their conversations were always limited to the progress of the bank and Laure's concern with finding suitable jobs or husbands for the girls who still resided at the Union House. Now, this early July evening, after supper at Moreau's, as the strong coffee was being served along with snifters of fine brandy, Laure declared, "Gabriel Mercier tells me he has a young cashier who wishes to make a change. He would like to work for us, Luke. Have you done anything yet about securing tellers and clerks for our bank?"

He tried not to show that her use of the word *our* had roused his suppressed hopes of having her share in all aspects of his life. "Last week when we went over John's accounts, I found the dossier on all the Brunton employees. Most of them left New Orleans when the bank closed, as you know. But this morning I located Jason Barntry and Edgar Maxton, of whom John apparently thought very highly. They're in their forties now, married, and

Barntry is working for a greengrocer at a pitifully inadequate wage, while Maxton has had to find work as a laborer. If you've no objection, I'd like to look them up and offer them a post at the bank." It was only with the slightest hesitation that he substituted the word *the* for *our*. To hide his emotion, he quickly sipped from the snifter and exhaled a sigh of content. Then he added, "I must take this high living easy, or I'll soon put on a paunch and become a dullard."

"If you're fishing for compliments, Luke, don't expect it from me. I've never accused you of being dull, only sometimes exasperatingly predictable. And now, to leave the banking business for a moment, have you considered what's to be done with our charming inhabitants of the Union House? I certainly don't want there to be any association between the bank that bears John's name and a house of pleasure. It's served its purpose, and as you know, these girls are not just doxies. For some of them, it was a matter of survival, a much more pleasant way than having to-sell themselves on the street or to some brute of a carpetbagger."

"Didn't you tell me that one of the girls has a lovely voice and can play the mandolin?"

"Oh yes, Aurelia Dubois. She was in the parlor with that fat Union captain the first time you visited the Union House to see John." As she spoke, there was a sudden warm glint in her green eyes, which vanished almost as swiftly as it had come, just enough to remind him again of the hour they had spent together.

Again Luke strove for composure, for Laure's swift, deft mockery had evoked sensual images that he had sought to banish from his mind. He paused long enough to finish his brandy with deliberate casualness, then replied, "As it happens, I lunched yesterday at a new restaurant on Eglantine Street, owned by a middle-aged Creole named Felix Brissart. He's a capital chef in his own right. His restaurant seats about fifty, and it's charmingly decorated. I happened to mention that perhaps a little music would add to the conviviality, and he was quite taken with the idea. You might have Mademoiselle Dubois call on him; it's just possible he might have a place for her."

Laure's lovely, sensitive face brightened as she leaned forward. "Why, that's marvelous, Luke! I'll tell her to go there tomorrow. But there's also Madelon Fortier, the one with the long, dark brown hair, very slim and charming. She's just twenty-two, the daughter of a sugarcane plantation owner who committed suicide after losing his whole fortune at Pierre Lourat's gaming table. Madelon might have been thrown into debtor's prison or worse if John hadn't paid off her father's principal creditors and then suggested that she come live at the Union House. She insisted on paying him back, so she became one of the girls, but she asked that she be allowed to select her partners and not feel that she had to accept all comers."

Luke nodded. "Girls like that are the inevitable and innocent victims of every war. Perhaps we should try to find her a good husband who wouldn't be concerned with her past."

Again a mocking smile fleeted across Laure's soft lips. "Luke, you're very naïve. Most men would look upon Madelon as a *putaine*, even though a very high-class one, and their male vanity wouldn't permit them to forget what she had been—particularly if they had occasion to have a domestic quarrel with her."

"I have heard it said," Luke observed wryly, "that very often women who have served many men's pleasures make the best wives precisely because they understand the animal nature of the species."

Laure leaned back and this time regarded Luke almost with fond amusement. *"Viens donc,* perhaps I've misjudged you, *mon cher.* Perhaps living out in the wilds and fighting off bandits and Indians has made you a little more human."

"That, *ma belle,* is exactly what I have been trying to tell you since I came back to New Orleans."

Quixotic in her moods, the golden-haired young widow held up a warning hand and shook her head. "Oh no, not that again, *je vous prie!* We are partners now, Luke, but in business only. You shan't trap me with honeyed words or play upon my maternal sympathies. So let's consider what can be done for poor Madelon and also for Virginie and Odette Nourmain, the charming red-haired sisters. Do you remember them from your first visit, when you saw that drunken Union officer with an arm around each of them?"

"Indeed I do, Laure. I believed them to be twin sisters, they looked so much alike."

"They are—they were born within two hours of each other. Their father was a hard-working drygoods merchant in the French Quarter. Their mother became dissatisfied with her husband's station in life, and she took lovers, choosing only the wealthiest and most distinguished men of New Orleans. One afternoon her husband came back from his shop on some errand or other and found her and her latest paramour, and killed them both, then himself."

"How horrible!"

"And there was worse to come. Their uncle took them into his house, gambled away what little money their father had left them, and then gave them the alternative of sleeping with him or being turned out in the street. John learned of this some months after the uncle had made them his mistresses by force—and by that I mean being locked in the cellar and whipped till they accepted their uncle's desires—and decided to take them away from that vile man."

"How did he manage?"

"By playing faro with their uncle and taking every sou he had till finally he offered to put them up as stakes. John won those stakes, too. He brought them to the Union House, and set up the money he had taken from their uncle into a trust fund. But it isn't much, perhaps six thousand dollars. What concerns me is what's to become of them after the lives they've had to lead. At the Union House, John made it very clear that if they wished to take clients, they alone should have the right to determine who their partners would be—regrettably, thanks to their uncle's teachings, both Virginie and Odette had developed an unhealthy appetite for physical pleasure, shall we say?"

"I quite understand. And it seems to me that what they both need now is a chance to regain their dignity and self-esteem. Are they well educated?"

"Oh yes. Both read in several languages and speak as fluently. They know their sums and have quick minds."

"Perhaps the bank would be the solution. They might act as intermediaries. By that I mean, when a customer enters the bank, they could greet him at the door and inquire how the bank could be of service and then direct him to the proper clerk or teller."

"That would be a novel idea! And it would certainly give our bank a distinction—I don't think there's another bank in New Orleans that has women employees."

"On display in that manner each day, it's possible that they may attract handsome, well-to-do husbands," Luke added.

Laure suddenly frowned. "The one danger would be, of course, that some of the customers might have visited the Union House and would recognize them. That might be embarrassing for all concerned. Then too, Luke, they might even continue to accept assignations, and the affairs of a bank certainly shouldn't be entwined with those of a bordello. Perhaps it isn't such a good idea after all."

"Well, why not use Madelon as our official hostess at the bank and try to find husbands for Odette and Virginie?" Luke proposed.

"Now that seems much better to me. Madelon, besides being older, has a certain poise and dignity that would make her well suited to such a serious enterprise. But how shall we go about finding husbands for our two wayward sisters?" Now her tone was almost bantering, and the smile on her face was delightfully provocative—just as it had been that never-to-be-forgotten afternoon last year. Then, before he could begin to answer, with the same teasing *diablerie* that had so provoked him then, she added, "Since you tell me you're looking for a wife to comfort you in your loneliness, Luke, why shouldn't you be a candidate for either Odette or Virginie? I'm sure, *mon cher*, that if you married the one, the other would be a most complaisant sister-in-law to you. *Voilà*—you would have your own little *ménage à trois* in such an arrangement."

Luke could not help blushing, especially as he observed Laure's smile. But he stoutly defended himself: "That would be a marriage of convenience, not of love. Moreover, madame, I am not a Turk seeking a ready-made harem."

Laure shot him an arch look from under her thick, curling lashes as she demurely sipped her brandy. "But you must admit, *mon cher*, that it would solve both your problems and those of Odette and Virginie. Most of all, I think it would keep you young—you would have to be to keep up with their demands upon you."

Luke felt his cheeks burning like a schoolboy's as he testily answered, "Take care now, Laure, teasing like that once cost you a good spanking."

She tilted back her head and uttered a soft, husky giggle that set his pulses pounding, and then, making a moue with her soft red lips, she saucily retorted, "*Va t'en!* That shan't happen twice. Have you never heard the proverb that lightning never strikes twice in the same place, Luke?"

"All I have to say to that, my dear, is: never tempt Providence by flying in the face of it. And even proverbs have been proved wrong on occasion."

CHAPTER EIGHT

On July 24, 1866, a curious crowd stood in front of the building on Greenley Street to observe the official opening of the Brunton and Associate Bank. Paddy Quinlan's work crew had done wonders, working after supper through most of the night the final week so that everything would be ready. Paddy himself had contributed the ingenious idea of setting up a marble counter about fifty feet beyond the entrance to set off the desks and offices of the bank officials. He had been able to find some quarried marble in an abandoned old mansion just upriver, in superb condition despite its age and the attack of the elements upon it. The marble had once decorated the front of the veranda of the old house. Many of the desks and the fine Oriental rugs and tapestries that ornamented the section for the bank's officials had come from the Union House.

There were private offices for Laure and Luke, and two others for Jason Barntry and Edgar Maxton. Luke had sought out both men and found them overjoyed at the prospect of returning to the business where they had spent so many rewarding years. Laure herself had interviewed them, and agreed with Luke's judgment in giving them responsible positions as an investment counselor and a trust officer. John Torrance, a personable, rather dapper man in his late twenties, who had worked previously for Gabriel Mercier, had been hired as a teller. He had confided to Laure and Luke that his reason for wishing to leave the Mercier bank was that he was infatuated with Mercier's private secretary, an attractive young woman, only to learn that she was intolerably fickle. He believed that by changing his job it would be easier to break off with her entirely.

It was indeed a gala opening. The flower shop and the bakery, which flanked the new bank, had contributed their wares for the occasion. There were bouquets everywhere, and boutonnieres for the customers who entered to open accounts or even to find out more about the bank. There were fresh brioches and dainty little petits fours, and even a lavish birthday cake with colorful frosting and letters that read BRUNTON AND ASSOCIATE BANK. At a table near the entrance, lovely Madelon Fortier presided, graciously offering the refreshments and porcelain cups of chicory-flavored coffee to all who entered. In a fashionable green muslin frock with full skirt and modest neckline, she lent a touch of feminine hospitality that drew enthusiastic comments from everyone there. Still more gratifying to both Laure and Luke were the nearly forty persons who decided to favor the Brunton and Associate Bank with their accounts.

To cap the end of a highly gratifying day, a young courier from Gabriel Mercier's bank brought to Luke's office, just before closing time, an envelope bearing the banker's own personal seal. It contained a draft for twenty-five thousand dollars and a note declaring Gabriel Mercier's desire to invest in his old friend's bank at the current rate of interest.

Luke had plunged himself into his new life with as much energy and discipline as he had shown in adapting himself to life on the Texas range. Having by now moved into his refurbished house, he spent many of his evenings poring over all the books on banking, investment, and finance that he could find in the New Orleans bookstores. Well before the opening of the new bank, he had paid several visits to Gabriel Mercier's flourishing establishment and made a friend of the somewhat foppish forty-two-year-old financier. At times he had taken Mercier to lunch at Antoine's or Moreau's, and, frankly admitting his novice role in this new profession, he had asked Mercier for advice. This candor had allayed Mercier's initial suspicions. Luke realized quite early in the friendship that Mercier had thought of paying court to Laure and inducing her, if she married him, to turn over John Brunton's considerable fortune to his bank. Gabriel Mercier had lost his wife to yellow fever two years earlier, and he now maintained a quadroon mistress in a little house on Rampart Street. His late wife, who had been ailing and fragile through much of their married life, had been unable to give him children. Mercier was eager to have a son and heir before much longer, and the fact that Laure Brunton was widowed and had an infant son had increased his interest in her.

During their luncheon exactly a week before the Brunton Bank opened for business, Gabriel Mercier had delighted Luke by declaring, "You are older than I, M'sieu Bouchard. From your experience, tell me why it is that the more desirable a woman is, the more unattainable she always seems to be."

"Perhaps because she learns early in life to realize her potential worth as an investment, to use banking terminology," Luke said with a chuckle as he lifted his glass to toast his guest across the table.

"True enough." The banker touched the tips of his carefully waxed mustache, then brought the crystal goblet to his nose to sniff at the bouquet before warily sipping it. "Excellent. You don't find it too tart, perhaps, M'sieu Bouchard?"

"One would not look for sweetness in such a vintage," Luke observed wryly.

Gabriel Mercier burst into a hearty guffaw, then took a long draft of his wine. "I like you, M'sieu—*par Dieu*, let us have done with all these formalities and call each other by our first names. Now then, you suggest that Madame Brunton seems to have as superb a bouquet as this wine, yet lacks the sweetness of compliance which a mature man like me desires."

"If that is your inference, Gabriel, you know

more about women than I do. But after all, that's only natural, since here in New Orleans you have so many belles that beauty becomes almost commonplace."

"I foretell that you will rapidly rise in prominence in the banking field, Luke, with so diplomatic an evasion as that," Gabriel Mercier said, laughing. "But I will be honest with you. You know of my interest in Madame Brunton, and it was not entirely to complete a merger between our two banks. But I daresay that you too have found the widow maddeningly desirable."

Luke nodded, not wishing to comment on a subject so close to his heart.

"Well then, set your mind at rest if you have similar aims, Luke. I was blunt enough to propose marriage to Madame Brunton, and she bluntly declined. I admire her spirit and independence. Perhaps we're not ready yet for the emancipation of the female, but I should say that when that day comes, Madame Laure Brunton will be in the vanguard of those who champion the movement."

"Then you have withdrawn from the lists, I take it?" Luke suggested guardedly.

Gabriel Mercier nodded. "I confess I'm at the time of life when I seek acquiescence and comforts. Besides, the advantage is all in your favor now, since you're associated with her in business. It was a clever move not to insist that your name be added to Brunton's, I'll give you that, *mon ami*."

"I did it only out of loyalty to John. Besides, it was Laure's wish."

"Of course, of course, *ça se voit*. All the same, Venus has suddenly smiled on me. Yesterday an attractive young woman visited my bank in search of employment. She happens to be the daughter of a retired banker who had a small plantation up-river; he was obliged to sell it for whatever he could get before the Yankees took it over. What money he garnered from that sale was spent almost entirely on medicines and doctors. The gentleman died a few months ago and Mademoiselle Clarice is penniless. She is in her mid-twenties, gentle and demure and modest, with an excellent education, and I think that she may well be my future wife. I have put her to work in the bank until I can begin to court her in earnest."

"It is gracious of you to tell me about your affairs, Gabriel. And let me thank you for the excellent advice you've given me. I've decided to buy some tracts of land in the American section, and also to lend money to sugarcane planters—but only those who seem capable and have a good crew. There are still too many stories circulating of the cruelties and tyranny practiced on many Louisiana sugarcane plantations."

"Ah, you're quite right. Before the war, the *Nègres* feared most of all being sold down the river and ending their days cutting cane under the lash of the overseers in the boiling Louisiana sun. Besides, there are new methods of refinement now, and there's a growing market for sugar. I do not think cotton will be very stable for the next few years, and I've heard some rumors about the blight that is likely to affect this year's crops."

"Again I thank you for your advice. As soon as my house is in order and I've engaged a housekeeper, I should like you and the future Madame

Mercier to be my guests for dinner." Luke offered the banker his hand, and Gabriel Mercier shook it warmly.

Aurelia Dubois had worn her plainest dress for the interview with Felix Brissart. Entering the restaurant on Eglantine Street, she self-consciously bit her lower lip as she watched the short, gray-haired man direct his waiters and busboys to set up their stations for the luncheon service. His gruff manner and resonant voice had made her some-what fearful, since, upon her hesitant entry into the restaurant, he had glanced irritably at her and snapped, "A moment if you please, Mam'selle, I'll be with you directly."

"A fresh tablecloth on that table in the corner, Adolphe—*vraiment, tu es un imbécile!*" He pointed a stubby forefinger at a gangling busboy. *"Vite, vite, pas de temps à perdre, tu sais!"*

Seeing his order being carried out, Felix Brissart turned toward the young woman and came forward with a gracious smile. "Forgive me, Mam'selle." With the utmost gallantry, he took her hand and brought it to his lips. "In forty minutes we open our doors for *dejeuner*, you see. Now then, M'sieu Bouchard has told me that you sing the old French songs. Now that I see you, I am sure that my patrons will be as enchanted as I am."

Aurelia Dubois blushed furiously and lowered her eyes. "You're much too kind, M'sieu Brissart," she murmured. "Perhaps if you've time to hear a song or two, you might not think so highly of my talents."

"When someone is modest and beautiful into the

bargain, Mam'selle, that already tells me much about her talents. Come now, let me hear a song."

Turning back, in a loud voice he exclaimed, "Listen, you imbeciles, but keep working. Make sure all the silverware shines like the morning sun and that there are plenty of *serviettes!*" Smiling, he seated himself and nodded. "Whatever you wish, Mam'selle Dubois."

Somewhat reassured, Aurelia tuned her mandolin, closed her eyes so that she would not be distracted by the scurrying waiters and busboys, and began to sing one of the songs of the Auvergne in a sweet soprano voice:

Lo, lo, lo, lo,
Passo pel prat, beloto,
Ieu possorai pel bouos;
Quon li seras pouloto,
M'esperoras se vouos!

Felix Brissart uttered a sigh, and then, before Aurelia could sing the next verse, himself proffered it in a hoarse, scratchy voice, his homely face radiant with pleasure:

Nous porloren, filhoto,
Nous porloren toui dous;
Qu'os toun omour drouloto,
Que me foro hurous!

"Oh, M'sieu Brissart, you know it too!" Aurelia exclaimed.

"Should I not, *ma petite fille?* I, who am from fair Provence, should I not know the songs of the Auvergne, the loveliest region in all *la belle* France? Do you know what the words mean?"

"Some of them, yes," Aurelia timidly confessed, her cheeks flaming from the intent look that Felix Brissart shot her. "It means, 'Come through the meadow, my beautiful one, I shall come through the wood.' Isn't that right?"

"Decidedly. And the verse I sang, 'We will talk, little girl, we will talk together. It is your love, little one, which will make me happy!' Ah, mam'selle, you could not have chosen a more delightful song to cheer the heart of an old widower. And your voice, such sweet purity! But now then— naturally, you are engaged. Would forty dollars a week and meals be enough to offer so accomplished a singer? Mind you, mam'selle, that is only to begin with. My restaurant flourishes, as perhaps M'sieu Bouchard has told you."

"That's most generous of you, sir. I shall work very hard to make your customers like me."

He rose from the chair, took her hand, and kissed it again. "I foresee that you will do much more than that, Mam'selle Dubois."

Luke had purchased a two-wheeled, light, low calash with a folding top, and had trained his stallion to accept harnessing. At first, he went on test rides along quiet residential streets to accustom the horse to the new burden, and within ten days him was able to move easily, without distraction from other carriages and the noise of passersby. It was nearing the end of July now, and many of the wealthier citizens of the Queen City had left for their summer homes upriver to avoid the humidity and the ever-present threat of yellow

93

fever, a threat that intensified during the heat of the summer.

Yet, there was more than yellow fever to threaten the citizens of New Orleans this summer. The Louisiana legislators, under congressional direction, were attempting to introduce Negro suffrage into the Louisiana Constitution. Already the *Times-Picayune* had thundered out its denunciation of Northern insistence upon this measure, which must necessarily prove odious to Southern sympathizers. There had been civic meetings and unrest among both shopkeepers and industrialists. A number of legislators, fearful of the angry reaction of their constituents if they were obliged to pass so unpalatable a measure, had asked influential members of Congress to urge a gradual approach to the issue rather than insistence upon immediate compliance.

But the anti-Southern faction, led by the virulent and vengeful Thaddeus Stevens, refused to tolerate delay. Stevens, who had proposed the Fourteenth Amendment, had already been named to the select, joint Committee of Fifteen, which tyrannically controlled the readmittance to the Union of the Southern states. In his view, the South was a "conquered province which must be taught its folly in breaking away from our beloved Union, even if it means imposing the shackles of servitude upon it." And President Andrew Johnson's attempt to bring about a sane Reconstruction policy only goaded Stevens into initiating legislation that would reduce Johnson's influence upon a war-torn nation. The President's words upon taking the Oath of Office— "The only safety of the nation lies in a generous and expansive plan of conciliation, and the longer this is delayed, the more difficult will it be to bring the North and the South into harmony"—seemed to fall upon increasingly deaf ears.

On the evening of July 29, Luke had taken Laure to supper at Moreau's, to outline to her his plans to purchase several small sections of land in the American Quarter. They also discussed the problem of Odette and Virginie, and when Laure mentioned that they were quite adept at designing their own hats, Luke replied, "You said that John won a trust fund for them by playing faro with their uncle—why not use that money to help them start a millinery shop? There's plenty of room in the rear section of the bank—and that way you and I could watch over them and make certain they tended strictly to business."

"That's a very good idea. I'll talk to them this evening about it. I'm sure they'd like to be independent and earn their own livelihood in an honorable way. Of course," she added as an afterthought, "women who buy hats often bring their husbands to see if they approve; I hope Odette and Virginie won't make eyes at the husbands."

"I'm sure that if you take them aside and warn them of the dangers, they'll listen to you, Laure. And, being so close, it'll be easy for us to visit from time to time and see that they're behaving themselves."

"Maybe some widower or nice young bachelor will visit the shop out of curiosity and fall in love with one or the other; that would solve their problems permanently."

"That, as Shakespeare might have said, is a consummation devoutly to be wished," Luke said, laughing. "And when that happens, there will have been a happy ending for everyone."

Laure regarded him, her eyes momentarily narrowing, then the curves of her soft lips took a deliberate, teasing moue as she remarked, "You should have been a writer of stories, Luke. You wish to contrive happy endings for everyone, and it's much easier to do that in stories than in real life, n'est-ce pas?"

Once again her verbal barb had pierced his composure. "There's nothing wrong with a happy ending, Laure," he said. "I look forward to the pleasure of calling for you in my calash about ten tomorrow morning, if that's not too early."

Once again Laure had the last word: "A widow with a child and a business to look over, M'sieu Bouchard, has no time to lie abed of a morning. Come even a few minutes earlier, if you like."

Early in the morning on July 30 there had been a brief but heavy rain, and the humidity was stifling as Luke's horse trotted up to the curb in front of the Union House. The top was pulled down over the calash to afford what protection it could from the heat, and Luke wore his derby as a further precaution. He had propped his swordcane in the back, against the seat. As he brought the horse to a halt and stepped down onto the banquette, he thought that it would do no harm to take fencing lessons. It was a fine blade, and a fencer whose wrist was quick and supple would find it a valuable weapon in time of danger. Despite the civil guards who patrolled the more rambunctious areas at nightfall, there were still many ruffians who roamed the streets and terrorized the gentry.

The door of the Union House opened and Laure appeared, dressed in a long-skirted black frock with puffed sleeves and a black bonnet to signify her mourning. The sombre hue seemed to make her golden hair more resplendent.

"Good-morning, Madame Brunton." Luke doffed his derby and bowed slightly, having decided after last night to adopt a strictly formal demeanor for this business appointment.

"And to you, M'sieu Bouchard," was her blithe answer as she came toward the calash. He helped her into the back seat, then mounted the driver's seat, took the reins, and started along the circuitous route that led to Greenley Street.

Laure had carried a little parasol in the event of the expected blazing July sun, but now, disconsolately glancing up at the gray, overcast sky, leaned to the left to place it beside Luke's swordcane, then settled back for the ride as the calash turned down Mirabeau Place, then turned left toward Canal Street. There was a faint rumble of thunder in the distance, but it was drowned out by the far more ominous sounds of angry voices: "Goddamn, no nigger's going to vote like a white man while I'm alive!—Blame it on the damned carpetbaggers—and on that dirty Yanke-lover Governor Wells—let's burn down his house!—Let's find us a nigger and show the Northern bastards how we liberate 'em down here, boys!"

"*Mon Dieu,* what is it, Luke?" Laure exclaimed

in alarm as she turned to look down the street in the direction from which the angry cries had come. Luke drew in the reins as he saw a milling crowd on the banquette opposite the office of the *Times-Picayune*. On the edge, a bewhiskered man in a silk top hat and light frock coat stood conversing with an equally well-groomed Creole dandy, each turning to glance back at the hostile crowd, which had begun to shove and push toward the doors of the newspaper office.

"Sir, can you tell me what's happening?" Luke called.

"The legislature is voting to give the *Nègres* the vote, m'sieu!" retorted the man in the silk hat. "It's a bad business. It looks like a riot down the street. There's already been fighting on Bourbon Street. A few poor fellows have been killed and others taken to the hospital. You'd best not go down this way, it might be dangerous for you and the lady."

As he spoke, there was a crash of glass as someone flung a brickbat through the window of the newspaper office, and jubilant cries arose. "Smash the presses, see if they've got any niggers working for them—drag them out here, we'll hang them to the lamp posts—you're right, that's the way to show that damned Northern Congress we've got in Washington that we Southerners won't be a nigger's slaves!" came the approving shouts.

"This is terrible, Luke," Laure said anxiously. "Can't we drive on?"

"I think so. The street's a little muddy from the rain this morning, and I don't see very many carriages on either side. We'll chance it. It's the most direct way to the bank, anyhow. Giddyap!" Luke called and shook the reins. The stallion tossed his head, snorted, and moved forward, his hooves impeded by the thickening mud along the side of Canal Street.

They had proceeded as far as the Rue de Jacques when Luke suddenly reined in his horse and stood up to watch as a tall, sturdy black man in his mid-twenties, his back against the window of a draper's shop, tried to defend himself against four white men, one of whom had lifted a malacca cane and was maneuvering for position to bring it down on the victim's head.

"Let him go!" Luke cried out angrily. As he spoke, two of the men lunged at the black man and seized his wrists, while he kicked and twisted with all his strength. Laughing cruelly, they dragged him away from the window and out to the middle of the banquette. "Now you can brain this black sonofabitch, Henri!" exclaimed a pockmarked, corpulent, shabbily dressed man in his early fifties.

With a muttered oath, Luke reached back into the seat of the calash and seized his swordcane, sprang down onto the banquette, and drew out the blade. "Let him go, I tell you!"

"Here's another fancy nigger-lover, Henri," the pockmarked man snarled. "Why, he's got a sword; a gentleman trying to defend a nigger like this one—maybe he's got a touch of the tarbrush hisself, hey? Give it to him good, Henri!"

The man with the malacca cane growled as he made a sudden swipe at Luke's face with the knobbed head of the cane. Ducking under the blow, Luke thrust deftly; his assailant uttered a

99

yowl of pain, dropped the cane, and clutched his bleeding wrist. "D'you see what he did to me? Call the civil guard; he tried to murder me!" he yelled.

The pockmarked man drew out a Bowie knife from the inner pocket of his threadbare frock coat. At the same time, one of the two men holding the young black launched a savage kick at Luke's shin.

"Look out, Luke!" Laure cried.

But Luke had seen the kick coming. Nimbly stepping to one side, he put the point of the gleaming sword up against the pockmarked man's throat. "Drop that knife! Drop it or I'll run you through, I mean it," he said between his teeth.

Cowed, the man stepped back and dropped the Bowie knife. "Fer Gawd's sake, mister, put that thing away!" he whined.

Luke stooped to retrieve the knife, gripping it in his left hand while he held the sword angled up at the man's throat. "That's much better. Now you and your friend Henri get out of here as fast as you can. And you two, let go of that man and join your cowardly friends!"

Glowering at him, the two men exchanged a disgruntled look, then ran down the banquette.

"Thank you, mister," the black man said, breathing hard as he tried to button his torn cambric shirt. "God bless you for what you did. But you sure got yourself into plenty of trouble over somebody you don't even know."

"You don't deserve to be torn to pieces by stupid brutes just because the color of your skin is different from theirs," Luke retorted curtly. "Get into the calash; I'll drive you to the bank where we've business, and then we'll get you to safety. For the

100

time being, you'll be out of this riot. My God, I didn't dream things would come to this—"

"I shouldn't rightly go with you, not sitting next to your fine lady, mister," the black said hesitantly.

"Nonsense," Laure said, leaning forward. "Do what M'sieu Bouchard tells you before another gang of fools tries to kill you. There's plenty of room beside me, get in!"

"Bless you both. My name is Marius Thornton. I won't ever forget you in my prayers."

Luke sheathed his sword, flung the Bowie knife into the muddy street, then mounted to the driver's seat and started down the street to the bank. The young black man, seated beside Laure, drew himself as far away from her as he could, as if fearing that his presence was odious to her.

But Laure did not notice this. Her eyes were fixed on the back of the tall man who sat in the driver's seat of the calash, and her lips were curved in a soft smile.

CHAPTER NINE

The race riot over the proposed black suffrage had gone on till evening, quelled by the civil guard on some of the main streets, only to break out again in other quarters. At noon there had been a brief but violent thunderstorm, as if the elements were echoing the hatreds that had created the Civil War and were still nurtured by the bitterness of the aftermath.

There was little business at the bank that day, for news of the riot had spread like wildfire and many citizens were afraid to leave their homes or places of business. Laure had a long visit with Madelon Fortier and saw for herself how admirably the young woman was adapting to her new situation. Thereafter, Luke closeted himself with Laure, Jason Barntry, and Edgar Maxton, to discuss the bank's policy in making loans and in issuing shares at a given parity that might be attractive to wealthier investors. Because of the inflation, as well as the obvious shortage of specie, several of the private banks had been obliged to set exorbitant interest rates on their loans. Luke declared that he was in favor of backing reliable merchants and landowners to help them build toward a solid future. "I would rather help industrious persons toward building the kind of security this city must have, than to be greedy and deal only with the very wealthy or indulge in risky speculation for the sake of big immediate gains."

"I quite agree with you, Mr. Bouchard," said Edgar Maxton, a stocky, black-haired man with weatherbeaten features and a straightforward manner. "Naturally, some of our customers have asked if we're going to support the cotton crop, and I told them, as you suggested, that sugar and land are more likely to turn a profit for them this year."

Luke nodded. "Mr. Barntry, if things continue slowly the rest of this week because of the riot, it might be a good idea for you to make a tour of the city and seek out pieces of property that are up for sale. Find out who owns them, what sort of liens still exist, and let me have a report as to your opinion of their potential value. And I'd like you, Mr. Maxton, to inspect the warehouses on the levee and talk to some of the shipping people to see what quality of cotton and other goods is coming into the port. Also, find out as much as you can about the tariffs on these goods. My grandfather used to tell me that one reason Mobile didn't have the same volume of trade as New Orleans was that the Spanish, who controlled it for so many years, imposed such outrageous tariffs. And I think, too, we ought to talk to someone from the *Times-Picayune* to see if they'll print a story on our modest lending rates and our plans to help New Orleans rebuild its financial structure."

At about three-thirty that afternoon, Laure and Madelon had left the bank together, Laure wanting to inspect Madelon's new living quarters. In her desire to begin a new life, with no association with the bordello on Honoree Street, the orphaned young woman had found a room in a boarding house on the Rue de Lucette run by a motherly Irish widow.

Marius Thornton had, at Luke's insistence, stayed in the bank, seated in one of the vacant private cubicles in the back. After Laure and Madelon had left the bank, Luke went in to talk to the sturdy young black man.

"You been mighty kind to me, Mr. Bouchard." Marius Thornton had risen, out of respect, as Luke walked into the little office.

"Please sit down, Mr. Thornton. I'd like you to tell me something about yourself. Were you a slave before the war?"

"Yes, sir. My mammy and daddy worked for old Mr. Eames, who had a sugarcane plantation upriver. I was born a slave. By the time I was freed, my folks had died. Mr. Eames took the war mighty hard, and started drinking and cursing the Yankees that had stolen his niggers and all his profits from the cane. Most of the slaves ran away as soon as the news came about the Emancipation Proclamation, but I stayed on till he killed himself one night—he couldn't stand it anymore, I guess. Well, sir, after that I got some work here as a handyman, running errands and such, doing odd jobs."

"Until today," Luke interposed.

Marius Thornton shrugged, and made as if to rise. "I better be getting back now, Mr. Bouchard. I guess it'll be safe enough."

"Don't be in such a hurry, Mr. Thornton. You said that you worked on a cane plantation—but the way you talk indicates that you've had a good deal of education."

"Well, sir, the last few years I was with Mr. Eames, he figured there wouldn't be any more work on the plantation, so he let me borrow some of the books in his library and showed me how to read and write. I was mighty grateful to him for that. I guess at the end he saw how things were going and wanted to make up for it to me, if you know what I mean."

"Yes, I do. And I take it you know a good deal about land, since you worked on it from the time you were a boy; is that correct?"

The young black nodded. "I had some ideas about making the work easier and getting it done faster, and once in a while the foreman would pay attention and try the idea out. Mostly, though, he liked to use his whip. It was good land, too, except the foreman made everybody pick a quota of cane, and thrashed those who didn't make it. And he set it a lot higher than it should have been. If he'd divided up the work better, I think Mr. Eames would have made more money."

Luke pursed his lips as he thought for a moment. "I'll be frank with you, Mr. Thornton. I'm here in the banking business now, and I came here from

105

Texas where my son founded a cattle ranch. But originally all of us came from Alabama, near Montgomery. The man who used to run this bank, John Brunton, was able to buy back some of the Alabama land and the house that was on it and have it held by a black freedman. What I'm hoping for is to go back there one day soon and try my hand at farming again, with improved methods and fair wages for all my workers. It won't be just cotton, because the price has dropped so badly; I'm thinking about raising cattle and also crops like barley and some other produce. Would you be interested in working my land for me when I get it back?"

Marius Thornton's eyes brightened. "I surely would, Mr. Bouchard. I've a hankerin' to work some land—I know it sounds silly, but I even thought of saving a little money out of what I made and putting it aside so that maybe one day I could buy a piece of land all for myself."

"Here is what I am proposing, Mr. Thornton: It'll be at least a year, maybe two, before it's possible to buy back that land of mine; meanwhile, I'd like to hire you to do some errands for us here at the bank, and also, if you've no objection, to be a kind of caretaker for my house farther down the street. I'd be willing to pay you twenty-five dollars a week, plus board, if that's acceptable to you."

"Mr. Bouchard, that's more money than I've ever seen at any one time! Besides, after what you did for me today, I'm your man. You know, there's a saying that when you save somebody's life, that person is just about bound to you—I don't mean like a slave in the old days, but—" He shifted in his chair and lowered his eyes.

"I know what you mean," Luke answered. "I tell you what. We're going to close the bank in an hour or so, and then I'll drive you over to your room. You can pick up your things and come back to my house and settle in right away. Maybe you could work mornings here at the bank and carry messages and take drafts over to some of the people who do business with us."

"I'd like that fine, Mr. Bouchard. I can't begin to thank you enough for all you've done—"

Luke held up his hand. "No need for thanks. I think you're going to be a great help to me, Mr. Thornton. Just one more question—do you know how to cook?"

The black man beamed from ear to ear. "That's something I can do right smart, Mr. Bouchard. Why, I was cooking old Mr. Eames's meals for him all the last year of his life, and he seemed to think they tasted pretty good. I know how to shop and I'm careful with money—I've learned that, being on my own this last year."

"That's fine! You'll be my cook as well as my caretaker, and if I like your cooking, I'll add a few dollars to your weekly pay. Have we agreed on terms, then?"

For answer, Marius Thornton stood up and held out his hand, which Luke Bouchard enthusiastically shook.

It rained again about eight o'clock on the evening of the street violence, but by ten o'clock the sky was clear and a full moon shone down over the

Queen City. Luke had taken the second floor of the little house for his own quarters, and installed Marius Thornton in one of the bedrooms on the first floor. A stairway just inside and to the left of the front door led to Luke's rooms. He was seated now in the parlor, poring over a book on banking and finance. In addition, he referred from time to time to the old account ledger in which he had recorded his transactions with John Brunton's bank. In this ledger he had retained some of the pages of the prewar account from the trading house in Mobile.

He opened the back of the ledger, drew out these pages, and studied them. Thousands of dollars in credit had been wiped out by the defeat of the Confederacy, money that might well have gone to his son Lucien Edmond and to little Carla and Hugo, money that might have been paid to the workers who had accompanied him from Windhaven Plantation. And all of that money represented years of toil, of methodically planned crops. What gave him heart for the future was the fact that, according to the figures for the last few years before the war, Windhaven Plantation had not been financially dependent upon cotton. The diversification of crops clearly indicated that if he could ever regain Windhaven Plantation and have a free hand to continue his experiments, those rich acres would produce bounteous harvests.

Dressed in a comfortable cotton robe, Luke leaned back in his chair with a sigh, shoved the ledger aside, and stared out the windows. He was suddenly very tired. It had been a nerve-wracking day and he needed a good night's sleep. This morning's fracas had drawn his mind back to those

108

days of the Underground Railway when he and Djamba had fought for their lives against the vicious James Buffery and his two cronies. How long ago that had been, in the days when he was still a comparatively young man!

He turned from the window as he heard footsteps, and smiled as Marius Thornton entered with a glass of hot milk. "Marius, you're going to spoil me!" he said, chuckling.

"Now I like that fine, Mr. Bouchard, you calling me Marius instead of Mr. Thornton, just like I asked." The young black carefully set down the glass with a napkin under it. "You'd best drink it while it's hot, Mr. Bouchard. It'll help you sleep."

"Thank you, Marius. Now you go to bed and get your rest."

"Just as you say, sir. Good-night."

Luke lifted the glass to his lips as he slowly walked to the window. Then he started with surprise as he saw a hansom cab pull up in front of the house. It was driven by an old black man wearing the livery of the Union House. As he stared, the door opened and a woman emerged, wearing a black domino mask and black velvet cloak, her dainty feet shod in silver cloth slippers. He caught a glimpse of elegant silk hose as the hem of the cloak lifted above her slim ankles.

He leaned forward as he saw her heading toward the door of his house, and then he hastily went down the stairs to admit her himself so that Marius Thornton would not be disturbed. As he opened the door, the lustrous golden hair of his nocturnal visitor at once revealed her identity.

"Laure—" he began, his voice taut.

109

She put a finger to his lips and whispered, "Hush. Am I disturbing you, coming so late and unannounced?"

The delicate scent of jasmine reached him and he trembled. It was the same exquisite scent she had worn on the afternoon they had spent together so long ago. It was with an effort that he forced himself to reply in a level tone, "No; I was going over some books, just to keep abreast of the banking business."

"Good!" She playfully tapped his nose with the tip of her forefinger. "You know what they say about all work and no play. Aren't you going to show me your new house?"

"I might be curious enough to ask why you're wearing a mask, Laure."

"Oh! Well, it's so as not to compromise a very upstanding banker whose character is beyond reproach. And also, from my viewpoint, so that no one would think that Laure Brunton, who is now carrying on her husband's bank as he would have wished it, is the kind who has secret assignations with one of her business associates. My, this is a charming little house. Please—show me where you live. . . . I told the night porter at the house to call for me about midnight; that should give me ample time to see your new quarters, don't you think?"

Already, flashing him a sultry glance from her ardent green eyes, Laure had begun to ascend the narrow, winding stairway to the second floor. Luke followed her, digging his nails into his palms as he tried to exorcise the sensual images that the graceful movement of her body aroused in him. The black cloak clung about her and, with each step she took, lifted to reveal the sleek curves of her lower calves.

As he reached the landing, she turned to face him and murmured huskily, "Am I really such an unwelcome visitor, Luke? You haven't kissed me yet."

He clenched his fists as he replied in a voice quivering with the turmoil within him, "This isn't fair of you, Laure. I asked you to marry me, and you rejected me. Now you visit me at night without warning, masked like a beautiful courtesan who goes secretly to meet her lover, and then you reproach me for not kissing you."

"Why, I should think that if you desired me enough to want to marry me, you surely wouldn't hesitate over a simple kiss of welcome."

"As you say, a kiss of welcome, Madame Brunton," Luke replied. Taking her by the shoulders, he gave her a brief kiss on the cheek.

"Where's the courage you showed this morning, *mon ami?*" Her voice was a whisper as she unbelted the cloak and let it slip down to the floor, the domino mask attached to it, and stood before him in the same red silk wrapper that she had worn on that fateful afternoon.

Luke sucked in his breath, his temples pounding feverishly. The wrapper hugged her voluptuous body like a cocoon. What made her all the more exciting to him was the contrast of her boyishly short golden hair where once it had tumbled nearly to her waist in a burnished silken cascade.

He stared at her like one bewitched by a Circe-like enchantress, his loins throbbing with desire.

"Has your courage come back to you yet, *mon*

ami?" she murmured. Turning to look into the parlor, she said, "The rest of the apartment is so dark; I'll use this candle to light my way. Since you seem indisposed to escort me on my little tour, it seems I must do it for myself."

"No—Laure—oh, God—why do you torture me like this?" he said, groaning.

But already the golden-haired young woman had gone to the mahogany table, lifted up the candleholder, and returned to walk slowly down the hall, provocatively glancing back over her shoulder with a faintly mocking smile.

"Torture?" she echoed, her dainty brows arching in feigned surprise. "Who spoke of torturing you, *mon vieux ami?* Ah, here, I believe, is your bedroom, *n'est-ce pas?*"

She crossed the threshold of his bedroom and set the candleholder down on the little night table beside the bed. "How very austere it is," she mused aloud. "I really must send over one of the canopied beds from the Union House. It's dreadful to think of you working hard at the bank all day and then trying to sleep on such an uncomfortable-looking bed."

He could bear no more. Striding to her, his face twisted in anguish and desire, he grasped her by the hips and drew her to him, his mouth coming down hard on hers.

With a delighted little giggle she reached up and wound her arms tightly around his shoulders, her lips opening to his, moist, soft, alluring with the promise of total acquiescence.

His hands stroked her deeply hollowed back, moving around to brush against the sides of her

112

swelling bosoms. With a wordless sigh she closed her eyes and clung to him, returning his kiss with burning ardor. Her body arched to his, and then it was her turn to quiver at the awareness of his furiously aroused maleness.

"Laure, Laure, does this mean you'll say yes?" he asked hoarsely as he drew away from her soft lips.

"It means—what it means, nothing more, Luke. Must you always have a reason for everything? Have you forgotten that afternoon when I wore what I'm wearing now, and you forgot yourself long enough to be a man any woman would want as her lover?"

With a cry of joy, Luke turned and bent toward the candle, but Laure stopped him with a gesture. "No, *mon ami*. Let us see each other as we are at this moment. This is our moment, not the future, and perhaps not any other time but now. Now, because this morning you thrilled me, because you didn't think of the dangers but tried to save that poor black man, because you would have fought for me to defend me—"

"Yes—oh, God, yes, Laure—now!" He groaned as he turned back to clasp her in his arms and fuse his lips to hers again. He could feel the heaving of her round breasts flattened against his chest, and the scent of jasmine was like an aphrodisiac. He scarcely felt her soft hands unbutton his robe and then shove it off his shoulders till it slithered to the floor. Now emboldened by her passionate candor, his hands cupped the sides of her breasts as he drew her still closer to him, till they seemed to merge, till he could almost feel the eagerness of her flesh to meet his.

113

Then swiftly she broke away from his embrace, her fingers deftly opening the sequinned belt that fastened her wrapper. Straightening her shoulders with a beautifully proud gesture, she lifted her wrapper from her tawny-skinned body and stood before him, her palms turned upward.

The thin flame of the candle flickered and cast eerie shadows on the walls, dappling her nakedness with its glow. She stood now in only the tan silk hose held at mid-thigh by elastic green-satin rosette garters, exactly as she had been that timeless afternoon that seemed an eternity ago. Spellbound, Luke knew only the glory of her tempting body. He stripped off his smallclothes, stooped to lift her with his arms around her back and thighs, and carried her to the bed. Then, mounting beside her, his hands revering the swelling globes of her sumptuous breasts, he bent his head to take her mouth and taste its honeyed sweetness as her arms reached up to cling around his neck and draw him down upon her.

He uttered a stifled cry of ecstasy to feel himself sheathed within her core, to feel her thighs entwined around his, to feel her warm moist skin at oneness with his own. His hands explored the remembered yet now marvelously new wonder of her body, molding her hips and buttocks, caressing her quivering inner thighs, cupping her luxurious round bosoms.

It seemed to him that he had never known such ecstasy before, never known the passionate, searching intensely joyous and abandoned act of love. Her hands caressed him, and her soft gasps and little sighs tutored him in the spontaneous and imaginative fulfillment of her own needs, which clamorously became his very own.

He heard her cry out in joyous abandon as his own shattering fulfillment came upon him, and they lay entwined and fused for endless moments. And then there was the exquisite and languorous rediscovery of each other, the flattering words and soft whispers, the touches and kisses and caresses that are such an integral part of the physical communion of love.

As he stared down into her luminous green eyes, tender and warm as they had not been until now, he heard the faint chimes of the old grandfather's clock in the hall.

"I must go, *mon amour*," Laure whispered as she sat up and swung her lovely stockinged legs to the floor.

"Oh no—not so soon—Laure, my darling—"

But already, very primly and demurely, she was drawing on the wrapper, then the cloak with its domino mask. "It's midnight, Luke."

"But you haven't told me yet—"

She laughed softly and shook her head. "There you go, being the old dull Luke I met last year. I must say, I much prefer the new one. But the answer is still no—I'm not ready to marry you yet. And you mustn't think you've trapped me by giving me a child tonight; it's not my time, you see."

As he awkwardly drew on his robe, he said in a strangled voice, "That's damnably unfair of you, Laure, and you know it."

"Perhaps. But why should a man have all the advantages? Tonight, *mon ami*, was what I said it was—no more and no less. Now I really must go or

115

old Moses will think you're keeping me against my will. Sleep well, and I'll see you at the bank tomorrow."

She blew him a kiss, and with a gay, soft laugh, went down the stairway to the waiting hansom cab.

CHAPTER TEN

Maybelle Belcher ladled out a spoonful of stew from the big pot in the open stone oven that her husband had constructed for her. Satisfied with its flavor, she wiped her forehead with the hem of her apron, then called, "Henry, supper's ready. Make sure Timmy and Connie wash up before they sit down at the table!"

"Sure, honey," Henry Belcher called back. "All right, kids, you heard your mother."

"Oh, all right, Pa," the freckle-faced, twelve-year-old boy assented gloomily.

"And let your sister wash up first; you just remember that, Tim, ladies go first in this house," Henry said, loud enough for Maybelle to hear.

Maybelle sighed happily. Just two weeks after Luke had bidden his family farewell and ridden off to Corpus Christi, she and the middle-aged widower had ridden to San Antonio to be married. In this short month she had managed to forget all the lonely years back in Alabama after Mark Bouchard had abandoned her and gone to work for Pierre Lourat. All that she regretted was that she could not give the kindly man from Sedalia a child; the miscarriage that had followed the news of Mark's permanent separation from her had left her barren. Even if that had not been the case, she was forty-five, past the age for childbearing. Yet, Tim and blond little Connie had already taken to her as if she were their real mother, and indeed called her that without being told to do so by their father. Daily, she rejoiced that fate had brought Henry Belcher and his two motherless children to this isolated part of Texas.

Henry continued to praise the courage she had shown in killing the comanchero Merle Kinnick, who, with his bandit and renegade Indian allies, had tried to raid Windhaven Range. And although her waistline had begun to thicken and her once-flaming red hair had begun to show streaks of gray, in Henry Belcher's eyes she was one of the most beautiful women he had ever seen. Their conjugal union had served to restore all her joy and pride in being a desired woman. In the days of her youth, Mark Bouchard had used her like the lowest chattel, demeaning her and rebuffing all her pathetic attempts to prove her love for him. But in Henry Belcher's almost humbly grateful embrace, her womanhood had blossomed anew. She was learning, for the first time, the meaning of warm, easygoing companionship and the sharing of emotions, which was more truly love than she had ever known before.

"There now," she said happily as she bustled in with the bowls of stew, setting the largest portion before her beaming husband, "and there's lots more where that came from. But you'd best leave room for the apple pie I baked this afternoon."

Henry dipped his spoon into the bowl, tasted the stew, and smacked his lips. "Maybelle, getting a beauty like you, and finding her such a scrumptious cook into the bargain, is more than I deserve."

Maybelle had served herself and now sat at the other end of the table. "Now, Henry," she chided, "you're going to spoil me if you keep making sweet talk like that. But I'm glad you like my cooking. I could do lots better if supplies weren't so far away. You know, with these hundred acres Luke Bouchard helped you claim, we can plant fruits and vegetables for our own table and have whatever we like, the soil is so rich."

"That reminds me, honey, I want to plough that fifteen acres on the west side and get it ready for some corn and melons next summer. When I go to San Antonio I'll bring back some seeds and show you what real farming is, the way I used to do it in Sedalia."

Maybelle smiled warmly at him. He was five years younger, and lately she'd taken to primping a bit when he wasn't looking, so that she could look as young as possible.

"Well, I'll say one thing, Maybelle," he concluded as he reached for one of her biscuits, "you don't know how good it is not to have to worry

119

about abolitionists and slaves, but just work the land with the hands and the brain God gave me. And to have a home like this and a wife like you to look after me and Tim and Connie—"

Maybelle's look was radiant. "I just hope Mara is as happy with Ramon as I am with you and the children."

"They're supposed to be married as soon as Ramon gets his house built, aren't they?"

"Yes, dear. You know, it's so nice to see Ramon's companions helping him build the house. And he picked a lovely place on the two hundred acres Luke gave him."

"When I went by this afternoon, it looked to me as if Ramon's house will be ready in about a week."

"Well, for sure we'll be invited to the wedding, Henry. I'm going to bake Mara the biggest, tastiest cake in all Texas," Maybelle promised.

By the end of the first week of August 1866, Ramon Hernandez and his vaquero companions, together with Djamba and his son, Lucas, completed the house where Ramon would live with his new bride, beautiful, twenty-nine-year-old Mara Bouchard. It was a one-story ranchhouse, with a specially fortified roof that rose in a triangular peak to minimize the effect of the intense heat. The huge cedar tree and the clump of pecan trees on the other side would give shade against the almost intolerable summer sun. Ramon himself had diligently toiled on a little stable; his beloved mare, Corita, would occupy the most spacious stall.

The house faced west, and there was a small

veranda at one side with a sloping, thin-planked roof where the young couple could sit and look out over the land. As a wedding present, Sybella Forsden, whom Mara lovingly called Grandmother, had promised the young couple her cherry-wood rocking chair, one of the few pieces of furniture to be saved from the fire that had destroyed Windhaven Plantation. As a personal gift, Sybella had given Mara an exquisite cameo brooch that had been given to her by her own mother.

Lucien Edmond Bouchard, a year younger than his sister, had promised to pay for the wedding and even for a honeymoon in San Antonio, or, if Mara wished, even as far away as New Orleans, so that she might visit their father.

On the Sunday evening after the house was completed, Mara and Ramon stood alone on the veranda, watching the sun descend. The air was still, and the droning of cicadas made a soft, drowsy hum.

"*Querida.*" The wiry young Mexican took Mara's hand and brought it to his lips. "Your brother is very generous. I know you would like to see your father, but it is I, not Lucien Edmond, who should pay for this honeymoon. I told you before, I am still a poor man, but your love has made me rich. And if you will give me a little time, I will make this new house of ours a palace for you."

Mara Bouchard was dressed in riding skirt and blouse, boots, and a wide-brimmed hat. Knowing that Ramon loved her luxuriously glossy black hair, she had pinned it up in a thick oval knot at the back of her neck, although the summer heat had often made her wish to cut it short. "My dearest,

I'm not asking you to be rich for my sake. We've the two hundred acres Father gave us as a wedding present, and you're one of the best horsemen I've ever seen. There'll be money in the years ahead, but right now we've all that matters: being together, starting our lives in our own little place, with our own land to grow crops on or to graze cattle."

"Mi esposa, te quiero mucho," Ramon huskily murmured as he drew her to him and kissed her tenderly. "I have sworn that I will not make love to you again until we are man and wife. You do not know how I have longed to love you just as we did that first time after you rode out so foolishly."

Mara stiffened for a moment, then tilted back her head and laughed softly. "You'll never stop reminding me of that, will you, my dear one? And I shan't forget that it was a lash from my quirt which began our love. I thought you were impertinent to tell me what to do, because you were—" She blushed, lowered her eyes, and pressed her forehead against his chest.

He chuckled delightedly. "I don't mind hearing you say it now, *mi querida.* Yes, because I was a greaser, a *Mejicano."*

"Shall I tell you how I really feel about you, Ramon?" Mara raised her eyes to meet his and spoke in an intimate, vibrant voice. "I've wanted to be yours, to have you take me just the way you did after you saved me from those Comanches. And then, after I'd agreed to marry you and told Father when he left for New Orleans that we were to be married by the priest in San Antonio two weeks later, I could hardly wait too be yours again. Oh,

Ramon darling, why did you suddenly change your mind and make me wait so long?"

"My sweetheart, my adorable one, *mi esposa*," he murmured tenderly as he drew off her wide-brimmed hat and gently unraveled the thick knot of her hair, letting it fall in a rich cascade below her shoulders. "I hunger for you more than you can for me, my dearest one. But I will tell you why I changed my mind. Your father once told me, when we were riding the range, how his father came from France to that Indian village and fell in love with the daughter of the chief. And how, before he could claim her as his wife, he had to till his own land and build a house for her. And I thought to myself that I, who had so little to offer so beautiful a señorita, should do no less. But now our house is truly built and ready for us, *querida,* and I will do whatever you wish. If you truly wish to see your father in New Orleans, I will borrow the money from your brother, but I swear I will pay him back as quickly as I can—"

Mara shook her head and put her fingers to his lips. "No, my dearest. I was being selfish again. Of course I'd like to have Father see us married. But he's gone back to New Orleans and he's busy making a new life for himself. I'd only be in the way. What I'd really like is to bring the priest here. I'll ask my brother if he can arrange it. Then we could be married in our own little house, Ramon. For our honeymoon I'd like us to go out on horseback, away from everyone. We could camp out under the stars and be alone and learn how much we really love each other, without feeling embarrassed by other people around us."

"Mara, *amorcito*, that too I would want with all my *corazón!*" Ramon exclaimed as he gently stroked her tumbling black curls and kissed her forehead, then each cheek in turn, and finally her lips.

Mara trembled, closing her eyes, her fingers clutching his sides as she shared the exquisite moment of their communion. "Do you remember what I promised my father, Ramon?" she whispered.

"I am not sure—I think so, *querida*," he stammered and flushed as she opened her eyes to stare ardently at him.

"Now you're being sweet and modest and making me feel like a shameless woman—which I'll gladly admit I am because I want you so much, my darling," Mara Bouchard laughed softly. "Don't you remember how Father hoped we would be very happy and we said that if we have a son and name it after him, it would please him greatly. And I promised him I'd do my very best." Then, in a fierce whisper, as she cupped his sun-bronzed face and brushed his lips with hers, she added, "I want to bear your son, Ramon, and that's why I've been so impatient."

Ramon kissed her tenderly, while the first shadows of evening began to creep along the grass, gradually, as if not wanting to plunge the lovers into darkness yet.

He was stirred by a profound emotion, evoked by her avowal of trust, passion, and love. He was remembering the little village of Miero, where he'd been shot in the back and left for dead by the self-proclaimed *Juarista* General Diego Macaras. He had come back to consciousness in the hut of a

124

handsome peasant woman, Magdalena Abruta. She had nursed his wounds and given him most of her own food so that he might regain his strength. He would never forget how, on the night before he was to leave the village, Magdalena Abruta had come to him and asked him to give her a son. Her husband had been killed in the raid on the village, and, barren during her twelve years of marriage, she longed for a child to help fill her empty and lonely life. Ramon had felt humble and unworthy in the face of such a powerful primitive yearning. Here was the eternal cycle—the desire, almost an instinct, to bring forth life to take the place of death.

He would never tell Mara about the heroic woman in the village of Miero. When he had gone back to the village to return the crucifix and the chalice that Diego Macaras had stolen, and which he had vowed to get back for the church, Magdalena told him she was with child and that a kindly, elderly man of the village had consented to marry her. She had said that if the child was a son she would name it Ramon after him. But he would not go back, for once he married Mara he would renounce all ties with the past. He held Mara close, almost reverently, and prayed to God to give them a son who would one day inherit the fruits of his labors upon the land that Luke Bouchard had so generously given him.

Lucien Edmond Bouchard had ridden to San Antonio and brought back a priest whose energy belied his sixty years, Father Bartolomeo Andraga, from the Mission of Dolores. A Franciscan friar, he regaled Mara's brother with stories of his travels, all of them imbued with naïve enthusiasm. He had come from Madrid thirty years ago with six other Franciscans to spread the teaching of Christ among the Indians of the plains. He had lived for a time with the Aiyuta Sioux and then the Ojibways before coming with two of his group to help found the mission in San Antonio. He was eager to see more of this fertile, varied country, and since he had never before visited the southeast boundary of Texas, Lucien Edmond's request had coincided with his own adventuresome spirit.

And so, not quite two weeks after Mara and Ramon had stood on the veranda of their new house and pledged their troth each to the other, they stood there again on a bright August day to be married by *Fr*. Bartolomeo Andraga. Mara's family—Sybella, Maybelle and her family, Lucien Edmond, and many others—were there, along with Ramon's friends and compatriots. Also present were the young Indian scout Simata, Andy Haskins, Joe Duvray, and Djamba, Lucas, and Celia.

At Sybella's request, *Fr*. Bartolomeo Andraga agreed to remain as a guest on Windhaven Range for a few days so that he might give communion to her and the other Bouchards who wished to reaffirm their faith. "It would give us great joy and peace, Father," Sybella said to the kindly little Franciscan, "if you would bless our house and also that of the young couple you have just joined. And I ask also that you pray for the happiness of my stepson, Luke Bouchard, who has gone to New Or-

126

leans and intends one day to return to the home where he was born in Alabama."

As the sun set in majestic splendor, Mara and Ramon waved farewell to their assembled guests and rode off toward the southwest, toward the place where Mara had been captured by Comanches and Ramon had followed to save her life. They had packed their saddlebags with provisions and blankets, and Ramon rode astride Corita, while Mara rode her pinto mare, Tamisen. This time, defying all conventions in order to show her young husband that she wished to share in their life together as an equal partner, Mara wore the trousers of a vaquero, boots, a white blouse, and her broad-brimmed hat.

They rode in silence until they reached the arroyo. The looks they exchanged, however, spoke eloquently of their admiration of and desire for each other.

Before he had crossed the border into Mexico, the Comanche chief Sangrodo had told Simata, the Windhaven Range scout, that messages had been sent to the Kiowas and the Comanches in this part of Texas, urging them to respect as friends the people in the ranch house. Sangrodo regarded Luke as his white-eyes brother and had given him the great talisman of the tribe. Nonetheless, Ramon carried a Spencer repeating rifle attached to his saddle, though he assured Mara that it would be used only to bring down game for their cooking fire.

At the top of the arroyo there was a clump of cedar trees framing a small, moss-covered ravine.

127

Tethering their mares to one of the sturdiest trees, Ramon and Mara unpacked their saddlebags and spread out two blankets to make their bridal bed.

Ramon built a small campfire from leaves and twigs and some of the moss of the little ravine, while Mara took out the piece of freshly slaughtered beef they had brought with them and roasted it over the fire. While Ramon heated coffee in a small iron pot, his young wife went back to the saddlebag for handfuls of dough, which she had mixed that morning, and used it to make frijoles. As they ate their simple meal, the mournful howl of a distant coyote sounded from the north of the arroyo, and Mara instinctively shivered, sidling closer to Ramon and putting an arm around his waist.

There was stillness and peace here, and the tireless feeling of an isolated world in which they were the only inhabitants. The moon was full and bright, and it cast its rays down upon them as they sat talking while the fire dwindled and at last went out.

"I wanted to come here for our honeymoon," Mara said softly, "because it was here that I learned the lesson of false pride and snobbery, and found out that if a man is brave and kind and considerate, it doesn't matter from what station in life he comes. I'll try to be a good wife to you, Ramon."

"*Amorcito*, my dearest *querida*, *mi esposa*," Ramon murmured huskily as his hands sought the thrusting globes of her firm breasts and his lips merged with hers. With a happy sigh, Mara locked her arms around his shoulders and lay back against the blankets, whispering, "Take me, make me yours again, *con fuerza, hombre!*"

She arched to him as his fingers deftly unfastened her trousers and drew them from her, and then the cambric undergarments. Unbuttoning her blouse, he knelt above her, and the moon touched her creamy flesh, making her nipples seem stiffer and darker with her surging desire. He bent to kiss each firm bud in turn as Mara gasped in exquisite anticipation, her thighs shuddering as she readied herself to accept him.

At first his fingers stroked her naked body, caressing its contours and feminine mysteries, till Mara could bear no more. "Oh, my husband, take me now!" she pleaded brokenly.

Yet it was with a lingering and gentle embrace that he possessed her for the first time since they had become man and wife. Holding himself back, accustoming himself to the eager, throbbing rhythms of her fully awakened body, the young vaquero at last grasped the firm resilience of her writhing hips. Her cries of joy resounded through the arroyo, and her nails dug furiously into his muscular back as her teeth clenched the flesh of his shoulder.

And then there was the blissful aftermath, the quiet, secretly shared delight of finding each other's sensual longings and aspirations, of shared and spontaneous kisses and caresses, till again they were renewed for their resurgent rapture. And this time, hearkening to Mara's exhortation, Ramon possessed her indeed as she desired, *"con mucha fuerza,"* and then both of them cried out in the tumultuous frenzy of communal fulfillment.

So enraptured were they, and so truly did they feel part of the very earth on which they lay and of the sky and the air above them, that they did not hear or see the six Kiowa riders a hundred yards to the east. At the head of the hunting party rode the old Kiowa chief Setangya, with one hand holding the reins of the black stallion that carried his mourned son's bones. He held up his hand and the five braves halted their horses as he spoke softly. "They are friends. They come from the ranch of the white-eyes to whom I gave the belt of wampum. They follow the custom of our people and of the Apaches, seeking their own secret lodge where no one shall disturb their coming together. Let us pray to the Great Spirit to look upon them with kindness."

CHAPTER ELEVEN

When Mara and Ramon Hernandez returned from their week-long honeymoon, Luke's black-haired daughter was certain that she was with child. Whatever doubts she might have had as to her impulsive decision to make amends to the handsome young vaquero by giving herself to him, only to discover that she had fallen deeply in love with him, had been completely dispelled by the magical and romantic interlude in the isolated ravine atop the arroyo. The primeval silence of the land had nurtured their thoughts and emotions. The words they spoke to each other seemed to have taken on new meaning, as if they were discovering language for the first time. At night, when the campfire was out, when only the moon intruded upon their ardent fusion, Mara and Ramon learned how well they were suited to each other.

Mara, who had been an iconoclast back in Alabama and a spirited believer in the emancipation of woman, found in Ramon not only a strong and passionate lover but also a man of quiet yet deep inner convictions of justice, decency, and honesty. She had already observed how companionable he was with the members of the Bouchard household, and his way with horses had from the very outset won her admiration.

On August 20 President Andrew Johnson proclaimed that the insurrection in Texas was at an end and that "peace, order, tranquility, and civil authority exist throughout the United States." This earnest, misjudged man, a scarred veteran of Tennessee's dark and bloody political grounds, farsightedly put the Union first. From his Senate seat in 1860, he had declared, "I love my country; I love the Constitution. Senators, my blood, my existence, I would give to save this Union." When the Civil War broke out, he alone, among twenty-two Southern senators, remained steadfast to the Union. But in the eyes of the radical Republicans, headed by the embittered Thaddeus Stevens, such a conciliatory attitude toward the conquered South was a "puerile, soft notion not worthy of a President of this strong Union." And the speculators, carpetbaggers, and Union sympathizers—the only ones who seemed to have a supply of money—had descended upon the South like a swarm of hungry locusts.

In New Orleans, Luke Bouchard continued to receive harrowing reports of the ruinous interest rates charged by the wealthiest of these speculators. To provide a bulwark of security in these troubled times, he placed advertisements in the *Times-Picayune* announcing that the Brunton and Associate Bank was ready to lend money at moderate rates to merchants and landowners of good character and sound judgment. He pointed out that his investment and trust counselors would make investigations to determine the soundness of the venture and the integrity of the borrower.

After that unexpected nocturnal visit, Luke had seen Laure only occasionally at the bank. With the full heat of a New Orleans summer sweltering down upon the city, she and Lucien, along with Mitzi, her nursemaid, had accepted an invitation from one of John Brunton's old friends who owned an attractive summer retreat about eighteen miles upriver. When she did see Luke at the bank, her manner was gracious yet impersonal, and she gave no sign of their passionate reunion. Luke in turn kept up his simple and healthy life. Marius Thornton took pains to buy the freshest meats and vegetables, and when he could, Luke saddled his stallion and rode out to the edge of the city to keep himself in shape.

A warm friendship gradually grew between Luke and the young black whom he had saved from the hands of the mob. Marius confided one evening that he was in love with a pretty nineteen-year-old mulatto named Clementine. She worked at starvation wages as a seamstress, and Marius hoped to save enough money to be able to marry her and free her from a bondage that in some ways was worse than slavery.

"Be patient, Marius. I'm going to suggest to Madame Brunton that you receive a small increase by this fall, and you know you'll be my foreman on Windhaven Plantation when it's feasible for me to return there," Luke said.

Marius stopped as he was clearing away the supper dishes and replied, "Mr. Bouchard, I can't wait for such a happy time as that'll be for me, married to Clemmie and working hard on good land. I surely hope it won't take you too long to go back to Alabama."

Luke rose from the table and went over to the window to look down at the deserted street. From a distance, a solitary gas lamp post tried valiantly to banish the dark shadows engulfing the street. There was silence, not even the clatter of a horse's hooves. Luke uttered a quiet sigh and turned back to face his young caretaker. "I've even more reason than you do for wanting it to be soon, Marius."

The possibility of handling foreign financial transactions was greatly increased, much to Luke's satisfaction, by the news that a trans-Atlantic cable between the United States and Great Britain was being laid and was expected to be completed by the following summer. Luke foresaw that if city banks became shaky because of the risky mortgages and loans they were compelled to make to compete with wealthy speculators and carpetbaggers, investments could be made in stable banks like the Bank of Liverpool.

Other bankers, such as Gabriel Mercier, shared Luke's hope that President Andrew Johnson would be able to effect his stabilizing Reconstruction program despite the hostility of Congress. If that could be done, parities and moderate interest rates could be offered to clients, and business would prosper. But already there were ominous signs that the president's program was doomed. On September 3, Southern Republicans met in convention at Philadelphia and declared themselves in favor of the Reconstruction policy of Congress. Three days later, President Johnson laid the cornerstone of a monument to Stephen A. Douglas in Chicago, paying tribute to the "Little Giant" who had stumped Illinois and debated against Lincoln. This commemorative act was part of a political "swing around the circle" in which the president intended to appeal directly to the voters to support his program. He spoke with fervor and honesty, but each such speech cost him votes and gradually lessened his power.

Although the Soldiers' and Sailors' Convention, meeting in Cleveland, supported the president's wish to hold out an olive branch to the conquered South, the Republican war veterans in their Pittsburgh convention declared their mandate in favor of Congress. And the final ominous sign that any conciliatory measures toward the South would be squelched came in the results of the autumn congressional elections. These returned anti-Johnson majorities to both houses, large enough to override any presidential veto.

On the last day of September an elegantly dressed gentleman, with silk top hat and malacca cane, entered the Brunton and Associate Bank. He seated himself in a comfortable chair against the wall and waited his turn to see the head of the bank. That was what he had told Madelon Fortier, who had gone directly to Luke's office and informed him of the presence of this new client.

Laure Brunton was not at the bank this week. She, Mitzi, and the baby remained as houseguests upriver, for the summer had been an exceptionally humid and oppressive one. Luke did not recognize the man who sat calmly observing the business at the tellers' windows. His dark brown eyes were mildly contemptuous as he took in the scene.

"May I be of service to you, M'sieu?" Luke asked.

"You are an officer of this bank, I assume?"

"I am, shall we say," Luke permitted himself a wry smile, "the associate. John Brunton's widow Laure is carrying on the bank as her husband wished, and retaining his name; she has engaged several of his former employees and been kind enough to designate some little authority to myself. How may I serve you?"

"I am Armand Cournier." The Creole rose, watching Luke attentively, his eyes narrowing for a moment. Then, with a bland smile, he added, "Till now I have done much of my business with the City Bank of New Orleans. However, after reading the interesting advertisements in the *Times-Picayune*, I decided to give your bank a chance to make some money for me. I should like to set up an account—rather, two accounts, one for investments and the other for depositing of a certain portion of my business profits."

"If you will be good enough to step into my office, we can discuss your affairs more comfortably. My name is Luke Bouchard."

Armand Cournier's eyes again narrowed, and he plucked thoughtfully at the point of his goatee. "Bouchard—Bouchard, hmm. Would you be related to the Bouchards of Windhaven Plantation?"

"Indeed I am, M'sieu Cournier. I have the honor of being the grandson of the founder of that enterprise."

"I congratulate you, sir. I have heard something of Windhaven Plantation and of the Bouchards. And now you are in the banking business, eh? I suppose one would say that those were the fortunes of war."

"Yes, one might say that. Yet the working of land and the prospering of a bank are very often related, M'sieu Cournier," Luke replied as he led the Creole to his private office.

Armand Cournier came directly to the point. "I want to transfer part of my funds to a bank which I believe to be more reliable. Besides, I know John Brunton's reputation for protecting his investors. Do you plan to issue shares of stock which an investor could purchase?"

"In the event that we need capitalization, should our own reserve be depleted through purchases of land or other investments, it is possible, M'sieu Cournier," Luke replied. "Of course, such stock would not be offered on the common market. And at least half of it would be retained by the bank so that no single investor would be able to gain control—that's simply common sense."

The suave Creole chuckled softly. "I had heard rumors that Madame Brunton had decided to re-open her husband's bank, but I was not aware that the real power behind the throne, so to speak, would be yourself, M'sieu Bouchard. And you appear to have an excellent view of the banking business. Yes, decidedly, I think I can entrust you with my affairs. But perhaps I had best outline my holdings to you, so that you will see that I am solvent, unlike so many of my unfortunate neighbors. General Butler, after looting our fair city, went off to Washington as a rich thief who will never be prosecuted as he deserves."

"That is exactly what we are trying to counteract, M'sieu Cournier," Luke replied. "We have already attracted enough new depositors so that our bank will be in a position to make calculated and reasonably sound investments. We want to help those who are good credit risks in spite of their financial losses from the war."

"Amen to that, M'sieu Bouchard. Now, as you may or may not know, I was the partner of a fellow Creole, Pierre Lourat."

At this statement Luke maintained a bland composure. Inwardly, however, his pulse quickened and he regarded the dapper Creole with more than nominal interest. "I knew the gentleman," he remarked in a casual tone.

"But of course you did!" Armand Cournier chuckled. "Everyone in New Orleans did and a great many more beyond our little world here. Naturally, the war brought an end to the very profitable slave-trading venture in which Pierre and I were engaged. There are, however, several first-rate *maisons de luxe* whose operation I have taken over since my partner's death. I do not presume to inquire as to your moral stance on this subject. But my feeling is that with a city of this magnitude, and a port which is certainly the finest in the United States for American exports, we shall always be compelled to provide the pleasures of the flesh for those who work so industriously to keep New Orleans ahead of New York and Pensacola and the Carolina ports."

Luke did not answer, but inclined his head to indicate that he had understood.

"Also," Armand Cournier continued, "I own several warehouses on the levee, and have converted the auction rooms, where we formerly sold slaves, to shops which are just beginning to show a profit. I also own a house downriver. Now then, M'sieu Bouchard," he reached into the lapel pocket of his thin white frock coat and drew out two drafts, "I have here drafts in the amounts of fifty thousand and twenty-five thousand dollars, as the basis for our first transaction together. I wish you to place the larger amount in a savings account under my own name. The other, if you agree, you may feel free to use in your investments, so long as I can make a little profit."

Luke Bouchard glanced at the drafts, noted that they were in order, and nodded. "We are grateful for your patronage, M'sieu Cournier. I will personally handle this transaction for you. While you are waiting, might I have Madelon bring you some coffee and a brioche?"

"By all means. She's a delightful young woman." Armand Cournier winked slyly. "If ever you should be forced to discharge her, I should be quite willing to install her in one of my *maisons de luxe*. Most likely the Jeux d'Amour, which caters only to the most fastidious and affluent clients."

Luke frowned; then in a level tone of voice he replied, "Mademoiselle Fortier is quite happy with us, as we are with her. Moreover, it is my hope that she will soon be under the protection of a worthy gentleman who will make her his wife."

"Touché!" said the suave Creole, laughing. "I have found this little interview most refreshing, M'sieu Bouchard. Indeed, you have impressed me greatly with your savoir faire, and I am quite certain that my financial affairs will prosper at this bank. But by all means, let the charming Mam'selle Fortier bring me the refreshment you offered."

Luke nodded, and was about to leave the office when the Creole added, "And you won't forget, will you, *mon ami*, to let me know as soon as your bank is ready to issue shares of preferred stock. I should very much like to acquire some, if only as a memento of our most illuminating meeting."

"You will certainly be informed when such a thing comes about, M'sieu Cournier."

As Luke explained the new client's wishes to Jason Barntry, his mind was deeply troubled. At last he had met Pierre Lourat's silent partner, the man who, according to the barber at the hotel, had acquired the mansion of Three Oaks for the ridiculously low sum of two thousand dollars in gold. How long had Armand Cournier been associated with Lourat? And how much did Cournier know about the devious plan to entrap his willful half-brother in marriage to Louisette Entrevois, in order to gain Lourat a foothold at Windhaven Plantation? The Creole's last, casually voiced remark concerning the purchase of preferred shares had kindled Luke's suspicions. If Cournier was really the power behind Lourat's influence, then might he not seek to gain control of the bank in which he had just discovered that Luke Bouchard was an associate director?

Finally, Cournier's visit seemed to have been perceptively timed. Only yesterday morning Luke had discussed with Jason Barntry and Edgar Maxton the advisability of offering shares at a parity of one hundred dollars in order to attract fresh capital to be used for land investment. Once the bank announced such a policy, he could not legitimately refuse Cournier's request to buy such shares. But he resolved that at least half of them would be held back in Laure's name so that it would never be possible for this wily entrepreneur to acquire control of this new and increasingly stable enterprise.

Laure Brunton, Mitzi, and little Lucien returned to their quarters in the Union House on Honorée Street on the last day of September, and Laure visited the bank to confer with Luke and the two officers. The day was unseasonably warm and humid, and there were few customers, so Luke was able to give Laure an extensive report on what had been accomplished during her absence. He also told her of the bank's plans for issuing preferred stock.

When he mentioned that Armand Cournier had

invested seventy-five thousand dollars, two-thirds of it in savings and the balance to be entered in the bank's investment funds, Laure remarked disdainfully, "Of course his money is welcome, and we haven't the right to refuse it, Luke. But I find the man utterly distasteful. You know, he bought Three Oaks from poor old Horace Amberley. The Jessups, at whose place I was staying, were shocked to hear how little that parvenu paid for such a beautiful old place. He just took advantage of him, and the last I heard, Mr. Amberley had moved to Baton Rouge to live with his cousin. And Mr. Amberley's family dates farther back in New Orleans than M'sieu Cournier's."

"I'm aware that he's an opportunist, Laure, but we do need the money. I have several projects in mind for which we'll have to lay out quite a bit, but with a very minimal risk. See here," he said, unfolding a surveyor's markup and placing it before her. "There's this warehouse on Tchoupitoulas, and this one on Union, and then there are two pieces toward the northwestern section, not far from the swampland where John Dewton used to live—"

"John Dewton?" Laure interrupted. "Didn't some of your workers stay with him while you were getting ready for your journey to Texas?"

"Yes. He was a good friend. He died of a heart attack just a week before I came to New Orleans. But as I was saying, these parcels of land could be converted for industrial use. They're more expensive than I'd like to see, but my opinion is that we can still afford to buy them and get a good return on our investment within, at the most, eighteen months."

"I'll leave it to you, Luke. So far you've done very well with John's bank. I'll approve the purchase of the buildings and land you have in mind, and also the issuance of stock. But please do be sure that we don't attract more customers like M'sieu Cournier. I don't want to lose control of John's bank."

"It can't possibly happen, Laure. If we issued a thousand shares at a hundred dollars apiece, we'd all see to it that at least five hundred one were retained by the bank. You would thus control a majority, no matter what kind of speculation or double-dealing might go on."

"Good. I feel much better. Luke, do you know that M'sieu Cournier had the audacity to visit the Jessups, and after I'd been introduced to him, he invited me to visit him at Three Oaks. Imagine how outrageous it was, suggesting that a widow spend a weekend alone with a bachelor in his house and that it would be all right because he had a few servants there! He also mentioned that when he was in town, he stayed at one of the small hotels in which he has an interest. I was very polite, but I let him know I wasn't interested."

"I'm glad to hear that," Luke said, and Laure gave him a sharp, probing glance that made him flush; he shuffled the papers before him in an attempt to change the intimate subject that had almost come up between them.

At closing time Luke turned to Laure and asked, "May I take you home in my calash?"

"I'd appreciate that. Little Lucien's nose has been running the last day or two, and I'm anxious to get back to him. Not that Mitzi doesn't make a wonderful nurse—you'd think the baby was hers, the way she carries on about him!"

Inwardly, Luke winced to hear this maternal gossip. He could not very well reveal his feelings about Lucien in front of Jason Barntry and Edgar Maxton. So he rose, tucked the papers away in the drawer of his desk, and remarked, "Jason and Edgar, that'll do nicely for today. Let's hope tomorrow's cooler."

When the two men left, Luke retrieved his swordcane from the corner and offered Laure his arm. With an enigmatic little smile, she took it, and the two of them walked out of the bank.

On the other side of the bank, construction work was completed on the shops Luke expected to rent. Paddy Quinlan and his workers had partitioned off a long, stall-like section where he would keep the carriage and allow the horse a comfortable resting-place out of the broiling sun. Laure walked with him around the building, then waited while Luke harnessed his stallion, and helped her into the calash.

As the calash turned down Honoree Street, Luke heard screams and saw a little boy running down the narrow banquette on his side. From farther down the street, a woman's cries resounded: "*Cours vite*, Robert! *Le chien fou, gare au chien fou!*"

The boy was towheaded, chubby, perhaps ten years old, and his face was twisted and flushed

144

with fear and exertion as he glanced back over his shoulder. Loping down the banquette about twenty feet behind him came a yellow-hided cur, with long tail waving frenetically, its jaws slavering and dripping with froth, its eyes bloodshot, uttering high-pitched yaps and snarls.

Luke drew to a halt, seized his swordcane, and leaped down from the calash just as the boy stumbled and fell full length on the wooden banquette. Unsheathing the sword, Luke faced the rabid animal, and as it lunged at him he thrust the gleaming blade into the dog's throat. There was a horrid gurgle, then the animal jerked convulsively and slumped onto its side, its teeth bared, its tongue swollen and black.

Dropping the sword, Luke knelt down and lifted the sobbing boy in his arms. "It's all right now, son, it won't bite you, it's dead. There now, it'll be fine."

Down the street a young black-haired woman ran, sobbing distractedly. "Oh, Robert, *mon fils, tu es sauvé! Méchant, j'ai eu grand peur à cause de toi!*"

Luke gently lowered the boy to the banquette and pushed him toward his mother, who knelt down and seized him, weeping hysterically.

"He wasn't bitten, Madame. He'll be all right."

The young woman looked up at Luke as she clutched the boy to her bosom. "Oh, M'sieu, God will bless you for what you've done! That naughty boy of mine, I told him it was too hot to go out, but no, he wanted to get some pralines at M'sieu Douadier's shop around the block. And when I looked out, I saw that horrible *chien fou*. I wanted

145

to save him—but I was afraid—oh, thank God you were there, M'sieu!"

"I thank God I was here to help, Madame. Take your son home now, and here," Luke fished in his trousers pocket for some small pieces of silver, "buy him and yourself all the pralines you want."

The young woman rose, one arm around the boy's shoulders, as she hesitantly extended her other palm for the coins. "You are so good, M'sieu, God will be good to you, too. I will remember you always in my prayers. Come, Robert, *méchant que tu es!*" Then, giving Luke a last look of gratitude, she herded the boy back down the banquette, scolding him for his thoughtlessness.

Luke turned back to help Laure down out of the calash. She stood there looking at him a long moment. There were tears on her long lashes, and her green eyes were luminous as they fixed on his tense, weatherbeaten features. "I was so wrong about you, Luke," she said at last in a husky voice that vibrated with emotion. "The way you held that boy and comforted him—now I see what a wonderful father you'd make."

"I couldn't let the dog bite him, Laure—". Luke began awkwardly, deprecating his own impulsive act.

She shook her head. "Not every man would have done that, and you know it. Now I see you as a man I can love. And I'll tell you one thing more— just as you believed, Lucien *is* your son."

His face was transfigured with wonder and joy, and he could not speak, only look at her.

"We're home, Luke. That is, unless you want me to move into your little house on Greenley Street after we're married? Yes, *mon amour*, I'll marry you, and when you wish, I'll go back to that plantation of yours in Alabama and help you fulfill your dreams."

CHAPTER TWELVE

Luke Bouchard and Laure Brunton were married by the archbishop on October 16, 1866, at Holy Trinity Church in downtown New Orleans. After the simple ceremony, Luke and Laure knelt before the prelate to receive his blessing, then went to the yard outside to do their reverence before the city's only open-air Stations of the Cross. They moved slowly from one to the other of the fourteen niches, silently communing with each other, each immersed in the solemn yet joyous thoughts of their new life together. They lingered at each station to see how the vines twisted about the beautifully ornamented wood and how here and there a flower blossomed along the frames of imposing statuary.

Madelon Fortier had been maid of honor, and as bridesmaids Laure had invited the sisters Odette

148

and Virginie as well as Aurelia Dubois. Mitzi had brought little Lucien to watch his mother being wed to his true father, and more than once, before the ceremony had begun, Luke had looked back with pride to see his infant son cradled in Mitzi's arms. The baby hadn't cried or fretted once during the ceremony, as though somehow he understood the solemnity of the occasion.

After Luke and Laure emerged from the Stations of the Cross, Madelon and the bridesmaids hurried up to them to congratulate them and to shower them with rice. Laure, exquisite in yellow organdy and a becoming veil, impulsively thrust her bouquet of jasmine at Aurelia Dubois, saying, "Dearest Aurelia, may you be the first to find true happiness, and then to follow quickly dear Madelon, Odette, and Virginie!"

Aurelia shook her head and turned to Madelon Fortier. "Here, *chérie*, you'll be the next." Then, turning back to Laure, she murmured, "You see, I've already found my happiness. Only yesterday Felix Brissart asked me to marry him, and I said I would. But I'll go on singing at his restaurant, because that's where I met him and grew to love him."

All of them then boarded hansom cabs to be driven to Antoine's for a gala wedding supper. Terrapin, pompano, and roast chicken were among the entrees served, accompanied by fine French wines. The pastry chef had surpassed himself in creating a sumptuous wedding cake, on the top layer of which he had designed a recognizable replica of the bank, with two tiny figurines representing Luke

149

and Laure standing at the entrance with clasped hands.

Luke cut the cake and presented the first slice to Laure, who gaily exclaimed, *"M'amour,* you've given me the black bean!" It was true: there, clearly visible in the fluffy yellow cake, was a black bean, the symbol of fertility and a happy marriage, according to old French legend. And when Luke looked at her adoringly, Laure blushed and lowered her eyes, while laughter rang out from the girls over whom Laure had once presided as *maîtresse* of the Union House.

This time, when Luke and his wife left the restaurant, it was to take a hansom cab back to his house on Greenley Street. Luke unlocked the door, then carried the golden-haired young woman across the threshold. "Laure, my dearest Laure," he murmured, and kissed her tenderly.

"My husband," she said slowly, as if relishing the words, her eyes wide as she studied his face. "There's so much for us to plan, to think about. I'll bring little Lucien over here tomorrow—but will there be room for Mitzi to stay and look after him when I'm at the bank? And maybe we should sell the Union House. I'm sure we could get a wonderful price for it, and—"

"Hush, Laure. Tonight is before us, and it's not the time for anything but ourselves, for learning about each other, for beginning our lives together," Luke softly interrupted as he bent to kiss her eyelids and to cup her satiny cheeks with his palms. In the darkness of the little foyer, her jasmine scent was stronger because of the bouquet she had carried at the church, and it made him quiver with anticipation.

Laure reached for his hands and pressed them against her swelling breasts as her lips met his. Then, breathlessly, with just a hint of the saucy flirtatiousness that he had observed at their first meeting, she whispered, "Perhaps it wouldn't be such a good idea to have Mitzi, at least not till our honeymoon is over. She has eyes only for you, and I don't ever want to be jealous about that little minx!"

"You'll never have cause to be jealous, Laure, I promise you. Come, my dearest one!" he said softly. "You see? Marius is a perfect caretaker. He's left a candle burning at the top of the landing so that we can find our way in the darkness to our bed chamber. And he's most discreetly gone to bed."

"Then let us do the same, *mon amour*," Laure whispered, and then, giving him a teasing look, gathered her skirts up in both hands above her slim ankles and hurried up the steps, glancing back at him and goading him to follow with a roguish wink.

Marius had lit a candle in the bed chamber too, and Luke watched with unabashed delight as Laure divested herself of her wedding gown and at last stood proudly and gloriously naked before him. Then, in an audacious mood, she came forward to help him undress, playfully chiding him for becoming such a dandy. "You know, my dear one, when you walked into the Union House in your Indian buckskin, I think I was already a little bit in love with you. And how much easier it would be

151

tonight if you'd worn that same thing instead of this fancy cravat and the ruffled shirt and—wait a minute, don't be so impatient, my darling, I shan't run away—there now—come to bed, my husband!"

But this time, turning to the little night table beside the bed, Luke blew out the candle before joining his young bride. When she laughingly protested, he silenced her with a passionate kiss, cupping her breasts in a way that left no doubt as to his ardor and virility.

"I wanted to begin in darkness, in the timeless darkness of the night, my Laure," he whispered as he began to make gentle, almost reverent love to her. "Let this room in darkness be our pledge to each other, my promise that you are and will always be my beloved woman."

Much later, as they kissed and caressed, their first sweet frenzy having been allayed, Luke whispered, "Let your hair grow, my darling—let it be long and shimmering to your waist as it was when I first met you."

"Oh yes, Luke, anything you wish—oh, my dearest one, how could I ever have thought you dull and predictable? Oh, take me again, make me yours!"

Two days after his wedding, Luke Bouchard sent letters to Sybella and his son, Lucien Edmond, in care of the San Antonio bank, knowing that his son went there periodically when it was time to acquire supplies for Windhaven Range. He wrote also to Fleurette Wilson in Pittsburgh and to Arabella Hunter in Galveston, as well as to Laurette Douglas in Chicago. In the letters he expressed his profound joy with his new wife and son, who would one day journey with him back to Windhaven Plantation. He wrote of his plans to restore the chateau and land to their former splendor, and to make the plantation thrive again. In the meantime, they would be in New Orleans for at least another two years, and so he hoped that these scattered members of his beloved family might be able to visit him and his family during that time.

As might have been expected, Mitzi refused to be separated from her little charge, and moved into a room on the first floor of Luke's house to continue her duties as nurse to Lucien. By the end of October, Aurelia Dubois and Felix Brissart were married in the Church of the Angels, a ceremony that Luke and Laure attended, as did Madelon Fortier and Virginie and Odette Nourmain. It was obvious that despite the disparity in their ages, the lovely young chanteuse and the aging restaurateur were deeply in love.

The hat shop operated by the Nourmain sisters was beginning to prosper. This was in large part due to the tasteful millinery displays and the beauty of the two young proprietresses, but it was also due to Luke's recommendations to friends and associates. It became known that the Nourmain shop offered the loveliest hats in all New Orleans. Already two young men, who had accompanied their well-to-do mothers to the shop, were showing more than casual interest in Odette and Virginie. Madelon Fortier had graciously but firmly rejected many offers from the bank's affluent clients to become their mistress, but she had not yet met the man to whom she would eagerly give herself in marriage. Her poise and charm as hostess at the bank led Luke to believe that this happy conclusion was not far off.

As he delved more and more into the intricacies of finance, Luke found that treasury notes issued by the city were the most frequently used currency in New Orleans. They were acceptable in the country sections of Louisiana as well, though they were not as commonly used there as were state treasury notes. The year before, city notes had been discounted by less than one percent in relation to greenbacks, but by the end of this year the discount rate was beginning to rise. State treasury notes were discounted much more heavily, from three percent to more than ten percent at various times during these two troubled years, although retail merchants generally accepted them at face value. The major problem was that, although state and city notes were valuable because they were acceptable as tax payments, they were not interchangeable—the city would not accept state notes, nor would the state accept city notes. Luke and his associates wisely sought to keep as much specie on hand as possible for clients who wished to make large withdrawals. Already two of the first patrons had withdrawn half their funds in order to speculate on cotton and sugar.

Toward the end of November, after consulting with Laure as well as Jason Barntry and Edgar Maxton, Luke decided to attract more capital by issuing preferred stock. Remembering his interview with Armand Cournier, he initiated the issuance of a thousand shares with a par value of one hundred dollars per share, and retained in the bank vault a majority of five hundred fifty shares. Three of the original depositors purchased a hundred shares each, and Armand Cournier bought the remainder.

Luke had not forgotten his concern over the Lourat-Cournier partnership and the recollection that the Creole dandy Edouard Villiers had once been a factor for the New Orleans gambling and slave-trading businesses. It had been just twenty-three years ago this last May that Villiers had disembarked from the *River Queen* at the Windhaven landing to deliver in person a packet of letters addressed to Luke Bouchard from the Rigalle Bank in the Queen City. Antoine Rigalle, knowing that he was about to die, had appointed as his successor John Brunton. Villiers had brought the letters for the purpose of introducing himself and courting young Arabella Bouchard. A subsequent letter from Brunton, however, informed Luke that Arabella's foppish suitor was actually in partnership with Pierre Lourat and Luke's half-brother, Mark. When Luke had confronted Villiers, the Creole had given him a look of undisguised hatred and gone back to New Orleans. There had been no news of his whereabouts since.

Luke had made several discreet inquiries among some of his friends and the older businessmen of New Orleans, but they did not recall anyone by the name of Edouard Villiers. At first he had thought of examining the files of the *Times-Picayune*, but the newspaper's old files were incomplete and there were many gaps in the forties and fifties. Yet, a nagging instinct told him that somehow Villiers's role as Arabella's suitor had been part of the scheme to gain control of Windhaven Plantation, and that in some way the plan had not perished with Pierre Lourat.

Luke found that he was beginning life anew at fifty. Although Lucy had been taken from him after twenty-five idyllic years, there was ample compensation in Laure's complete devotion to him. And, even more, in the knowledge that he could claim little Lucien as his true son, as a descendant who might one day bring Windhaven Plantation to the zenith of its worth.

CHAPTER THIRTEEN

The Bouchards celebrated Christmas Day, 1866, with joy and gratitude for the bounties that this year had brought. For Luke and Laure there was a richly companionable sharing of ideas, work, and planning for the future, as well as their increasing conjugal delight in each other. Seeing little Lucien grow, sturdy and sound, increased Luke's dedication to his new family at so advanced a period in his life. Now he could face the long months of waiting before it would be feasible to try to regain Windhaven Plantation. Until then, he could use the time to great advantage in mastering the banking business, and putting aside hard-earned profits to ensure his family's future.

He had sent gifts of bank drafts to Fleurette in Pittsburgh, to Laurette at her Prairie Avenue address in Chicago, to Arabella Hunter in Galveston, and to his son, Lucien Edmond, in care of the San Antonio bank. In that last letter he had added a sizable amount to the draft, and he requested that Lucien Edmond use the extra money to buy a gift for Sybella. And to Sybella he wrote a separate and very private letter, sharing with her his joys and hopes for the future and the pride he felt for his little son, and urging her to write him as frequently as she could about the activities at Windhaven Range.

Just before he posted these letters, Luke heard that there was talk of a railroad to be built from Kansas to Chicago, for the purpose of bringing beef to the new stockyards. Philip Danforth Armour, who had made a fortune selling pork to the Union Army, had just established a packing house because he felt that postwar city populations would demand huge supplies of meat. It was even possible that beef would be bought from ranchers at as much as eight to ten cents a pound.

Luke had added a postscript to his letter to Lucien Edmond, urging him to investigate the possibility of a cattle drive through Indian Territory into Kansas, with good grazing all along the way to fatten the animals before they could be weighed and tallied by the buyers. There would still be a market in Fort Sumner, where meat was needed for the Army as well as for the Navahos on the New Mexico reservations, but the price paid for beef on the hoof led him to believe that if a connection could be made with a railroad carrying cattle into a city like Chicago, the profits would far surpass those in the Santa Fe area. There would probably be greater risk of Indian attacks, he wrote, but with sufficient weapons and the acquisition of a few more trustworthy vaqueros, Luke felt confident that his son would more than triple his earnings over last year.

At Windhaven Range, the last holiday of the old year was equally one of rejoicing. The only shadows to mar that happiness were the deaths of Harry, who had followed his wife, Betty, by three months, and of old George, who had always been extremely fond of Celia's daughter, Prissy. Lucien Edmond's wife, Maxine, was expecting another child by spring. Sybella's good health continued, and her never-failing optimism and hard work around the ranchhouse set an example for everyone.

During the week before Christmas, Sybella was delighted to receive a letter from Fleurette, telling her that her husband, Dr. Ben Wilson, had been admitted to practice in Pittsburgh. He had worked at General Hospital for a time, and was continuing his studies to be a surgeon. Ben was also hoping to found his own clinic for the poor and needy, and he had already approached several wealthy citizens to outline his plans. They had shown only moderate interest, but he was still optimistic about the project. During the war, the gentle Quaker had seen too many men die of their wounds because of lack of proper medical treatment. Since settling in Pittsburgh he had observed how many babies died in childbirth and how many families who could not afford a doctor, much less hospitalization, lost husbands or wives or children because illnesses or injuries were improperly treated. Fleurette happily wrote that their son, Thomas, was a year old and resembled his father more and more every day.

From Galveston, Arabella's chatty holiday letter to Sybella, as well as her briefer note to Luke in New Orleans, reflected a growing discontent with the unexciting life she was leading. True enough, Andrew and Melinda were her chief concerns and occupied a good deal of her time. But James was taking on more responsibilities at his cousin's cotton mill, and was now being sent on trips to several of the ports to which the processed cotton was being shipped. Arabella, approaching forty-three, had begun to feel that her beauty was fading and that her husband's interest in her was waning—that much Luke could easily read between the lines of her scrawled letter.

Laurette's letter had also reached Luke before Christmas, but hers was radiant with enthusiasm for the bustling, growing metropolis of Chicago, where she and her husband, Charles, and their twin sons, Arthur and Kenneth, made their home. Charles was doing so well at the department store that the owner had already sounded him out about taking full charge of merchandising, buying goods as well as displaying and selling them. Laurette suspected that the owner had it in mind to sell the store and move west. He had come to dinner at the Douglas house several times in the past few months and had talked of the as-yet-untapped opportunities in places like Los Angeles and San Francisco.

Before the beginning of the new year, Luke had purchased the two warehouses on Tchoupitoulas and Union streets, as well as the two pieces of land in the northwestern part of the city, using the funds acquired by the sale of the preferred stocks. The total cost of these purchases was thirty thousand dollars. Luke had reserved a portion of the proceeds from the sale of the stock for the rehabilitation of the newly acquired warehouses. Paddy Quinlan and his crew were set to work on this new project.

Many in New Orleans, particularly around the levee, had little protection against the elements. Luke had already learned that cane-sugar production in Louisiana had reached ten thousand pounds the previous year, doubling the 1864 production, and that there were already indications that the 1866 crop would be well over twenty thousand pounds. Prior to the Civil War, planters had begun to use guano in their fields to increase the yield; at the same time, cane rot had notably decreased production by as much as two-thirds in the five years before the war. To anyone who had worked in the fields, it was obvious that if planters took greater precautions to avoid rot and loss of quality, it would mean better agricultural methods and improved working conditions for the laborers in the cane fields. In Luke's estimation that was a desirable goal. He remembered how old Lucien had countered the objections of neighboring planters to his own benevolent treatment of his black workers by answering, "Gentlemen, all of you work toward a single purpose—to make money from your crops. Well, my profits are even greater because of the better yield of my land, and it is my black workers who have made this possible through following my methods."

Paddy Quinlan and his labor gang finished the remodeling of the two warehouses by the end of January, erecting low cement stands along one side of the floor where perishables such as cotton bales would be protected from dampness. This protection was necessary because humidity from the levee would rapidly dampen the floor, thereby endangering any supplies set upon it. There were also partly closed stalls to protect other types of cargo for export. Luke's argument was that the difference between profit and loss for the planter very often depended on the degree of deterioration of his crops by the time they reached market. If proper storage methods maintained quality along the way, the planter's investment would be profitably returned to him. Without that, there would be little incentive for him to improve the quality of his crops.

The prospects for cotton were not very encouraging. Luke had visited the plantations of several upriver cotton planters who were trying to cope with rebuilding practically from scratch. Two of the owners, Peter Henton and George Cressy, who had originally come from Maryland, were Northern sympathizers and had been able to purchase two confiscated plantations soon after the end of the war. The other planter, Emile Sourvois, was also a Northern sympathizer. After taking the oath of amnesty, he had been permitted to retain his plantation, for he had proved that he had manumitted his slaves well before the Lincoln Proclamation.

These planters had experienced difficulty in getting workers for their cotton fields. They had tried freed blacks but found few who wanted to return to that kind of arduous labor; even the prospect of good wages did not lure them. Emile Sourvois had even tried hiring a dozen Chinese laborers whom he recruited in New Orleans; they were hardy enough to withstand the heat and the back-breaking toil, but the problem of finding a capable Chinese foreman who could understand English and translate the planter's wishes to his compatriots was proving insurmountable. Worst of all, insects had destroyed a good part of the crops of all three planters, and both Marylanders doubted that they would be able to restore their fields to any kind of ample productivity even by the end of 1867. Moreover, the price of middling cotton was down to fourteen or fifteen cents a pound in New Orleans.

Yet, because these three men represented the best possible potential for the prosperity of Louisiana, Luke decided, after discussion with Laure and his two trust officers, to advance them several thousand dollars each to help meet their production costs for the ensuing year, taking in return notes payable on demand after the nominal fall marketing of the crops. "If we don't help men like these," he had said to Edgar Maxton and Jason Barntry, "they may fail. Those who replace them may be greedy for immediate profits, not capable of offering their workers decent treatment, and not having the wisdom to rotate crops and give the land a chance to regain its fertility. To my mind, a loan must depend as much on the character and integrity of the applicant as on his financial stability. The issue is, gentlemen, whether my judgment of human nature is sound enough; if it is not, this bank will not prosper, and I should be the first to tender my resignation if I found that I was indulging in risky speculation."

It was a rainy afternoon in the last week of January when a stocky Comanche brave, riding bareback, brought his horse to a halt in front of a gate in the stockade that enclosed Windhaven Range. Andy Haskins and Joe Duvray, who had been working in the corral nearby, hurried toward him. The young Indian scout Simata had taught the two young Southerners a few words of his own tongue and that of the Comanche, and Joe Duvray addressed the brave in the Comanche language. "Ho, you have ridden far. Whom do you seek?"

Dismounting, the brave replied, "I, Timanka, seek him who is called Taiboo Nimiahkana. My chief, Sangrodo, sends word to summon him."

Jubal, the hound that Djamba had saved from fighting the bear in New Orleans and brought to Windhaven Range to act as a watchdog and to help herd cattle, ran up, barking, but Andy Haskins shushed him with a wave of his hand. In reply to Timanka, Haskins said, "He has left to go back to the land of his birth. But his son is here, and you can give the message to him."

The brave grunted his assent to this, and Joe Duvray went into the ranchhouse to bring out Lucien Edmond, who introduced himself to the Comanche rider.

"Sangrodo will be sad to learn that his white-eyes brother has gone from this land," the Comanche said in his own tongue, with Joe Duvray translating for Lucien Edmond. "Now this is what I am

164

sent here to tell your father. That my chief wishes him well and prays that the Great Spirit will smile down upon him. And that our warrior Jicinte has had his first man-child from the squaw he took from here. The child and the squaw are well."

"He means Prissy!" Lucien Edmond exclaimed after the brave's words had been translated for him. "Ask him if there is more to the message."

The Comanche nodded. "The squaw asks if her family will not come to visit her in the village of Sangrodo and see her son."

"I'll tell Djamba at once," Lucien Edmond said to Andy Haskins. "Ask him where the chief's village is."

When the young Southerner had translated Lucien Edmond's question into Comanche, the brave replied, "It is a journey of three days and three nights from here, near a village of *Mejicanos* called Miero."

Andy Haskins hurried out to Djamba in the corral, and the tall, gray-haired Mandingo came running up to the gate before the ranchhouse. When he was told the news, he turned to Lucien Edmond and said, "I know Celia would love to visit Prissy and see her little grandson. So would I and my son, Lucas. But, Mr. Lucien Edmond, could you spare us for a week or so, what with our getting ready for the cattle roundup?"

"I think so, Djamba. I got a letter from Father saying that we might be able to drive our cattle to Kansas this summer. They're building a railroad line from Chicago, or at least that's the rumor. We know we aren't going to go by way of Baxter Springs and be turned away by those bushwhackers who'd head us off from Sedalia. From the way Father talks, we'd make a great deal more money if we hold off until that railroad is ready, instead of going to Santa Fe again. So take the week, and more if you need it, Djamba."

CHAPTER FOURTEEN

Maybelle Belcher had eagerly volunteered to replace Celia as the Bouchards' cook during the latter's visit to the Indian village. Djamba, knowing that Sangrodo's village was near Miero, where Ramon Hernandez had been nursed back to health by the widow Magdalena Abruta, sought out the young vaquero, after he had hitched two horses to the wagon that he and Lucas would drive, with Celia resting comfortably in the back. It was early morning of the following day, and the Comanche brave Timanka was waiting impatiently, astride his mustang, to act as guide and escort for the journey to the secret stronghold of his Comanche chief.

Ramon had sectioned off the two hundred acres of land that Luke Bouchard had deeded to him as a wedding gift, building a fence to enclose seven acres that he planned to plant with vegetables and fruits. It had been Maybelle's husband, Henry, himself an enthusiastic farmer, who had urged Ramon to use some of his land to produce food for his own table, and he had offered to help him cultivate. The remaining acreage provided excellent grazing for the thirty steers and cows that Ramon had already roped and branded. He would keep several as stockers and fatten the rest to be sold at the market to which the next drive would go.

"You're up early, Djamba," Ramon cheerfully greeted him as the Mandingo came toward him. He laid down his hoe and shook hands with Djamba. "Are you going to San Antonio for supplies?"

"No, not for supplies. That brave over there came to us yesterday with a message from Sangrodo. After his village was massacred by Captain George Munson's troops, Sangrodo went across the Rio Grande so that other soldiers would not find him. We did not know where Sangrodo settled until now, but Timanka says he will lead us to the new stronghold. Prissy's just given Jicinte a son, and my wife is dying to see them both."

"Is it very far?"

"A few days' journey." The Mandingo glanced toward the little house to make certain that Mara was not there to hear his next words. "Sangrodo's stronghold is only about thirty miles from Miero."

Ramon Hernandez stiffened, his eyes widening. *"Por Dios!* If I were not already married, I would go with you—"

"I know you would, Ramon. I know how you feel about that fine woman who saved your life, and I came to say that I'd be pleased to look her up for you and take her a message."

Ramon excitedly grasped Djamba's hand again. "Her name is Magdalena. When I returned to Miero to bring the crucifix and the chalice to the church from which Diego Macaras had stolen them, she told me that she was going to marry a kind old man and that she would name her child, if it was a son, after me. Tell her that I shall never forget her. Tell her that I shall pray for her and her child and for her husband, too. And that I am married now to a fine girl, a *gringa*, but that I could not have had this new life if she had not cared for me back in Miero. And if you see the priest, tell him I thank good *Señor Dios* each day and night for the kindness that was shown me in the village, and that I shall try always to be worthy of his prayers for me. Ask him to pray also for my *esposa*, my lovely Mara."

"I'll see that it's done, Ramon. Here comes your wife, you'd best get back to work with that hoe, I'm thinking," the powerful Mandingo chuckled, and courteously tipped his sombrero to Mara.

Ramon glanced appealingly at Djamba. The Mandingo gave him a meaningful look, then said, "Good morning, Mrs. Hernandez. I was just telling Ramon we're going to visit Prissy and Jicinte and their new baby."

"Why, that's just wonderful! Then Sangrodo must have sent word where he and his people are staying?"

"Yes, Mrs. Hernandez. Mr. Lucien Edmond was very kind to let us visit Prissy, and we ought to be back in two weeks. Just in time to rope and brand the cattle to get them ready for the next drive. Well, Timanka is making signs he wants to start, so I'd best say good-bye to both of you." And then, to Ramon, "I'll take care of that matter, you can depend on me."

"*Vaya con Dios, amigo,*" Ramon replied gratefully.

Djamba stood a moment looking after him, then strode to the wagon and hoisted himself into the driver's seat, while the Comanche kicked his heels against his mustang's belly and headed south toward the Rio Grande.

Much to Timanka's disgust, the wagon journey to the stronghold of his chief took a week, not the three days and nights that he had said was needed for the journey. They came at last upon a slightly upraised stretch of plain framed to the west by a row of irregularly shaped hills. There were tepees and some adobe huts; Djamba quickly counted about forty of such dwellings. As Timanka rode into the little village, Djamba saw several young Mexican women emerging from the tepees, holding their babies in their arms and staring curiously at the wagon and its occupants. Dismounting, he and Lucas helped Celia down from the back of the wagon, and the three walked toward the largest tepee, at the end of the village, before which Timanka now stood respectfully inclining his head and lifting his right arm in salute to his chief, while he held the reins of his mustang in the other.

From the tepee Sangrodo emerged, followed by the beautiful Mexican woman Catayuna, who had once been Sangrodo's captive, forced to watch the torture-death of her husband, the *alcalde* of a Mexican village. She had not known then that her husband had sold Comanche scalps to the government, and so she had at first hated Sangrodo. But when Prissy taught her how to weave, as a distraction from her captivity, she had begun to learn the legends and the history of the Comanche people, and she found herself fascinated by them almost against her will. Then, after Captain Munson's troops had descended upon Sangrodo's Texas stronghold and massacred many of its inhabitants, Catayuna, despite her own wound, had ridden to find Sangrodo and tell him of the slaughter of his people. Luke Bouchard had lent weapons to Sangrodo's braves and sent his scout, Simata, to help lure Captain Munson's troops into the *Cañón de Ugalde*, where the Comanches had exacted a pitiless vengeance for that massacre. And when Sangrodo had come back to Windhaven Range to tell Luke that he must take refuge in Mexico for what he had done, beautiful Catayuna had resolved to accompany him as his squaw.

Comely, dressed in buckskin, her face radiant with joy and pride as she glanced at her tall Comanche husband, Catayuna eagerly greeted the newcomers. She hurried toward Celia and hugged and kissed her, shook hands with Djamba and Lucas, and then gaily exclaimed, "Come see Prissy and Jicinte and their little one, whom they have named Moukara—it means Little Rabbit."

She led them to a tepee midway down the right side of the rows of lodgings. An attractive quadroon emerged from one of them with a cry of joy and flung her arms around her mother. Jicinte,

171

looking ill-at-ease, carried a child in his arms, and gravely nodded to Djamba and Lucas. Prissy turned, took the child from Jicinte, and showed it to her father, mother, and brother, boasting of the child's sturdiness and disposition. "He's such a darling baby," she exclaimed, "and he almost never cries—isn't that right, Jicinte?"

"Yes. Little Rabbit grow to be strong warrior," the Comanche brave declared proudly.

"Prissy, are you truly happy here?" Celia asked, looking around the Comanche village with its desolate landscape beyond.

"Oh yes, Mother! Jicinte is a wonderful husband. I'm teaching him English, and he taught me to speak Comanche very well. Even the chief says I am almost one of their people now."

After the trio had visited with Prissy and her Comanche husband, Catayuna said to Djamba, "Sangrodo would talk with you. He has just had some news which is not good for your people at the ranch."

The powerful Mandingo followed the Mexican woman back to Sangrodo's tepee, where the chief had been standing, watching the reunion. He now held out his hand in friendship to the Mandingo. "Timanka has told me that my white-eyes brother has left the land and that he goes back to fulfill the prophecy of the shaman Mingride. Come, let us sit and smoke a pipe."

Catayuna hastened to fill the long, ornamented calumet with coarse tobacco while the two men seated themselves cross-legged, facing each other, in the large tepee. Then, going outside to the cooking fire, she deftly took two sticks and plucked a

172

small burning coal out of the fire. She hastened back inside with the calumet, which she presented to Sangrodo on her knees, and touched the coal to the tobacco while he drew on it till it was ignited. Then, bowing her head to him and to Djamba in gesture of ceremonial welcome as an honored guest, she withdrew.

Sangrodo puffed at the pipe and then handed it to Djamba, who inclined his head in thanks and drew on the pipe, sending clouds of strongly aromatic smoke to the top of the tepee.

"It is good to smoke the calumet of friendship with my black brother. Tell me now of my good friend," Sangrodo commanded.

Djamba told him of Luke's marriage to Laure, his restoration of John Brunton's bank, and his plans to return to Windhaven Plantation with his new wife and son.

"And my white-eyes brother is happy in his new life?"

"Yes, he is happy. And he writes that when it is time, he and his new squaw and their child will go back to the land of his grandfather and work upon it as his grandfather did with the Creeks."

"Ho, it is as Mingride said." Sangrodo took the pipe and puffed contentedly, his eyes bright with satisfaction. Then, laying it down, he said gravely, "Seven suns ago, Ipiltse, my war chief, rode near the village of Maxtime. There he met an old sheepherder whose mother was Comanche, and the old man told him that an evil *Mejicano* has boasted that he will avenge the death of his brother, that he will learn who it was of the white-eyes that killed him and so many of his followers."

Djamba frowned. "Ipiltse is sure that the old man said it was the brother of a *Mejicano* who swore that he would take vengeance?"

"Yes, it is so. And I will tell you the name which the old sheepherder told him. It is Carlos Macaras."

"That is indeed bad news, Sangrodo," Djamba replied. "It was Diego Macaras and his men who attacked the wagon train of your white-eyes brother when we were on the way from Corpus Christi to find the good land for the ranch. He returned, after we had built the ranch, to attack us. Ramon Hernandez killed Diego Macaras with his own hands, and I had thought that all those bandits died in the raid, so that this Carlos could not know who had killed his brother."

"I remember the raid on the ranchero, for my white-eyes brother told me how it was. But not all of the bandits were killed, for some deserted their leader when they saw that all was lost. The old sheepherder told Ipiltse that this man Carlos now seeks through the *Mejicano* villages for the men who rode with his brother, so that they can tell him where it was that his brother died. You must go back to your people, Djamba, and warn them to be ready for an attack if ever this bandido finds his brother's men and is led back to the ranch by them. Ipiltse says that the old sheepherder told him this man Carlos is younger than the bandido whom your vaquero killed, and that he is cruel and reckless. He tries even now to gather an army of followers, and he will grow rich and strong by raiding villages as his brother did, saying that he fights to save Mexico from the foreign king and queen who were placed there on the throne by the French."

"That is the trick his brother used. Ramon Hernandez had become an officer in his army, thinking that Diego Macaras was fighting for the liberty of his country. So Carlos Macaras will call himself a *Juarista* as his brother did, to gain followers. In the name of Benito Juarez they will kill and steal. Sangrodo, I thank you for telling me this. I shall warn my people on Windhaven Range. And because we will soon round up our cattle and drive them many miles to sell them, it is well that we hire more vaqueros to guard the ranch while we are on the drive."

"If I hear that the bandido has found out about your people, I will send my warriors under Ipiltse to fight with you. I give you my word, the word of a Comanche chief."

"The son of your white-eyes brother is in command of the ranch now, Sangrodo. I will tell him what you have said to me today, and I thank you in his name for your pledge of help. I pray God it will not be needed. And I pray too for Maximilian of Austria and his wife, Carlotta, whom the French have compelled the Mexicans to accept as their emperor and empress and who, when the French troops leave Mexico, will be at the mercy of the true *Juaristas*. They are good people, and they do not deserve what will happen to them."

"Smoke the pipe again with me, my brother, before it goes out." Sangrodo picked up the calumet, drew on it, and handed it to Djamba, who imitated him.

As he handed it back, the Mandingo paused to

175

ask, "Will you stay long at this stronghold, San-grodo?"

"It is as the Great Spirit wills. You know that many of my people were killed by the white-eyes soldiers. The men who lost their wives and their mothers have found Mexican squaws here. Our tribe is small now, and there were more braves than squaws left alive after the soldiers had left our stronghold across the river. We shall wait here and get back our strength, but there will be no war between us and the white-eyes. For I do not think we can go back safely across the great river to the land where once we hunted and lived in peace."

Djamba sighed. "I'm afraid you are right, San-grodo. New settlers and more soldiers are coming to Texas, and the settlers are afraid of the Coman-ches, as they are of the Kiowa and the Kiowa Apaches."

"Ho, and they are right to be afraid!" For a mo-ment Sangrodo's dark eyes blazed. "If the white-eyes and the soldiers had come to us and said, 'We wish to hunt and to build dwellings upon your land, and we wish to be at peace with you, and we will help you hunt so that there will be meat for your cooking fires,' then we might have had parley with them. But they came upon the land without asking us, and they lied to us and made treaties on paper, and then they killed us even when we were at peace. Aiyee, it is a bad thing. But you are right, there are too many soldiers for us, and we tire of killing. We shall settle here and we shall marry the Mexican squaws and have sons by them so that the proud birthright of the Comanche will not be for-gotten after we are gone. But that is enough of such talk. Will you and your wife and son not stay with us as guests in our village?"

"I thank Sangrodo for his kindness. My wife would like to stay a day or two with her daughter and little grandson, but I have a promise to carry out, and I must go now to keep my word."

"One thing more—when you go back to your ranch, tell the son of my white-eyes brother that I have sent word to the other tribes of the Comanche and to the Kiowas as well that I have given our sacred talisman to the Taiboo Nimiahkana, and that it was given to protect not only him but also all of his people on the ranch. They will honor my pledge, for they are my allies and my red brothers. But I warn you, there are many renegades from the tribes who will not heed the pledges of the chiefs and who will walk their own paths in the sun. Tell the son of my white-eyes brother that he must be always watchful, for to prepare against an unknown enemy is to be strong against him."

"Again I thank Sangrodo for his wisdom and his warning. And after I have carried out my promise, I shall return to smoke the pipe again with the mighty chief of the Comanches."

Djamba rose, saluted the tribal leader, and left the tepee.

As he went to unhitch one of the horses from the wagon to ride to Miero, he saw Catayuna coming toward him. "And you, Catayuna, are you happy here?" he asked gently.

"Oh yes, Señor Djamba! He is a good man, and he thinks of peace now." She touched Djamba's hand, and there was an exquisite smile on her lips as she added, "I have asked the Great Spirit to let me bear Sangrodo a strong son who will be both wise and brave like his father."

Djamba genuflected before the altar of the little church of Miero, then rose as the priest came toward him. *"Buenos dias,* my son," *Padre* Antonio greeted him. "How may I help you?"

"Father, I have come from Windhaven Range, on the part of Ramon Hernandez, the vaquero. He remembers the time you and a woman of your village cared for him after he was wounded by the bandit who stole the crucifix and the chalice from your church," Djamba replied.

Padre Antonio crossed himself, then turned to the altar, his face radiant with joy. "I pray each day for that good man, Señor. The vaquero is well?"

"Yes, Father. He asked me to tell you that he has married the daughter of the founder of our ranch across the border, near Carrizo Springs. And he wishes to send greetings to the woman who nursed him in her hut."

"Yes, my son. She is now Magdalena Burcano, the wife of our good and kind *alcalde* Tomas Burcano. She is happy with him, and their little son Ramon has blessed their home."

"I will tell Ramon that she kept her promise to name her son after him. Please tell her that although Ramon has married, he will think of her always and pray God to bless her and her husband and child because she gave him back his life."

The priest smiled and nodded gently, and made the sign of the cross over Djamba. "It will be done, my son. God will not forget Ramon's goodness;

178

praise be unto Him who judges all men and knows what is in their hearts!"

The tall Mandingo bowed to the priest. "Amen, Father Antonio. May He protect your church and all your people from harm. I will tell Ramon Hernandez what you have said."

CHAPTER FIFTEEN

The new year of 1867 carried ominous portents that served to endanger the uneasy peace that had followed Appomattox. Luke Bouchard had already observed the racial hatred that had flared when the Louisiana legislature tried to pass the black-suffrage law. When Congress enacted a law on January 31 that would establish the black's right to vote in the territories, he wrote Lucien Edmond, "You and I steadfastly believe in the equality of men under God. Yet I cannot rid myself of the fear that while this swift transition from slavery to suffrage was accomplished through the purest of humanitarian motives, it will be used by a number of spiteful Northern radicals purposely to rub salt into the raw wounds of the war-torn, helpless South."

Greed as well as vindictiveness motivated the victorious North. The Union Pacific Railroad directors formed the Crédit Mobilier Company to build their railroad with fat profits for themselves, and sold shares at par to congressmen to ward off possible investigation.

By March of this new year, the controversial Fourteenth Amendment had been rejected by twelve of the thirty-seven states, including all Confederate states except Tennessee, and was defeated for the time being. Nebraska entered the Union as a state, over President Johnson's veto. On March 2, two bills were pastsed over his veto that destroyed his hopes of a conciliatory peace and served notice that henceforth his attempts to rehabilitate the weakened South would earn him only condemnation and eventually impeachment. First, on March 2, the Tenure of Office Bill became law over his impassioned veto. It prohibited him from removing any civil officer without the consent of the Senate. And on the same day, his hostile Congress passed the new Reconstruction Bill, which stipulated that the ten states not restored to the Union were to be governed in five military districts, and that restoration to the Union was to depend on the efforts of reorganization on the basis of black suffrage, rebel disenfranchisement, and ratification of the Fourteenth Amendment. For Luke Bouchard, who dreamed of restoring Windhaven Plantation, this punitive bill loomed as an almost imponderable obstacle.

It was the end of January when Djamba, Lucas, and Celia returned to Windhaven Range from the Mexican stronghold of Sangrodo. Djamba at once told Lucien Edmond what Sangrodo's war chief,

Ipiltse, had learned from the old sheepherder about Diego Macaras' vengeful brother. Lucien Edmond immediately sent for Ramon Hernandez and urged him to go across the border to hire more vaqueros who could not only drive cattle but also were expert with weapons. Lucien Edmond proposed to ride to San Antonio to purchase more repeating rifles and ammunition so that the ranch could be properly defended in the event of attack, and so that the trail riders likewise could be provided with sufficient arms to ward off the raids of bushwhackers or hostile Indians. Also, remembering Luke's letter mentioning the extension of railroad lines into Kansas, he commissioned Simata to ride northward through Indian Territory into Kansas to learn which railroad town was being readied for the coming spring cattle drive.

Before riding across the Rio Grande to recruit vaqueros to work on the ranch, Ramon Hernandez sought out Djamba, who was working in, the corral with his son, Lucas. Astride his beloved mare, Corita, the young vaquero glanced around to make certain that no one could overhear him, then beckoned to Djamba. "Did you see her? Is she well, Djamba?" he asked anxiously.

"I saw Father Antonio, Ramon. Yes, she's very well, and she's married the man who they chose as mayor of Miero. She had a son, and she named it after you. Father Antonio says he will always remember you in his prayers, and he promised me that he'd give her your wishes for her happiness."

"*Gracias, amigo.* My mind is easier now, though I wish you'd seen her so you could have told me how she looks—and the baby—"

"She'll know how you feel, Ramon, never fear," Djamba said understandingly. The young vaquero nodded, then saluted the Mandingo, wheeled Corita to the south, and rode off on his mission.

Lucien Edmond had concluded his business in San Antonio; in addition to arms and ammunition, he had purchased several sacks of flour and coffee, slabs of smoked bacon, and sacks of pinto beans. At the general store where he customarily bought his supplies, he had left a list of items that he would need for his chuckwagon, to be picked up by early April at the latest. John McArdle, the gruff, bearded ex-Virginian who ran the store, had said: "Be glad to see a former Southerner like myself making out in this wild country. If you don't mind my saying so, I heard how you handled yourself in Austin last year when you got suckered into a shoot-out with those dirty comancheros. The goods will be here waiting for you, Mr. Bouchard. Just send for them."

Because of the weight of the arms and supplies, Lucien Edmond had saddled two of his strongest stallions to a sturdy wagon, constructed by an old New Orleans wagonmaker for the Bouchards before they had set out from Corpus Christi to find their new home. Three days out of San Antonio, he camped at night behind a low hill in a grassy knoll obscured by tall cedars. After watering and feeding the horses, he prepared a quick, simple meal and then stretched out in his blanket and fell asleep.

A little after midnight, he stirred in his sleep at the sound of horses' hooves, and as they came closer, he came awake swiftly and reached for his

183

repeating rifle, cocking it and crouching behind the nearest cedar tree.

The moon emerged from behind a cloud, silhouetting half a dozen Kiowa braves on wiry mustangs. Its rays shone also on the canvas side of the wagon where Lucien Edmond had traced in tar the initials W.R. to designate it as the property of Windhaven Range.

The first brave in the single file of horsemen, evidently the leader, turned back to his companions and spoke in the guttural Kiowa tongue, of which only a few words were comprehensible to Lucien Edmond. Then he pointed the tip of his lance at the wagon, raised the lance in salute, and gestured to his followers to ride on. Lucien Edmond rose and lifted his gun in grateful acknowledgment, as the Kiowa brave turned back to regard him and responded by again lifting his lance skyward. It was proof that Sangrodo's friendship had been relayed to the allies of the Comanches, just as Djamba had been told.

In Mexico, the final tragedy of Maximilian and Carlotta had begun. She, who had been Princess Charlotte of Belgium and who at first had been lovingly called Carlotta by her new Mexican subjects, now heard her name parodied in a viciously bawdy song that derided and abused her. She showed the first symptoms of the madness that was to plunge her into a shadowy dream world in which she would exist for sixty years after Maximilian's death. Napoleon III had already telegraphed Marshall Bazaine with orders not to force Maximilian to abdicate, but on no account to delay the embarcation of the troops. And in Washington, Secretary of State Seward kept insisting on a speedy evacuation of all foreign troops from Mexico. At nine o'clock on the morning of February 5, 1867, the French army evacuated Mexico City, with Bazaine riding ahead of his men followed by a brilliant galaxy of staff officers. And although Maximilian's General Miramon had carried out a bold and brilliant attack with only four thousand men against Zacatecas, the seat of Juarez's government, Juarez himself had escaped only by a miracle. The relentless, overwhelming forces of the *Juaristas* would soon foretell Maximilian's doom. General Escobedo, commanding a vastly superior force, outflanked Miramon and his exhausted soldiers and cut them to pieces in the massacre of San Jacinto. No mercy was shown to Imperialists and especially to over a hundred prisoners, most of them French Legionnaires who had volunteered to stay on in Mexico. At that ferocious battle, the Imperialists lost their war chest of twenty-five thousand pesos, and over three thousand men were killed, wounded, or captured.

Hearing this news, Bazaine, then on his way to Orizaba, sent a special courier to Maximilian, urging him to abdicate and promising to wait a week for him at Orizaba. But Bazaine's messenger passed another courier, who bore the news that on February 13, Maximilian had left his capital for Queretaro to put himself at the head of his army for a final stand. That army, supposed to have numbered ten thousand, was comprised of only sixteen hundred troops. Seven thousand had been left behind to defend Mexico City. And Escobedo, with an army of sixteen thousand, was advancing on Queretaro from the north, while Corona and Regules, with another ten thousand, were approaching from the west.

When his messages to Juarez went unheeded, Maximilian vowed to die bravely on the battlefield. On March 14, the *Juarista* troops launched a full-scale attack against Queretaro. Brigands like Diego Macaras and his brother, Carlos, who had posed for so long as liberators of oppressed Mexico, no longer counted in the scheme of things. An impractical idealist, a humanitarian who could not judge character, tricked by wily Napoleon III into proclaiming himself emperor of Mexico, Maximilian was destined to stand with his generals Miramon and Mejia on the Hill of the Bells on June 19, 1867, before a firing squad.

Simata did not return until early April from his scouting expedition to Kansas. Along the way he had met friendly Kiowas and Comanches, and had learned from them that a half-breed Cherokee trader, Jesse Chisholm, had hauled goods over what had once been known as the Black Beaver Trail, which ran directly south from Kansas for several hundred miles through Indian Territory, thence to the Red River and on to Texas. Black Beaver had been an old Delaware scout who had guided Colonel William H. Emory's Union forces in Indian Territory when the outbreak of the Civil War trapped them amid hostiles. He had guided the soldiers to safety in Kansas, just as he had once used the same route to guide exploring parties in the gold-rush days of 1849.

As soon as Simata had washed his dust-grimed face and eaten a hasty meal, he entered the ranch-house and reported to Lucien Edmond. "I heard much talk of a Joseph McCoy, a stockman from Illinois who had gone to Junction City and Salina to have the people there build a stockyard so that cattle could be shipped on the Kansas Pacific Railroad. They turned him down, but near a town that is called Abilene, I met a railroad man who says that McCoy thinks he can get that town to build his stockyard. It is a good place, Mr. Lucien Edmond. It has a river full of water for thirsty cattle, and on the prairies for miles around is much grass for keeping and fattening the stock at the end of the drive. Best of all, Fort Riley stands near there, so it can offer protection from raids, and the soldiers there are hungry for good beef."

Lucien Edmond smacked his fist into his palm. "Then it's worth trying for, Simata. Where there's a railroad, there's certain to be good prices for beef. Do you think it is a dangerous trail?"

"There are rivers to cross and much barren land, and it is a long journey—it would take you three months, I think, without pushing the cattle too hard. Maybe even four. They should not go more than seven or eight miles a day, and should have time to graze. In the Indian Territory there are many friendly tribes. I have talked with their peoples. You will have to give them some of your cattle for their campfires, but they will let you pass through. I was told that there is a band of Kiowa Apaches not far from the Red River, and they are hungry because they find no buffalo. They have raided some of the white settlers' farms. But if you

187

have enough vaqueros and weapons, you can get through to Kansas. I will go with you on the drive, for I can speak their language, and perhaps I can keep them from attacking."

"Ramon has hired thirty-two vaqueros, and I have enough rifles, carbines, and ammunition for all of them. We'll leave a force here to defend the ranch in case of a raid by Carlos Macaras, and the rest will guard our drive. You've done well, Simata. Tomorrow morning we'll start rounding up the cattle and branding what unmarked cattle we can flush out of the chaparral and mesquite. By the end of the week we should be ready to move out."

CHAPTER SIXTEEN

During these weeks of early spring, while the men of Windhaven Range waited to begin the roundup for the cattle drive, Ramon Hernandez, Djamba and his son, Lucas, Andy Haskins, and Joe Duvray spent much of their time working out the remuda of horses that would accompany the drive. It was vital to train cutting as well as roping horses for the work of driving at least twenty-five hundred head of cattle from Texas to Kansas.

Mara often came out to the corral to watch her young husband at work, and saw how he broke in the wild horses with patience and gentleness rather than brutality. When a horse had been properly tamed, Ramon rode him into a grazing herd, teaching him how to cut out a particular heifer or steer, then how to run on a loose rein that was to be used only when Ramon pulled him up or stopped. Much of this direction was done with words, leg action, or a slight jerk of the reins. Ramon put in a great deal of effort to train a "peg horse," one that was able to stop short when galloping, change direction, and instantly gallop off on a new course. Often a horse's ability to turn swiftly without endangering his rider could mean the difference between life or death, especially during a cattle stampede.

Djamba, who had long ago proved his skill with animals, worked with his son, training rope horses. Once a steer was roped, the rider had to take in slack at once and keep it taut. The horse had to be trained to gallop to the steer's left but never past him. He would stay there until the rider cast his lariat, and then with the slightest pressure on the rein, a well-trained rope horse would stop, his hind feet well under him, his forefeet braced out in front enough to balance the shock of holding the steer. The slightest pressure with the reins on the side of his neck would make him turn instantly to face the roped steer. A good rope horse never permitted a steer to get a side run on him, nor an inch of slack to let the rope wind him up. The moment the roped steer fell, the horse pulled against the rope, holding the dead weight of the steer on the ground.

Good night horses were invaluable on such a drive. Good vision, gentleness, dependability, surefootedness, and an unerring sense of direction were their prized attributes. Tests of a night horse's stamina and ability came during a stampede at night in the rain, thunder, or lightning, when the rider would give the horse his head and depend upon the animal's many senses to see him through. Such horses were used only at night, and their vision was such that they could see a cow or a calf straying from the herd and turn it back without being guided, or find their way back to the wagons on the darkest night.

Many of the horses in the remuda had to be trained for river work, for leading or driving a herd through water, and to know where it was swimming depth and where the bottom was firm and safe. Nervousness in such animals was a sure sign that they could not be trusted. The sureness and calmness of good river horses would encourage the more timid animals of the remuda to follow. And the same psychology was used in training docile steers, which would be used as leads or decoys to direct the rest of the herd.

Celia had pleaded with Lucien Edmond to let her run the chuckwagon, insisting that her good cooking would hearten the vaqueros. Lucien Edmond had pointed out the hazards—Indians or bushwhackers, withering heat, drenching rain and thunderstorms that would cause stampedes—but the gray-haired mulatto woman whom young Mark Bouchard had ravished and over whose possession Mark's father, Henry, had died, remained adamant. "I'm not afraid of danger, Mr. Lucien Edmond," she had stated firmly. "It won't be any worse for me than for Djamba or Lucas. And you know I can use a rifle or a carbine 'bout as well as any man. Anyhow, Miz' Maybelle will take care of all the vittles at the ranch here."

Lucien Edmond had consented, and now Celia bustled about, ordering the vaqueros to load the supplies into the chuckwagon with a bossiness that amused and delighted them. Several of the Mexican riders whom Ramon Hernandez had hired had been on cattle drives to New Mexico and remembered only too well the unpalatable fare; having already enjoyed Celia's meals, they carried out her orders with good-natured chaffing. Lucien Edmond was encouraged by this acceptance and saw it as a sign that there would be amity among all the workers on the drive.

The night before the drive was to begin, Ramon Hernandez knocked at the door of the ranchhouse and was admitted by Lucien Edmond. He beckoned to one of the new vaqueros. "*Adelante, Miguel!* Señor Bouchard, this is Miguel Locado. He was born in Cuernavaca, in the province of Morelos. I was talking to him just now about the bandido Diego Macaras, and he says he knows the two men who escaped after the raid on the ranch."

"*Es verdad, Señor Patrón,*" said the stocky little Mexican, in his mid-thirties.

"Are you sure, Miguel?" Lucien Edmond asked anxiously. "Do you know for certain that they belong to the band of Diego Macaras?"

"*Sí.* Their names are Ernesto Valdez and Humberto Dondero. You see, they had families in Cuernavaca, where I lived, and they had come back to see them. I was in a little *posada* one night and they came in with some señoritas. They were boasting how they had ridden with the great *jefe* Macaras and how they had attacked a *rancheria* of the gringos. Ramon tells me that this Macaras and his men raided your ranch, *Señor Patrón,* and

I am sure they must have been the two who escaped after the raid here."

"Are they still in Cuernavaca?" Lucien Edmond asked.

"I think not, *Señor Patrón*. I heard one of them say that they were going to Nuevo Laredo to see if they could steal gold and women in some of the little villages near there. I do not know where they are now, I am sorry."

"Let us hope," Lucien Edmond said fervently as he glanced at Ramon Hernandez, "that Carlos Macaras does not find them, now or ever. But Nuevo Laredo is not far from here, so we must leave plenty of men to guard the ranch. What is the least number of vaqueros that will be needed on the drive to Kansas?"

"It would be best, Señor Bouchard, to have fifty men for twenty-five hundred cattle. But I have seen how the horses work and how well Djamba and Lucas handle them, and the cattle. Perhaps thirty men would be sufficient, and of course they will all be well armed."

"A good many of the blacks who came from Windhaven Plantation with us are ready to defend the ranch, and we can use the rest of the vaqueros. Simata will come along as scout, to show the others the trail. Andy and Joe are chafing at the bit to be off on the drive—but perhaps I'll leave them here to defend the ranch. We'll see tomorrow." Then to the stocky little Mexican he added, "*Muchas gracias*, Miguel, for the information you've given me."

"*De nada, Señor Patrón.*"

The last day of April was bright and sunny, a good sign for a cattle drive that would wind over eight hundred miles through northwest Texas and across the mighty Red River, which bordered Indian Territory (one day to be called Oklahoma), and thence on through Kansas toward Abilene. Lucien Edmond would lead the drive, with Simata riding well ahead to sound out possible danger for the herd and the riders. Ramon Hernandez had insisted that he go along to act as translator between Luke's stalwart son and the vaqueros, many of whom spoke only a few words of English. Besides Djamba, Lucas, and Celia, who proudly presided over the chuckwagon, twenty-six armed vaqueros would ride along, with Ramon in charge of the remuda. Andy Haskins and Joe Duvray would remain behind to guard Windhaven Range, along with fourteen vaqueros, ten of whom had joined the outfit a year ago. The four blacks who had joined Luke Bouchard on his trek from Windhaven Plantation to Carrizo Springs—Dave, Frank, Ned, and the tall Ashanti, Carl—would stay home to guard the ranch. Because of their experience as point riders on last year's drive to Santa Fe, Lucien Edmond had named Felipe Rodriguez and his brother Manuel to flank the head of the herd.

The evening before the departure, Lucien Edmond had ordered a last-minute inspection of the supplies, wagons, remuda, and weapons and ammunition. He had also ordered a final tally of the already branded cattle: 2,852 yearlings, steers, heifers, and cows, none older than four years. The vaqueros had already cut out of the herd the stockers, the scrubby calves and yearlings, and the lean, old steers. Felipe and Manuel Rodriguez had, in the past two weeks, trained half a dozen docile, well-fed steers to lead the other cattle behind them and to settle the herd. There was an extra wagon to carry provisions so that Celia would not want for supplies to feed the hungry riders.

Twenty head of cattle from Ramon's own small spread would go to market, branded with his own initials, RH, with two bars above and one below. And because Mara had whispered last night, "Be careful, *querido*, come back to me safely after the drive. We're going to have a child, a child of our love," the young vaquero had vowed that half of the money he received from the sale of his twenty head would be banked in an account in his son's name, for he was sure that Mara would give him a son.

Maybelle and Henry, with their two children, Tim and Connie, had come to the Bouchard ranchhouse to watch the start of the great drive. Maxine Bouchard, with Carla and Hugo clasping her hands and watching eagerly beside her, smiled as her tall, handsome husband mounted his horse and rode up to her. "I'll send word back by courier when we're safe in Abilene, sweetheart," Lucien Edmond told her gently. "Andy and Joe will be on guard here to look after you and the children and the others. You're not to worry, now."

"Of course I'll worry, Lucien Edmond." Maxine tried to fight the tears. "If it weren't for the children, I'd go along with you."

He smiled lovingly at his beautiful wife. When he had first met her, back at Windhaven Plantation before the war, she had been Maxine Kendall, the intellectual young bluestocking from Baltimore. But she had gradually become much more than that to him. She was not only the mother of his children and an impulsive, eager lover, she was also an intrepidly courageous woman, even in the midst of danger. She had proved that courage when the comanchero Merle Kinnick had abducted her, planning to give her to the renegade chief Norvito.

As gently as he could, Lucien Edmond said, "It's too much hardship for a woman. I almost wish I hadn't let Celia talk me into letting her come along. Now then, Carla and Hugo, you be good and look after your mother. When I get back from Abilene, I'll have presents for both of you."

Maxine lifted the little girl first, then the boy, and Lucien Edmond kissed and hugged each of them as he bade his family farewell. Then he turned to Sybella.

"Grandmother, you'll be in charge of the ranch now, and that's another reason I'm not worried about things here. The way you handle a gun, no bandit or hostile Indian would dare to come within twenty miles of our spread!"

Sybella laughed heartily and reached out her arms to him. Lucien Edmond leaned down from his saddle and kissed her. "God bless you and keep you and all the others safe," she murmured to him as his lips touched her wrinkled cheek.

He drew a deep breath, adjusted the strings of his sombrero, then rode to the head of the long line of milling, lowing cattle to take his place.

At twenty-nine, an inch over six feet, Lucien Edmond Bouchard rode tall in his saddle. Long-legged and wiry, he looked indeed as a trail boss should. His warm blue eyes now showed serious attentiveness to the beginning of a drive that could mean either prosperity or failure for Windhaven Range. He glanced around, making sure that all the riders were in place, waved a last good-bye to Maxine, then raised his hand. At his signal, Simata spurred his horse and rode on ahead, as Lucien Edmond called, "Let's get them moving, amigos!"

The long line began to move, with the chuck and other wagons at the back. Behind them were Ramón and two riders with a remuda of a hundred well-trained horses. The noise of hooves and shouts and the lowing of the cattle rose on the peaceful range under the clear blue sky. A thick cloud of dust rose to hide the procession from the watchers who stood at the gate of Windhaven Range. Sybella, her hands clasped in prayer, looked up at the sky and her lips moved silently. Mara had come to stand beside Maxine and Carla and Hugo. Her eyes were bright with tears, but she rejoiced in the secret knowledge that she carried a child of her own. Maybelle waved, then put her left arm around her husband's waist, her other arm affectionately hugging Tim and Connie. The two young Southerners, disappointed at having to stay behind, looked enviously at the vaqueros who threaded their horses expertly alongside the longhorns.

They watched until the cattle, wagons, and men dwindled on the horizon, until only a faint cloud of dust marked their passage to the north. And then Maybelle, wanting to break the sudden lonely silence that had fallen on all of them, exclaimed,

"Come on, all of you, I'm going to make a pot of coffee and bake some biscuits with lots of that wild honey Henry found in an old log down by the creek!"

CHAPTER SEVENTEEN

By nightfall of the first day on the trail, the herd had covered a leisurely five miles, stopping to graze here and there, with Lucien Edmond quite content with the orderly behavior of the cows and steers. The vaqueros whom Ramon Hernandez had engaged were expert at their work, and a spirit of camaraderie pervaded the drive. Celia, bustling with self-importance, even flirtatious with the sturdy Mexican cowboys who sought to ingratiate themselves in the hope of getting an extra portion of food, lost no time in starting the evening meal. Pots were set up over quickly readied fires. The odors of good strong coffee, beans cooked with molasses, and tangy bacon filled the air. The swing riders had seen to it that the cattle were bedded down for the night. There was no real haste, for if Simata's information was correct, the cattle pens at

Abilene would not be ready before July, which would leave plenty of time for grazing on the rich grass of Indian Territory just before reaching the railroad market.

Lucien Edmond leaned back against the stump of a lightning-shattered cedar and savoured the hot, strong black coffee and the frijoles that one of the vaqueros had taught Celia to make. The night was still, and from the distance came the mournful howl of a solitary coyote seeking a mate. There was a cooling breeze to lift the stickiness of the warm day. But it had not been an arduous one, and the easy, if slow, progress was heartening.

Lucien beckoned the young Indian to him. "So far, so good, Simata. We have a good crew here with us."

"They are happy. I think they appreciate the touch of a woman in preparing their food. And she works as hard as any man."

"That she does, Simata. I've been thinking—seeing that we haven't pushed the cattle at all, and that we ought to keep this pace up all through the drive, we probably won't reach Abilene until August."

"That will be good. By that time it will be a drier heat when we come to Indian Territory, and there are plenty of creeks and rivers all along the trail. Some of the rivers are too deep to ford, but I remembered as I came back what will be the shallower places for the cattle to cross without danger."

"It's good to have you with me, Simata. A hunting band of Kiowas rode up on me while I was camping on my way back from San Antonio. They

recognized the brand of our range, which I'd painted on the canvas of my wagon. That's why I had
the same thing done with our chuckwagons."

"Mr. Bouchard, there will be renegades who wan-
der all over the plains and who have not been to
the council fires to hear the message from Sangrodo that all those on your range are to be treated
as friends. When we reach the Red River we will
have to watch out for their attacks. Now, with your
permission, I'll go ride out a few miles along the
trail and see how it is for tomorrow." Respectfully
saluting Lucien Edmond, he rose, mounted his
horse, and rode off slowly toward the north.

Once again the call of the distant coyote floated
through the darkness. Lucien Edmond smiled to
himself. If Jubal were here now, he'd be running
off to investigate that noise and to give warning if
it meant trouble. But Jubal was home at the ranch,
and, as he had done once before, would bark his
warning if enemies approached. Finishing his
coffee, Lucien Edmond wrapped himself in his
blanket, turned over onto his side, and soon was
fast asleep.

In the dusty little town of Sabinas, on the banks
of the sluggish Rio de la Babia, fifty miles north of
Nuevo Laredo, a tall, swarthy Mexican shoved
open the door of a little *posada*. He squinted at the
men standing at the bar and sprawled in rickety
chairs at the discolored wooden tables, then entered with an arrogant show of self-importance. He
was in his late thirties, and the hollow sockets of
his glittering black eyes gave a cadaverous look to
his angular face with its broad, hawk-like nose and

thin, sneering lips. There was a fading purplish scar on his right cheek, the souvenir of a knife duel in Cuernavaca, and a mottled scar around his neck, from dangling a long minute from a rope strung up to a tree by a platoon of Imperialist soldiers. His band of guerrillas had ridden up in time to cut him down before he strangled to death, but he would wear that mark of the rope till his dying day. Around his waist was strapped a gunbelt with two Belgian pistols, hung low and widened for swift access, and as he strode to the bar, the spurs on his black boots jingled. Untying his wide-brimmed black sombrero and laying it down on the bar beside him, he called hoarsely, "Tequila, *pronto!*" to the bald, frightened-looking bartender, who was conversing in whispers with two young vaqueros.

"*Sí, jefe.*" The bartender poured a generous measure into a glass and scurried with it toward his customer. "It is on the house, *jefe.*"

"*Gracias.*" The gaunt, pockmarked man drained the glass in a single gulp and set it down with a clatter. Then, taking out a pouch of tobacco and the papers, he rolled a cigarette as he squinted around again at the occupants of the *posada.* Taking a lucifer match out of the vest pocket of his olive-green soldier's tunic, he scratched it on the bar and held it to the cigarette till the end glowed. Then he gestured toward the glass and tossed the smoking match into it. "A clean glass, *por favor.* This one has a crack at the lip. I have shot men for less than that, amigo."

"A thousand pardons, *mi jefe,*" the little bartender babbled as he swept away the glass, seized another from behind him, and polished it with his apron. "Is that better, *mi jefe?*"

"It will do," the stranger drawled. He watched as the bartender, with shaking hand, took up the bottle of tequila and poured again, then nodded when it was enough. "*Digame*, I am seeking two men I have been told come here to drink your poor tequila. They are Ernesto Valdez and Humberto Dondero. Even if you do not know their names, amigo, you may recognize them when I say that they boast of having served under the illustrious General Diego Macaras."

"*Pero sí, mi jefe!*" The bartender's exclamation was one of relief at being able to appease his terrifying customer. "They were in here just last night!"

"And you think they may come again tonight?"

"It is possible, *mi jefe.*" The little bartender had begun to sweat profusely; covertly he made the sign of the cross, while the newcomer turned to stare slowly at the others in the *posada*.

"*Bueno.* I have a little time to waste. I will take one of these tables, and when these two men come in, you will nod to me. *Comprende?*"

"I swear it, *mi jefe!*"

"Do not try to trick me or to warn these men. You see this medal?" The stranger touched a gaudily ribboned medal on the chest of his tunic. "It is that of a French sharpshooter who aimed a rifle at me and had both his eyes blown out by these two friends of mine—*mira!*" His hands darted down to the holsters, and the bartender uttered a strangled cry to see the two barrels leveled at his face.

"No, no, *mi jefe*, I will tell you, I swear it on the cross!"

The man holstered his pistols, picked up the glass and the nearly empty bottle of tequila beside it, then sauntered over to one of the tables and seated himself facing the door. The other patrons eyed the stranger for a time, then went back to their conversations, cards, and drinking. When he had finished what was left of the bottle, he drew a cigar out of the pocket of his tunic, bit off one end, lit it, and leaned back to wait. In about twenty minutes, three men entered the *posada.* The bartender stiffened, then shot a frantic glance at the stranger and nodded. Languidly the man rose, adjusting his sombrero with one hand, the cigar clenched between his teeth at the side of his mouth, his right hand hovering near the holstered pistol as he drawled, *"Momentito, señores, por favor.* I am looking for Ernesto Valdez and Humberto Dondero."

One of the three newcomers was tall, angular, with a coiled reata around his neck. The other two men were short and squat, both in their early thirties, wearing boots and spurs like the pockmarked stranger, and wide red sashes wound around their waists. They stopped and glanced at each other nervously, then one of them moved slowly toward the stranger and said, *"Soy* Ernesto Valdez. What do you want with me? My friend there is Dondero."

"You rode with the late General Macaras, I am told."

Once again the two men exchanged a nervous look, then Ernesto Valdez nodded. *"Sí, verdad.* And what is that to you, señor?"

"Only that I am Carlos Macaras," was the answer, "and I think that both of you are *cobardes* and *ladrones*."

The angular man uneasily put out a hand and began, "Señor Macaras, I know nothing of this—"

"Get out, then. Go somewhere else for your tequila. I have business with these two *hombres*."

The cigar still clamped between his teeth, Carlos Macaras dipped both hands toward the butts of his pistols. The angular man turned and ran out of the *posada*.

"Señor Macaras, believe me, it is not as you think—" Ernesto Valdez stammered, looking around for aid from the other patrons and the bartender. But the bartender had already ducked below the bar, and the other patrons had moved in unison to the back of the *posada*, anticipating a shoot-out.

"So, it is not as I think. Suppose you explain to me, then, how it was that you left my brother to die. You see, Señor Valdez, I have heard of your boasts in Cuernavaca, how you rode with the great General Diego Macaras and how you attacked a *ranchería gringa*. Then you said, as I am told, that your leader was captured by the gringos, and because you and your *compadre* were the only ones left, you rode away and swore to take vengeance for your great leader. I believe that to be a pack of lies, and I believe you to be a coward. Do you wish to argue?"

Ernesto Valdez was trembling. He bit his lower lip, his eyes fixed on the hovering hands of Macaras. "No, no, Señor Macaras, but you have heard it all wrong—"

"If you wish to live a little longer, you and your friend, you would do well to tell me where this *rancheria gringa* is located. You have had several months now to raise a band of men to avenge my brother. That you have not done, so it only proves that you are both liars and cowards."

"I swear, Señor Macaras—" the other man began, his voice breaking with fear.

"Do not trouble yourself. Either you or your amigo will tell me at once the location of this ranch, or I will shoot you down like the dogs you are for leaving my brother to die at the hands of those gringos!" He gripped the butts of his pistols and drew them halfway out of the holsters.

"No, no, *por Dios!*" Ernesto Valdez exclaimed. "It is near the Nueces River, where the pecan trees and the tall reeds grow, near Carrizo Springs."

"*Sí, es verdad, por todos los santos!*" Humberto Dondero hastily chimed in.

"Very well, amigos. I am going to give you both a chance for your worthless lives."

"Anything, Señor Macaras, anything you say!" Ernesto Valdez babbled, energetically nodding his head.

"It is a pleasure to find you both so reasonable. You, *hombre*—" Carlos Macaras took his cigar out of his mouth and gestured at the cowering bartender, who had just emerged from the space below the bar— "bring a fresh bottle of tequila and two glasses. Be sure they are clean, not like the first time, *comprende?*"

"At once, senor!" The bartender turned back to grope for a bottle, then grasped two glasses and hurried over to the table to set them down before Carlos Macaras. "Will that be all, Señor Macaras?"

"For the moment, yes. But you, Ernesto and

Humberto, surely you will not let this worthy bartender stand treat for the tequila? Pay him,
hombres!"

The two squat Mexicans frantically delved into
their pockets, while Carlos Macaras looked on in
mocking amusement, puffing at his cigar. He had
seated himself again, sprawling nonchalantly
against the back of his chair. "Sit down, but first
take out your pistols and lay them on the table before me, the butt first. *Bueno.* Now you, Ernesto,
open the bottle and fill my glass. Then you and
your friend Humberto may fill yours and drink a
toast with me."

When it was done, Carlos Macaras lifted his
glass and declared, "Before all my compatriots
here, I swear to avenge my murdered brother at
the hands of those gringos. And you, Ernesto and
Humberto, you will join me in this oath. And by
taking it you will agree to come with me and help
raise a band of men who are not afraid of gringos.
When we have found enough men with enough
weapons to kill all the *gringos* and take their
women and their gold, then you will lead me to
this *rancheria.*" In his contempt for the whites,
Carlos Macaras had used the word *rancheria*—
meaning a group of huts—rather than *rancho*—the
Mexican word for ranch. And from the curl of his
lips and the glitter of his narrowed eyes, there
could be no doubt of his murderous intentions
toward the inhabitants of Windhaven Range.

CHAPTER EIGHTEEN

By the third week of May, Lucien Edmond and his riders had reached the little town of San Marcos and had already forded the shallow waters of the placid San Antonio River. Simata reported that the trail was clear ahead, and, judging by the average pace of five miles a day, the cattle would reach the powerful Colorado River within ten days.

From his experience on the Santa Fe drive last year, Lucien Edmond had learned that a good wagon boss never beds his cattle on rough ground or near gullies or trees, but chooses a level place such as the cattle would naturally pick for themselves if unattended. At night he walked among the campfires, stopping to chat with each of his vaqueros, to establish a bond that would draw them closer together in the long days ahead. Now that Ramon Hernandez was his brother-in-law, Lucien

Edmond saw the intense pride and dedication of the Mexican horsemen. He realized that they prized above all else their freedom and enjoyed the sense of power gained by riding alongside a steer with its curved, sharp-pointed horns, which could cause death should the animal veer suddenly. Courage and an outward show of indifference toward danger characterized their daily, monotonous work and quickly won Lucien Edmond's admiration. And because he was still new to this venture, an even more formidable cattle drive than last year's had been, he quietly listened to the vaqueros' conversations, gleaning many useful bits of information.

Tonight, Lucien Edmond determined that before they crossed the Colorado, he would kill one of the fattest cows so that the riders could enjoy a feast of fattened beef, made the more delicious by Celia's preparations. As he propped himself up in his blanket, the gentle hum of laughter and conversation came to him, an indication of the good mood that pervaded the camp.

Ramon Hernandez had seen to the comfort of the horses in the remuda, and walked over to Lucien Edmond, seated himself on the ground, and proffered a cigarette that he had just rolled. Lucien Edmond accepted it, watching the young vaquero roll one for himself. "How peaceful it all is, Ramon."

"Sí, Señor Bouchard. If we can get across the Colorado without losing any of our herd, we shall pass the first real test of this drive."

"Ramon, now that you're my brother-in-law, stop calling me señor. It makes me feel a good deal older than I am." Lucien Edmond took a puff on his cigarette. "This draws very well, and it's strong tobacco. Grandfather used to tell me that the fine Virginia leaf tobacco had ruined the land long before he came to Econchate. That's all they planted for years, until the soil didn't have any power left to it. But with cattle it's a different story."

"That is true, señor—I mean, Lucien Edmond. If you have water and grass, the cattle will breed, and there will always be more cattle, and people will always eat beef. And there will be more people soon on this land, even in the Indian Territory. I see good years ahead for Windhaven Range."

"I feel the same way, Ramon. And I think Father did too. That's why it was easier for him to leave us and go back to where it all began. This cigarette reminds me of those early days when I was a boy out there with him. He was always interested in trying out new crops, new planting methods, and giving the land more strength so that it could return a better harvest with each new year. It will be a challenge for him, and I think that's why he decided to go back after he lost Mother."

"I shall not forget what a good, kind woman she was, and I say prayers for her sweet soul, Lucien Edmond," Ramon said softly.

"As I do, Ramon. And I hope one day Father will come back and see our range as you and all the others will help me to make it, one of the greatest in all Texas. You know, these Texas long-horns are what we have to start with. But one of these days I want to bring in some Herefords, do some crossbreeding, get a better quality of beef for the market. These animals are lean and tough, but because of the many Army posts and the Indians on the reservations, just about any kind of beef is welcome. But when there are more railroads and more settlers out in the western part of this country, there's going to be a demand for prime quality. And what we are learning on this drive is going to help us make Windhaven Range strong and rich—and you will have a part in it too, now that you're part of our family."

"You are very kind, and I won't forget how your father took me in and gave me a chance. I promise you, Lucien Edmond, I will be a good husband to your sister. I love her very dearly."

"I know that, Ramon. I've seen how happy she is with you. You've treated her exactly the way you do the horses you train—gently, without breaking the spirit—and that's exactly what Mara needed all along." Lucien Edmond took a last puff of his cigarette and crushed it out in the dry ground beyond the blanket. "I can't help worrying about Carlos Macaras. You remember how his brother sent those two poor girls Isobel and Dolores ahead of him to beg for help so that we'd open the gate to his band?"

"Yes. I think of Carlos Macaras too, Lucien Edmond. But it may be a long time before he finds those two men who escaped our marksmen. Mexico is very large. Let us pray that he does not find them until we come back from Kansas."

"Amen to that, Ramon. Now we'd better turn in. Oh, one thing—you might tell the men that just before we get to the Colorado, we're going to have a feast. The better men eat on a drive, the more they'll keep their stamina for the really tough part."

"My *compañeros* are very happy to be with you as their wagon boss, Lucien Edmond. Jorge Feliz, who took a bullet in the shoulder when Diego Macaras attacked the ranch, is one of our riders now, you know, and last night he said to me that he was glad he fought for you because you treat him and his friends like equals. We have been peons for so many years, it is good to stand on our feet and breathe in the air and know that we are free men again." Ramon Hernandez rose, hesitated a moment, then added, "*Buenas noches*, Lucien Edmond. Sleep well."

The weather was sultry all the next week, with intermittent rumbles of thunder to the northwest, and at times flashes of heat lightning darted across the sky. They had come now to hillier ground, with good grazing for the cattle. Three more days, Simata reported, and they would be on the bank of the surging Colorado River. With the humidity came a swarm of heel flies, plaguing the cows, steers, and calves. Early in the morning, one of the lead steers made for a shallow creek nearby to escape the blackening swarm on his withers, and got caught in a narrow bed of quicksand. Two of the vaqueros, José Mendez and Felipe Murciano, rode to the creek, swiftly surveyed the situation, and began their arduous work. They managed to free the steer's hind legs, and the trapped animal stumbled onto the bank. At last the steer righted himself and staggered back to the herd. The drive resumed, slowly, methodically, the riders calling out and waving their sombreros to keep the herd in formation. He had reverently crossed himself and muttered a prayer to avert any repetition of that harrowing experience.

Another three miles, and the burnished blue of the sky gradually darkened and became overshot with the orangish red tinge of sunset. The cattle were lowing, for water was only a hundred yards ahead at a little creek. They stopped there to water the animals, then allowed them to graze on the thick grass along the bank. There was a small hill to the right, where Lucien Edmond could post lookouts for the camp at night, and he gave the order to slow the herd.

After supper, Ramon Hernandez inspected the remuda. All the horses on the cattle drive were geldings; stallions fought and disturbed the peaceful remuda, and it was well known that mares were failures as saddle horses. Ramon's own Corita was an exception, for his training and gentle care of her had turned her into a constant friend, with as much stamina as a stallion. She had already proved her mettle when he had ridden her from Miero along the desolate Texas plain to overtake the Bouchard wagon train and warn them of the proposed attack by Diego Macaras and his bandit followers. Lucien Edmond, not wishing to defy the traditions of the cattle drive, had left his prize stallion back in the corral at the ranch, and Ramon had chosen for him a sturdy piebald gelding, whom Lucien Edmond had whimsically named Spots.

The horses were quiet in the rope corral, and the night was still except for the sounds of the cattle

213

lowing as they rested. There was a hazy ring around the full moon, dulling its brightness, and there were dappled shadows on the long grassy plain before it dipped into the Colorado.

Carefully making his way between the vaqueros who had laid out their bedrolls, Ramon approached the chuckwagon. Two of the vaqueros were bantering with Celia while they helped her clean up and get the equipment ready for breakfast the next day. Ramon grinned to himself; a male cook would have been obliged to do his own cleaning up without any assistance.

"How does it go, Señora Celia?" he asked pleasantly.

Celia, flushed and smiling, wiped her forehead on the sleeve of her open-throated blouse. "It's lots of work and lots of fun. The boys seem to like my cooking."

"Much more than that, Señora Celia. They tell me that they won't go out on any drives from now on unless you're around to see that they're well fed."

"I might try to whip up a batch of sourdough biscuits. I know it sounds silly, but maybe some of the boys could look for wild honey if they've got a moment to spare. I saw some bees a while back, buzzing around an old oak tree, so there's bound to be lots of combs of honey as we go further north."

"I will keep an eye open for that. Biscuits and honey and your strong coffee—that's enough to make me work twice as hard all day!"

"Go on with you, Señor Ramon," Celia bridled, lifting her apron to her mouth to stifle a giggle of pleasure at this excessive flattery.

Suddenly there was a flash of light and a crash of thunder. Ramon's face tautened with anxiety. "*Por Dios!* I've got to round up the men—there might be trouble!"

Hardly had he finished the last words when another jagged bolt of lightning slashed across the sky and an even louder clap of thunder resounded. There was a wild bellow from a steer near the head of the herd and then another and still another. As the rain began to pelt down, there was the sound of the milling of restless cattle, and then the long, wailing bawl of frightened steers and cows as they rose suddenly and, wheeling toward the left, began to run.

"*Muchachos, pronto!*" Ramon yelled. There was another bolt of lightning and a prolonged rumble of thunder as he ran for Corita and mounted her.

At his call, six of the vaqueros had sprung up from their blankets and raced to their tethered mounts, inspecting for lariats and shouting words of direction to one another.

Lucien Edmond sprang up just as Ramon drew Corita to a halt and leaned down to call at him, "Stay out of this, *patron!* You're not used to night riding, so you can't get too close to the herd. We'll handle it!"

Then, kicking his heels against Corita's belly, he broke her into a gallop to follow the stampeding herd.

The noise was deafening as cows, steers, yearlings, and even calves joined the pell-mell flight from the sharp detonations of thunder and the blinding streaks of lightning across the leaden sky.

A torrential downpour made the horses' footing even more hazardous as the vaqueros rode along either side of the thundering herd, shouting and waving their sombreros, letting the cattle run but trying to keep them in a northerly direction.

Pedro Tolivar, one of the newly hired vaqueros, was riding on the right side of the plunging cattle when suddenly his gelding stumbled in a gopher hole. With a shriek of terror, the plump little Mexican tried to clutch his saddlehorn, but he was flung to the ground. He had time only to throw up his hands and begin a prayer when three lean long-horn steers trampled him. When the herd had passed, he lay lifeless and crushed. His gelding, screaming in pain, lay crumpled on its side, waving one front hoof, the other foreleg torturously twisted under its body.

Ramon dismounted, crossed himself as he looked at the dead vaquero, then unholstered his pistol and put a merciful end to the gelding's agony. Then, remounting, he urged Corita on.

Now, as suddenly as it had begun, the rain stopped, and only the distant rumbles of thunder were heard, drowned out by the onrush of twenty-five hundred head of cattle.

It was not until he first purplish streaks of dawn lightened the angry sky that they stopped, exhausted, and lowed in weakened protest against the shock and terror of the night.

When it was over, Ramon Hernandez sadly counted eighteen dead calves, cows, and steers. Before breakfast, the somber, silent vaqueros gathered while Djamba and Lucas dug a grave for

Pedro Tolivar, and Lucien Edmond bowed his head as, with the sound of the Colorado River a faint murmur in the distance, he intoned the prayer for the dead.

CHAPTER NINETEEN

Three days were consumed in the crossing of the Colorado River, for Lucien Edmond let his vaqueros and cattle rest almost all day following the nocturnal stampede. Moreover, the tragic death of Pedro Tolivar cast a shadow on the mood of the drive. Even to these experienced vaqueros, the loss of a *compañero* was a personal blow that made each man reflect on his own mortality.

Simata went ahead that next day to select a fording place where the water would be shallow and less turbulent. The recent thunderstorm had swelled the waters at a place he had already considered, but there was a bend at the river two miles west, which seemed relatively safe for both cattle and riders. Lucien Edmond therefore directed the point riders to swing the herd in that direction.

The young Indian's judgment proved unerring. Nonetheless, the crossing was arduous. Thanks to the patient hours that had been spent training the lead steers, they hesitated only a few moments before essaying the stream, and, bawling and lowing as they swam forward, induced the rest of the herd, urged on by the tireless vaqueros, to follow them to the other side. Even so, the crossing was not without peril: Pablo Toldano's gray gelding lost its footing, stumbled, and threw him into the water, then screamed in fear as it swept downstream. The vaquero righted himself and agilely mounted a bellowing steer, then leaped off onto the bank as the steer scrambled to safety on the other side. But Pablo's gelding drowned, a victim of its own panic.

The night before the crossing, true to his promise, Lucien Edmond had slaughtered two of the fattest cows, and the vaqueros had had a feast. The meal fortified the men for the arduous work of lifting at least a dozen scrawny calves into the extra wagons, since they did not have the stamina to swim against the current. But once the crossing had been made, the spirits of the drivers lifted noticeably; the first grim hurdle had been cleared, and now with early June's hot days upon them, they looked forward to the northerly drive to Kansas. "Most likely, Lucien Edmond," Ramon said as they made camp after the crossing, "if this Señor McCoy gets his stock pens built at Abilene, he'll send riders down through Texas to tell the cattlemen where to come. The closer we get to Kansas, the more likely we'll be to come in first with one of the big herds and get good prices for our beef."

"That's exactly what I'm hoping for, Ramon. When Simata came back to tell us about Abilene, he mentioned that prices for beef at the railroad might be anywhere from five to ten dollars a head. If we can tally twenty-five hundred sound cattle, that would mean twenty-five thousand dollars. But I don't think we'll get that much, and probably two or three hundred of these animals will be too scrawny to be of interest to quality buyers. But it'll be much more than we made in Santa Fe last year—enough to pay each of the vaqueros a bonus of at least a hundred dollars, and with enough reserve to import some shorthorns for breeding. Once the demand for meat stabilizes as the population grows, and once the railroad lines expand, we're going to be rewarded well. I wouldn't be surprised if, in our lifetimes, the railroads extended their lines all the way to Texas."

"Nor I, Lucien Edmond," said Ramon Hernandez, nodding in agreement. "But we've had to slow down a little because of the river, and it'll be about a month before we get into Indian Territory."

"Speaking of Indians, Ramon, thus far we haven't seen any at all, not even hunting parties."

"Manuel Rodriguez told me he thought he'd seen a small band of Kiowas off to the southeast yesterday afternoon, but he couldn't be sure."

"Well, I hope Sangrodo's message to his allies has reached far enough north to keep us out of danger," replied Lucien Edmond.

By Thursday of the third week of June, the ambling herd had reached the dusty high plain near Mineral Springs. The intense heat of the day had caused Lucien Edmond to call a halt before sundown and set up camp. The land was barren, with stretches of mesquite, chaparral, and wind-blown tumbleweed. The sandy soil was reddish-brown and sparse, dry grass grew under the cloudless sky. Throughout the day, the point riders had reported seeing small bands of Indian riders, too far distant to make out their tribal identity or whether they were garbed for war or for hunt. Consequently, Lucien Edmond warned his vaqueros to make sure their pistols were loaded and to inspect their rifles and carbines. Simata had suggested the camp for the night, about half a mile to the northeast, near a small creek, set off from the barren landscape by a semicircle of tall mesquite bushes.

As the sun descended, Celia industriously began her preparations for the evening meal. The vaqueros tethered their horses and inspected the resting herd, while Ramon conferred with the two Rodriguez brothers, who had ridden the point since the beginning of the drive. He reported to Lucien Edmond that the cattle were watered, had sufficient grazing, and were settling down for the night.

Gradually, the soft hum of conversation died down as the night advanced. One heard the occasional call of a nightbird, and again, hauntingly, from a distance, the mournful, long-drawn howl of a coyote. Bedrolls were unpacked, blankets laid down, and the vaqueros stretched out with weary sighs. Dusty from a day on the desolate trail, their thoughts were on the Red River, which ran its winding course between Texas and the yet-unknown Indian Territory.

Lucien Edmond, seated cross-legged, smoked a cigarette as he watched the campfire dwindle. Djamba and his son, Lucas, who had been working the drive as swing riders with the other vaqueros, approached him now and squatted beside him. "Evening, Mr. Lucien Edmond," Djamba greeted him. "Lucas and I are going to stand guard tonight. Everything seems quiet enough."

"Let's hope it continues that way, Djamba. How do you and Lucas like the cattle drive? It's a little different from working the fields at Windhaven Plantation."

"Quite a bit, Mr. Lucien Edmond." Djamba chuckled, his arm around his son's shoulders. "But you know, sir, back there I had a hand with horses and cows and bulls and the like, so I don't feel out-of-place at all. Matter of fact, I'm might glad that I'm still spry enough to do a good day's work in the saddle and still look forward to the morning. Lucas here, of course, he's one of the youngest men in the outfit, so he doesn't have such problems." Djamba grinned at his sturdy son. "Well, we'll leave you to your sleep, Mr. Lucien Edmond. Going to be mighty hot tomorrow, judging by the way that old red ball of the sun looked when it was going down tonight."

"Good-night, Djamba, Lucas." Lucien Edmond slid down onto his blanket, stretched and yawned, then rolled onto his side, pillowing his cheek against his palm, as bone-weariness claimed him.

It was well past midnight, and the night air was humid with the promise of morning rain. Djamba and Lucas walked slowly and carefully among the sleeping vaqueros, pausing a moment beside the

222

second chuckwagon, which Celia transformed at night into her sleeping quarters. The canvas flap at the back was drawn, and Djamba patted it tenderly, then turned to his son and nodded. They walked on to the outskirts of the camp. Clouds had begun to form, irregular and scattered, sometimes dimming the moon for a long moment.

Djamba turned to his son and put an arm around his shoulders. "Do you feel at home out here, Lucas?"

"Sure, Father. Where you and Mama are, that's good enough for me."

"I know, boy. But you see, back in Alabama, I was mighty restless till I met your mama. I had freedom back in Africa, for I was king of a pure-blooded tribe that was looked up to over in that country. But then things happened, and I became a slave. And it was Miz Sybella who made me a man again—you know what I think about her, boy, it doesn't bear repeating. All the same, what I'm getting at is, I've got your mother, but you're in your prime now, and it's high time you were thinking of settling down and finding yourself a nice girl to give you children. There hasn't been much chance back there on the ranch with so few people around, least of all no blacks like us."

Lucas self-consciously rubbed the toe of his right boot back and forth against the dusty ground. "I haven't done much thinking about anything like that. Maybe I'll find someone up there in that railroad town in Kansas."

Djamba shook his head. "Most likely you won't, boy. You remember old John Brown and his way of liberating folks—liberating them from their lives, mostly. They didn't hold with slavery in Kansas, but they won't take kindly to having blacks settle up there, boy; and even around where we live, there are plenty of people that'll look down on you. The old-time plantation folks from the South won't ever see you as anything but a slave, even if you get to have your own spread and money in the bank. That's the way of some folks. The war didn't teach folks like that everything there was to know about human beings, I'm thinking. Hush now, didn't you hear something just then?"

Djamba turned toward a clump of mesquite a hundred feet away, knelt down, leveled his Spencer repeating rifle, and cocked it.

"No, Father, I—*aaaah!*" Lucas's words turned into a cry of agony as an arrow whirred through the air out of the clump of mesquite and pierced his left upper arm. He flung himself down on his side, wincing with pain, while he cocked his carbine and turned to aim at the clump of mesquite.

"Don't shoot till you have to, boy—you might stampede the cattle. If they do it, they'll rush us, thinking we're going after the herd, and they can pick us off one by one. Just hold your fire!" Then, seeing the arrow protruding from his son's arm, he swore in Mandingo, then muttered, "Lie back, boy. Let's see if I can pull it out clean—hold still now—there—thank God it's not barbed or poisoned, the way arrows were in my country. You're lucky it's just a flesh wound." Djamba tore off a piece of his shirt and bandaged his son's arm. "There now. You crawl back and wake up Mr. Lucien Edmond while I cover that mesquite."

Lucas nodded, his face drawn with pain. He began to crawl toward Lucien Edmond's blanket while his father, squinting through the darkness, kept his rifle aimed at the clump of mesquite. Beyond Lucien Edmond, east of the camp, the horses had been tethered for the night. Farther east were tall clumps of mesquite and chaparral. Just as Lucas reached the sleeping Lucien Edmond there came the sound of a screech owl, twice, and then the silence of the night was shattered by shrill war whoops as a dozen war-painted Kiowa Apaches came running out of their hiding place in a deep ravine just beyond the mesquite and chaparral.

"Wake up, Mr. Lucien Edmond, for God's sake!" Lucas cried, shaking him by the shoulder. Lucien Edmond propped himself up on an elbow and blinked his eyes; then, hearing the cries of the attackers, he sprang to his feet and seized the rifle lying beside him.

"They'll stampede the horses and cattle, Mr. Lucien Edmond, and they'll expect us to go after them. We've got to stand here and pick them off. I'll go wake the others!" As Lucas spoke, a tall brave, naked to the waist and with the cabalistic red and ochre signs of war painted on his chest, sprang out of the darkness with upraised tomahawk. Lucien Edmond had no time to fire his rifle, but swiftly reversed it and struck the onrushing brave across the forehead, the heavy butt making impact with a sickening sound. The Kiowa Apache dropped his tomahawk, fell down on his back, twitched a moment, and lay still.

Already the cattle were stirring, and now there was the sound of an old buffalo gun as one of the braves, attacking from the east of the camp, knelt

225

and aimed at one of the vaqueros who had stumbled up from his blanket, dazed and bleary-eyed from sleep. There was a shriek of agony and the Mexican plummeted backward to the ground, his face blown away by the heavy charge. Lucien Edmond whirled, knelt, took aim, and triggered his Spencer. The stocky brave lifted his buffalo gun, whirled halfway around, then dropped in his tracks.

The shrill whinnying of the horses and the bellowing of the frightened cattle drowned out the Indians' war whoops. An arrow whizzed past Djamba's ear to pierce a blanket just quitted by one of the vaqueros, who had grabbed his carbine and, crouching behind the chuckwagon, was firing at a young brave who ran at him with a feathered lance. The carbine momentarily jammed just as the brave thrust his lance at the vaquero, piercing his heart; as he died, the vaquero's finger twitched against the trigger, the carbine fired, and the brave, uttering a gurgling scream, sank to the ground, still clutching the haft of his lance.

A dozen painted braves now rushed out of the thick clump of mesquite that Djamba had been covering with his Spencer, thus attacking the camp from both sides. Djamba squeezed the trigger again and again, and three of the braves dropped in their tracks. Lucas hurried back to stand by his father, and, taking quick aim with his carbine, snapped off a shot that dropped a heavy-set, grimacing Kiowa Apache who had lunged at Djamba from the left. The brave whirled around, dropped his tomahawk, and fell inert in a welter of blood.

Simata and Ramon Hernandez hurried to the remuda to try to calm the horses. Half of them had broken away from the rope corral and were galloping northward, whinnying shrilly at the hideous sounds of battle. One of the geldings stumbled in a gopher hole and fell, and the thundering steers crushed and trampled it in their frantic flight. Simata held his clasp knife in his right hand and a six-shooter in his left; Ramon was armed with a repeating rifle. Suddenly, weaving through the milling horses, a young Kiowa Apache brave made for Simata with upraised knife. "Friend!" Simata cried in Kiowa. "White-eyes friend of Sangrodo, whose talisman he bears!"

But the young brave snarled his defiance as he crouched to face the Indian, and in a guttural voice he replied in the Athapaskan tongue, which derived from both Kiowa and Apache of the southern plains, "Tanipa our chief, all white-eyes enemies, Kiowa-dog!"

As he feinted with his knife in a wide slash aimed at Simata's belly, the young Indian pulled the trigger of the six-shooter. But the weapon jammed. Simata leaped back, flinging away the useless gun as he pulled out his knife, and circled his adversary. Again the young brave lunged at Simata, and again he parried the thrust. There was a clash of steel as they stood for a moment glaring at each other, their knives locked together and held high in the air. The brave kicked out with his right foot, but Simata had anticipated this maneuver and nimbly leaped to the right. With a straight, swift thrust, he pierced the brave's side. A strangled cry was torn from the Kiowa Apache as he staggered back and dropped his knife, and the light in his eyes dimmed as he pitched forward at Simata's feet.

Djamba and Lucas, kneeling side by side, reloaded their weapons as the remaining eight attackers, loping toward the south, circled past them to take a hiding place behind another thick clump of mesquite. Lucien Edmond was reloading his rifle as one of the braves from the east side of the camp stealthily crawled on his belly till he was hidden under the chuckwagon in which Celia slept, then leaped up and tore open the canvas flaps. Lucien Edmond fired but missed the brave, who had begun to clamber into the wagon. Celia, long before awakened by the hubbub of the attack, seized a heavy iron frying pan and smashed it against the brave's face, breaking his nose and sending him tumbling to the ground. Once again Lucien Edmond leveled his Spencer, and as the brave dazedly struggled to his feet, he dropped him with a bullet through the neck.

Some of the vaqueros had run for their horses, cursing savagely in Spanish as they tried to quiet those geldings that had not broken free, and finally six of the men rode in desperate pursuit of the stampeding herd. The last of these, Jesus Lorado, pitched from his saddle as a well-thrown feathered lance buried itself between his shoulder blades. His gelding, with a squeal of fright at the sudden fall of the rider, galloped on after the others.

Djamba turned to Lucas and muttered, "Keep your eyes over to the south, boy—there's about eight of those redskins hiding off behind that big mesquite bush. How's your arm?"

"Sore, but I can manage the carbine. Look out

228

there—I see the gleam of a rifle out of that mesquite—"

A shot rang out and Djamba uttered a cry as he clutched his left shoulder and dropped his rifle. Lucas, with a snarl of rage, emptied his carbine into the distant clump of mesquite, and there was a howl of pain as one of the braves staggered out of the bushes, clutching his belly, took a few stumbling steps forward, and collapsed.

A flight of arrows whizzed out of the bushes, one of them burying itself in the dusty ground only inches from Lucas's foot. Lucas backed away, looking around frantically for his ammunition belt, only to discover that he had used it up. He hesitated, torn between uncertainty and alarm for his father. "Are you hurt bad, Father? I'm going to get more ammunition—it's in one of those wagons!"

"Never mind me, boy. I've still got enough, I can hold them off till you get back!"

Lucas nodded, then ran, bending low, toward the second chuckwagon. As he was about to enter it from the back, a bullet creased his skull; Djamba's sturdy young son dropped his carbine, clutched at the canvas flaps with both hands, then sprawled, unconscious. Djamba returned the fire into the mesquite bushes, and another scream of pain attested to his marksmanship as a gaudily painted Kiowa Apache, through whose red bandanna a black crow's feather was thrust, staggered erect, just his head visible for an instant and his face twisted in death-agony, then he fell.

Lucien Edmond had turned toward the depleted remuda, where Simata and Ramon Hernandez were on guard. Satisfied that there was no immediate danger in that vicinity, he turned back to see Djamba raise his rifle again, and then drop it as he pitched forward, his bleeding wound having sapped his enormous strength. With bloodcurdling whoops, two braves, brandishing spears and tomahawks, ran out of the bushes toward the fallen Mandingo. Lucien Edmond uttered a shout, knelt down, and fired his rifle, killing the first brave. As he aimed again to pick off the other, the trigger clicked—empty. He ran forward at top speed, swinging his rifle by the barrel as the second brave lifted his lance and was about to plunge it into Djamba's back. There was no time to reach the Kiowa Apache: in desperation, Lucien Edmond flung the heavy rifle like a boomerang, catching the brave across the chest and making him stumble back. Running as he had never run before, Lucien Edmond wrenched the lance out of the dazed brave's hands, reversed it, thrust it into the Kiowa Apache's belly, then stepped back and tugged it out. The hideously painted, pain-contorted face turned to him, the teeth bared and the eyes glazed; then the brave sank to his knees, both hands clutching the gory wound, and fell forward, his forehead touching the ground as he died.

Four of the vaqueros who had stayed behind now sent volleys of rifle and carbine fire into the mesquite bushes off to the east, and yells of agony resounded through the night. Two Kiowa Apaches ran out of the bushes and made toward the remuda. One of them leaped astride a black gelding, wrenched the reins free of the tether, and galloped off toward the east. As the second brave mounted, he was instantly felled by simultaneous shots from two of the vaqueros' rifles.

The lone survivor hiding in the mesquite that Djamba and Lucas had so vigilantly covered now broke from his hiding place, and ran like a deer, bending low to the ground, toward a deep gully in which he had left his mustang. Lucien Edmond could make out a feathered headdress; retrieving Djamba's rifle, he aimed at it and fired twice. From the distance there came a mocking cry of derision as the mustang galloped off toward the south and was lost in the shadows of the night.

Lucien Edmond flung down the rifle and knelt beside the Mandingo. Gently he rolled him over onto his back and improvised a bandage for the bleeding shoulder wound.

As he finished, Djamba's eyes opened, and in a faint voice the Mandingo muttered, "Your father— saved my life once—now his son gives me back my life again. I, Djamba, once king of the Mandingos of Mopti, swear to be your man to the end of my days."

CHAPTER TWENTY

It took two days to round up the stampeded cattle after the attack—grim, sweaty days of riding, roping, and shouting, stopping only to chew at a piece of smoked bacon or cold biscuit. While the vaqueros moved the herd back to the besieged camp, Ramon and Simata went after the runaway remuda horses, bringing back all but a dozen.

Lucien Edmond, his face lined with sorrow, read burial services over the graves of the six vaqueros killed during the Indian raid, then helped to bury the Indian dead. Lucas had recovered from his head wound, though his arm was still swollen and sore from the arrow. Djamba would have shrugged off his clean shoulder wound, but Celia scolded him until he sheepishly agreed to rest in the second chuckwagon, and with some embarrassment submitted to her solicitous nursing.

Then they moved on again under the monotonous glare of the searing sun, over the more verdant plains that led to the Red River and the Indian Territory. Ramon Hernandez conferred with Lucien Edmond on the day the drive resumed, regretfully shaking his head as he said, "We didn't allow for delays like this, Lucien Edmond. Not only that, we've got to let the cattle graze and water to get back the fat they lost from that hard run. We'll be lucky if we average three or four miles a day for a couple of weeks till they're rested again."

"That would put us into Abilene sometime in September, then." Lucien Edmond scratched his chin and frowned. "Well, it can't be helped. But there'll certainly be cattle pens waiting for us by then. And in a few weeks there's bound to be a courier from this fellow McCoy to let us know if the market's really going to be open there. All we can do is push on. I know that you lost some dear friends during the raid, Ramon. They were good men, Pablo Toldano and Felipe Rodriguez."

"Sí, Lucien Edmond. Pablo was Manuel's cousin, and Manuel now rides like a ghost. Let me take the other point. Perhaps it will cheer him to work with a *compadre*."

"That's a good idea, Ramon. Take the other point, and have that rider drop back to the swing."

Ramon smartly saluted, then headed Corita toward the front of the herd.

At nightfall the vaqueros set up a double-roped corral to hold the remuda horses in place. After the raid, Simata had discovered that one side of the single-rope corral had been cut by the attacking braves and caused the horses to follow the stampeding cattle. Manuel Rodriguez, still taciturn and somber-faced over the deaths of his brother and his cousin, had pointed out to Ramon two of the steers that still showed jumpiness and might cause another stampede. They were both slaughtered and the meat was turned over to Celia. Simata had found a patch of wild onions, which was a welcome change from the by now unvarying menu. And Djamba had come upon some wild huckleberries, which Celia used to make tarts for the hungry vaqueros.

As if the fates sought to make up for the bad luck they had sent the way of the Bouchard drive thus far, the herd proved more durable than Ramon had expected. By the time the outfit made camp for the night, Lucien Edmond was agreeably surprised to find that they had covered eleven miles toward Abilene.

Now there was a closer unity to the outfit, one born of sharing adversities, the hardship of the elements, and the dangers of stampede and Indian attack. The deaths of their comrades had brought the vaqueros closer together, each more concerned for his *compañeros* than ever before. At night, as they savored the evening meal, they would tell stories of their exploits down in Durango or along the Santa Fe Trail. Even Manuel Rodriguez was drawn out of his self-imposed sorrow, and told an entranced group of vaqueros how he had been on a cattle drive in Mexico where the friction of the speeding steers caused weird blue flashes to quiver at the tips of their long horns, and how, during this same

234

stampede, a bolt of lightning had struck the ground and set the grass on fire just ahead of him.

At last, in mid-July, they reached the mighty Red River. They had traveled over four hundred miles through the dusty plains, dry gullies, treacherous ravines, and on through verdant, higher land where the grazing was good. Once again fortune seemed to smile on them: the waters of that treacherous river were low and they could see white sandbars glittering in the sun. The vaqueros could not help cheering at this welcome sight, and fell to their work with zest. All the same, with over two thousand head of cattle, some of them still shying at water, it took nearly two days to ferry the animals to the other side, where Indian Territory began.

Lucien Edmond called for a day of rest after this grueling passage, not only to let the men regain their energy for the last stage of the drive, but also to allow the herd time to get over its skittishness. The day lost in this way would, he knew, be made up in the weeks ahead as their destination came ever nearer.

Now they came to deep buffalo grass and the ever-rising plain of Indian Territory, where there was bountiful grazing for the eager cattle. They moved to the north, with the plains endlessly stretching out ahead, and the blue sky with only a few scattered clouds making the horizon seem ever more distant. There was a loneliness now, and they felt like the first pioneers who had crossed this land.

The cattle had more weight on them now than

they had when the drive began. Not all were the ungainly white-patched longhorns; there were also varicolored Spanish cattle with small short horns that glistened in the sun, and brown west-Texas cattle with faint stripes down their backs and long shiny blue horns. By now these cattle, varied as they were, had learned to rely on their primitive instincts. They quickened their gait when they smelled the waters of a muddy river or a creek ahead. They had lost a number of calves along the way, and one of the docile lead steers, bitten by a rattlesnake, had been shot to put it out of its misery. But now the men and the cattle seemed to move with a dogged purpose, slowly in the early morning when the herd was allowed to graze and have its fill. Simata rode two or three miles in advance to find a watering place for the noon camp, and behind him came the chuckwagon proudly driven by Celia, with Ramon Hernandez leading the string of remuda geldings. Then came the point with the lead steers in front and the point riders on their sides, and strung along behind was the flow of the surging cattle with the swing and flank riders. At the very end came the tail of drag riders, whose job it was to keep the lame and weak cattle moving. All day long they suffered the clouds of dust generated by the moving herd. But Lucien Edmond, wise now in the ways of the drive, changed drag riders each day so that no vaquero could complain that he was being singled out for the least desirable position on the trail.

Now they were making from ten to thirteen miles a day. Each evening they bedded down comfortably, and the night watch was assigned, the va-

236

queros working in shifts of two to four hours. And, his face still grim from mourning but now resolved to see the drive successful and thus justify the deaths of his brother and cousin, Manuel Rodriguez rode slowly around the herd at night, crooning Mexican songs to quiet the cattle and prevent the always-dreaded danger of stampede.

Halfway through Indian Territory, Lucien Edmond saw a lone, bearded rider galloping southward, and lifted his rifle and fired a shot. The rider veered and rode up to the herd. "You a Texan, mister?" the bearded man asked jovially.

"That's right. From Carrizo Springs."

"I'm Bill Sugg. Joe McCoy sent me down to meet the cattlemen from Texas and tell them that Abilene's ready and wide open for them."

"That's wonderful!" Lucien Edmond exhaled a happy sigh. "My name's Lucien Edmond Bouchard. I'd appreciate it if you could take a few minutes and let our vaqueros know about the good news you just brought us."

"Be glad to." William Sugg dismounted and shook hands with Lucien Edmond. "How was your drive so far?"

"We were raided by a war party of Kiowa Apaches, but we came through it pretty well. And the Red River was running low when we crossed it."

"You were lucky at that, Mr. Bouchard." The two men walked over to the chuckwagon where Celia was preparing coffee and biscuits.

"These are first-rate!" the bearded man exclaimed after he had taken a bite. "And a woman cook—that's new in these parts, I can tell you that."

"Well, Mr. Sugg," Lucien Edmond replied,

"you've just had a sample of what makes our vaqueros work so hard to get these cattle to market."

"I'll give you that, Mr. Bouchard! My compliments, ma'am."

"Thank you," Celia replied, with a broad wink at Lucien Edmond.

"We held off till the end of April, Mr. Sugg, till we were sure there would be a railroad market up at Abilene. My father, in New Orleans, wrote to me a while back that there was likely to be a Kansas market for good beef, but it was a gamble."

"Well, you won't be the first by a long shot to get to Abilene, but you'll do right well. There's a fellow by the name of Thompson, got his herd in first all the way from Texas, but he sold his herd in Indian Territory about twenty miles up ahead of you, to those big cattle buyers, Smith, McCord and Chanler."

"I see."

"I'd say that the first herd to get to Abilene was owned by Colonel O. W. Wheeler. He assembled his herd in Texas, twenty-four hundred head of good beef, and he had fifty-four cowboys with him, armed to the teeth to fight those damned redskins. He left San Antonio and headed north, thinking he'd go back to California over the South Pass route. But when he hit Kansas, he heard that there was cholera and hostile Injuns looking for scalps. So he bedded his stock down about thirty miles from Abilene, and when he heard of my pal Joe McCoy's shipping bins, why, he just drove in there and sold out."

"So long as I can sell these cattle, I'm not looking

to be the first man to reach the market. I'm just glad it's there, Mr. Sugg."

"It's there, waiting for you. You've got a good-looking herd, Mr. Bouchard. Might go as high as seven, maybe even eight dollars. 'Course, you'll have to expect to lose money on some of those scroungy-lookin' yearlings you've got, and I can see a couple of calves you might just as well have slaughtered for meat on the trail. What do you count, around twenty-five hundred?"

"The figure I had yesterday, Mr. Sugg, was two thousand six hundred eighty-three, and by that I mean sound and healthy and expected to reach Abilene."

"Well, next time you take a herd, Mr. Bouchard, weed out a few more. And don't get me wrong, I'm not meaning to pick faults. Any man that can stave off an Indian attack the way you did, I take my hat off to. Well now, you go tell old Joe McCoy that Bill Sugg sent you in. I've got to go on south and see if I can catch me some more cattlemen and turn them Joe's way. I get me a little commission, you un'erstan'."

He shook hands with Lucien Edmond, then mounted his roan mare and rode slowly down the line to tell the vaqueros that they would be welcomed with open arms in Abilene. Then, waving his sombrero in farewell, he headed south.

By noon of the second day after William Sugg's visit, Simata rode back to report to Lucien Edmond that there was a small Indian reservation two miles to the northwest and that he believed the inhabitants to be Creeks. "Tell the point riders to head the herd in that direction, Simata," Lucien

Edmond said. "I was born two years after the Creeks were driven out of Alabama, and I remember the stories Father used to tell me about their pride and courage and wisdom. If it hadn't been for the Creeks of Econchate, near where Windhaven Plantation was built, there mightn't have been a Bouchard family at all."

A few hours later the herd was halted near a small Indian village of tepees and wigwams, surrounded on all sides by a rickety waist-high wooden fence. Lucien Edmond dismounted and walked to the gate. From the nearest tepee there emerged a tall copper-skinned brave wrapped in a ceremonial blanket and wearing a bedraggled feather headdress. Lucien Edmond held up his hand in the sign of peace and nodded. By this time, women with their papooses, carried on their backs in buffalo-hide slings, and old men and curious children had flocked toward the gate to see the lowing herd and the vaqueros.

"You are Creek?" Lucien Edmond inquired.

The brave inclined his head. "I am Emataba, son of Turintaka, the *Mico* of this village."

"Then my father knew your father, Emataba," Lucien Edmond responded eagerly. "And my great-grandfather came to the village of Econchate and was made welcome by the great *Mico* Tunkamara, and was friend and blood brother also to the next *Mico*, Nanakota."

The tall Creek's face was wreathed in a smile as he extended his hand, and Lucien Edmond shook it warmly. Then Emataba said in a grave voice, "I have seen six and thirty summers come and go, and I remember that when I was a very little boy my

240

father told me how the white-eyes soldiers had driven the Creeks of Econchate to a less happy village near Tuskegee. I remember how the soldiers took us out of the beloved land and herded us like wild animals till we came here and were told it would be our home."

"My father, who is Luke Bouchard, told me how it was in those days, Emataba," Lucien Edmond replied.

The tall Creek chief sighed. "Before my people left in those days, many of us went about touching leaves and trees and rocks and streams in farewell. We wanted to remember the happy land where we hunted, fished, and built our lodges, and cooked our food and knew the love of our wives and children."

"That I can understand, Emataba. When I heard that the village of the Creeks was here, I turned my herd toward you because I wished to offer beef for your cooking fires, as a gift in the name of my father and my great-grandfather."

"That is a good thing. We are poor here, and we do not often have meat. The soldiers will not let us have guns to kill the buffalo or the deer, so we must use the old ways of the bow and arrow and the lance. And we may not go too far from this village, which is like a prison with its fence all around us. What you do is a very good thing. My people will ask the Great Spirit to look down upon you with favor and to protect you."

Greatly moved, Lucien Edmond turned to Simata. "Tell Manuel Rodriguez to turn ten of the fattest cows through the gate here." Then, turning back to Emataba, he said gently, "We must go on

241

north with these cattle, for we have brought them a long way. But when we have sold them and come back this way, I will ask the privilege of visiting with you and your people."

The tall *Mico* nodded, then pressed his right palm gently over Lucien Edmond's heart, and touched the top of the latter's blond head with his left hand, saying, "When I tell my people what you have done and what you have said to me this day, they will be proud once again. That is true especially for the children, who cannot remember when they were not looked upon with scorn and hatred by other white-eyes, and even by the soldiers who come sometimes to see that we do not go on the warpath. There are not many of us left now, oh my brother, and it is good that you have helped us remember what we once were. Come back to us when you have completed your journey, and we will share with you what little we have in a feast of remembrance."

The two men silently shook hands, then Lucien Edmond mounted his gelding, saluted the tall *Mico* of the Creeks, and gave the order to go on.

CHAPTER TWENTY-ONE

Shortly before noon on the second day of September, 1867, Simata galloped back toward the herd, waving his wide-brimmed hat and smiling from ear to ear. "It's ready, the railroad and the pens for the cattle! Abilene's just ahead!" he shouted.

Cheers broke from the vaqueros, who had traveled four months to reach their destination. Ramon Hernandez, spurring Corita, rode up to intercept Simata. "How big a town is it, Simata?" he asked eagerly.

"There isn't much. A shipping yard, a barn, an office, and a three-story hotel they call the Drover's Cottage. And there are lots of big white tents near the hotel, which isn't quite finished yet, where the cattle buyers are waiting. I'm going to tell Mr. Lucien Edmond. It shouldn't be more than two hours into Abilene now!"

Lucien Edmond had seen the young Indian heading back toward the herd, and started his gelding forward to intercept him. We've finally reached it, haven't we?"

"Yes, Mr. Lucien Edmond! I saw many wooden shipping pens and loading gateways for the cattle. There are already some railroad cars and they are marked for the Kansas Pacific. I'm sure you can sell the cattle right away."

"That's wonderful, Simata! Tell the vaqueros to speed things up—I want to get into Abilene before sunset."

As if this news had given even the herd new energy, the long procession of yearlings, cows, calves, and steers quickened its gait. There had been twenty-six armed vaqueros when the drive had started back at Windhaven Range. Now there were only nineteen. And of the 2,852 head of cattle that these tireless and courageous horsemen had driven all the way from Carrizo Springs, Lucien Edmond had counted only yesterday a total of 2,617. Over 200 had been drowned, slaughtered for food, given to the Creek reservation, or lost during the stampede. And of that count, Lucien Edmond estimated that he could offer the cattle buyers in Abilene at least 2,500 sound animals.

"I hope there's a telegraph line in Abilene," Lucien Edmond said to Simata as they rode on together. "I'd like to send a wire to Father in New Orleans, telling him that we've made it. It'll prove to him that I was worthy of his trust."

"I didn't see any telegraph poles, Mr. Lucien Edmond. Even the hotel isn't open for business yet. This Mr. McCoy had to work in a hurry, they say.

He's there now, and he knows that you're coming in."

"I'm as eager to see him as he'll be to see me," Lucien Edmond said with a grin. Then, turning his gelding back to the chuckwagon, he called to Celia, "You can be thinking about turning back and heading for home soon, Celia! If I sell the herd this afternoon, we'll rest up overnight and then head back in the morning."

"How long do you think it'll take us to get back home, Mr. Lucien Edmond?" she asked.

"Well, it's eight hundred fifty miles, and I think we can do thirty miles a day, which would put us back at Windhaven Range in a month—at the latest, by mid-October. I'm just as anxious as you are to get back south before the winter starts up in this northern country. So you can set your mind at rest, Celia. Look—there in the distance, you can just make out cattle cars along the railroad tracks! That's the loveliest sight I've seen this year!"

With a proud smile, Lucien Edmond rode forward to take his rightful place as owner and trail boss of the first Windhaven Range herd to travel the Chisholm Trail into the Kansas railroad market.

"Welcome to Abilene, sir!" Joseph McCoy came out of his office and walked up to Lucien Edmond. He was a stocky man, in rough, unblackened boots, slouch hat, and wrinkled clothes. "I'm Joe McCoy. Mighty fine herd you've got there. You'll be able to sell it as soon as you want. The first shipment's due to move east on the Kansas Pacific three days from now."

"Thank you, Mr. McCoy. I'm Lucien Edmond

245

Bouchard, out of Windhaven Range, near Carrizo Springs."

"My God, another Texan with guts. Say, did you meet my friend Bill Sugg?"

"Yes, I did. The fact is, we weren't sure exactly where to take our cattle this year. Last year it was Santa Fe and the army fort near there. But my father had heard that you were pestering the railroad to open up a cattle town."

Joseph McCoy chuckled. "Pestering is just the word, Mr. Bouchard. First I tried Junction City, but the local businessmen there didn't seem interested in building any kind of a stockyard. I was sure that somewhere on this Kansas plain there ought to be a railroad for shipping cattle. Well, sir, I went to St. Louis first and walked into the office of the president of the Missouri Pacific. He took one look at me and told me to leave. Then I went to the top dog of the Kansas Pacific, but he didn't feel like risking any of his company's money. So I came back here to Kansas, tried to sell the people of Solomon City and Salina, and you'd have thought, from the way they acted, I was a monster of a fellow threatening damnation and the plague. Now this Abilene is just about the end of the Kansas Pacific line. When I got here it was just about dead, with maybe a dozen log huts with dirt roofing. What business they did was in two of those log huts, and of course they had a saloon in another hut. It's still here, and it's doing a land-office business, I can tell you."

"But I see you've already got a hotel started, and you've certainly got cattle pens and cars for the herds."

"Of course," Joseph McCoy testily declared. "First I had to buy a piece of land right next to this dead little town; by then it was already July, and the herds were moving north from Texas. I gave myself sixty days to build a yard and a barn, and my office and the hotel you see over there. And I'd say I'm well ahead of schedule—'cept for the hotel, which won't really be ready till about the end of this month. I had lumber sent all the way up from Hannibal, Missouri, and I was able to talk those tightwads of the Kansas Pacific out of rail-road ties so I could build my shipping pens, strong enough to hold those wild longhorns of yours. Well, that's the story. But you don't want to stand here in the hot sun talking to me all day. Let's go over to those tents and meet some buyers from Chicago. Come on, I'll introduce you myself."

"It's kind of you to give us a welcome like this. Mr. McCoy."

"Not just kindness—good business and good profits for all concerned. I'm not exactly here for my health—well now, you aren't either. How'd you like me to stand you a drink in the saloon before you go in and talk business?"

"That's very kind of you, Mr. McCoy, but if you don't mind, I'd just as soon sell the herd so I can let my riders feel what it's like to rest after four months of hard trail driving."

"Sure, sure," the stocky man patted Lucien Edmond on the back, then took him by the elbow and steered him toward one of the tents. "But I'll tell you one thing, in a couple of years, that old Chisholm Trail is going to be worn as deep as a river, yes sir, from two to four hundred yards wide.

And there'll be bedding grounds at regular intervals trampled by all the herds that are going to come up from Texas in the next couple of years. You just mark my words!"

Inside the tent into which Joseph McCoy led Lucien Edmond, four men in shiny black leather boots, riding breeches and wide-brimmed Stetsons were seated at a long plank table. Joseph McCoy nodded to Lucien Edmond and announced, "Gentlemen, this here is Mr. Lucien Edmond Bouchard from Carrizo Springs in Texas. He's just driven his herd in here, so why don't you fellows come on out and take a look at what he's got, and make him an offer. Don't be too stingy, gentlemen. We want to encourage all these cattlemen from Texas to make a beeline for Abilene so they'll pass the word that it's a fairminded town that pays a good honest dollar for good beef on the hoof!"

The four men looked at one another, rose, and followed Lucien Edmond and Joseph McCoy to the clearing near the railroad track where the two point riders had halted the herd.

"I'm Ed Dade, and I buy for Mr. Armour back in Chicago," said one of the booted cattle buyers. Self-importantly, he took out a gold watch with chain and fob from his vest pocket, cleared his throat, and added, "I'm interested, and I'll give you a fair shake if those animals are in good condition. I'll take the whole herd, if we can settle on terms."

"I'm Jack McCready, out of St. Louis," said the second man, tall, gray-haired, with a bushy beard and thick sideburns. "I can tell you right off, Mr. Bouchard, all I can take is a thousand head. But I'll give you top price for them."

"I'd like to sell the entire herd and get it over with, gentlemen," Lucien Edmond announced to the quartet.

"Well, that lets me out." The third buyer, a fat, nearly bald man in his fifties, wiped his brow with a silk handkerchief, nodded curtly, and walked back to the tent. The last buyer, in his mid-forties, with beetling brows and florid face, shrugged and followed his companion.

"Well then, I'd best get back out of the sun," the St. Louis buyer declared gloomily. "Unless, of course, you're sure you wouldn't want to change your mind. I'd go fifty cents higher than the Armour man, but all I can take is a thousand. I've already promised another owner who's due in here any day now that I'd take his whole herd. I knew him before the war when he used to run a small ranch on the Missouri border."

"I think I'll stick with the Armour man, if you don't mind," Lucien Edmond replied politely.

"Your privilege, sir." The St. Louis buyer raised his hat and walked back to the tent.

"I'll just go back to my office and leave you two gentlemen to talk business," Joseph McCoy said. "Maybe you'll have a drink with me after you've done your business, Mr. Bouchard?"

"I might at that. Thanks for your help, Mr. McCoy."

"Now then, Mr. Bouchard," Ed Dade said impatiently, "can we look over the animals? What tally do you make of them?"

"Altogether, 2,617, including calves and yearlings. I haven't brought anything over four years old on this drive."

"Well now, so these are the famous Texas longhorns," Ed Dade commented as he walked slowly down the halted line of cattle. "Any stockers?"

"No, sir, my men cut those out of the herd before we started."

"Good! You're a cattleman, all right. But I don't like the look of some of those calves and a couple of those yearlings. You say 2,617. Well, allowing for rejects back at the Chicago stockyards—Mr. Armour tells us to keep an eye on quality just as much as quantity—why don't we say 2,550 at seven dollars a head?"

"I had heard the price was as high as ten dollars a head, Mr. Dade."

"That's asking price, sir, not taking price. Take it or leave it. Joe McCoy says there'll be a couple more herds in the next couple of days, and I'm a busy man."

Lucien Edmond frowned, then nodded after a moment and held out his hand. "Agreed."

"Good. That's the way I like to do business. Let's see now, that'll come to $17,850 in all."

Lucien Edmond Bouchard calculated a moment, then nodded. "To the penny, Mr. Dade."

"Fine, fine! I'll write you a draft on our Chicago bank—good as gold, Mr. Bouchard. You don't have to worry once you get an Armour draft, I can tell you."

"My vaqueros will want to rest up a bit for the night, and some of them may want to celebrate in the saloon over there. So, if it's no inconvenience, I'd appreciate some cash."

"I see." Ed Dade shifted his Stetson to the back of his head, scratched his forehead, then declared,

"And you'll want to pay off your riders too. They'd appreciate the coin of the realm, no doubt. How many riders have you got?"

"Nineteen vaqueros, Mr. Dade, my remuda wrangler, my scout, and three others. That makes twenty-four in all."

"Yes, I see that. Well now, what wages are you paying?"

"Twenty-five dollars a month, Mr. Dade. We've been four months on the trail, and I promised them each a bonus of a hundred dollars if we made it to Abilene," Lucien Edmond explained.

The Chicago buyer scratched his forehead again and scowled, while he rapidly made his mental calculations. "Well now, unless I misremember multiplication and addition, Mr. Bouchard, that would be twenty-four hundred dollars in wages and again as much for the bonus, am I right?"

"You certainly are, Mr. Dade," Lucien Edmond chuckled.

"Then you'd want about five thousand dollars in gold all told and the balance in the draft. Will that be satisfactory?"

"Very much, Mr. Dade."

"I've got a strongbox full of ten- and twenty-dollar gold pieces, and I guess I ought to be able to scrounge up five thousand out of that. Let's go back into the tent and I'll write you the draft, and then you can come with me and I'll see that you get the gold." His voice dropped to a whisper: "We've got a few boys in town I don't exactly like the looks of—hard, tough fellows that just seemed to drift in last week on their own, if you get my

251

meaning. I wouldn't want any of them fellows to get wind of our transaction."

"Of course not. I appreciate your concern, Mr. Dade."

Half an hour later, Lucien Edmond folded the bank draft and pocketed it, then followed Ed Dade to Joseph McCoy's office, where the strongbox was safely concealed. Lucien Edmond held a small burlap sack while the Chicago buyer methodically counted out 240 twenty-dollar gold pieces. The two men shook hands, then walked out to the herd. "Manuel, Ramon, you can start driving the cattle into those pens over there to the left," Lucien Edmond ordered. "We've sold the herd and I've got everybody's wages and the bonus I promised."

Then, holding the heavy sack of gold coins, he watched proudly as the vaqueros loudly and enthusiastically began to drive the cattle into the waiting pens, an act that symbolized the success of the new and flourishing Windhaven Range.

All the cattle had been rounded up out of the brush on the land that Luke Bouchard owned. They had cost only the wages of the loyal and courageous cowboys who had worked the Bouchard land.

As he watched the last of the herd being driven into the pens, Lucien Edmond was making mental calculations. He resolved that after paying the wages and bonuses, he would take fourteen hundred dollars from the net profit and give two hundred to each family of the seven dead vaqueros who had given their lives to protect their companions and the cattle on the Chisholm Trail.

CHAPTER TWENTY-TWO

Since the Drover's Cottage was not yet able to accommodate the men of the Bouchard cattle drive, Lucien Edmond told his vaqueros to camp just outside Abilene and make themselves as comfortable as they could with their bedrolls and blankets. They would go back to Windhaven Range the next morning, either stopping for supplies in Wichita or taking the southeasterly route to Baxter Springs.

When he made this announcement, some of the vaqueros looked disappointed. Most of them were used to celebrating when they reached the end of a drive, and in Mexico or Santa Fe would head for the nearest *posada* to drink and to dance with the girls of easy virtue who worked there. Then, as he remembered Ed Dade's warning, an idea occurred to him. After hiding the burlap sack of gold coins in Celia's chuckwagon, he turned to the men and declared, "I've got your wages and the hundred-dollar bonus I promised all of you, and I'm going to keep it hidden till we get back home, but I know that many of you would like to enjoy some tequila or whiskey, so I'm going to stand drinks for all of you out of my own pocket." With this, he took out a leather wallet and handed Ramon Hernandez a sheaf of federal banknotes. "Ramon, see that your *compañeros* have whatever they want. But remember, men, we want to get an early start tomorrow, so try not to overdo it. If you'd like, Ramon can buy some bottles to take back on our journey home."

A cheer went up from the Mexican riders, as Lucien Edmond drew Ramon to one side and said softly, "When I was in Mr. McCoy's office, the Chicago buyer told me there were a few strange riders in town who didn't seem to belong to any outfit. Keep your eyes and ears open in that saloon, and report back to me if you learn anything to alert us to any kind of ambush."

"I will, Lucien Edmond." Ramon Hernandez shrugged and winked. "These are good boys, but most of them aren't married, and they were looking forward to painting the town red once they got here. But there aren't any señoritas here to welcome them."

"If this town keeps growing, there probably will be by next year. But in the meantime they'll just have to be satisfied with all the liquor they can handle. I'll stand the first part of the night watch with Djamba and Lucas, while you take the men into the saloon."

Lucien Edmond went back to the chuckwagon, where Celia was busy preparing the evening meal. "Are we running low on flour and meat, Celia?" he asked.

"A mite on beef, and there's hardly any bacon left, Mr. Lucien Edmond. I've still got enough coffee to get us through a couple of weeks on the way back, though."

"Well, now that we've sold the herd, we'll have to depend on what game the men can shoot along the trail, till we can get to Wichita or Baxter Springs for provisions. You know, Celia, I'm still thinking about Diego Macaras's brother, Carlos, and praying to God that he didn't find those two survivors from his brother's band who could lead him back to Windhaven Range. That's another reason I'd like to get back there with our men as quickly as we can. If we take Baxter Springs route, we'll go about a hundred miles out of our way to the southeast, and even though we'll be traveling light this time, that would mean at least a week in getting back on the straight route to Carrizo Springs."

"Well, Mr. Lucien Edmond, you know best, of course. But some of the boys have told me they've seen wild turkeys and deer and even a stray buffalo every so often in Indian Territory. I think we can manage if we try to live off the land."

Lucien Edmond smiled. "Well, give the riders as good a meal as you can muster up this evening. The more they eat, maybe the less they'll drink, or at least the food will help keep them from getting too drunk to start back early tomorrow morning."

"Yes, sir."

"By the way, Celia, I'm going to pay you the same monthly wages the men are getting, plus a bonus of a hundred dollars. You've earned every penny of it, and I'm very grateful to you. You've helped more than you know by just being around to talk to the vaqueros and keeping them cheerful."

"Shucks, Mr. Lucien Edmond, it was easy." Celia giggled and self-consciously smoothed her apron as she turned back to the coffeepot. "All that attention from those strong, good-looking men made me feel like a young girl again. Not, you understand, Mr. Lucien Edmond, that I'd think of looking seriously at any other man except my Djamba."

"If you'll give me just a cup of that good strong coffee of yours and maybe a biscuit and a small piece of whatever meat is left, I'll make do just fine."

"Right away, Mr. Lucien Edmond. I hope that'll hold you till breakfast."

He nodded his thanks and walked over to one of the cattle pens, seated himself beside it, and attacked his supper. As he finished his coffee and rolled a cigarette, Lucien Edmond thought of the bank draft that represented the profits of this arduous but highly successful drive. Next spring there would be very few stray or maverick cattle left on Windhaven Range. True, the vaqueros could probably flush a hundred or even two hundred head out of the brush, but now was the time to plan for interbreeding and for producing beef that would bring better prices. For it was certain that by next year Abilene and perhaps similar towns along the railroad leading to Chicago would be welcoming even larger herds to keep up with the demand for meat in the East. And, from what Joseph McCoy had casually mentioned while they were in his office, it was evident to Lucien Edmond that cattle would represent not just fresh beef on the hoof but also tallow and lard, and even fertilizer for the farmers' crops. It represented a growing industry beyond even the wildest imagination, and that was why this first long drive from Windhaven Range was to his mind an omen of great things to come.

Probably this winter, he told himself as he crushed out his cigarette, he would have to go to Missouri to buy shorthorns—maybe five bulls and twenty-five or fifty heifers. Then Djamba and Lucas could help round up some longhorn cows and bulls as well, and cross-breed so that there'd be a good tally of sturdy, well-bred cattle ready for top prices. And he was convinced that it would not be many more years before the railroads would extend their lines down to the big cattle ranches—perhaps even to Windhaven Range.

The saloon was little more than a log hut, large enough to accommodate about twenty men at most. Behind the plank counter that served as a bar, a stolid-looking middle-aged bartender wearing a black bowler hat, his chin adorned with a pointed goatee and his mustache waxed at the upcurling tips, glowered at the vaqueros as they followed Ramon Hernandez into the improvised little saloon.

"Now, now gents," he bellowed, cupping his hands to make himself heard above the din of boisterous conversation coming from the two tables, "there's not room enough for all of you at once.

257

'Sides, all I got's whiskey. Take it or leave it, fifty cents a drink."

"And how much for a bottle, señor?" Ramon inquired.

"Can't sell you no bottles this time, greaser. Mebbe in a week the train'll bring in a fresh supply. What I got here is for my trade. How many greasers you got in your outfit?"

There was a low muttering among the vaqueros at this insulting term, but Ramon shook his head and held up a warning hand as he turned back to the bartender. "Well, then, señor, counting myself, there are twenty of us. If you like, we'll take turns. We've come four months on the trail from Texas, and I guess we can wait a few minutes more to have our first drink."

There were four men at the table to the left of the young vaquero, and they looked up from their game of draw poker. The man closest to Ramon had a straggly beard and a low, receding forehead, which was hidden by his dirty black hat pulled down to cover part of his face. Holsters were slung at each side of his belt. He swung himself around to face Ramon and drawled, "Brought in a herd from Texas, did you now, greaser? How many head?"

"That's my *patron*'s business, señor. We just work for him, we don't handle the sale."

"I don't like greasers nohow," the bearded man sneered, "least of all a whippersnapper who barges in here and tells me to mind my own business."

"I'm sorry, señor, I meant no offense," Ramon responded. Then, turning to the scowling vaqueros, he called, "*Muchachos*, half of you stay outside till

258

the others have their drinks. There's enough for all of you."

"Frank," the bearded man complained to the bartender, "are you going to serve these damn greasers? Most likely they brought in that damned Texas fever along with their mangy cows."

Ramon's lips tightened, but he controlled himself with an effort, and forced a polite smile as he countered, "I do not think that Mr. Armour of Chicago would buy mangy cattle, señor, and that is to whom my *patron* sold them. We have earned the right to drink here after the long trail, and we have money to pay for it. Allow me to offer you and your friends at the table a drink in friendship, señor."

"Well," the bearded man seemed mollified, "guess that's fair enough, greaser. Frank, bring a bottle over to the table. Ned 'n Jack 'n Tom 'n me'll enjoy this greaser's hospitality, seeing as how he's right eager to treat us. Thank the greaser, boys!"

His three companions tipped their hats and inclined their heads in derisive acknowledgment of Ramon's offer, as the bartender scurried to the end of the counter and brought out a bottle of cheap whiskey. The bearded man seized it, put the wad of tarred rag that served as a cork to his teeth, tugged it out, and spat it at Ramon's feet. "Thanks, greaser," he drawled as he filled his companion's glasses and then his own.

Ramon stared down at the improvised cork, glanced at his compatriots, and then, ignoring the deliberate insult, went up to the bartender and handed him a greenback for the bottle. "That'll just about cover the damage, greaser," the bartender grinned, obviously encouraged by the support of the men at the tables.

Ramon nonchalantly shrugged. "Well, señor, since this is a celebration, I shall not complain. Now then, amigos, step up to the bar and enjoy your drinks with the compliments of our good *patron*."

A number of the Mexican riders came forward, and the bartender, uneasily watching for the reaction of the four gunmen at the table to his right, reached for a bottle, opened it, and began to pour out whiskey. Of Lucien Edmond's crew, only two of the vaqueros had holstered six-shooters at their belts, but Ramon had taken the precaution of bringing his carbine into the saloon. From time to time, as the men drank, the bartender shot a worried glance at the polished, deadly weapon that Ramon held in both hands, the barrel pointing toward the floor but ready to use in an instant if need be.

The three men at the other table, nondescript cowhands who had just come in with a herd a few days earlier, turned away from their game of stud to eye the newcomers, but took no part in the scene. When the first four vaqueros had finished their drinks, they left the log cabin and were replaced by four more. Ramon himself did not drink, but kept close watch on the bearded man who had so openly insulted him and his friends. At last the remaining vaqueros finished their whiskey and left the saloon. Ramon tossed another greenback to the bartender and said, "That should be more than enough for very bad whiskey, señor. Perhaps when we come back next year, you'll have tequila for my amigos."

"That'll be a cold day in hell, greaser," was the bartender's jeering retort as he grabbed the bill and stuffed it into the pocket of his trousers. "Mebbe by next year Abilene'll have a law sayin' only white men can come into this here saloon. Now that you've had your liquor and paid your score, mister, whyn't you close the door real tight behind you, huh?"

There was a loud guffaw from the bearded man in the black hat. "Not that we want to rush you, you un'nerstan', greaser, but it gets to smellin' bad in here when too many Mexs take up breathin' space. *Adios*, greaser."

"And to you, señor." Ramon inclined his head and then slowly made for the door. As he heard a whisper behind him, he whirled, and knelt down just in time to see the fourth man at the table go for his holstered pistol. Swinging up the carbine, the young vaquero squeezed the trigger twice, and the ferret-faced, wiry gunman stiffened, stumbled backward against the wall of the log hut, and then slowly slid down to the floor, his head drooping.

"Why, you goddamned spic!" the bearded man swore hoarsely. "You murdered poor old Ned—"

"A moment, señor," Ramon coolly interrupted. "He drew on me first. The bartender saw it just as I did."

"Now you leave me out of this, greaser. I didn't see anything," the bartender snarled, glancing over to the bearded man for confirmation. The latter gave him a tacit nod, and then, turning back to stare at Ramon, growled, "Good thing for you you still got that carbine in your hand, greaser. Tom 'n Jack 'n me, we'd blast you for that if you just had a

261

six-shooter. Course, you wouldn't expect a side-winding spic like you to fight fair and square. Go ahead, beat it, but one of these days we'll catch up with you on the trail, and you won't die so easy as poor old Ned did. You can take the word of Bud Larkin—that's me!"

"Señor Larkin, I shall be at your service whenever you wish." Ramon again inclined his head. This time, gripping the carbine in his right hand, he groped for the door with his left, facing the men at the table, and then went out, slamming it behind him, and hurried after the vaqueros, who had gone back to gossip with Celia at the chuck-wagon.

Having heard the explosive sound of Ramon's carbine, Joseph McCoy had hurried out of his office to the saloon. A look inside showed him the three men in the act of lifting their dead companion's body onto the table where they had been sitting. "What the hell happened here, Frank?" he demanded of the bartender.

"Mr. McCoy, that damned greaser just walked in here, got mighty high and fancy, and then without any warning he turns around and fills poor old Ned Bender with hot lead. It's a damn shame we don't have a law in these parts. That greaser ought to be strung up sure!"

"I'll handle this, Frank. Guess you fellows will have to bury your pal—we haven't got an undertaker in Abilene yet. I'll go have a word with this greaser."

"We'll have something to say about what he did to Ned too, you can bet your last pair of boots on that." The bearded man's eyes were cold and narrowed as he tugged at his gunbelt. "Hell, it was a setup. Here this greaser comes in with more'n a dozen of his spic pals, flashes his money, and wants to be treated like a white man. Then he keeps lordin' it over us, and when poor Ned starts to speak up, this greaser just turns around and drills him."

At this, one of the three men at the table across the room stood up, shoving his chair to one side. "'Twarn't that way at all, Mr. McCoy. I saw the whole thing. I don't hold much with greasers either, but this fellow was polite as could be, and he paid hard cash for drinks for those fellows over there, and if you ask me, he got shortchanged some too. Anyhow, as he was going out the door, I saw that runty man they call Ned Bender pull his sixshooter, and I'm here to tell you that that greaser turned fast as lightnin' and snapped off his carbine. It was pure'n simple self-defense, that's what it was."

"You callin' me a liar, mister?" Bud Larkin thumbed his holsters, glowering at the mild-mannered cowhand.

"No, I ain't. I'm jist sayin' what I saw. That's the straight of it, Mr. McCoy."

Joseph McCoy scowled, rubbing his stubbly cheeks with a callused thumb. "I'm inclined to go along with you, Jimmy. So, seein' as how there's no law around here to make it official, I'm putting it down to self-defense. Case closed. Now you, Mr. Larkin, I don't know what your outfit is, but I don't want any more trouble in Abilene, *savvy?*"

"So you say. All right, we're sick of this lousy town anyhow. C'mon, boys, let's take poor Ned'n

263

bury him. Nobody else is gonna do it, that's for damn sure."

The trio lifted their companion's limp body and left the saloon. Joseph McCoy looked long and hard at the bartender, who flushed, looked away, and began to busy himself cleaning glasses. "Thought as much," McCoy said, then tipped his slouch hat to the cowboy who had spoken up in defense of Ramon Hernandez. "Thanks, Jimmy. That just about wraps things up. Only if I was you, I'd go back to my trail boss's camp and stay there. That Larkin fellow and his pals aren't characters I'd want to turn my back on on a dark night."

"I get your meaning, Mr. McCoy. Thanks. I'll look out for myself, and my pals Jeff and Don. But I wouldn't be surprised if that Larkin tries to bushwhack that greaser on the trail back to Texas."

"I'll have a word with Mr. Bouchard and tip him off. But I have a hunch that greaser isn't anybody's fool. He must have had a seventh sense to feel that Bender was going to try to drygulch him, and be able to turn around and get out of range that way."

"Quickest draw I ever saw in my life, Mr. McCoy."

"Well, it's all over now. Frank, you side with any more lowlifes like that Larkin fellow, I'll put in my own bartender—I mean it."

They had made good time on the trail back to Windhaven Range. The two chuckwagons brought up the rear, with the vaqueros riding on ahead and Lucien Edmond leading them, while Simata scouted a mile ahead. Behind the last chuckwagon, Ramon Hernandez and Manuel Rodriguez, who had formed a strong bond of companionship since the latter's tragedy, flanked the remuda. These horses were allowed to graze as it suited them, the two riders gently urging them to follow the trail when they seemed to lag too far behind.

Fortune favored them in their search for food before having to put in to Wichita or Baxter Springs. Shortly before noon of the second day, Ramon saw a small herd of buffalo grazing about half a mile to the west, and he and Manuel were able to bring down two before the rest of the herd took flight. That evening the Bouchard trail crew enjoyed a savory feast. And just before evening of the second day, Lucien Edmond rode up to a farmer working in his fields and was able to buy some fresh vegetables, two large sacks of flour, and several chickens.

When they camped at night, Lucien Edmond and Ramon chose sites that minimized the danger of ambush. Mostly, the men bedded down on open stretches of plain, nowhere near forests or hills. Ramon had not forgotten Bud Larkin's baleful threat of retaliation, and he saw to it that at least three of his compatriots stood guard during the night.

Toward evening of the seventh day of the return journey, they neared the little Creek reservation, and Lucien Edmond halted the crew and walked to the gate in the fence that encircled the little village. Emataba came out of his tepee, opened the gate, and shook hands with Lucien Edmond. "Welcome, my white brother!" he exclaimed. "My people will be glad to see you. They remember your kindness and what you said about our once-great nation. Your words gave them new heart because now they understand that not all white-eyes hate them. Will you accept hospitality for yourself and your men?"

"Willingly, Emataba, if you will let me share my food with you. This morning one of my riders killed a deer, and another replenished our store of meat by killing two buffalo."

"We will have a feast," the tall *Mico* joyously declared; then he called out in the Creek tongue for all to assemble. Several of the vaqueros carried in the deer and the rest of the buffalo meat from Celia's chuckwagon, and cooking fires were started as the Creek women and children crowded around the trail crew, smiling and nodding and whispering to one another.

Thus it was that nearly seventy years after Lucien Bouchard had come from the little Normandy village of Yves-sur-lac to share the bounty of the Creeks of Econchate, his great-grandson Lucien Edmond was made welcome in the far-distant, displaced village of that once-mighty nation. After they had eaten, the braves and the younger women performed a ceremonial dance in honor of their visitors, then Emataba lit the tribal calumet and solemnly handed it to Lucien Edmond, who imitated him and in turn passed it to each of the vaqueros, and then to Ramon, to Djamba, and to Lucas.

Emataba turned to Lucien Edmond and asked, "Can you not spend a day or two more with us and talk to my braves? It is the young ones I fear for most, for they have lost their spirit and sometimes I think even the will to live. The hunting is not good, and we feel like prisoners, always waiting for the white-eyes soldiers to inspect us as if we were wild beasts that they fear will break loose and run amuck. Your words would hearten them, help them remember the dignity and the pride of the Creeks who once were respected by all men. Without pride and dignity, my white-eyes brother, no man can be truly free or happy."

"I do not wish to refuse you, Emataba, and had I not had a premonition of danger for my family and the other workers whom I left back on my ranch in Texas, I should be honored to remain here as your guest. But because this is so, and because once we were attacked by bandits who came from Mexico to kill and to plunder, I am anxious to return home as quickly as possible."

"Now that you talk of danger, it comes to me that what I saw only yesterday should be told to you, my white-eyes brother," the *Mico* replied. "As the sun was setting, I was talking with our shaman, Equitaba, and we saw a group of horsemen riding toward the south. Equitaba said to me, 'These men ride as if the evil one pursued them, and their faces are filled with anger and hate. It is well they do not stop and see us.' I do not know these men, but it has come to me in thought that they may ride ahead of someone for whom they plan an ambush. Do you know of such enemies who might so behave toward you, my brother?"

Lucien Edmond's face hardened as he nodded soberly. "In the town where we sold our cattle, Emataba, the young Mexican who handles our horses was forced to defend himself against four men who insulted him. One of them tried to shoot him when his back was turned, and he had to kill that man to save his own life. What you tell me makes me think those three men may have been among the riders you and your shaman saw."

"Yes, it may be so, my white-eyes brother. And you are right to heed the dark cloud of fear which shadows your thoughts. Only a fool does not arm himself against a known enemy. Since you have these thoughts, let Equitaba cast the sacred bones, as was done in the days of our forefathers. It may be that he will see a portent of the danger you fear. And if his words bring comfort to you, then we will have repaid in some small part the kindness you have shown us."

"I will listen eagerly to the words of your shaman, Emataba," Lucien Edmond answered gravely.

The *Mico* rose, walked slowly to a nearby tepee, bowed low before the opening, and intoned in his own tongue, "Come forth, wise old man of our tribe. Give comfort to one who is our brother. Though his skin be not like ours, his ways are those of the white-eyes who still respect us!"

From the tepee emerged a feeble man in his late seventies, his face wrinkled, his sparse hair white, wearing a cape of buffalo hide, with the great horns attached to a band that encircled his forehead. In his trembling hands he held a pouch made from the skin of a coyote, and in a thin, cracked voice he replied in Creek, "It is long since I have heard of a white-eyes who remembers the strength and honor of our people. Bring me to him, that I may read his face, for the Great Spirit has taken the sight from my eyes but has left me my heart to know whether a man walks a straight or a crooked path."

Emataba reverently helped the blind old shaman toward Lucien Edmond, who rose to his feet and stood with his arms at his sides, while the vaqueros and the inhabitants of the village watched in an almost hypnotic silence. "He stands before you, Equitaba," Emataba gently said. And then, to Lucien Edmond, he added softly, "In his time, he was *Windigo* to the great *Mico* Tisoula in the land that the white-eyes called Georgia. He is the last survivor of the now-forgotten tribe that stood high in the ranks of the Creek Confederation. The others who came with him here have long since been summoned by Ibofanaga, the Giver of Breath."

Lucien Edmond felt an almost mystical shiver surge through him. And in the silence, as the old man put out his bony right hand to touch Lucien Edmond's face, the blond heir of the Bouchards sensed the spiritual kinship between himself and his pioneering great-grandfather who had harkened to the words of Tsipoulata.

Lightly the old man's fingers touched Lucien Edmond's forehead, cheeks, chin, and nose, then traced his lips and finally, almost with the delicate touch of a feather, his eyelids. Then he nodded and said in Creek, which Emataba translated in a whisper, "I see the face of a strong young man who walks straight yet heeds his elders. He has courage and pride, but he is wise enough to know that even these may be brought down by evil which is not of his own doing. He is worthy of our friendship, and for him I will cast the sacred bones."

Lucien Edmond glanced quizzically at Emataba,

who nodded and put a finger to his lips. Gently, then, the *Mico* helped Equitaba seat himself upon the ground and carefully untied the rawhide drawstrings of the pouch.

The old man took the pouch and the bones fell before him. They were the bones of an owl, a deer, and a coyote. After his fingers identified their position, he lifted his face to the sky and in his thin, reedy voice declared, as Emataba swiftly translated for Lucien Edmond, "He has journeyed far and now returns to his loved ones many miles from this place. He fears that they are in danger, but the danger has already come and gone like the sudden wind of the plains. Yet before he reaches them and finds them unharmed, he himself will walk near the shadows of death, yet not be touched by them. And this I see also—that his squaw will be with child before the winter which comes after this one. His life will be long and good and he will be loved by many. This is what the sacred bones foretell."

Lucien Edmond said to the *Mico*, "Say to Equitaba that I am grateful for what he has told me. And I shall heed his warning as I go back to my home. Tell him also that if the Great Spirit so wills that next year I come this way again with cattle, I shall share my good fortune with the Creeks of this village in the name of my great-grandfather, my father, and myself."

"I will tell him what you have said, my white-eyes brother." Emataba helped the blind old man to his feet and then solicitously led him back to his tepee.

The evening of September 2 was overcast after

an intermittent rain that had lasted throughout the day. The lean hound Jubal, having been penned up during the day, bolted outside as soon as Sybella opened the front door of the ranchhouse. Maybelle Belcher was busy in the kitchen, with young Tim and Connie helping her prepare the evening meal. Maxine Bouchard sat on the living-room couch, reading a fairy story to Carla and Hugo. Henry Belcher, restless because he had nothing better to do, had offered to help his wife in the kitchen, but she had impatiently shooed him out of the way. So he had disconsolately followed Jubal into the yard and squinted up at the ominous sky, then shook his head at the visible prospect of still more rain.

Andy Haskins, the one-armed young Tennessean, had left the bunkhouse to practice throwing his knife at a live oak tree some fifty feet away, while his Georgia friend Joe Duvray good-naturedly proffered disparaging comments on his friend's marksmanship as he stood whittling a toy steer for little Hugo.

As the sky darkened with the advent of night, an occasional low rumble of thunder was heard from the southeast, warning of an approaching storm. This was interspersed with the soft calls of the night birds preparing to take shelter from the anticipated rain.

"Tim, go into the living room and tell Aunt Maxine that supper's just about ready," Maybelle said as she inspected the wild turkey roasting in the oven and the pot of sweet yams picked from her husband's garden patch near their own house. Carl, the loyal and tireless Ashanti, had shot the turkey this morning, and it would provide a delightful change from the usual fare. She was smiling to herself, pleased with her life. Even in the midst of that contentment, she could still remember how desolate she had felt when she had left Windhaven Plantation to come out to this unknown country. Only yesterday Sybella had complimented her on how young she was looking these days. It was no wonder, with such a devoted, kind man as Henry who couldn't do enough for her and who praised her over the silliest little thing, and his dear children, who treated her as if she were their real mother. She didn't have to wait until Thanksgiving to feel grateful for all her blessings.

When everything was ready, she served Maxine, Sybella, and Henry and the four children, then went out to the back porch, rang the cowbell, and called, "Come and get it before I throw it out!"

Andy Haskins chuckled as he retrieved his knife from the tree and thrust it back into the leather sheath belted around his waist. "Don't guess we better let her do that, Joe," he told his friend. "I've been smelling that turkey since morning, and I'm starved."

"Reckon I could try a forkful myself," Joe Duvray admitted. "Come on, let's go take the chow out to the boys in the bunkhouse."

"You are sure this is the place, *hombre?*" Carlos Macaras hissed as he dismounted and tethered his horse to one of the pecan trees that grew near the Nueces River.

"I swear it, *mi jefe*, on my hope of paradise," Ernesto Valdez replied.

"Believe me, you will enter not that place but the one below sooner than you think if you have lied to me," Carlos Macaras said grimly. Unholstering one of his pistols, he gestured to Humberto Dondero. "*Adelante, hombre!* Your friend says we have come to the *rancheria* of the gringo who murdered my brother. Does he tell the truth?"

"*Pero sí mi jefe,*" the squat Mexican assented.

"With the two of you and myself, we have sixteen men. It should be enough. We will wait till it gets darker, and then we will take these gringos by surprise. Valdez, you have said you are sure there are young *mujeres* in that house. We shall not kill them—at least not yet, *mi compañeros.*"

By now the other men whom Carlos Macaras had recruited in Mexico had dismounted and tethered their horses to trees. Then, tying bandannas over their noses and mouths, they waited for the leader's signal.

"One thing is in your favor, amigo," Carlos Macaras said to Humberto Dondero. "As we circled the back of this *rancheria* I did not see many horses in the corral. Nor any cattle either. It is most likely that the vaqueros rounded them up and took them along to sell to the market far north. That means that most of the gringo's men are not here to defend the lovely *mujeres* we shall find and take back with us. So, amigos, you are both in luck for now; say prayers that your luck will continue. Do not think I have forgotten that you ran away like frightened dogs to leave my brother, Diego, to be killed."

The two Mexicans shifted uneasily and exchanged a frightened look, and Carlos Macaras

273

chuckled humorlessly, "There is still time, if you have anything left to tell me, amigos," he prompted.

"No, no, *mi jefe*," Ernesto Valdez protested, "Humberto and I have told you everything that we can remember, we swear it by the Blessed Virgin."

The bandit leader gave them a hard, long look and then answered, "Now I know that you will not see paradise if you have lied to me. For if you have, I shall kill you, and then the Blessed Virgin will damn you to the fires of everlasting hell for your blasphemy." Then, raising his voice, he ordered, "I see no one who is guarding the gate to the *ranchería*. One of you will go to open it, while the rest of us attack from the side nearest the river. When I give the signal, you will all begin to fire into the house. Before I have finished with these murderers of my poor brother, I will burn it to the ground and take their gold and their horses and their women, and even all that is not payment enough for the death of a great man like Diego Macaras, fighter for the *libertad* of our beloved Mexico."

Then, turning again to the two men who had led him to Windhaven Range, he jabbed his forefinger into each man's chest and growled, "One of you, I do not much care which, will go to the gate and try to open it. Choose between yourselves, but be quick. I cannot wait any longer for my vengeance!"

The two men turned pale and began to tremble as they helplessly eyed each other. Carlos Macaras drew a clasp knife from his belt, spat on the gleaming blade, and polished it against the sleeve of his tunic. Then, pressing the point against each man's belly in turn, he hissed, "Choose, or you shall both die now, and slowly!"

"I—I will go, *mi jefe,*" Humberto Dondero gasped.

"Then go and be quick about it! You, *hombres,* wait to see if this *cobarde* can open the gate for us. When I hoot like an owl three times, take your places along the fence on this nearest side of that *rancheria* and fire into it. It will draw them out, and six of you will go now around the other side and be waiting to shoot them down. *Comprende?*"

There was a muttered chorus of "*Sí, mi jefe!*" from the thirteen bandanna-masked men behind him. Six of them crouched low, like Indians, and, hurried toward the fence on the river side of the ranchhouse, the others waiting a moment and then circling to the left to take up their places on the other side of the enclosure. Meanwhile, his face damp with sweat, Humberto Dondero began to run toward the gate of the enclosure.

"You, *cobarde,*" Carlos Macaras turned to Ernesto Valdez, "stay beside me. And this time you will not run away, you will fight. I am an excellent shot."

"I—I will not run, *mi jefe.*" Ernesto Valdez's voice was hardly audible.

"*Bueno.* Watch now—I did not think the gate would open so easily. They have put a bar on the inside. Your amigo will have to climb it. There he goes, squirming his fat body up like a worm. Now, Valdez, take that pistol which one of my men laid on the ground there for you. Make sure that it is ready to fire. When your friend opens the gate, you and I will go to the door of the house and hide on each side to wait for the gringos to run out."

Humberto Dondero, alternately praying and cursing under his breath, forced himself out of sheer terror to clamber up toward the pointed tops of the posts; he swung himself over and landed on the ground with a heavy thud, stumbling and losing his balance as he fell to all fours.

"*Caramba*, the idiot, they will hear that sound indoors!" Carlos Macaras snarled. "Go on, son of a diseased burro, take down the bar and open the gate!"

But at that moment the hound Jubal decided to make a last circle of the house before going back in. He came toward the front of the house just as Humberto Dondero straightened himself and with trembling hands lifted up the heavy plank that was used as a bar. Then he began to bark angrily, and the squat Mexican turned, his eyes widening in fear, as he reached for his pistol, aimed it, and fired it. Jubal had already lunged forward, and the bullet whined past him to thud harmlessly into one of the posts.

Carlos Macaras cried out, "*Fuego, hombres!*"

When Jubal's angry barking first began, Henry Belcher started up from the table and hurried to the front door of the ranchhouse. He was just in time to see Humberto Dondero struggling to lift the heavy plank, while Jubal, growling, sprang at him and sank his teeth into his right thigh. With a yell of pain, the bandit let go of the plank and kicked Jubal. The hound rolled over, righted himself, and again sprang at his enemy. Henry Belcher seized his old Whitworth, which he kept against the wall inside the front door, took careful aim, and fired. Humberto Dondero staggered, uttered a cry of agony, then toppled over onto his side. Jubal nosed his inert body for an instant, then ran back to the house. At that moment, on Carlos Macaras's signal, the bandits on each side of the enclosure opened fire, and the fusillade tore through the windows of the living room. Henry Belcher whistled to Jubal, and as the hound sprang inside, he closed and bolted the door, then crawled along the floor, gesturing to Jubal to lie down, as still another fusillade rang out.

By now the men in the bunkhouse had grabbed their weapons and begun to emerge, crouching low to avoid the bullets. Carl, the tall Ashanti, flung himself down on the ground just outside the bunkhouse and readied his Spencer rifle, and when the next fusillade rang out, the position of the attackers marked by the flashes of ignited gunpowder, and triggered his rifle three times. A scream of pain answered him, and he heard one of the bandits call out, *"Jorge es muerto—fuego, mis amigos, muerte a todos los gringos!"*

Another shot rang out and Carl quickly answered it with another burst of fire from his Spencer. There was another hoarse cry, and then he heard running footsteps as the four survivors on the river side of the fence sought to find a new position.

In the dining room, the children had begun to cry in terror. "Don't cry, children, our men will protect us," Sybella urged. "Tim, Connie, you're the oldest, take Carla and Hugo and lie down under the table. We'll play a game of hide-and-seek, and nobody will get hurt."

"My God, Mother," Maybelle sobbed, "are those Indians or bandits out there? What if they have more men than we do?"

"Stop acting like a hysterical child, Maybelle," Sybella snapped. "In the closet in my bedroom you'll find a carbine and a six-shooter. Maxine, go with her and get them. Don't get too close to any of the windows. That's right, Tim and Connie, stay there on the floor till it's all over!"

"My God, Henry—he's out in the living room—" Maybelle suddenly remembered, wringing her hands as she turned, undecided, back to Sybella, while Maxine, an arm around her waist, gently tried to lead her out of the dining room.

"He'll be just fine. He's got his army rifle," Sybella said calmly. "Now then, Maybelle, are you going to make him proud of you, or are you going to stand there whimpering?"

"All right, Mother. Oh God—" This as another volley of shots rang out.

Andy Haskins and Joe Duvray had brought the vaqueros their supper and had gone back to the kitchen to get their own rations when Jubal's barking had warned them of the attack. Hurrying back to the bunkhouse, the one-armed Tennessean had picked up a loaded six-shooter and hurried out to join the four black workers, while Joe Duvray had grabbed his carbine and hastily loaded it, then followed.

Carlos Macaras, cursing at the failure of his men to storm the house and most of all at Humberto Dondero's inability to open the gate, primed and loaded an old Belgian rifle. Standing on a little grassy knoll near the riverbed, he was able to make out the slightly open front door of the ranchhouse, and he aimed the rifle and fired. Henry Belcher, having finished reloading his Whitworth, slipped out the door, knelt on the porch, and shot at the space between two of the upright posts. The bullet thudded into a live oak tree only a few feet from Carlos Macaras, who pulled Ernesto Valdez's pistol out of his shaking hand and fired. The bullet fell short, the range being well beyond that of the small handgun. But again the flash of light told Henry Belcher where the attackers were, and he squeezed off another shot. Ernesto Valdez spun around, then fell headlong at Carlos Macaras's feet.

"He has saved me a bullet, *cobarde*," the bandit leader said as he crouched down and rolled Valdez's body over. "I would have killed you even had we been successful. In my dead brother's name, *cobarde*."

Now, at the right side of the enclosure, the bandits began to scale the posts and drop to the ground, crouching low and moving toward the porch of the ranchhouse. Sybella, pulling the carbine out of Maybelle's trembling hands, knelt beside the window, squinted out into the darkness, and vaguely made out the shadowy forms of the bandits moving to her right. She fired three quick shots, and cries of pain attested to her marksmanship; one of the bandits fell dead in his tracks and two others sustained flesh wounds in the arm. Henry Belcher, again reloading, picked off a fourth bandit with a clean shot through the heart, then pulled the door to and bolted it, and lay flat on the floor to prime and reload again.

"Maxine, use the pistol—there's a man going around to the left, I can see him," Sybella whispered. Maxine nodded, knelt beside Sybella, and fired the six-shooter. The bandit stumbled but kept running and disappeared in the shadows of the night.

Jubal, barking, had run to the front door and back into the dining room, where the four children lay under the table. Tim and Connie were holding Carla and Hugo by the hand, doing their best to keep the two younger children from crying or moving, though they themselves were terrified.

On the side of the enclosure that faced the bunkhouse, two bandits scaled the posts and dropped onto the ground, only to be met by Ned and Carl, who had led the charge of the vaqueros out of the bunkhouse. Ned had brought from Windhaven Plantation an old Confederate saber, and, swinging it over his head, he brought it down with all his might into the side of the closest bandit's neck before the latter could regain his footing and fire his pistol. The dying man thrashed and kicked, uttering gurgling cries, and then lay still. Carl had drawn his six-shooter and snapped off a shot at the other bandit who had scaled the stockade, but the weapon misfired. With a triumphant chuckle, the bandit drew his pistol and leveled it at Carl, but the tall Ashanti flung himself forward, his arms locking around the bandit's knees and felling him to the ground. Scrambling over his adversary, Carl wrested the pistol away from the swearing, struggling Mexican, and, reversing it by the barrel, smashed the heavy butt down repeatedly against the Mexican's skull until his body slumped in death.

One of the vaqueros, Antonio Falzedo, was killed by a pistol shot as he moved toward the stockade to take up position against the attackers. His closest friend, Porfirio Gonzalez, uttering an agonized cry as he saw his friend fall before him, aimed his carbine through one of the shoulder-height firing holes in the stockade, and killed the running bandit, who was trying to circle toward the back of the ranchhouse in hopes of finding an easier entry. Several of the other vaqueros now moved around the back of the house in time to see one of the bandits trying to smash in a window, and their simultaneous fire dropped him where he stood.

Carlos Macaras ground his teeth in frustration and bawled, "*Retiro, retiro,* amigos! There will be another time, I swear it!"

He waited for a few moments, shuddering with thwarted rage and blood-lust, till two of his men stumbled onto the knoll, panting, and two more, their wounds bleeding, followed. "Take all the horses, quickly!" he commanded. "Next time, we'll come back with an army and kill all these dirty gringos, and their *niños* too, and we'll make their *mujeres* pay for the loss of your *compañeros!*" Then, mounting his horse, he galloped across the river, followed by the exhausted survivors.

Of the Bouchard family, only Henry Belcher sustained a wound from the bandit attack: it was only a scratch on the hand from a flying splinter of wood dislodged by one of the bandits' bullets. As

281

he picked up his rifle and turned to go back into the dining room, Maybelle came hurrying toward him, sobbing hysterically. "Oh, Henry darling, you're hurt—you're bleeding! Oh, my sweet husband, I was so afraid for you and the children! You let me bandage that wound right now!"

"Now stop crying, honey. I'm just fine, and so are you and the kids."

Maybelle looked up at him with a tremulous smile. "I'm just crying for joy because you take such good care of me, Henry Belcher. The luckiest day of my life was when you came by here in your wagon with Tim and Connie. And now you're going to let me bandage up your hand and make you some good strong coffee, and I think there's a piece of pecan pie left—you've earned it, darling."

CHAPTER TWENTY-THREE

On this same September evening, three miles east of what had once been the Williamson plantation, downriver from the red-brick chateau where old Lucien Bouchard had realized his fondest dreams, the night was dark and the thick clouds obscured the quarter-moon.

It was dense forest here, cedar and oak trees and cypress, with some Spanish moss entwined along the branches like vibrant serpents, dangling and immobile, yet with the illusion that they would strike. In the clearing in this dense forest, just beyond a copse of waist-high flowering bushes, there stood a huge wooden cross. It was ignited at the top and along the horizontal cross-arm. Before it stood a group of twenty men, dressed in white sheets that had been formed into hoods, masking their faces save for the eyes. Near the cross, his white hood marked from the others by the symbol of a black cross drawn with a tar brush over his left breast, a short, stocky man held up his hand for silence.

"Brothers of the Ku Klux Klan, I bid you welcome as your Grand Kleagle. We have sworn the oath, the sacred oath of fire and the sword, against the Northern oppressors. They have vowed to exterminate the South with their carpetbaggers, with the traitors in our midst whom we call scalawags, and with their reliance upon the freed blacks—whom we call niggers and who were slaves and whose brains will never be worthy of better rank in the society of good, free men."

There was a muttered chorus of agreement from the group that faced him, and a stirring among them as the fire flickered and lit up the clearing, making the ghostly figures seem part of some hellish gathering of warlocks. About them came the chirping of night birds, the droning of insects, and the soft rustle of branches as the humid wind touched here and there and then retreated as if in fear.

The robed leader held up his right hand for silence. "Brothers," he declaimed in an earnest voice, "each of you has sworn the oath, and each of you knows how we began and why. Those valiant men who followed heroes like Robert E. Lee and Stonewall Jackson, and who shed their blood against the Northern tyrants who wish to force the niggers upon us as our equals, came in holy dedication to the town of Pulaski, Tennessee, in May of last year. Their purpose, my brothers, was to oppose the vicious, despotic arrogance which the

Radical Republicans, in the name of Reconstruction, sought to force upon us. It is unthinkable that we should accept the horrid black apes who once toiled in our fields as being equals among us—free, my brothers, to rape our women, destroy our households, and swagger down our streets. They must not think that because that other ape, Abraham Lincoln, freed them, they may spring at once into the society of God-fearing, decent men."

Again there came the muttered chorus of agreement, but this time louder.

"Yes, my brothers," the leader continued, "that is what they would do to us. And now, thanks to the glorious courage of our Imperial Wizard, General Nathaniel B. Forrest, we have organized through the supposedly conquered and dying South. In this very year, in April, our Imperial Wizard organized local Klans through those states which have most to lose from the vindictive North. And this night, in our Klavern, united as one by the burning cross whose light shall terrify and drive forth our enemies, we swear to put confusion in their ranks. We must teach these ignorant black apes that they dare not think themselves our equals. We shall punish them!"

"We shall punish them, punish them!" The cry was loud and savage, piercing the gloomy night in the forest.

The leader waited, his eyes bright with joy at the instant approval of his followers. He extended his arms in the figure of a cross as he exhorted, "Wherever the burning cross is seen, these damned

285

Republican Reconstructionists and their black African dupes will have cause to tremble and to fear.

"No one knows who we are in public life, and no one shall. For we have taken the oath, my brothers, and he who betrays it will wish that he had never been born. Repeat after me, my brothers, the sacred oath we took when the great word came to us from Tennessee: 'I, who am sworn to uphold the right of free men in our beloved South, do, by the symbol of the burning cross, whose brightness clears the darkness from my eyes and whose sacred flame warms my heart, now before God and my sworn brothers take this new oath, which is binding upon me till my last breath.'"

He waited as the hooded men before him repeated the preamble, then lifted his arms, first to the sky, and then again in the figure of the cross. "'I do solemnly swear before my brothers and before God to drive forth our enemies, to cause terror and confusion among them, till finally they quit our beloved land and leave us to our own destinies. By fire, by sword, by the lash, by the gun, we shall exterminate our oppressors. Yet they shall never know as they walk the streets of our cities and our villages who it is that turns the wrath of the Almighty upon them through our holy society. This I swear, and may God strike me dead if I betray the oath. And I further swear that if one of my brothers of the Ku Klux Klan shall betray the oath which he takes now with me, I shall judge him as a traitor and so deal with him as with all our unholy enemies. This I so swear!'"

And once again, with voices growing louder in

almost ecstatic fervor, the men before him repeated the terrible oath.

The leader bowed his head and clasped his hands. "Let us pray to Him who will not let a sparrow fall without His notice, to give strength to our arms and to our hearts and our minds in this holy cause."

There was a long silence as the men bowed their heads and prayed. Then the leader turned to a pot of bubbling tar held up on a kind of improvised spit over a fire of moss and twigs, dipped a broken piece of wood into it, and moved to the lower upright of the cross, on which he inscribed K.K.K. "By these three secret letters, which spell the name of our holy and secret society, my brothers, we shall let our will be known to the traitors. The oppressors, the black apes. It will not be long before the sight of those letters upon the door of an ignorant nigger, who was once a slave and who now dares look upon our decent women as his rightful prey, will make him turn and run as if the devil were behind him till he has left the boundaries of our beloved state. And when this is done throughout the South in unison and with the loyalty of all of us, the South shall again be free."

"Again be free!" the voices eagerly echoed.

"Go now back to your homes. Go, and say none of this even to your wives or your dearest friends. We are men destined for a holy purpose. We may suffer the taunts even of those who know us for seeming to accept the perfidious shame and dishonor which the North has heaped upon us. But inwardly, in our hearts, we shall glory in the knowledge that it will not long be thus. I declare the business of this Klavern now officially at an end. When next we meet, it will be to take forthright measures against our enemies. Till then, be faithful, be loyal, and swear unwavering vengeance upon those who abuse and dishonor us!"

And from the hooded men who faced him there came once again the chorus, almost savage in its ferocity: "We so swear!"

They had gone three days southward after leaving the Creek reservation. Each night vigilant watch was maintained, and pains were taken to camp on level ground with neither hills nor forests close by, in order to further decrease the danger of ambush. Lucien Edmond had been comforted by the words of the old blind shaman, Equitaba, and yet he could not dispel a sense of anxiety and foreboding as he rode at the head of his men, his eyes scanning the horizon. Ramon Hernandez also was sure that the friends of the man whom he had shot in the Abilene saloon were still to be reckoned with. When Lucien Edmond told him what Emataba had said about a group of riders galloping southward about a day ahead of them, the young vaquero was certain that it was these men and their accomplices, and that they would lie in ambush and attack when it was least expected. Because of this, Lucien Edmond slightly altered the homeward route from that of the Chisholm Trail.

They had had good luck in finding plenty of game on the way back. Simata flushed a covey of partridge out of the bushes the next day, and that evening the vaqueros feasted on the roasted fowl. Celia, during a halt to water the horses, had discovered patches of wild red berries on the banks of the creek. She had filled several pails, and that evening, using her flour sparingly, she provided the hungry riders with a finale to a meal that, in contrast with what they had eaten while driving the cattle, seemed worthy of a Lucullan banquet.

After another week they came within sight of the majestic Red River. At first it seemed an easier task to ford it now that there were no cattle, but the waters were higher, and because they had varied their approach to it by several miles, the shoals were unknown and hence more dangerous. They made camp that night about five miles from a precipitous bank, choosing again as level a terrain as possible, with only a small stretch of straggly oak and poplar trees several hundred yards to the right. Simata, having scouted ahead, said that in the morning they would have to go down along the bank about three or four miles to find an easier fording. From what he had seen, the waters were much too high, almost at flood level at this particular spot. Yet, westward, there were thick bushes and clumps of trees lining the bank for as far as the eye could see.

This time Lucien Edmond himself stood guard with a Spencer repeating rifle, while Simata, Ramon Hernandez, and Manuel Rodriguez accompanied him on the first watch until after midnight. Then four vaqueros replaced them, all armed with rifles, but the night passed without incident.

It had begun to rain slightly and the skies were a dreary gray as they woke the next morning. Grumbling, the vaqueros rolled out of their blankets. Just beyond where the remuda horses were tethered in a single-rope corral, Pasquale Ruíz, a lean, peaked-faced Mexican in his late thirties, whom Ramon Hernandez had recruited for the cattle drive, yawned and let his carbine lower butt-first toward the ground. He had been standing guard duty about two hundred yards from the camp, facing west, between three in the morning and six-thirty, and the thought of a hot breakfast was uppermost in his mind, for the night had been exceptionally cool.

Suddenly there was the crack of a rifle from the direction of the trees along the bank to the west. Pasquale Ruíz grunted, put out a trembling hand, then sprawled on his belly and lay still.

Galvanized by the sound of the shot, Simata caught the repeating rifle thrown to him by Ramon Hernandez and rode off toward the river. Flattening himself along the back of his mount to make a harder target for the hidden sniper, he sought to draw the unknown enemies' fire. A volley of shots rang out from the distant trees but missed their mark as Simata wheeled his horse back toward the camp. What he had seen in that brief instant was a group of ten masked riders crossing the river to the east and spurring their horses toward the left side of the camp. "Vaqueros, take your places alongside the corral, ten horsemen come at us from that side!" he cried. There was the sound of another rifle shot from the trees, and the bullet whistled past the young Indian's head as he reached the safety of the chuckwagons.

"They must have some sharpshooting Whitworths in the woods over there," Lucien Edmond, kneeling beside the wheel of the first chuckwagon, muttered to Ramon.

"I think so, Lucien Edmond," the young Mexican agreed. "Poor Pasquale Ruíz was killed by a bullet from long range, and that's the sort of gun that could hit such a distant target." Then, raising his voice, he called out, "*Muchachos*, stay on the ground like sharpshooters and pick off the horsemen as they come. They will want to distract us so the others over to the west can come closer and attack!"

The horsemen from the east had begun to open fire as they neared the camp, riding in a wide circle Indian-style in a galloping maneuver aimed at overwhelming the defenders by the sheer surprise of the attack. At the same time, the hidden snipers to the west increased the intensity of their own volleys. "At least two of them have long-range rifles with sights," Lucien Edmond explained to Djamba, who lay at his side behind a front wheel, their Spencer repeating rifles trained on the trees. "Watch for the puffs of smoke after they shoot to locate them, Djamba. Our Spencers ought to be able to carry that far—there's one now!"

The gray-haired, powerful Mandingo, squinting along the barrel of his rifle, pulled the trigger. Lucien Edmond saw the figure of a man stumble beyond the tree from the side at which he had fired, drop his rifle, then pitch forward to the ground. "That's one to pay them back for Pasquale Ruíz!" he exclaimed.

Five of the vaqueros, with Ramon joining them, had stretched themselves flat on their bellies near the whinnying, restlessly milling remuda horses, some of whom pawed the air with their front hooves and tossed their heads, frightened by the sounds of gunfire. As the attacking band swept past the eastern side of the camp, Ramon caught one of the bandanna-masked riders in his sights and pulled the trigger. The rifle dropped from the rider's hands, and he slid off his saddle, his foot caught in the stirrups. His horse dragged his dead body as it swept on past the camp. A second masked rider fell to a shot from Lucas's pistol, but in retaliation a third rider, half turning in his saddle and leveling his rifle, targeted Alfonso Diaz in his sight as the stocky, middle-aged vaquero knelt down to fire at the circling attackers. The Mexican dropped his carbine, then leaned forward to retrieve it, his fingers scrabbling at the stock. Then his mouth opened, and blood spurted from a bullet in his lungs as he rolled over, twitched for a moment, and lay still.

The rifle fire from that cluster of trees to the west succeeded in pinning the defenders down. Manuel Rodriguez, in the act of reloading his repeating rifle, winced and groaned as a bullet shattered his left wrist. One of his companions dragged him to safety behind the front wheel of the second chuckwagon and hastily tore off a piece of his shirt to bandage the bleeding wound.

The attackers who had circled the camp drew off toward the north, leveled their rifles, and began to fire at the chuckwagons. Four of them had fallen in that first foray. Celia cried out in alarm as one of the bullets splintered an arm of the wooden frame supporting the canvas only two feet above her head, and flung herself down on the floor just as another bullet ripped through the canvas and sped past.

"How many men can you make out over in those woods, Djamba?" Lucien Edmond asked as he re-loaded his rifle.

"Maybe a dozen, maybe a few more, Mr. Lucien Edmond. It's hard to tell. But they've got plenty of ammunition, that's for certain. And if we make a run for it out in that open stretch of plain before we get to the river, they'll pick us off like flies."

"We can't just wait here for a standoff, Djamba. They've got six riders left from that first attack, well behind us and out of range. But at least two of them have Whitworths—whoever shot Manuel is a real marksman. I've got an idea—if we could hitch up one of those chuckwagons and drive it toward the trees there to the west, and have four or five of our vaqueros hidden inside with their guns trained through the peepholes, we could force their hand. And we could turn loose the remuda horses to follow us so those fellows wouldn't have any human targets to shoot at."

"I'll drive the wagon, Mr. Lucien Edmond."

"Are the reins long enough so you can lie back in the wagon and be protected by the flaps, maybe even lying flat, till the horses get momentum enough to charge forward without your handling the reins?"

"I think so, Mr. Lucien Edmond. I've trained those two geldings and they don't get panicky, not like some of the horses in the remuda," Djamba re-plied.

"Then we'll try it. Otherwise God knows how long we'll be kept from crossing the Red River. I'll go with you. Have Ramon pick about four of the best shots among the vaqueros."

"Right away, Mr. Lucien Edmond." Djamba crawled back toward the chuckwagon and Ramon Hernandez and quickly explained the plan. The young Mexican energetically nodded his approval of the scheme and beckoned to four of the riders who lay waiting on the ground near the restless horses.

Lucien Edmond and the four Mexicans got into the back of the second chuckwagon, while Djamba hitched up the horses and climbed into the driver's seat. He untied the knots on the reins to lengthen them, and moved carefully backward just inside the two wide flaps that served as doorway. Lying on his belly, he tugged at the reins and gave the order, "Giddyap, Hannibal, Merlin!"

Even as he spoke, Simata swiftly slipped between the horses, and, his rifle strapped to his side by a rawhide sling, he stretched himself out on the whiffletree and gripped it tightly. The wagon started off toward the western side of the riverbank, while Lucas and Ramon divided the remaining vaqueros into two teams. One would hold off the band of masked riders at the south, while the other would concentrate their gunfire at the trees lining the bank to pin the bandits down and give the charging chuckwagon a chance to reach the hidden attackers.

So effective was the vaqueros' fire that only a few stray shots were directed at the oncoming wagon. But the six riders who had drawn off to the south, seeing the wagon's advance, now began to gallop in a swinging arc to head it off. Lucas leveled his carbine and squinted along the sights as he watched the masked riders approach the wagon, then fired. The foremost rider was thrown from his saddle as his horse galloped on toward the wooded bank. One of the vaqueros on the ground beside Lucas took careful aim and brought down a second rider. The other four riders pulled up their horses, wheeled them around, and broke toward the northwest, apparently abandoning the uneven struggle.

Ramon now swiftly untied the rope of the corral, mounted his own horse, and shouted at the other horses to follow. Responding to the expert wrangler's command, nearly one hundred horses turned and galloped en masse after Ramon. Armed now with a Spencer carbine, Ramon crouched low and headed toward the thickets and trees to the west. He could hear the cries of alarm from the hidden attackers as they saw and heard the thundering geldings rushing toward them like a stampede.

Lucien Edmond and his four riders crouched at the peepholes of the chuckwagon. By now the fast-moving wagon had come within a hundred feet of the wooded riverbank, and Djamba gave a last flick of the reins and shouted to the thundering horses as he crawled back to retrieve his rifle and then moved back to the open flaps.

Carefully freeing his rifle, as he clung with his other arm to the whiffletree, Simata grabbed with his left hand for one of the traces, nimbly straightened, then leaped onto the back of the horse at the left. Flattening himself along it, he brought up his rifle and fired twice. From behind a dwarfed oak tree, one of the bandanna-masked men sank to his knees, then rolled over onto his side. As another man stepped from behind his tree shelter to take aim at the charging wagon, Djamba picked him off with a clean shot in the forehead. Lucien Edmond squeezed the trigger of his Spencer and another of the masked men sprawled forward.

On the other side of the wagon, the vaqueros kept up a steady and murderous fire into the bushes and trees on their side, killing three of the concealed attackers and wounding a fourth. Ramon brought down two men with his carbine, as the remuda horses thundered onward, creating confusion in the enemy ranks.

The bold charge of the chuckwagon had taken the bandits by surprise. Bud Larkin came out of a clump of bushes to kneel and level his rifle, just as Djamba squeezed the trigger and toppled the bandit leader onto his side. He tried to crawl, dropped his rifle, made a supreme effort to rise, and then sank back, his head turning to one side.

Farther down the bank, three of the bandanna-masked men broke from their cover and ran toward their tethered horses. Lucien Edmond killed one and wounded another, as Djamba crawled back to retrieve the reins and tugged on them to slow the charging geldings.

As Lucien Edmond rose to his feet, he saw a bullethole through the canvas just a foot above where he had crouched. The words of the venerable blind Creek shaman came back to his mind, and he touched the bullethole and smiled grimly.

"I think we've seen the last of them, Djamba. Let's turn the horses back to camp and then start across the Red River. Once across it, we're really on our way back home!"

CHAPTER TWENTY-FOUR

Ben Wilson's earnest, homely face was aglow as he leaned over the trundle bed in which his two-year-old son, Thomas, lay sleeping peacefully. Then he shook his head and turned to take the hand of his wife, Fleurette, who had come in behind him on tiptoe so as not to wake the child. "He's just as sturdy as can be, Fleurette darling," Ben whispered. "Let's go into the living room and talk for a bit before supper. I'm not hungry anyway."

Loving devotion to her husband and late motherhood had brought a serene beauty to Fleurette Bouchard Wilson's sensitive face. Now thirty-five, her only regret was that she had not met the kindly young Quaker years before the war. Even as a young girl she had been fascinated by the study of medicine. At the age of nineteen she had fallen desperately in love with Dr. Horace Phenley, who had set up practice in Montgomery, having come from Richmond. His father's death had summoned him back home, and there he had remained to look after his aging mother and only sister. At the age of twenty-five, Fleurette had been engaged to Dr. Jonas Morton, a thirty-two-year-old Quaker from Philadelphia. He had come to Montgomery two years before to visit his older brother and his wife, stayed on to aid her through a difficult pregnancy, then decided to set up his practice in Alabama's capital. But on the day before his scheduled wedding to Fleurette, Dr. Morton succumbed to a fatal attack of scarlet fever.

Fleurette's bereavement had intensified her interest in medicine, and, more specifically, nursing. Soon after the outbreak of the Civil War, she had gone to Richmond to live with one of her friends who had made her house over into a hospital for the soldiers. It was there that she had met Ben Wilson, when he had been brought into the hospital with a bad shoulder wound, sustained while he had been bandaging the wounds of a Confederate officer. He had been a medical corporal in the Union Army, since his Quaker faith forbade him to take up arms against his fellow man. His quiet courage, together with his humanitarian act of saving the life of a Confederate officer, caused his captors to place him on his honor as a prisoner of war instead of sending him to the notorious Libby Prison. When the young corporal had spoken fervently to Fleurette of his desire to return home to become a doctor, and one day to establish a hospital that would offer clinical services to the poor,

Sybella's younger daughter had known at once that he had been sent to her to compensate for her two earlier denials of love.

He had passed his medical examinations a year before and was assigned to the Pittsburgh General Hospital on Traylor Avenue. There he frequently got into trouble with his superiors because of his constant advocacy of improved facilities and stringent hygienic measures.

Only last week, white-haired, bearded Dr. Elmer Drawley had summoned him to his office. There the sanctimonious doctor berated him for having told a young intern that fewer babies would die of puerperal fever if greater attention was paid to the sterilization of both bedding and surgical instruments. "Young man," Dr. Drawley had thundered, "Pittsburgh General is not and never will be a haven for malcontents, for dreamers who believe that their inheritance of the mantle of Hippocrates forces them to speak out in defiance of their wiser elders. I shall keep my eye on you, Dr. Wilson, and the next time I hear an expression of your extreme and unfounded views, you may be obliged to seek another hospital in which to dispense your impertinent nostrums!"

Fleurette leaned down toward the sleeping child, her green eyes warm with love. She formed a kiss with her full lips and touched them with two fingers, which she lightly brushed over Thomas's neck, then left the bedroom. Her sweet round face was bright with tenderness, but her high-arching forehead wrinkled with concern as she saw her husband pacing back and forth before the couch in the darkness.

"We'd best have some light on the subject, don't you think, Ben dear?" she said softly as she went to the kerosene lamp and turned it up. "There, that's better. Now stop that pacing before you wear out the rug."

Ben Wilson, two years younger than his wife, was six feet tall, with unruly, light brown hair that invariably fell in a curl over one side of his forehead. His face was lean, his chin a trifle sharp—Fleurette teasingly called it a sure sign of stubbornness—and there were faint pockmarks from a mild attack of smallpox as a child. His voice was soft, in keeping with his self-effacing manner, except when he was violently agitated by the subject of improved medical aid to the poor. The adoring look that his quizzical brown eyes sent Fleurette as she came toward him was indeed what had first drawn her to him in the improvised Richmond hospital.

"Do sit down, darling," she urged as she came to him, gently took his hand, and led him to sit beside her on the couch. "Now, what's troubling you so? Is it that pompous old Dr. Drawley?"

"No, I'm used to dealing with that. It's something else. It's both a temptation and a curse, because out of the clear sky I've been offered the chance to run a hospital of my own."

"But that's wonderful!" Fleurette exclaimed, turning toward him and putting her arm around his waist. "Isn't that what you've always wanted?"

"Not the way it's been proposed, Fleurette. I told you about George Hardesty, didn't I? He's a bigwig at the Bessemer iron plant, and he's got the

301

most luxurious suite of offices in downtown Pittsburgh you ever saw in all your life."

"But it would take a rich man to help found a hospital, darling. And if money is used in that way, it can't be so very evil."

"Dear Fleurette," he took her hands in his and kissed her tenderly on the cheek. "You make life sound so simple. You've almost become a Quaker, like me, in refusing to believe that there can be wrong even in right. But there is, believe me."

"Why do you say that?"

"Because George Hardesty is a vain man, and he wants to perpetuate his name. He'll have plenty of publicity in the newspapers when he announces his plans for the new hospital down near Clarendon Street, just past the bridge over the Monongahela."

"So far I see no harm in all this, darling," Fleurette said calmly. "Perhaps it's because I'm just a little bit more worldly than you that I wish you wouldn't always be so terribly idealistic. Please don't misunderstand me, dearest, but does it really matter if this Mr. Hardesty wants to build a hospital and have his name on it, so long as it offers the very best of medical care? And if he's chosen you to be the head of it, then at last you'll have your chance to do all the things you've tried to do at Pittsburgh General."

"Yes, Fleurette, I understand all that," Ben Wilson said patiently, shaking his head and frowning, "but the whole point is that this hospital won't have any clinical facilities at all. Mr. Hardesty said that in his opinion, the people who mattered in this city ought to have the very finest hospital there is, and I took umbrage at that remark. I told him that what I really wanted was a clinic to serve those who couldn't afford to go to the hospital, those who couldn't even afford to pay the doctor for a visit when their children are sick. Don't you see, Fleurette? He's rich, and he wants to have a hospital just for wealthy people. I'd never accept the post of director of such a place. I'd be a liar and a hypocrite if I did."

He uttered a bitter laugh and looked away, biting his lip. Then he added, "I know, I must sound just the way Dr. Drawley accused me of sounding last week. He threw in that business about the Hippocratic Oath and how I mustn't think that just because I was a qualified doctor, everything I thought up had to be put into practice. But the fact is, I do feel that way. I feel consecrated to help people who can't afford decent medical treatment. Do you know how many families there must be all over this country who still rely on midwives to deliver their babies, in the dirtiest possible surroundings? And how many others have a sore throat and don't know that it's the start of diptheria because they're too poor to go to a doctor? Even if they could go, the doctor himself can't necessarily recognize the symptoms!"

"There, there, darling, don't get so excited!" Fleurette soothed. "What did you tell this Mr. Hardesty?"

"Why, what I'm telling you, Fleurette." Ben rose and walked over to the window, then turned back to face his wife. "I told him it was very kind and very flattering of him to think of me, but that I didn't even want to be on the staff of such a hospital."

303

"Ben! That was rude, even insulting!"

"Well, I just can't be a hypocrite. You're forgetting how many people I saw wounded and die in the war. I had to serve my country, and I did what I could for those who were in pain. There too, I saw so many die because the doctors on the battlefield were short of painkillers and even proper surgical instruments and clean bandages."

"Yes, sweetheart, but all that's past now. Why didn't you try to be more tactful with Mr. Hardesty, perhaps ask him if, when the hospital was doing well, he wouldn't allow you to open just such a clinic?"

"Oh, I thought of that." Again he uttered a bitter laugh. "Know what he said to me? He said, 'Ben Wilson, you're a fool. Do you think I want the riffraff of Pittsburgh flocking down to my new hospital? Do you think people of that sort matter very much in the world's affairs?' Well, Fleurette, when he said that, I got so angry—I know it's against my religion, but I almost hated that man. I just walked out and slammed the door of his office behind me."

"Poor darling!" Again Fleurette kissed him on the cheek, but Ben cupped her face and put his mouth to hers in a long, ardent kiss.

"You don't know what you've done for me, Fleurette," he said at last. "Sometimes I think you're the real Quaker in this household. But I think I knew how much you might mean to me that first time you came over to my bed in Richmond and brought me a glass of water and asked if my wound was still hurting. Your touch was so gentle, and I've never forgotten how beautiful and soft and full of pity your eyes were."

304

Fleurette blushed and kissed him quickly on the chin, then declared saucily, "I never dreamed I was going to marry a man who'd kissed the Blarney Stone. Now you let me go fix supper and we'll talk some more about Mr. Hardesty."

"There's really not much to talk about," he said as he rose, entwining his fingers with hers and smiling tenderly at her. "I guess with my little dramatic flourish in his office, I just about burned my bridges behind me. Pittsburgh's an industrial town, and I keep thinking about those poor souls who live out on the fringe of the city, who have to slave in the iron works, under terrible conditions and at low wages, and have to kowtow to their bosses for the privilege of working there. I heard of a case where a fellow in the mills tried to organize a labor union; he was waylaid in an alley and beaten up by men paid by the bosses to keep all the workers in line. That's what I'm really fighting for, Fleurette—justice, compassion, and medical help that won't cost poor people every penny they've got."

"Hush, my darling, that's enough talk for one evening. I've got a wonderful beef stew for you, and you're looking so peaked lately, you need all the nourishment you can get. Ben dear, I wonder if some of the beef that Lucien Edmond is raising way down there in Texas will one day find its way to Pittsburgh?"

"I shouldn't be surprised. They're building railroad lines into Kansas. One of these days, there'll be tracks from here to Los Angeles and San Francisco."

"Wouldn't that be wonderful? Then, instead of

taking a boat, we could go by train to visit Luke in New Orleans and his son on that ranch they have in Texas," Fleurette mused. Then, again entwining her fingers with his, she urged, "Now that's enough talk for sure. You just come on in and get ready for supper."

Nodding curtly at the butler who opened the filigree-scrolled walnut door of his elegant mansion on Castleton Drive, George Hardesty growled, "Is Mrs. Hardesty at home?"

The butler, a tall, gloomy-faced man in his early fifties, had been imported all the way from London because an agency had recommended him to his intended American employer. He respectfully inclined his head and replied, "Yes, she is, Mr. Hardesty. However, she asked me to tell you that she's not feeling well and wishes to be excused from joining you at supper this evening."

"Oh, very well, Jefferson. Where's my son?"

"Daniel is in the study room with his governess, Mr. Hardesty. Miss Prentice, if I may say so, sir, was most distressed over his lack of attention to his arithmetic lessons in school. She felt it best to give him some coaching before supper."

"Can't hurt at all. I didn't have too much schooling myself, Jefferson." George Hardesty, a powerfully built, florid-faced man of fifty-five, removed his overcoat and handed it to the dignified butler. "But one day young Dan'll take my place at the works, and he'd better know production figures and how much ore it takes to smelt down to how many tons of iron, or he'll be in real trouble. Well,

I guess just my son will be dining with me, and of course Miss Prentice, eh?"

"Quite so, sir. Shall I tell Cook you'd like your supper started at once? She wasn't sure what time you were going to be home from the office, but it won't take long. There are pork cutlets and a trifle."

George Hardesty grimaced and gave the butler an irritated look. "Look, Jefferson, what impressed me into hiring you and paying your way over here in style was that you worked for a genuine duke back in England. But that's not to say that my stomach is going to be converted to English food, not by a damn sight! Trifle indeed! Give me a good suet pudding with plenty of raisins, or plum duff or just an old-fashioned apple pie, and you'll find me easy to deal with. And you'd better tell Cook exactly that."

"Very good, sir." The butler nodded and left the foyer, while George Hardesty walked into the living room and flung himself down on a thickly upholstered couch, drew out a cigar, bit off the end, and spat it into a silver cuspidor.

As he puffed at his cigar and scanned the newspaper, he glanced up at the ceiling and muttered something under his breath. His wife, Cora, was pampering herself again. This would be the third evening in a row she had asked to have a supper tray sent up to her room. And the boy wasn't much better.

George Hardesty stood up, stretched, and yawned. He was stocky, about five foot nine, with a visible paunch. He had ladled hot pig iron in the mills as a young man, and by dint of brawn and

307

shrewdness he had been elevated at the age of forty-five to a vice-presidency of the Bessemer Ironworks. Because of his gregarious, outgoing nature, his superiors were quick to see that his real forte was in sales, and that was why they had installed him in an expensive suite in one of downtown Pittsburgh's newest buildings, a veritable skyscraper, five stories high. He ate and drank with much gusto, despite occasional warning symptoms of a rapidly fluttering heart, which he attributed to having shoveled coal for many of his younger years. He continued, even at his desk job, to attack sizable portions of meat and potatoes and pies and cakes and to wash them down with good Irish whiskey and occasionally a beer chaser.

His wife, Cora, nineteen years his junior, had been the only daughter of a sawmill owner. Brought up in a finishing school, Cora Semple had been overwhelmed by the vitality and gusto of her suitor. But she had always been of delicate health, and they hadn't had a child until late in their marriage. Daniel, who had celebrated his tenth birthday two months ago, was blue-eyed, blond, and, to his father's disgust, quiet as a mouse and "picky" with his food.

Business was good in Pittsburgh and would keep getting better. That cunning young Scot, Andrew Carnegie, was going to make things hum for coal, iron, and steel one of these days, or his name wasn't George Hardesty. And Carnegie's success would carry all the other smart ironworks operators along with him. One of these days Pittsburgh was going to be the wealthiest industrial city in the nation.

The thought of profits momentarily dispelled his fretfulness over the health of his wife and son. When the butler discreetly stood on the threshold and announced, "Supper is ready, Mr. Hardesty," he was more than ready for it.

The dining room was ornate, with marble statuettes on exquisite cherry-wood tables, and oil paintings and tapestries on the walls. George Hardesty liked to boast that although his own schooling had been comparatively neglected, what he had learned of the world after going out into it and making his living was of far more consequence. One of his favorite sayings was, "What good does it do a fellow to know everything about art and books and paintings and such if he can't afford to have them in his house?"

Now he scowled again as he seated himself at the head of the dining table. Cynthia Prentice, his son's middle-aged governess, was leading Daniel in and fussing over him as usual. As she pulled out the boy's chair, he said to her, "Let Dan stand on his own two feet and do something for himself for a change. He's big enough to pull that chair out. My God, woman, you'll turn him into a sissy before much longer!"

"I—I beg your pardon, Mr. Hardesty. Daniel hasn't been feeling well lately. I didn't want to worry you about it, but he doesn't have much appetite and he's losing interest in his lessons—which is most unlike him, sir." Cynthia Prentice was forty-six and a spinster who had always longed for children of her own. She had been engaged by George Hardesty because she, like the butler, had come highly recommended. Her previous employer had been the wife of one of New York's wealthiest importers. Tall and angular, her graying mouse-brown hair was done up at the back in an enormous oval bun. Her features were those of a frightened rabbit. Cynthia Prentice was as cowed by her new employer as was his own fragile, reticent wife.

He stared coldly at the thin, blond boy who sat primly, hands folded and ready for grace, then sarcastically demanded, "Aren't you going to say good-evening to me, Daniel?" His use of the boy's full name was an indication of his irritation, and Cynthia Prentice, as if on cue, promptly leaned toward the blond boy and whispered, "Daniel dear, we mustn't forget our manners, you know."

"Good-evening, Father," he said in a quavering voice.

"That's better. Now then, suppose you say grace, young man. After that, I'll ring for supper." George Hardesty unfolded his napkin, opened his frock coat, and tucked the edge into the top of his vest.

The boy, without glancing up at his father, began: "Bless, O Lord, this food to our use and our lives to Thy loving service, for Jesus Christ's sake, Amen," in a kind of singsong.

"Do you know what all those words mean, Daniel?" his father pursued.

"Why, yes, s-sir."

"Well, I hope so! We'll talk about it another time." He rang the silver handbell and a timid-looking young Irish maid, in black uniform with white apron and cap, hurriedly entered. "Tell Cook we're ready, Molly," he said without looking at the girl, who bowed and disappeared as promptly as she had come.

She returned with a tray on which were three bowls of Scotch broth, as thick as porridge and extremely greasy. These she set down before George Hardesty, his son, and finally the governess. She returned to bring the German cook's freshly baked bread and a porcelain crock of butter.

The industrialist reached for the still-hot loaf, broke off a large chunk, liberally smeared it with butter, then bit off a piece and followed it with a spoonful of the broth. Smacking his lips, he nodded. "At least Gretchen knows how to make a good soup. Eat up, dammit, boy!"

The boy lifted the silver soup spoon and hesitantly brought it to his lips, tried it, grimaced, and put the spoon back into his bowl. "I—I'm not very hungry tonight, I guess, F-Father."

"Nonsense. You're thin as a rail. After you finish your schooling, you're going to spend a month or so in the mill—that'll make a man of you. Now eat that broth!" his father boomed. He bit off another enormous piece of bread, washed it down with three spoonfuls of broth, then belched and patted his belly. "What are you waiting for, Dan? Eat up!"

Once again the little boy tasted the broth, and once again he made a face and shoved the spoon back into the bowl. Cynthia Prentice, a worried frown on her pallid features, sought to soothe matters by delicately cutting a piece of bread, buttering it, and handing it to Daniel. This he began to nibble at, casting quick, nervous glances at his father, who had decided to ignore him and proceed to the full enjoyment of the first course.

Presently the young Irish maid entered with a large Dresden china serving bowl filled with pork cutlets, fried in batter and heavily spiced. Setting this down on the table, she hurried back to the kitchen to return with an even larger bowl of mashed potatoes and another containing turnips and carrots. She stood dutifully by George Hardesty's side, offering the serving dish of cutlets while he helped himself to half a dozen. He piled the mashed potatoes in a towering mound beside them, then snapped at her, "Can't you see I don't have a dish for the vegetables, girl? Whatever gets into you these days? Look alive and pay attention!"

"Yes, sir. I—I'm sorry, sir." Molly, coloring hotly, turned and ran back to the kitchen.

Cynthia Prentice put one of the thickest pork cutlets on the little boy's plate and helped him to mashed potatoes and vegetables. Glancing almost fearfully at her employer, she permitted herself a single pork cutlet, though her wistful glance at the depleted serving dish indicated that she would have given much for another one. Then, leaning over to whisper to the boy not to pick at his food, she began to eat daintily but heartily.

When he had finished, George Hardesty belched again, then rang the silver handbell and said to the flustered maid, "Molly, what the devil do you mean by forgetting to serve a good hock or claret? No, no, girl, it's too late now for wine. Bring in that decanter of whiskey and a glass." As she hurried off to execute the order, he shook his head and commented, "The help you get these days is atrocious. Born shirkers, that's what they are. Take a man's money and give nothing in return." Then, noticing that his son had eaten only half of the cutlet, none of the mashed potatoes, and only a few of the vegetables, he snapped, "Daniel, what's the matter with you tonight? Isn't the food good enough for your lordship?"

"I—I said I wasn't very hungry, F-Father," the boy stammered; then he began to sniffle.

"You know, I really am worried about Daniel," Cynthia Prentice said quietly. "I think it might not be a bad idea if he saw a doctor."

"Now don't you start coddling that boy again, Miss Prentice!" George Hardesty countered angrily. "He's as bad as his mother these days. I don't understand why people can't stay healthy like me."

"Please, Father, may I be excused now? I really don't want any trifle," Daniel said. He was perspiring now, and his face looked almost green under the flickering light cast by the candelabra.

"You may as well go to your room with your governess, boy."

Cynthia Prentice took the boy by the hand and led him out of the dining room. She turned at the doorway to send one final, almost pleading glance back at her employer, but George Hardesty was at the moment savouring the whiskey that Molly had brought to him.

CHAPTER TWENTY-FIVE

After George Hardesty had finished dinner that evening, he went into his study, fortified with another glass of whiskey and a fresh cigar. His son's listless appetite had irked him, as had his wife's continued absence from the dining room. As he glowered over the rest of the paper, extracting what useful bits of information he could find in the stories dealing with Pittsburgh industries, his mind went back to that impudent young whippersnapper of a doctor, Ben Wilson, whom he had summoned to his office early that afternoon. Angrily, he puffed at his cigar till the study was filled with pungent blue smoke, then gulped down a third of his whiskey and flung the newspaper onto the floor.

He had done very well this year, with his stock and the huge Christmas bonus that he knew he could count on. There had been a few little rollback deals in which his bank account had been impressively increased, and that was something the company would never know about. It wasn't cheating at all, the way he thought. Just good business. He did a fellow a favor by giving him a sound tip where he could latch on to a piece of land. And when he bought construction iron from you, he showed his gratitude by seeing that you got yours. The company made a good profit, so how could there be any cheating involved?

But what he couldn't abide was the smug, dedicated fellows who, like Dr. Wilson, went around preaching the gospel of helping the poor. Dammit, he'd known what it was to be poor, living as a boy in a Liverpool slum, his father out of work most of the time and coming home drunk when he got his wages. If it hadn't been for his own gumption in stowing away on a ship bound for New York, he'd probably have ended up like his father, dead in the gutter after a night of carousing.

When he arrived in New York, he lied about his age, changed his name, and went to work shoveling coal for an old skinflint who ran a coal yard and paid him all of seventy-five cents a week. He'd trimmed the old skinflint at his own game, upping the price of a scoop of coal when he came across a well-to-do householder who didn't bother to count his pennies. He pocketed enough to give himself a fresh start and to leave New York for the brighter prospects of Pennsylvania. First he'd worked on a farm, then in a coal mine, and finally in the first big iron mill near Pittsburgh. He'd risen to foreman and finally managed an office job. Rubbing shoulders with older men who'd had more education than he could shake a stick at had given him the polish he needed to exploit to the fullest his natural cunning and resourcefulness.

Now he was worth more than a million dollars in cold cash, and it hadn't come by helping the poor. The sort of people that Dr. Wilson was talking about would never amount to anything. You could give them the world with a fence around it, and in a year's time they'd be back in their miserable hovels, whining about being poor again. It was all a matter of brains and toughness and perhaps just a bit of luck.

He hadn't told that pigheaded young doctor why he really wanted to build a hospital. There was only one thing George Hardesty was afraid of: death. Somehow he had the feeling that if he built a shining new hospital with plenty of beds and comfortable rooms for those who could afford it, he'd be making a bargain with the Almighty and putting off his own death for a few more years. There were things he wanted to do—travel, see some of the famous museums and all the paintings in the Louvre he'd read about. And now, well on his way to sixty, he wanted a little more fun with women than he'd been able to get with sickly Cora. When the doctor had told him that he'd better not let her have another child, he'd known right away that what little pleasure she'd been able to give him was at an end. Every month or so, when his animal urges demanded release, he'd go to a discreet two-story brick building at the southeast end of the city where he could be certain that his name and reputation would be protected. But there was always the danger of having his carriage seen just once too often at that address, because it was becoming much too popular with the youngbloods of the city. What he'd really like to do was to set up some attractive young woman in a little house, where he could visit her even during business hours when things were slow. The trouble was, he hadn't been feeling quite fit the last few weeks. It was probably because Cora and that finicky boy were acting like invalids.

He took another puff of his cigar and a swig from the whiskey glass. Maybe he'd send Cora and Daniel to Europe for their health. It wouldn't hurt the boy to get a little European background early in life. Then maybe he'd appreciate what was going on here in Pittsburgh and how people who really mattered got things done in this country. You could travel in any town in Europe and all you'd see would be a few rich people's homes and then miserable hovels where the poor spun out their unimportant lives. The best thing he'd ever done in his life was to stow away on that ship bound for New York.

Yes, that wasn't a bad idea at all, giving Cora and Daniel a little vacation. Then maybe he'd have a chance to see if that pretty new maid, Molly, could be taught a few things apart from her household duties. She was a fetching little baggage, soft pink and white skin and curly black hair. And her shy ways were exactly what he liked in bed. A girl like that, once she was trained to know what pleased a man, would do everything she could to keep her place in an important house like this.

He chuckled at the prospect, had another swig of whiskey, and then scowled again. He was remembering his interview with Ben Wilson. The fellow was a crackpot, a dangerous radical. Just let the doctors and the lawyers and the priests go around preaching the doctrine of having the rich support the poor, and the first thing you knew, you'd have a country of peasants and serfs the way it was in Russia or Germany or Italy. The next thing you'd see would be free soup kitchens all over the country with lines a mile long. And people like him would have to pay for the laziness of people who would rather accept charity than work. Yes, just let more people like Ben Wilson keep talking, and you'd have total anarchy.

He opened the drawer of his desk, took out a sheet of paper, and began to write a letter to the leading Pittsburgh newspaper. It would go on the editorial page, all right. The *Globe* was extremely cooperative. And he wouldn't have to name names, either. That pious old Dr. Drawley would recognize right off to whom he was referring, and he'd give that young man a talking-to that he wouldn't forget. George Hardesty's mouth curved in a sardonic, satisfied smile.

Dr. Elmer Drawley was livid with rage as he waited for Dr. Ben Wilson. Spread out on his desk was the morning edition of the Pittsburgh *Globe*, on whose editorial page George Hardesty's letter appeared verbatim, and with an editorial postscript after it.

There was a knock on the door and the director of Pittsburgh General Hospital barked, "Come in! Sit down, Dr. Wilson."

The young Quaker seated himself and inwardly

318

winced at the angry look on his superior's face. Dr. Elmer Drawley wasted no time in getting to the point: "Have you read this morning's *Globe*, young man?"

"No, sir, I haven't."

"Let me edify you, then. This is a letter signed by George Hardesty, an extremely important man in our city. As a matter of fact, it had been my wish to induce him to make a considerable contribution to our hospital. But after this letter, I am afraid I shall have to abandon any such notion. Thanks to you, I may say."

"To me, Dr. Drawley?" Ben straightened in his chair.

"Precisely! This is a letter to the editor. In it, Mr. Hardesty laments the radical and, to use his own term, almost anarchical attitude of many so-called humanitarians, idealists, and do-gooders. He believes, as I do, that the promulgation of such nonsensical ideas as supporting the poor and giving them free medical assistance is tantamount to overthrowing the government. What makes it even worse, Dr. Wilson, is that he referred to Pittsburgh General."

The bearded hospital director paused for effect, then resumed: "He says here, 'Not all these notions come from known malcontents or professional agitators. When we find them expressed by a member of the staff of Pittsburgh General Hospital, we view with alarm the very real danger which such impracticable ideas can create among the working classes.' I told you before, Dr. Wilson, this hospital is no place for misguided nostrums. I have no alternative but to discharge you from the staff. Mind you, I do not question your ability as a doctor, but I simply cannot have any personnel whose inflammatory ideas will endanger the high ethical reputation of this institution. And a final word of advice, Dr. Wilson. In your next post, wherever it may be, I strongly advise you to keep your thoughts to yourself and your mouth firmly shut when you practice medicine. That is all I have to say to you, sir. If you will stop by this afternoon, I shall have your salary ready for you."

"It's so unfair, so unjust, darling!" Fleurette's lovely green eyes filled with tears as she stood looking down at her husband. He sat on the couch, his face buried in his hands, his shoulders slumped in despair. She reached down lovingly to touch his unruly hair, then seated herself beside him. "Never mind, at least Dr. Drawley said he wasn't questioning your medical ability. He'd better not, either. I've helped you as a nurse several times, and I know how capable you are, how devoted you are to people in sparing them pain and making them well. I'm sure you'll find something."

"But don't you see, Fleurette, I know I'm right. Why, even at Pittsburgh General there's an alarming percentage of deaths after surgery, as well as childbirth. You remember that woman who had twins in September, Mrs. Ferrinetti?"

"Yes, that poor woman!" Fleurette's voice was hushed.

"First off, it was a difficult delivery. And she was practically starving because her husband had been out of work for over a month. And then, after I made sure that the babies were as healthy as one could expect with a mother suffering from malnutrition, they died two days later. And Mrs. Ferrinetti died the next night from puerperal fever. And Dr. Drawley condemns me for my radical notions about hygiene and greater precautions!"

"Hush, dearest." Again she stroked his hair, and her other hand reached for his and squeezed it. "It won't always be this way. A fine doctor like you won't go without work. God will look after us, and besides, I can work as a nurse. There are advertisements in the *Globe* begging for experienced help in private homes."

"No! I don't intend to have you work to support the baby and me, Fleurette! Before that happens, I'd go to the mines and shovel coal or even be an orderly in an insane asylum," Ben said fiercely as he rose from the couch and took her in his arms. Then his face softened as he said gently, "I thank God every waking moment for you, Fleurette. You're my life, my hope, my courage."

With the advent of November's raw weather, little Daniel Hardesty's health worsened. At first his father was annoyed, but finally annoyance gave way to worry. Just before the end of October, Cora Hardesty had caught a head cold, which persisted, and her appearances at the supper table were even more infrequent during the next two weeks. Finally, one blustery night in mid-November, George Hardesty sent his butler by carriage to the house of his own personal physician, Dr. Hugo Cawkins, a venerable septuagenarian who had presided at the birth of his son, and who on that occasion had

321

taken him aside and intimated that it would be best for his wife never to have a child again.

Dr. Cawkins had dined at home this particular evening, and so was able to accompany Cyril Jefferson back in the carriage to his employer's home. George Hardesty met him at the door, scowling with anxiety. "I want you to look at the boy first, Dr. Cawkins. Then I'd appreciate it if you'd visit my wife. She's had a wretched cold and hasn't been able to get rid of it in several weeks."

"Of course, Mr. Hardesty. Just let me catch my breath. Dear me, how dreadful winter is—I keep telling my housekeeper that I'll retire next year, but I owe a duty to my patients. There now," said the fussy little man, slowly removing his scarf and winter overcoat, which the butler promptly accepted. Then the doctor picked up his black satchel and trudged slowly up the stairway to Daniel Hardesty's room.

George Hardesty stood outside, his hands clasped behind his back, pacing back and forth as he heard Miss Prentice's voice and then the doctor's. Presently, the bewhiskered and bespectacled man emerged, stroking the tip of his nose. "He seems sound enough, Mr. Hardesty," he declared in a thin, cracked voice, "but his color's bad, you know. He doesn't seem to have a fever or a cough or a cold, but the governess tells me that his appetite has been very poor of late."

"Yes, but he was always a picky eater. Can you cure him, Dr. Cawkins?"

"I really think the boy should have rest in a warmer climate."

"I'd thought of sending him to Europe with his

mother in the spring," George Hardesty admitted. "But what else would you suggest? Dammit all, he's so puny—and look at me, strong healthy stock. He's the only son I've got, you know, and one day I hope he'll take over my place at the firm. Are there any medicines you can give him?"

"I did prescribe a tonic, and I left a bottle with Miss Prentice. It's iron, for the blood, and it certainly can't do him any harm in his present condition, Mr. Hardesty. Now, with your permission, I'll visit your wife. Possibly Miss Prentice should come with me?"

"Of course, of course," the industrialist replied testily. "Just go back and tell her to come along with you."

Half an hour later, the elderly doctor emerged from Cora Hardesty's room.

George Hardesty was waiting impatiently for him. "Well, man, how is my wife?"

"It's a bad cold. And I don't like the sound of her cough. She complains of sleeping badly, so I've given her a prescription for laudanum. In very small doses, though, I must warn you, Mr. Hardesty. She too could certainly do with a warmer climate. But then, so could all of us."

"Then you don't think my wife's illness is serious?"

"My dear sir," the little man drew himself up as if affronted, "the slightest scratch or insect bite can be dangerous in our modern times. There's always the unknown factor in medicine. Sometimes a patient lacks the will to live no matter what may be done for him or her. Then again, sometimes there are unhealthy vapors in the house or outdoors which may make a person sicken."

"Yes, yes, I understand all that, Dr. Cawkins, but what else besides laudanum are you prescribing for my wife?" George Hardesty's voice was strained and irritable.

"Rest, liquids, and I daresay she should be made to eat sensible meals. You know our saying, starve a fever and feed a cold."

"Is that so? I thought it was the other way around. Well, no matter. Of course she'll eat sensibly in this house!"

"Good gracious, Mr. Hardesty, you seem very upset this evening!" The elderly doctor squinted through his thick lenses at the industrialist. "I don't like your color either, Mr. Hardesty, now that we're on the subject. In my professional opinion, sir, you really should be bled. I have a bottle of leeches, as it happens." He delved into his satchel and produced a jar. George Hardesty grimaced at the sight of the black worms clinging to the inside of the glass, and made an abrupt gesture with his hand. "Put that away! You're not going to put those slimy things on me. There's nothing wrong with me except a little aggravation and worry over my wife and son. Send me a bill, and come back in a day or so if there's no improvement. My butler will take you back home."

"I'm sorry I can't be of more help, Mr. Hardesty. Of course, there's always the hospital, if you're not satisfied with my opinions." The little man seemed hurt as he readjusted his scarf and was helped on with his overcoat by the solicitous butler.

After he had left, George Hardesty tramped angrily back to his study, lit a cigar, flung himself into an armchair, and pondered the bad luck that had plagued his marriage. An ailing wife who hadn't comforted him the way wives were meant to for more years than he cared to remember, and a sickly boy who disgusted him every time he watched him try to eat. Here he was, influential, rich, in the full prime of life, but saddled with a joyless menage. Of course he'd send Daniel and Cora to Italy in the spring. It wasn't a question of not being able to afford it. Money should be able to buy everything, including health. Yes, including love as well. Since Cora hadn't been downstairs in weeks, it might do no harm to sound out that pretty little bitch Molly and find out if she knew what side her bread was buttered on.

He picked up a handbell and rang it, and a few moments later the pretty black-haired Irish maid entered and curtsied. "Molly, would you bring me some whiskey, please," he said ingratiatingly.

"Yes, sir. Is that all?" she asked timidly.

"Well now." He rose from his chair with an effort, the exertion of forcing himself up by his palms making him temporarily short of breath. "Perhaps you'd like one for yourself. I've been wanting to talk to you in private, Molly girl. Now's just as good a time as any."

"Oh, sir, I—I wouldn't dare drink that stuff. My father always said it was fit only for strong men, and even he didn't dare touch more than a wee dram himself!"

"Well then, bring me mine, at least. And then come sit down there on that settee and we'll have a little chat. After all, girl, you've been here almost a year now, and it's high time we got to know each other better."

Flustered, the young maid turned crimson, curtsied again, and went to the library, where the decanter of whiskey was usually kept. She measured out half a glass and brought it to him, nervously twisting the hem of her apron as she watched him take a hearty swig.

"Sit down, Molly," he said, waving her to the settee as he seated himself in the armchair. "Now then, I've been thinking for quite some time what a lovely colleen you are. Are you happy here, Molly? Do you like your room, and does Cook feed you properly?"

"Oh yes, sir, I—I haven't any complaints at all, sir. You—I mean—everybody here has been awfully nice to me."

"That's fine, Molly. I've been thinking about giving you an increase in your wages."

The young maid clapped her hands, her eyes wide and shining with pleasure. "Oh, that's so good of you, sir! That way, I'll be able to send off a little something every month to my poor brother Hughie. He's crippled, sir."

"I'll see that it's enough so that you'll have something worthwhile to send the boy, Molly. Now then," he said as he leaned forward, with a slyly confidential wink, his eyes taking in her trim young body in the close-fitting black uniform, observing the fine, sleek calves sheathed tightly in black worsted stockings. "Do you have a gentleman friend on your day off?"

Molly shook her head, her joyous look replaced by a frightened one. "Oh no, sir. I don't know a soul here, excepting of course yourself and the missus and the boy and of course Miss Prentice and Cook and—"

"Never mind." He waved her to silence. "Come over here and stand by me a minute. I don't like that dowdy uniform you've got on. Maybe we can do something about that. Maybe a pretty new dress and some nice things a girl wears under it to complete the outfit, eh, Molly?"

Molly rose from the settee, and nervously walked over to stand before him. "Come closer—that's right. No need to be afraid of me, my girl. There now, that's fine. Yes, you're very pretty. You've nice color in your cheeks, and fine white skin, and very beautiful eyes—did anyone ever tell you you had beautiful eyes, Molly?"

"N-no, sir." Her voice was faint as she shook her head and shifted nervously from foot to foot.

He took hold of her wrist then and suddenly drew her down onto his lap. "Now it's all right, Molly girl," he soothed. "You be nice to me, and I'll give you fifty dollars a month more in wages, and all the pretty clothes your heart could wish for."

"Oh no—oh please, sir, I—I'm a good girl— please—Mr. Hardesty, you shouldn't—your wife's upstairs—"

"Botheration!" he exclaimed angrily as she struggled free of him. "For all the good she does me, she might as well not be in this house at all. Come back here, Molly—" As he made a lunge for her wrist, he suddenly stiffened, groaned, put his other hand to his heart, and sank back into the chair.

"Oh, sir—oh please—what's the matter? I hope I didn't do that—oh, sir!" Molly wrung her hands, tears glistening in her widened, dark brown eyes.

"Wh—whiskey—give me my glass—" he said hoarsely.

Molly quickly proffered the glass to his lips. George Hardesty seized it with both hands and greedily held it to him as if it were the elixir of life. He sucked down a mouthful, choked and gasped, then blinked his eyes and gave her back the glass. "That—that's better. That was a bad spell just then. Look, Molly—you'll find a little book on the desk over there. See if you have Dr. Ben Wilson's address. Hurry!"

"Yes—yes, sir!" Molly ran to the desk, brought back the little black book, and thumbed through it. "Here it is, sir, 327 Susquehanna Street."

"Good—Molly—get—get Jefferson. Have him take the carriage around to Dr. Wilson and bring him back here. Don't you leave me now, girl. Come back as soon as you've told him, hear?"

"Oh, I will, sir! I'll tell Jefferson right this minute!" Molly cast him a frightened look, then turned and ran toward the hallway.

It was an agonizing black void, and slowly, degree by infinite degree, he felt himself being drawn up to the surface, as if he were a swimmer sucked down into a giant vortex and then slowly spewed back into life. Opening his eyes, blinking them to clear the blur, he saw an anxious, kindly face bending over him. "I—is it—" he whispered hoarsely.

"Don't try to talk, Mr. Hardesty. You've had a

328

heart attack. Just lie still. I've made you as comfortable as I could."

"You—it's—"

"Ben Wilson, Mr. Hardesty, yes. I was home when your butler came for me in the carriage, and it's a good thing I was. Do you feel a little better now? No, don't talk, just nod your head slowly."

George Hardesty obeyed. He blinked his eyes again to clear them, trying with all his might to focus on the face of the young doctor. The features seemed to waver, blurred again, then came back into sharper focus.

"Good. You're going to get a good night's sleep, and while I'm here I'm going to look at your wife and your boy. Your maid told me about them too, Mr. Hardesty."

"Please—help—help them. I—I'm sorry as hell—I made a mistake about you—don't h-hold it against—"

"I told you not to talk. And there's no need for an apology. I'm a doctor, you're my patient. That is, I know you have a family physician, and ethically I shouldn't try to take his place—"

With a visible effort, George Hardesty, his face damp with sweat, shook his head. "N-no—I want you. You know why!"

"Please—"

"No, I have to—I have to say it. In my—in my office that time—" His breath wheezed as he forced himself to speak, his eyes fixed intensely on Ben Wilson's face. "You said, even the poor had the right to live, had the right to—to have capable doctors save them—from—unnecessary death. Can you—can you save me too? I'll make it up to you—I swear to God—"

"Now that's quite enough. I shan't listen to another word. Close your eyes, try to go to sleep and forget everything. I'm going upstairs now to see your wife and your boy, Mr. Hardesty. This is an emergency, so I can replace your family physician for the moment. Now you just rest."

George Hardesty uttered a long, faint sigh and fell asleep. His last thought was that it was strange that the words of a man he had hated and condemned in public print should so console him and give him confidence and strength.

It was noon the next day when George Hardesty awoke. Again he saw Ben Wilson standing before him, the kindly face now lined with fatigue but the eyes sharp and bright. "You—how are they?" he asked softly.

"I want to talk to you in a day or two when you've got your strength back, Mr. Hardesty. By the way, I've already given your cook some orders about your diet. Both she and the maid told me what your diet consists of when you're at home. It's a wonder you didn't die from that attack—and I predict you certainly will if you keep on eating and drinking as if it were your last meal on earth. You'll find it might well be, Mr. Hardesty."

"What—how do you—"

"Shh, now. I told you we'd talk about it in a day or so when you feel better. But there are some things besides diet I mean to mention to you, Mr. Hardesty. And I don't care whether you think I'm impudent or not. In all conscience, as a physician I have to tell them to you."

"Are they—"

Ben Wilson nodded. "Your wife's cold is hanging on because she's weak. She has to change her diet, but there's something much beyond that, which we'll talk about when it's time, Mr. Hardesty. As for your son, I'd say almost the same thing, except even more strongly. But the boy feels better, and he's keeping down some clear broth. I've also prescribed a tonic that I think may help him get back his appetite and then his strength."

"Thank you—thank you, Dr. Wilson," George Hardesty mumbled, and again his eyes closed in sleep.

George Hardesty sat up in bed, two pillows propping his head, while Molly spoon-fed him chicken broth. The butler came into the bedroom and announced, "It's Dr. Wilson, Mr. Hardesty."

"Yes, send him right in, Jefferson."

Ben Wilson entered, seated himself on a stool beside the bed, and reached for George Hardesty's wrist to take his pulse. "It's stronger and more regular now. As I told you before, Mr. Hardesty, you had a very serious heart attack. And it's possible that you may have recurrences. We don't know everything we should about the human heart, but we do know that when it's overloaded and overtired, when it's under stress from business or domestic problems, and especially when it's weakened by overloading your stomach with rich foods and far too much liquor than your system can stand, it's going to react unfavorably."

"Am I—will I die?"

Ben permitted himself a grim little smile. "All of

us will, Mr. Hardesty. But now that you know what your condition is, you can at least take sensible measures to prevent a recurrence. For one thing, stop eating greasy foods, all those potatoes, and those extra helpings of dessert. And no more whiskey, except perhaps a very small amount no more than a few times a week. Of course, you don't have to take my advice. But if you want to live, you'll find you have a better chance by taking it."

George Hardesty nodded, his eyes anxiously fixing on Ben's face. "I don't want to die. I'll do it."

"Good. Your cook knows what kind of diet you should follow for the next several months. If you wish, I'll come in from time to time to look you over. And of course if you need me before then, I want you to feel free to send for me as you did the other night."

"Yes. I—I was wrong. You'll find that I can be very grateful, and I want to make amends for the harm I did you."

"You needn't feel beholden to me, Mr. Hardesty."

"But that letter—did Dr. Drawley read it?"

"Oh yes. He discharged me the morning he read it."

"I'll make it up to you. I swear before God I will!"

"I told you before, you owe me nothing, except of course the bill I'll render to you after my services have been concluded. Now, Mr. Hardesty, I think you're strong enough for me to talk some common sense to you. I'm going to do it because I'm a doctor and because I can see things laymen can't. Your wife and your son are, to put it bluntly, browbeaten by your domineering nature. That's really the long and the short of it. You're angry because Daniel isn't sturdy like you, and because he picks at his food. The more you point this out to him, the more withdrawn he becomes. So the upshot is that he has a nervous stomach—entirely due to nerves, not to any constitutional defect in him, believe me."

"I see." George Hardesty clenched his fists, a look of abject supplication in his eyes.

"And the same thing is true of your wife. She feels she's just a servant, an ornament. When was the last time you told her you loved her, Mr. Hardesty? Yes, I know I'm interfering in your private life. But that's just it—you don't really have a private life. You're one of the most important men in Pittsburgh, but when you come home, try letting your family know that you love them. You'll be surprised how they'll stand by you and give you strength, if you'll only give them a chance, Mr. Hardesty."

George Hardesty bit his lips, then lowered his eyes. After a moment he said hoarsely, "You hit hard at a man, Dr. Wilson. Well, I guess I had it coming. I gave you a dirty low blow, didn't I? And I guess maybe you're right. I just want everything to be so perfect—"

"Nothing can be perfect in this life, but we can try hard to improve it. That's about all we're here for, Mr. Hardesty. Now, with your permission, I told your cook just what sort of meals your whole family should have for the next month or so. And when you come to the table, try to say something from the heart, something nice to both of them. I think you'll be pleasantly surprised how they'll react to you. You see, they're both afraid of you, Mr. Hardesty. Now, go to sleep again and I'll be back tomorrow."

It was two weeks before Christmas, and the cobblestone streets of Pittsburgh were covered with thick, feather-soft snow. In the little frame house on Susquehanna Street, Fleurette Wilson was decorating the Christmas tree, with little Thomas watching wide-eyed from the playpen that Ben had made in his spare time. Fleurette reached up to pin the gilt star at the very top of the tree, then stepped back to admire it. "See, Tommy? It's the Star of Bethlehem. It'll watch over all of us, just as it did over the Christ child."

"M-Mama, pwetty—Mama!" the little boy lisped.

"Oh, you darling! It's not Mama who's pretty, but the star!" Fleurette lifted him up in her arms, her face shining with tender joy. As she heard the key in the front-door lock, she hurried to meet her husband.

He took off his hat and shook the snow from it, then his overcoat. He was dazed, his lips quivering; his eyes had almost a startled, disbelieving look.

"Ben, what's the matter? You look so strange—is anything wrong?"

"No, Fleurette. I just can't believe what's happened. Wait till I hang up my coat and hat." He came toward her, took his son into his arms and kissed him, then set the boy on his shoulders and walked quickly back and forth, to the child's delighted squeals. Setting Thomas down, he led him

334

to the couch and seated himself, taking the boy in his lap and holding out his right arm to Fleurette, who came quickly to sit beside him. "I went to Hardesty's house to give him a checkup, Fleurette. First of all, he gave me an envelope with a check to pay for my house calls. He said I wasn't to open it till I got home. But—but I couldn't help opening it just before I unlocked the door—my God, look at this!"

He took out of his inner coat pocket an envelope and handed it to Fleurette. She opened it, then uttered a cry of disbelief. "It—oh, Ben!"

"But read the note that's attached, that's the best thing of all," he urged, as tears began to roll down his cheeks.

Fleurette unfolded the note beside the check in the envelope, and read it:

Dear Dr. Wilson:

The check for $5,000 will, I hope, balance my debt to you for your many house calls on behalf of my entire family. However, now that I know how valuable your services are, I want all the city to be able to benefit from them as I did, and as certainly my wife and boy did. Therefore, this is to tell you that next spring I intend to donate the sum of $250,000 for a new hospital which will bear my name. I wish you to accept the appointment of chief of staff of this hospital, with the understanding that you will be free to open a clinic for the poor and the needy, just as you have always wanted.

Let me close by wishing you and your family a very merry Christmas. You have certainly made mine such, and you have taught me a lesson into the bargain.

                    Yours truly,
                    George Hardesty

"Oh, Ben, it's like a dream!" Fleurette sobbed as she flung her arms around him and kissed him ardently.

"You were right, my dearest, when you said that God would look after us. And do you know what we're going to do with some of that money? This spring we'll use some of it to visit New Orleans and Texas so that you can see your family. That'll be my Christmas present to you, my sweet wife."

CHAPTER TWENTY-SIX

For Laurette Douglas, her husband, Charles, and their twin sons, Arthur and Kenneth, Christmas of 1867 promised to be their happiest holiday ever. Charles, now thirty-two, and two years older than his flame-haired wife, was now the owner of the three-story wooden frame department store at the corner of Lake and Wabash. His former employer, Levi Tallon, had decided to move to San Francisco to live with his younger sister and to open a new store in the City by the Bay. The terms he had offered his former manager were incredibly generous: sixty-five thousand dollars, of which he had stipulated that only a fourth need be offered as a down payment, the balance to be included in a promissory note with a five-year redemption period. Since Charles had saved his money back in Tuscaloosa and had prospered in Chicago, he had been able to meet the first stipulation, and now looked forward to running his own store and to changing its name to Douglas Department Store.

The Douglases had moved also, from their former Prairie Avenue address to a new house on Schiller Street near Wells. It was more isolated and also in a far more fashionable neighborhood. Of course, it meant a walk to work of over a mile and a half, but the old house on Prairie Avenue had been even farther away from the store.

As he helped his wife trim the Christmas tree, the brown-haired, good-natured Charles Douglas was almost lyrical about the future. "Just imagine, Laurette honey, if we'd had to stay in Tuscaloosa! Now that the war is over and the North is trying to force the South to her knees, we'd have just vegetated. But this city has nearly tripled since the beginning of the war. And I can see right in my own store how much more goods we can sell in a place like this than just about anywhere else, except maybe New York, Boston, and Philadelphia. And with the railroad lines extending, and the big stockyards, this is only the beginning of what's in store for Chicago. Potter Palmer, who made a fortune on wartime cotton speculation, is arranging to buy three-quarters of a mile along State Street and is going to make it a street of shops."

Laurette smiled and playfully tweaked her husband's nose. "I declare," she said, laughing, "I don't think you're ever going to slow down. Here it is two weeks from Christmas and we're in a lovely new house, and all you can think about is the future of this big city." But the fond, affectionate

338

tone of her voice and the devoted look in her eyes belied her mild reproof.

At thirty, Laurette Douglas had never been more beautiful. She had already been mentioned in the society column of the *Chicago Evening Journal* as one of the most attractive women in the city, and her husband had been referred to as "that leading young merchant prince from the South who has become a true Chicagoan."

"No," Charles replied, "and I don't intend to slow down. You know how people talk about the sleepy South. But even when I was working in Tuscaloosa I had big ideas for selling people what they needed and making them know about it. In Chicago, there isn't time for sleep. I'm thinking of hiring boys after school to pass out handbills about some of our specialty sales items, and big signs, maybe even in some of the residential areas, telling people about the Douglas Department Store." He grinned boyishly. "That was really a great Christmas present to myself, seeing my name go up on the store and Levi's go down."

"Aren't you the least bit afraid that people might stop coming because somebody else owns it and they think he won't be as nice to them as Levi was?"

He chuckled, pulled her to him, kissed her, and gave her a playful spank. "Just let them try not to come, honey, once they start seeing my advertisements in the *Evening Journal*. They'll be lined up hours before the store opens, wanting to buy what I've got on sale—you just watch and see! And you know something else, Laurette?"

Coloring deliciously, she shook her head, looking at him as if in total ignorance of his projects.

"Well now, Mrs. Douglas, this is just my first store, you know. It's just a start of the Douglas chain. Before I finish—and I hope that won't be for a long, long time, with you beside me every step of the way—I'll have stores in New York, Boston, Philadelphia, Pittsburgh, even Los Angeles and San Francisco. And one in the biggest city in Texas, which will give you an excuse to go down there and visit your mother. How is Maybelle, by the way?"

"Oh, just wonderful, darling!" Laurette took his hand and drew him down beside her on the ottoman. "I had a letter from Grandmother Sybella just the other day, and if you think you've got exciting news about the store, listen to what happened to them a few months ago! They were attacked by bandits, and Grandmother helped rout them with her rifle."

"She's an amazing woman. So full of optimism and vitality," Charles Douglas mused. "If she ever gets tired of Texas and ranch life, you might just write and tell her that I could give her a wonderful job up here in Chicago. You know what? I'd make her personnel manager over all the female clerks."

"At that," Laurette replied somewhat cattily, "I think she'd show herself to be a better judge of character and human nature than you, darling. You're so trusting, you think everybody who works for you is just bound and determined to have the same enthusiasm and zest for what you're doing."

"Oh, Laurette," his face fell, "you really don't mean that, do you? I thought I had a pretty fair

340

group of clerks, and they're doing a wonderful sales job for me."

"Yes, I'll admit that, from all the figures you keep impressing me with every month. But I went down to your store last week, and some of your sales ladies were standing around gossiping. And others were just primping themselves, not showing the interest they should in the customers. Certainly not for the wages you pay them. And that's another thing. You're awfully generous, Charles. And I love you for it. But if you start them at such a high wage, they'll be expecting more money than they're worth before very long."

"I don't agree with you, honey. My theory is that if you treat people well and give them an incentive, they'll give their best for you. And I haven't been wrong so far."

"Well, I hope it'll always be that way, darling. I'm really very proud of you and all you've done in that short time since you left Tuscaloosa. I like Chicago too."

"Does your mother say anything about the bandit raid?" Charles asked as he stroked her glossy, bright red hair and then kissed her on the ear.

"Grandmother Sybella said Mother was awfully scared but she got over it. You know, the best thing in the world to happen to Mother was meeting Henry Belcher. And she's still a very handsome woman too, I'll have you know. After all, she was just seventeen when I was born."

"And you still don't look a day over twenty." He drew her to him and gave her a long, ardent kiss.

"Charles Douglas, you're just dreadful!" Laurette exclaimed as she disengaged herself, smoothing her hair and sending him a mock-stern look. "You're neglecting the twins, and that's not like you."

"No I'm not, I'm paying attention to their beautiful, seductive mother, without whom there wouldn't have been any twins." He kissed her again.

"Now, Charles, that's enough," she protested. "Just look at how you've mussed my hair."

"Hair like yours was meant to be mussed, sweetheart. Know what I'm going to get you for Christmas? One of the sheerest nightgowns I can find, and then I'll insist that you let down your fiery hair and let me just stand there dazzled."

Laurette giggled, gave him a playful pinch on the thigh, then sprang up from the ottoman. "You come right along now and say good evening to your sons."

She led him to the children's playroom, where Kenneth and Arthur Douglas stood in a wide, rectangular playpen, gaily painted, with a profusion of toys from Charles Douglas's store scattered around their feet. He leaned down and took Arthur and Kenneth into his arms, beaming as they responded enthusiastically. "Hear that, Laurette? They can both say *daddy* now."

"Didn't I tell you our sons were good? Oh, I'm so glad your old boss let us rent this house. It's so nice and clean, with just enough neighbors to make it cozy."

"You wait, Laurette, because in another year or two you're going to see this city expand on all sides. There'll be many more buildings along the north shore of the lake, and they'll go pretty far south, too—miles beyond where we were living.

342

That's progress, honey. And maybe by next year I can have gas light installed in my store. I've been talking with some engineers, and there's a fair chance we can do it. That'll really show off the merchandise to its best advantage."

"Don't you ever think about anything except that store of yours?" Laurette reproached, smiling.

Charles set the children back in their playpen and turned back to take her in his arms. His mouth met hers, and Laurette at first tried to push him away, then locked her arms around his neck and passionately returned his kiss.

After a long moment she whispered, "I take it back. You *do* think about other things. But just don't ever let me catch you making eyes at one of those pretty sales ladies down at your store, because all redheads are jealous, and don't you ever forget it!"

"Now that's one thing you'll never have to worry about, I promise." He laughed softly as he kissed her again. Laurette sighed happily, closed her eyes, and abandoned herself to her husband's ardent and flattering wooing.

Carrie Melton, an opulently formed, chestnut-haired young woman of twenty-three, had grown up in a Chicago tenement. Born of a drunken, sadistic father and a mother who hated her, Carrie had survived by her wits. At sixteen she had attracted the attentions of a well-to-do young bachelor, and induced him to rent for her an attractive house at Twenty-ninth and Prairie, leading him on with promises she knew she would never fulfill. When he tried, at last, to claim his reward, Carrie ran out of the house shrieking that she was under-age and he had tried to rape her. The young man's ardor had cooled quickly, but, fearing for his reputation, he had continued to pay the rent on the house for a full year, as well as giving Carrie a considerable sum of money.

Carrie continued for some years to use to full advantage the same sort of tactics that had stood her in such good stead with her first suitor. Her appearance and manner proved to be of invaluable help in such ventures. Her sumptuous breasts could not be fully concealed by the compressing corsets of the day. Also, she had learned early in life that the adoption of a naïve, little-girl tone of voice instantly made an impression on the opposite sex. She was both worldly and shrewd, and because of this she survived for some time simply by the use of her physical charms and her quick mind.

After several years, however, having spent much of her money on clothes and entertainment, she went to work at the Tallon Department Store. It did not take her long to set her cap for Levi Tallon, but she soon discovered that he was not only a widower with five children but a man of the most stringent moral outlook. So the news that Charles Douglas had taken over the store made her ponder how she could profit from this change of employer.

On the day before Christmas, Carrie decided to make Charles aware of her flamboyant charms. Seeing him talking to a plainclothes store detective, she waited until the man had left, then went up to him, wearing her most endearing smile and using a little-girl voice.

"Oh, Mr. Douglas, sir, I do hate to disturb you,

but I couldn't help noticing how terribly tired you look. I think you work harder in the store than any of us girls. I'm so grateful for this job, and I'd really like to make up to you for the chance you've given me."

Charles blinked, taken aback by the forwardness of this attractive young woman. "Why now, Miss—Miss—?" he began.

"Carrie Melton, sir. I've been here over a year. But I guess"—this with a rueful little laugh—"you have so many pretty girls working for you, you'd never notice me."

Charles blushed with embarrassment and nervously shifted his feet. Carrie Melton leaned forward, her eyes wide and humid, her lips parted and quivering.

"It's very thoughtful of you, Miss Melton," he finally replied. "But if you want to thank me for your job, I suggest you try to make these busy shoppers as happy as you can."

"Yes, sir. But you know, I'm all alone in the world. I thought—please don't think me too forward—I thought that maybe you might like to take me to supper, and you could tell me all about the store and teach me how to be a better salesgirl."

Now Charles really blushed. "As it happens, Miss Melton, I'm very happily married. I'm sure, attractive as you are, you'll have no trouble finding someone who is interested in you and who is also available, which I assuredly am not. Good morning to you!"

Carrie watched him turn and walk down the aisle, then made a spiteful grimace at him and went back to her counter.

It was the same spiteful motivation, together with her discovery that her money had almost entirely dwindled, that led her, early in January, to try to steal an expensive bracelet from the jewelry department. She quickly concealed it in her bodice, but she was seen by the plainclothes detective who had been watching the counter. Going up to her quickly, he muttered, "Not a peep out of you, sister, if you know what's good for you. Now we'll go right upstairs to see Mr. Douglas."

Shaken and pale, Carrie Melton accompanied the house detective to the top floor where Charles Douglas had his private office. He listened silently to the detective's explanation, then turned to stare at the crestfallen young woman. "Is it true, Miss Melton."

"Yes, sir, but—"

"You will kindly give the bracelet to Mr. Rogan. I am afraid I shall have to discharge you, Miss Melton?"

"Please—you can't—" Carrie began desperately.

"I'm afraid I can't change my decision, Miss Melton. It's a very serious thing you've done, and if I let you off this time, how could I be sure you wouldn't try it again? No, I'm afraid you'll have to leave the store."

With a sneer, the handsome young woman thrust her hand into her bodice, took out the bracelet, and flung it at the store detective. "There's your stinking bracelet, you bastard!" she stormed. "You'll be sorry for this. And you can take your wages and shove them, too, for all I care."

Carrie Melton paused for breath, then resumed her tirade, but Charles Douglas had already turned his attention back to the papers on his desk. The detective reached for her elbow, and she haughtily jerked away, saying, "Don't you dare touch me!"

As she sauntered insolently out of the office, she turned back to call, "You'll be sorry you lost your chance with me, Mr. Douglas. You just watch—I won't forget this!"

By the middle of February, Carrie Melton had caught the attention of Dalton Haines, a prominent officer at the Chicago Commercial Bank. Having learned that this bank handled the Douglas Department Store account and that there was a position open, she applied for the job. When she was ushered into the office of old, fat Mr. Haines, she observed that his eyes stealthily glanced down at her trim ankles. She determined to make the most of his interest.

As soon as she had seated herself she leaned forward, clasping her hands in an attitude of intense concentration. Widening her eyes and curving her full lips in a dazzling smile, she confided in a husky voice, "I've always wanted to work in a bank, Mr. Haines. It's so dignified, and it's so valuable to people."

She could not have chosen a more felicitous beginning for the interview. Dalton Haines, just past sixty-three, passionately loved two things in life: the banking business and women, though not always in that order. After having been put to work in an English bank by his father, in an attempt to curb his son's lack of interest in anything but gambling and girls, Haines had discovered that he was fascinated by the work. His interest in the fair sex continued to be a complication, however, and his father finally sent him off to New York, ordering him never to return to England.

From New York, Haines moved to St. Louis, and finally to the Chicago Commercial Bank, where he was quickly made an officer. Carrie Melton seemed to him infinitely more desirable than Josie Wentham, his current mistress. Carrie's fascinating look and smile therefore elevated her, in his mind, from the other applicants, though most of them were more qualified. From the moment she walked into the office there had been no question in his mind—Carrie was hired.

By the end of February, Carrie had set herself to work diligently under the approving supervision of Dalton Haines. One raw February evening, as the bank was closing, Haines glanced over to the desk where his attractive secretary was working, and beckoned to her. Forcing an eager smile to her lips, she hastened over to his desk and stood attentively beside him.

"Perhaps you would do me the favor of having supper with me this evening, my dear?" Haines asked hesitantly.

Carrie had been so bored with her job and the lagging way in which her elderly mentor had pursued her that she could hardly believe her ears. "Oh, Mr. Haines, that would be just wonderful!" she replied.

Suddenly conscious of anyone who might overhear their conversation, Dalton Haines said in a loud voice, "I should be indebted to you, Miss Melton, if you'd remain after the bank closes to help me with a few letters I'd like you to take in longhand."

"Of course, Mr. Haines," she replied, a twinkle in her eye.

As she demurely sat beside him, taking a letter that he had no intention of sending, she continued to send him melting glances from under her fluttering lashes. As soon as he was sure the bank was empty, they left for Davidson's Chop House, where Haines ordered the best wine in the house and insisted that Carrie drink most of it. His intention was so blatantly obvious that a child could have seen through it. But it didn't matter. Tonight she was ready, willing, and able to sacrifice her virginity in order to bring vengeance upon Charles Douglas.

Thus, at the conclusion of the meal she accepted without hesitation Dalton Haines's suggestion to accompany him home. Half an hour later, when the carriage stopped in front of his elegant house, he clutched her slim hand in both of his as his eyes devoured her.

Once inside the house, Carrie patiently sipped port and listened to boastful tales of Haines's widely traveled past. Finally, it was she who led him to his bedroom and helped him undress. She then began to undress herself slowly, with the grace of a practiced houri. When she was naked except for her stockings and cloth garters, she clambered into bed beside him, turned on her side, and, stroking his chest with a soft hand, began to sob.

Instantly Dalton Haines sobered. "Oh come now, my pretty! What's the matter?"

"Oh, Mr. Haines—it—it's not you—no, it's that awful man I worked for before I began working at the bank."

Awkwardly the elderly bank officer caressed her, but his curiosity got the better of his lechery. In a tone of righteous indignation he demanded, "Tell me the name of the scoundrel!"

"It—it was Mr. Charles Douglas. He—he approached me several times when I worked in his store, and he asked—" Once again she burst into tears of feigned anguish.

"There, there, my precious," he mumbled. "Do you mean—why, that fellow has an account at our bank! To think of such a dastardly rogue approaching you!"

"Why—yes, Mr. Haines," she said, sniffling.

"Oh come now, my pretty, call me Dalton. I'll make you happy, my darling, and do you know what else I'll do?" Now his desire for her supple body began to get the better of him. "I'll have a talk with him and tell him what I think of a rascal who lures decent young women and tries to enslave them to satisfy his own degenerate urges!"

"Oh, D-Dalton—I love you so much! I—I think I fell in love with you when you first interviewed me for the job!"

With a groan he mounted her, and, gripping her shoulders until she winced, attempted to possess her. But his age and excitement, to say nothing of the wine he had consumed, left him far short of his goal, and Carrie Melton remained technically a virgin.

By now, the impending battle between President

Andrew Johnson and the antagonistic Congress was reaching a crescendo. On January 13, 1868, the Senate voted to refuse to concur with the president's suspension of Secretary of War Stanton. The next day Grant surrendered the office back to Stanton. On February 21, the president again dismissed Stanton, and appointed General Lorenzo Thomas in his place. Three days later the House of Representatives resolved that President Johnson "be impeached for high crimes and misdemeanors in office."

Impeachment proceedings began on March 5, with Chief Justice Chase in the chair. The trial would formally open on the thirteenth. During this same period, the Fourth Reconstruction Act, designed to "facilitate the restoration of the late rebel states," was enacted. Its provisions would further suborn those who had fought for the losing cause.

It was during this same week that Dalton Haines, basking in his at last effectual enjoyment of Carrie Melton's long-prized virginity, determined to denounce Carrie's former employer as a perfidious scoundrel. Carrie, wanting to cement their relationship, had resorted to the age-old artifice of the timid, virginal female. Having removed her garments and then helped him doff his own, she had suddenly blushed and burst into tears.

"Oh, don't, I shouldn't—it's sinful for me—but I love you so much!" she had professed.

"There, there now, precious, I want to protect you, to shield you from anything that can hurt you, Carrie."

351

"But truly—I shouldn't let you do this—that other time, even though I was so excited—I knew it was sinful for me—you see, I've never had a man before."

"And you shan't need one after now either, my precious," he had said, his hands roving over her opulently rounded buttocks and pressing her against him. "I—yes, by God—I'll marry you, Carrie. There now, it won't be sinful, will it, my precious darling?"

"Oh, Dalton, Dalton, do you really mean it?" she had asked softly, looking up at him and fluttering her lashes.

"Yes, yes, of course I will—oh, Carrie, hurry!"

And so that night, her face turned to one side and her head pillowed on her arm, Carrie had at last made Dalton Haines the gift of her maidenhead. And when he lay spent and panting in her arms, she had stroked his head and patted his shoulder, and then murmured, "I'm so glad I saved myself for you, dearest Dalton. When I think how that wicked Mr. Douglas tried to force me to love him, I could just die."

"That despicable wretch! I'll avenge your honor, my beautiful wife-to-be, I promise you."

And so, on this sunny May morning, Dalton Haines left the Chicago Commercial Bank to go to the Douglas Department Store, taking with him a current statement of the store's account. He was ushered into Charles Douglas's office and wasted no time in coming to the point: "Sir, although you have been a valued customer of the bank I represent, I feel it my duty to inform you that you

352

have behaved most reprehensibly toward my fiancée."

Charles's jaw dropped. "Excuse me, Mr. Haines, but I'm not sure I heard you correctly."

"Sir, there's nothing wrong with your hearing, but a good deal wrong with your conscience." The fat, elderly banker drew himself up in an attitude of righteousness. "I have brought an up-to-date statement of your account with us, sir. It is apparent that you are an extremely successful businessman, and of course the bank values your patronage. But I could not in all conscience keep silent in this personal matter. You see, sir, Miss Carrie Melton has done me the great honor of agreeing to become my wife. Only by tactful means, and the greatest spiritual anguish to her, sir, I may add, was I able to draw from her unwilling lips the story of how shamefully you behaved toward her. Now, I confess that I myself am attracted to pretty, young women. But I should never go so far as to take advantage of my position as an employer to coerce one of my female employees into catering to my depraved carnal desires."

"Now wait just a minute, Mr. Haines, that's a little strong! Also, it happens to be an outright lie."

"How dare you, sir!" Dalton Haines's face turned an angry red. "Do you imply that I am a liar?"

"Not at all. I think only that your fiancée has duped you into believing her nonsensical fabrication. The fact is, Mr. Haines, I discharged Carrie Melton for stealing a bracelet. The store detective caught her in the act of tucking it into her bodice. I recall that she said that she would get even with me, and this apparently is the way she has chosen."

"I can't believe it—I won't believe it!" Dalton Haines stormed.

"You are at liberty to make your own judgment, Mr. Haines. However, I will tell you that I recall at least two occasions when she came to me and intimated that she was alone and seeking a protector. It was, as any man of intelligence and worldliness would see, a rather bald attempt to offer her amorous attentions in return for material advancement."

"Now you go too far, Mr. Douglas! Miss Melton—Carrie—would never lie to me."

Charles shrugged. "I don't want to argue her veracity, Mr. Haines, and I certainly don't question yours. I say only that there isn't one shred of truth in what she told you. Now, am I to infer that because of this unfortunate misunderstanding, your bank no longer wishes to service the store's account? If that is the case, I shall regretfully take my business elsewhere."

Dalton Haines realized that he had gone too far. Though his faith in Carrie Melton was still unshaken, his dedication to banking momentarily overrode his chivalrous instincts. He put out a placating hand. "Mr. Douglas, I was a little hasty, I confess. No, sir, our bank is quite happy to handle your business. You are a valued customer. I came only to talk to you about a private matter, which of course has nothing to do with the transactions between your store and my bank." Dalton Haines was remembering that Frederick Tyson, the old and venerable president of Chicago Commercial Bank, not only outranked him but also had the final word on the acceptance or rejection of a commercial account.

"Very well, Mr. Haines. I'm relieved that there'll be no need to transfer my account. I'm also sorry that this misunderstanding has had to strain our relationship. But I do hope you will further investigate the motives behind Miss Melton's charges."

Then, to show that there was no rancor between them, Charles Douglas held out his hand. Dalton Haines looked sheepish, then at last shook it. "Very well, sir. I did not mean to offend you, be very sure of that. I shall question my fiancée at length. Good day, sir."

When Laurette Douglas heard the news of that incredible interview, she burst out laughing. "Oh, Charles, it's so ridiculous it's funny! What a blind, trusting idiot that fat old man must be. It's plain the girl's nothing but a schemer!" Then her green eyes narrowed. "But a dangerous schemer, too, darling. Imagine the harm she could do if she keeps spreading that dreadful lie. And the worst of it is, that man's actually going to marry her!"

"Oh, come now, Laurette," he said, chuckling as he put his arm around her waist and drew her to him. "She can't do me any harm. The only one I really feel sorry for is that trusting, bumbling old man who insists he's going to marry her and make an honest woman out of her."

"I'll bet my boots it'll be the first time in her life she ever was that," Laurette retorted, her eyes flashing with an angry glow. "Blackening your reputation like that—even if he marries her, she'll go on saying such things till the word gets all around

Chicago that you're forcing your girls into white slavery." Then, in keeping with her mercurial moods, she drew away from him and shook a finger at him. "I know this is a deliberate lie on her part. Just the same, Charlie Douglas, you'd just better not let me catch you making eyes at any of your sales ladies, or you'll have me to deal with."

"As if I ever would." He laughed softly and pulled her to him again. "You're all the woman I want, all the woman any man in his right mind would want."

"Well," she sighed contentedly as she nestled into his arms, "as long as you put it that way, I guess I'll have to keep on putting up with you. Kiss me hard, Charlie darling. Don't stop now, sweetheart—"

It was warm and sultry the morning of May 16. Today the Senate would vote on the eleventh article of impeachment in the trial of President Andrew Johnson. And that vote would stand at thirty-five to nineteen, and Johnson would escape conviction by one vote. That deciding vote against conviction was to be cast by freshman senator Edmund G. Ross, an obscure Kansas Radical who later said, "I felt that I was literally looking into my open grave." (And indeed, in a sense, he was, for at the next elections Ross was defeated, like the other six Republicans who voted for acquittal.) It was a solemn and a shameful day in the history of the United States. Secretary of the Navy Gideon Wells declared, "Those who may vote to convict would as readily vote to impeach the president had he been accused of stepping on a dog's tail." For among the "high crimes and misdemeanors" of which Andrew Johnson had been accused, one of them was for giving speeches "in a loud voice which disturbed his hearers." But now at last honor had prevailed, if only by a single vote.

Laurette Douglas waited until her husband left for the store that morning, then went out into the street and hailed a carriage. "Stop at a livery stable first, if you please, sir," she told the driver. "Then take me to the Chicago Commercial Bank."

The grizzled old Irish driver eyed her in surprise, then tipped his cap and clucked at his horse to start down the cobblestone street. At Kinzie and Wabash there was a livery stable, and Laurette went inside and said to the ruddy-faced proprietor, "I want you to sell me a horse whip."

"A horse whip, ma'am?"

"Oh, I'd never dream of using a whip on horses. It's for a costume party I'm giving next week."

"Oh, yes, ma'am, I see. Very good, ma'am." He went back into the rows of stalls behind the shop and came back with a braided horse whip with a double-thick handle. "Will this do, ma'am?"

"Perfectly." She took a five-dollar gold piece out of her reticule and put it on the counter, then marched out, with head held high and a mischievous little smile curling the corners of her lips. She got back into the carriage, and when it stopped in front of the Chicago Commercial Bank, Laurette told the driver to wait, then headed straight for the door. She determinedly made her way past the astonished uniformed guard at whom she flung a

357

"Good morning!" and glanced around in search of the object of her mission. Carrie Melton had just risen from her desk and was about to enter Dalton Haines's office when Laurette called to her, "Miss, are you by any chance Carrie Melton?"

"Why, yes, ma'am, I am. May I do something for you?" The young woman came forward to the counter.

Laurette held the horse whip behind her back, and with a sweet smile replied, "Indeed you can, Miss Melton. Would you step out here so that I can have a word with you in private?"

The unsuspecting chestnut-haired young woman nodded, lifted up the hinged section of the counter, and came out onto the floor of the bank. "What did you have in mind, ma'am?"

"This!" Laurette hissed, as she drew back the horse whip, stepped back at the same time, and launched a whistling stroke that wound the braided thong around Carrie Melton's waist.

"Oww! Goddamn you, you must be crazy, you bitch!" Carrie cried out.

"No, you're the one who is, Miss Melton, daring to lie about my husband! There—there—now, take it all back!" Laurette exclaimed as she brought the whip down again and again. The chestnut-haired young woman, retreating, her hands raised to protect her face, writhed and twisted as the braided thong stung her voluptuous body. But the victim's hoopskirt was in Laurette's way; lowering the whip, she lunged forward and ripped the skirt off. The guard stood as if petrified, his mouth open, not believing what he saw. Again Laurette resumed the

358

lashing. "Tell the truth! I'll whip you raw till you do! Well?"

"Arrrhh! God—stop it, I can't stand it—yes—yes, I lied about him, he never touched me, he never asked me—oh please stop, I'll do anything—" Rolling over on the floor, still holding up her hands to ward off the stinging cuts, Carrie Melton capitulated.

"That's what I thought," Laurette triumphantly declared. Then, seeing Dalton Haines rush out of his office, his face a mask of consternation, she turned and said, "Your fiancée has just testified in public that she's nothing but a conniving little liar! Didn't you, Miss Melton? Speak up or I'll give you some more!"

"Yes, yes, it's true—I—I did lie about Mr. Douglas—oh don't hit me any more, I can't stand it!"

"I think," Laurette said to Dalton Haines, "that concludes my personal business with this bank."

Charles Douglas's face was wet with tears of laughter that evening as Laurette proudly related her escapade. "Good heavens, honey," he said when he was at last able to control his mirth, "you might have been arrested! Just think of the headlines!"

As she cuddled closer to him on the ottoman, she replied, "All I could think of was making her confess her wicked lies before they stopped me— and they didn't, thank goodness."

"You never cease to amaze me, Laurette." He took her into his arms and kissed her tenderly.

"Charles," she murmured, "I think we ought to

have another baby right away. Not only because I want to give you a daughter this time, but so I can keep on being sure I'm the only woman in your life."

CHAPTER TWENTY-SEVEN

It had taken Carlos Macaras six months to effect his plan for another attack on Windhaven Range. The survivors who had gone back with him across the border had deserted him. They had denounced him as a man unworthy to be the *jefe* of courageous bandidos. Indeed, they had spoken loudly of his cowardice, since he himself had not charged the stockade that guarded the ranchhouse; nor had he, so far as they had observed, inflicted a single casualty on the gringos. And since his four accusers had confronted him as one with their decision, he could not, livid with fury though he was, shoot them down like the dogs they were. Instead, inwardly smoldering, digging his fingernails into his palms to hold back his temper, he had stolidly heard them out and then cynically replied, "If that is the way it is, *muchachos, vaya con Dios*. I will find other men, never fear."

In order to find other men, enough men to overwhelm the gringo stronghold, Carlos Macaras well knew that he would need gold and not simply promises of it. Now that Benito Juarez had driven the foreign usurpers from Mexico and sent the ill-advised Maximilian to die before a firing squad, Carlos Macaras could not hope to recruit peons for his guerrilla band. His brother, Diego, had been able to enlist men in the name of the cause of Mexico's liberation, but that would not work this time. What he needed were savage fighters, men without a conscience, who enjoyed killing and plundering for its own sake. He needed a band of outlaws with Indians among them, for it was well known that the Indians were the most savage killers of all and masters of the art of slow torture. Many a night since his ignominious retreat, he had relished the vengeful dreams that haunted him. He saw the women of that gringo ranchhouse stripped naked one by one, tied to their own fence, and tortured with fire, the knife, and the lash, before they were ravished. Then, if some of them seemed humbled enough to wish to satisfy him, he would spare their lives and make them lower than the worst *puta* in the most squalid crib in Mexico City.

Carlos Macaras, now thirty-eight years of age, was seven years younger than his brother, Diego. From boyhood both of them had been dedicated to living by their wits and, as they matured, by violence. Even the old priest who had baptized them had declared that the devil seemed to covet their mortal souls, judging from the constant mischief and wrongdoing that they perpetrated. By the time Diego was twenty, he had killed a man over a game of cards and fled all the way to Guadalupe, where for some years he had settled down and married a handsome young girl who bore him two sons. She brought him as her dowry a small piece of land that her father, the *alcalde* of the village, had managed to own outright after years of peonage.

In time, Diego's restless, greedy nature made him abandon his wife and children, never to see them again, and to go to Chihuahua to become a member of a gang of smugglers. He had killed at least a dozen men and was a wanted outlaw by the time Benito Juarez came into power and rallied the Mexicans against the Austrian ruler whom Napoleon III had sought to impose upon them. By that time, Diego's reputation as a valiant, reckless leader of bandits was so well known that many outlaws flocked to his camp to enlist, lured there by what seemed a guarantee of money and women.

Carlos's career was less spectacular but quite as vicious. He had had smallpox in his youth, and its lingering marks had darkened his nature and made him distrustful and secretive, a loner who sought the association of others only in order to use them for his own purposes. Even Diego had infuriated him with taunts that with his pockmarked face he would hardly find the lovely señoritas willing to accommodate him, while he, Diego, would have no such difficulty.

After leaving the little town of his birth, Carlos Macaras had worked for a brief time as a laborer in the silver mines near the town of Jalisco, then gone to Monterrey to seek his fortune. But the pickings had been lean for him, and he had had to kill a man after having been revealed as a cheat at cards. Thus he had become an outlaw like his brother.

From Monterrey he went to Guadalupe, where he settled for several years. There, like his brother, he married a pretty young girl and had a son by her, who died a year later. But he had begun to be unfaithful to his wife well before that tragedy, as if to disprove his brother's taunts. A year after his son's death, Carlos was making love to the wife of a minor government official, when the latter entered the bedroom. In the scuffle that followed, Carlos strangled him, and then had to flee Guadalupe, one step ahead of the soldiers whom the tearful widow sent after him.

Finally, he had gone to Nuevo Laredo after several years of wandering through the provinces, and there he had been reunited with his brother, Diego. He had learned that the latter had made a lucrative arrangement with a corrupt Union officer in New Orleans, who had sent him gold and weapons to help him stage raids upon villages suspected of harboring the hated French soldiers who alone had kept Maximilian on the throne of Mexico. This officer received a share of the loot, Diego had told him. Diego had invited him to join his band, but Carlos had refused, and had ridden away to form his own band of guerrillas. But when he had returned to Nuevo Laredo, at the *posada* there he had determined to avenge him. It was not entirely out of fraternal love: the prospect of robbing, raping, and killing gringos was much more tempting than trying to plunder poor little Mexican villages.

Now that he had seen this gringo ranch with his own eyes, he was certain that the family who owned it must be very rich indeed. He did not mourn the loss of so many men killed in that attack; they were replaceable, and none of them had been his friend, nor he theirs. Nonetheless, after those four erstwhile *compañeros* had decried his tactics and his valor, Carlos Macaras knew that he must raise enough money to attract to him ruthless, capable followers. And that was why he thought of Cuernavaca, where a dozen years ago he had had a knife duel with a man who had accused him of cheating at cards. He still bore an ugly scar on his right cheek as a souvenir of that fight to the death. On the outskirts of Cuernavaca there was a small bank. Occasionally burros with sacks of silver from the mines were driven to it by a guard of soldiers employed by an English mine owner who delegated his authority to the pompous, overbearing Mexican tax collector at Cuernavaca. This collector, Alejandro Barenda, first had the silver weighed, subtracted from it the government tax, then slyly took a little more as his own commission before sending the rest of the rich ore on to the bank.

Curious to know whether this same procedure still existed, Carlos Macaras rode to Cuernavaca after his defeat at Windhaven Range. He used what little gold he had saved from his raids to rent a modest hacienda and engage a cook and her attractive young daughter, who had just been widowed. Then, playing the role of a well-to-do man about town, he visited the *posadas* of the city and learned all he could by eavesdropping on the conversations of others. He was soon rewarded by overhearing two men grumble over their low pay as escort guards for the silver-laden burros. He found that the pompous tax collector, Alejandro Barenda, had died and been replaced by a younger man. He learned also that there were only six or eight men who rode with the burros to the Cuernavaca bank, since a larger force might attract attention. Best of all, he learned the route that they took from the mine to Cuernavaca.

Near the bank, Carlos had already discovered, was the building in which the smelting of the silver ore took place. The ore itself would be useless unless it was refined. It would therefore be necessary not only to steal the ore but also to find someone who could process it for him, turning it into bars or coins. Forgery of government coins was an offense punishable by life imprisonment or by death. But once the bars were used as pay for the kind of men he proposed to recruit, they could very easily be smuggled across the border and taken to a bank there for assay and payment. He would need to find a hearthmaster who could be trusted and who would have access to what was needed to melt down the ore and extract the silver from it.

Because Carlos Macaras had all his life been a lone wolf and not one who ran with the pack, his inclination was to believe that every man had his price. For some it would be limitless tequila; for others, women, or simply enough *dinero* to buy whatever they wished. And because he believed

this cynical philosophy, his first act was to ingratiate himself with the hearthmaster of the Banco de
Cuernavaca.

It was now early October and he was a thousand
miles away from Windhaven Range. Yet the very
audacity of his plan flattered his twisted ego. For,
once he had implemented his present plans, those
men who had called him a coward would, he was
sure, stand in awe of what he had done to keep his
vow of vengeance. It would be a legend throughout Mexico. Thus he would avenge his brother and
at the same time possess whatever riches he
desired. Having the silver to pay a band of savage
mercenaries would mean that he would be able to
go where he chose, and loot and plunder where he
would.

More patient than he had ever been before, Carlos Macaras bided his time. He made guarded,
seemingly harmless inquiries, and pieced his information together like a woman who carefully
threads beads to make a necklace. One evening the
hearthmaster of the Banco de Cuernavaca entered
the *posada* and was pointed out to Carlos Macaras
by the proprietor.

The man was squat, in his mid-forties, his com-
plexion a reddish-brown and his brows and beard
singed by the intense fires of the hearth. His fingers were thick and pudgy but enormously strong,
and Carlos observed that the man had a tic that
made the left side of his face convulse. As the
hearthmaster seated himself at the adjoining table,
Carlos rose and introduced himself. "Señor Alazar,
will you do me the kindness of sitting at my table
and letting me buy you a drink?"

"You are very kind, señor." The hearthmaster lumbered over to Carlos's table. "And you know my name?"

"Everyone in Cuernavaca knows the name of Tomás Alazar. Yours is the most important job in all the city. Indeed, you could be famous throughout all Mexico with your skill."

The hearthmaster essayed a smile that changed into a horrible grimace as the tic struck him. Apologetically he mumbled, "Excuse me, señor—"

"Teofilo Manos," Carlos lied. "I have come from Nuevo Laredo to visit my cousin."

"That is a very long way, Señor Manos."

"Sí, es verdad. As you see, I amuse myself. Your pleasure?"

"Tequila, por favor."

Carlos signaled to the proprietor to bring a bottle of tequila, and after he himself had poured out a glass for the hearthmaster, he resumed: "I have always admired men who have the skill to turn that which is dug from the good earth into dinero. It is a hard life, though."

"Ah, sí." The squat man mopped his sweating forehead with a piece of dirty rag and nodded agreement. "But you see, Señor Manos, I do not stand before the hot fire every day. It is only when the ore is brought here that I labor."

"And for low wages, I'll be bound." Carlos winked slyly.

The hearthmaster nodded, began to speak, then grimaced again as the tic came upon him. "I do not disgust you, Señor Manos?"

"I see in you cleverness and strength, not the affliction which God may have visited upon you. Each of us has afflictions, *hombre*."

"Yes, it is true." The hearthmaster gulped down part of his tequila, then shook his head. "Sometimes I think I will leave this dirty, smelly town where I have few friends and, as you yourself have said, Señor Manos, little money to show for all my work." He finished the rest of the tequila, whereupon Carlos at once refilled his glass. "Do you know how much they pay me, those officials at the bank? Fifty pesos a month, Señor Manos. It is hardly enough to live in Cuernavaca, and one does not enjoy tequila such as this very often, I assure you."

"Nor the señoritas either, I daresay," Carlos suggested.

"Do not even speak of such things!" The hearthmaster sighed, then seized his glass and took a copious swig.

"But that is not to be tolerated, my good friend." Carlos Macaras pretended the deepest indignation. "Without your services, Cuernavaca would have no *dinero*. Why, in recognition of what you do for the city, the *alcalde* himself should provide you with a sweet and willing companion, a house, fine clothes, and plenty of tequila."

The squat little man's eyes grew dreamy at the vision. "Yes, but not on this earth, I fear, Señor Manos."

"Tell me, *mi amigo*, suppose I were to invite you to visit my own humble house, and there you could enjoy a fine young *mujer* who would do whatever you wished in bed?"

"I would be your friend for life, Señor Manos!"

369

The tequila had loosened his tongue, and the little hearthmaster became voluble: "You understand, Señor Manos, I am a man like all men, except for this accursed affliction of mine. And yet, when the fire is in my veins, I must satisfy myself with some dirty little *puta* who will close her eyes and ask me to blow out the candle before I come to bed with her. It is a shame that a man must suffer so!"

"Of a certainty it is, Tomás. But tonight you may enjoy as lovely a *mujer* as you have ever seen. She is my housekeeper's daughter and she will do whatever I tell her." Carlos Macaras spoke the truth: out of his waning hoard of gold, he had bribed the mother to go back to her own hovel and to leave her daughter there as his housekeeper and concubine. And a single night with the young widow Margarita had been sufficient to cow her into surrender to all her sadistic employer's carnal whims.

"Truly? You would not try to have fun with poor old Tomás Alazar?"

"As heaven is my witness, Tomás, you shall come home with me now and see that I am telling you the truth. And I will buy another bottle of tequila so that you can enjoy it after you have slept with Margarita."

Margarita Santorce slept in a room at the back of the house. Carlos lit a kerosene lamp and led the hearthmaster down the hall to the young widow's bedroom. Kicking the door in, he bawled, "Margarita, get up, you lazy bitch! I have a visitor for you!"

The young woman, her long, glossy black hair tumbling down to the bodice of her thin cotton shift, sat up with a cry of fright as she saw the leering hearthmaster. "*Que pasa,* Señor Manos?" she asked. Carlos had adopted this name not only to keep the authorities from learning that he was a wanted man but also to further his ingenious scheme of raising money to hire mercenaries.

"Take off your shift, Margarita. You are going to entertain my friend Tomás. And you'd better make him happy, or I'll take my belt to you. You've had a taste of it already, and you know I mean what I say." Carlos touched his black leather belt and Margarita shrank back against her pillow with a stifled cry.

"Didn't I tell you she was a sweet, ripe morsel, Tomás?" He nudged the hearthmaster in the ribs. "Go on, man, I'll leave you here with her. Do what you will. When you've finished, come tell me if she satisfied you." Then, shoving Tomas toward the bed, he burst into coarse laughter and left the room.

He waited in the hall a few moments, chuckling as he heard Margarita's tearful pleas mingled with the hearthmaster's hoarse interjections. Then there was a piteous scream, and a moment later the lewd snigger that proclaimed the hearthmaster's penetration of the young woman. He went back to his room, lit a cigar, and thought of the triumph that awaited his cunning plans and patient preparations.

When Tomás Alazar staggered out of Margarita's room an hour later and effusively babbled his thanks, Carlos knew that he had achieved success in the first part of his plan.

Tomás Alazar paid several more visits to his

new friend's house, and each time Margarita Santorce was compelled to submit to him. Once,
indeed, to show the hearthmaster how totally he
had dominated the black-haired young widow,
Carlos Macaras knelt over her, cruelly pinning her
arms behind her as he compelled her to satisfy him
orally while the grunting panting hearthmaster violently copulated with her. By the end of the week,
Tomás Alazar had told Carlos what he wanted to
know and had also agreed to aid him.

There would be a shipment of silver from the
mine within ten days, the hearthmaster declared.
Since they had done away with that Austrian emperor, things had been peaceful in Cuernavaca.
There were no bandits in the vicinity so far as the
rurales knew, so the burros would be accompanied
by at most six *soldados,* and it would take three
days from the mine to reach the bank. The last
shipment of ore had been smelted down into the
equivalent of twenty thousand pesos, and this time
it might be more than that.

To Carlos Macaras's final question as to whether
the hearthmaster could find a new place in which
to melt down the stolen ore, the answer was even
better than he had hoped: Tomás Alazar had a
brother in Coaxtil, a little town near San Luis Potosí, a poor blacksmith but one with a new forge
and the skill to smelt ore.

It had not been difficult to discern that the
hearthmaster of Cuernavaca had often thought of
becoming rich by stealing the ore. But, lacking the
enterprise to plan such an undertaking, Tomás Alazar seemed a tool that fate had handed to Carlos

Macaras. Each time he welcomed the hearthmaster as a guest in his house and compelled the unfortunate young widow to service him, he plied him with promises of riches beyond his wildest dreams. When he was confident that Tomás Alazar was devotedly bound to his project, Carlos set out to find the men who would rob the burro train and convey the ore to the little town where Tomás's brother lived.

It took him the rest of his gold, and all but two days before the next shipment of ore was due, to find four ruffians in a squalid little *posada* on the outskirts of Cuernavaca. Poor Margarita served them as she had the hearthmaster, and when they had glutted themselves on her bruised, welted body, Carlos Macaras calmly strangled her so that she could not bear witness to the plot that they had discussed while awaiting their turns with her. He buried her under a little shed at the back of the house, then he and his four new aides rode off toward the hilly trail along which the ore-laden burros would come to Cuernavaca.

One of these four men was Pablo Asira, a poor wagonmaker, gaunt-faced and surly, whose wife had run off with a handsome soldier. Once again Carlos Macaras was convinced that fate was smiling on him to have met such an accomplice: a wagon and at least four horses would be needed to carry the heavy ore the long way to Coaxtil. Yes, indeed it was fate that had made Pablo Asira despondent with his lot in life and eager to cheat the government whose young representative had taken his wife from him.

Before departing to overtake the burro train,

however, Carlos had one last piece of unfinished business. He bribed a boy to take a message to Tomás Alazar, urging him to come at once to the *Cañón del Diablo,* a tortuous dirt road about five miles east of Cuernavaca, for final instructions on where to meet Carlos Macaras for division of the spoils two weeks after the theft of the ore. Tomás Alazar gave the boy a coin for his trouble, dressed hastily, and saddled his horse, his tic more hideously active than ever at the knowledge that soon he would be a wealthy man. Taking a little-used road out of Cuernavaca so that he would not be detected, he rode toward the *Canon del Diablo.*

As he spurred his horse past a jagged boulder that marked the beginning of the canyon, a shot rang out. Tomás Alazar stiffened in his saddle, then pitched forward to the ground, while his frightened horse bolted and ran.

From the top of the boulder, Pablo Asira blew the smoke from the barrel of his pistol and chuckled as he rejoined his new *jefe.* "It is done, *mi jefe,*" he told Carlos with a crooked grin. "Right through the back of the head, an easy shot."

"*Bueno,* amigo! You have earned a little extra, and you shall have it when we melt the ore down," Carlos promised. "Now, on to the pass of Tenancingo, where we shall meet the burros and the *soldados!*"

CHAPTER TWENTY-EIGHT

The sun had just set on the evening of the next day, and eerie shadows were etched upon the boulder above the winding, narrow trail of the *Canon del Diablo*. Beyond the boulder were thick manzanita bushes, flowering cacti, and closely clustered trees. The wagon and four horses, which Pablo Asira had brought for the transfer of the ore, was concealed well beyond this protective covering and could not be seen from the road below. Here, at the very start of the narrow canyon, the north wall that framed it did not begin for about a hundred yards. Carlos Macaras had chosen this site for the attack so that the soldiers would see the end of the canyon, and, with only flat ground between themselves and the distant town of Cuernavaca, they would have no fears of ambush once they had passed it.

He had no illusions about the caliber of the four men who had agreed to take part in this venture. Between Cuernavaca and the little town of Coaxtil were mountains and desert. First, after the ore had been transferred to the wagon, his route would follow the rarely used and abominable roads to the east of Mexico City, in order to avoid interception by the *Juarista* patrols. He knew that his companions, once into the desert, would wait for their chance to kill him and take the ore. But he had not told them everything of the plan. They knew nothing of the village of Coaxtil, for he had said only that he had friends who could smelt the ore into silver bars and that it was not far from San Luis Potosí. They would, he reasoned, let him get within what they believed to be range of that place, and then dispose of him. But he had prepared for that just as he had for the disposition of Margarita and the squat hearthmaster. Once the silver was melted down by Tomás's brother, Pedro Alazar, he could move toward Nuevo Laredo and the other little towns around it and recruit other men to destroy the gringo ranchhouse.

Carlos lay flat on the top of the jagged boulder, armed with an old French rifle and two pistols. About fifty feet behind him, his four accomplices, armed, knelt behind the protective screen of trees and bushes. The darkness deepened around them in the silence of the early night. Manuel Lorza moved over to Paco Domingar and whispered, "I hear nothing. Perhaps this Señor Manos had wrong information. Perhaps the burros will not come tonight—or perhaps they have already come."

"No, Manuel, I am certain they will come. And

after we have taken the ore, what is to prevent our keeping it for ourselves? I do not trust this Señor Manos, and there may be more *dinero* here than he has said."

"In that case, I myself will kill him. But not here and not right away. We must first take the silver out of the ore before it is worth anything to us. We will have to find someone who can do that."

Lying on the top of the boulder, Carlos Macaras had overheard the whispered voices, and he grinned to himself. He knew what was in their minds, and it would be amusing to anticipate their clumsy, stupid plan. Then suddenly he stiffened, for there came from a distance the faint sound of hooves. Cupping his left hand to his mouth, he called back softly, "Be ready, amigos! I hear the burros!"

The noise grew louder, and suddenly around the bend of the narrow road there appeared a single line of about a dozen burros tethered together, with a sturdy peon leading the first by the bridle. There were only six soldiers and the peon to dispose of. Slowly lifting his rifle, Carlos took careful aim and fired. The shot reverberated through the canyon, and the soldier at the head of the line dropped from his saddle to the ground, rolled over, and lay still. With cries of alarm, the other soldiers reined in their mounts, just as the four bandits opened fire. When the last echoes of the volley had died away, the burros stood alone, squealing and nervous, the dead peon's hand still gripping the bridle of the first burro.

"Good, amigos! Now we have work to do. We must lead the burros up that sloping road to where the wagon is waiting and unload them. *Pronto,* before anyone comes!"

Manuel and Pablo slid down the side of the hill and a few minutes later were leading the burros up the gradually sloping path to the wagon and horses. Carlos also hastened down to the road, for he had noticed a repeating rifle lying beside one of the dead soldiers. It was a further sign that fortune was smiling on him.

He retrieved the rifle, found it fully loaded, and began to ascend the path back to the top of the little hill. With twenty men who had rifles like these, he could destroy those gringos in an hour.

Even the hunchback was helping load the ore into the wagon. Carlos, holding the rifle behind his back, called encouragements to his aides until the transfer was completed. Then, swiftly cocking the weapon, he triggered it until the magazine was empty. Agonized cries accompanied the staccato of the bullets, and then there was silence again in the *Cañón del Diablo*. All four of them were dead.

An hour later, Carlos Macaras was on the road heading toward the little village of Coaxtil. The money he had taken from the soldiers and his former companions would be enough to buy provisions and jugs of water in the little villages on the edge of the desert. It would take him nearly a month to find Tomás's brother, Pedro Alazar, but he was in no hurry now. In the back of the sturdy wagon was more than enough money to hire all the men he needed.

By day, the blistering sun beat down upon the vast stretches of desert, ruled by rattlesnakes, Gila monsters, scorpions, and centipedes. For miles he could see behind him only the ruts of the wagon wheels and the prints of the horses' hooves, and the same dreary, barren terrain stretched to the horizon. From Cuernavaca, Carlos had chosen the dusty, seldom-used road that led to Tlaxcala, where he had stopped to eat and drink at a little inn. He had haggled with the proprietor to sell him enough food to reach Pachuca, paid more than it was worth, and had filled half a dozen clay jugs with tepid water and paid dearly for those also. He had taken burlap sacks from the inn's stable to cover the ore, then covered those with straw and hay so no one would suspect what rich cargo the wagon bore.

Since he had let it slip that he might visit Pachuca, he had skirted that town and driven instead to the even smaller village of Ixmiquilpan. From there to San Luis Potosí, and to Coaxtil, he knew, there was a cruel stretch of more than two hundred miles to the northwest, across rugged country and mountain ranges.

It was not the desert alone that slowed his pace. He held to his resolve to make his own trail and to shun any semblance of a road to avoid being seen. He was certain that the bodies of the soldiers and Tomás Alazar had by now been discovered by the authorities in Cuernavaca and that a search had already begun. From time to time he would glance back, his heart beating faster at the mere hint of a cloud of dust behind him. But each time he would discover that it had been only the sultry, eddying breeze that had stirred the dust, rather than a posse of *rurales* bent on tracking him down.

What occupied his mind and kept him from going mad, day after day under that remorselessly blue sky and the furnacelike sun, were thoughts that he often spoke aloud, as if to an imaginary *compañero*. How, for example, would he dupe Pedro Alazar in the village of Coaxtil? How would he explain the rich silver ore hidden in the heavy wagon? What price would Pedro Alazar demand of him, and would the hearthmaster's brother not be suspicious enough to inform the local authorities? But beyond these soliloquies, in which the sound of his voice mockingly challenged the terrifying, consuming silence of the desert, there was a growing egotistical pride in his exploits. Even his brother, Diego, would not have dared to go alone with a wagon and four horses through the desert and across the mountains, even for the sake of vast plunder. He told himself that he was greater than any bandido leader who had ever set foot upon the soil of Mexico; that if he had been born to the right parents, he, not Benito Juarez, might even have become *el presidente*. And at times, when the sun made him feverish and his lips were dry and parched and he held back the maddened urge to seize one of the water jugs and drink his fill, he would laugh aloud and cry out, "I am Carlos Macaras, and I have a destiny to fulfill!"

Two weeks later he drove into the outskirts of Tamazunchale, and was at last able to buy fresh horses. The people of this village were simple peons who hated the government and, indeed, would have resented any government that sent authorities to tax them.

He stayed three days in this village, and was tempted to stay longer, having caught sight of a tall, sinuous black-haired girl whose thin cotton blouse and skirt limned the promise of hard-pointed young breasts and long, sleek legs. But when he learned that she was the ward of the village priest, he harnessed his fresh horses and set out along the trail again. Now only a hundred more miles of lonely, dangerous journeying lay in store for him before he would reach Coaxtil. When he had foresworn the temptation of the priest's young ward, it was not out of any sense of sacrilege, but rather that he feared the priest's curse. Carlos openly scorned superstitions, but inwardly he trembled with the fear that they might wreak their malice upon him if he defied their rules.

And yet the very sight of that vibrant young girl had renewed his determination to complete this grueling, solitary trek. As he drove the wagon out into the sun-baked stretch of uninhabited land, he closed his eyes. For a moment he could see himself in the fine gringo ranchhouse, with pistols thrust into his belt, and a whip in his hand, master of the household and lord over the *mujeres* whom he had captured. He would decide which one would kneel, wringing her hands, and beg him for mercy. He would take her to his bed one night and another captive the next. He would glut himself, wallow in their shame and degradation.

And so, where many men wandering across the lonely desert might have seen mirages, Carlos Macaras saw kaleidoscopic visions of young girls and handsome women, their clothing in disarray, their white flesh besmirched by red welts from his lash, which would compel them to offer themselves as might a whore to a masterful conqueror.

Such visions made the scorching days seem shorter and the nights cooler, with each new morning bringing a fiercer resolve to drive forward. Now he no longer had to look back over his shoulder after imaginary pursuers; none would follow so far. By the time he reached the little town of Cardenas, he knew he must follow a directly westward course to skirt San Luis Potosí—where there was a telegraph line and to which news of the events in Cuernavaca might well have been sent—and arrive at Coaxtil for the meeting with the hearthmaster's brother.

At Cardenas he replenished his food and water, rested a day, and enjoyed an evening of fiesta. It was a wedding celebration, and the sight of the pretty girls in their low-cut blouses and swirling, colored skirts made him shiver with longing. He half wished that he had forced Margarita Santorce to accompany him and release him from the maddening desires that at night sometimes made him sweat as with fever. But then he consoled himself by thinking how much tastier the gringa captives would be once their men had been killed and the ranchhouse burned to the ground. He could spin out his pleasures with them, savoring their revulsion in having to comply with his commands.

At last, on the second day of December 1867, Carlos Macaras reached the outskirts of Coaxtil, a village of scattered adobe huts and a little church. There was a water trough for the horses in the village square, and the sight that he most welcomed: the long rectangle of logs and adobe in front of which a heavyset, nearly bald man was shoeing a horse.

It was at the other end of the village, and although several men and women emerged from the adobe huts and glanced at him and his wagon, they had little curiosity over his presence. Doubtless they thought that he had brought his horses to be shod by their blacksmith. His only problem now, as he saw it, would be to convince Pedro Alazar of the truth of his story. He had come so far and through such hazards that in his mind he had blocked out any possibility that Pedro Alazar would refuse to smelt the ore. No, if he had escaped the *rurales* and the perils of starvation and thirst and the bites of insects and reptiles all this long way, it could only be because, just as he had shouted aloud in defiance to the lonely skies, he had a destiny to fulfill.

At last Carlos got down from the wagon with a sigh of sensual pleasure at being able to stretch his legs. "*Buenas dias, señor*," he greeted the blacksmith, who, he saw, was only a few years younger than Tomás Alazar.

"And to you, *hombre*," was the laconic answer. The blacksmith began to collect his tools and lay them away, then halted as if a thought had just struck him. "Perhaps your horses need new shoes?"

"Of a certainty, but before that, I am near dead with thirst. Could you spare a little water, *por favor*?"

"It would be my pleasure." The blacksmith nodded and disappeared inside his shop. His little house was at the other end of this rectangle of logs

383

and adobe, so close to it that it seemed a single building.

"Your water, *hombre*," the blacksmith said as he returned with a large clay dipper. As Carlos stared at it, the blacksmith explained, "I have made a little pump and there is a small well at the back of my shop. We are blessed at Coaxtil with a hidden spring. Our priest says it is the blessing of the *Virgen Santísima*, because we live at peace and farm the land around us and share with our neighbors when they are hungry."

"Then I am more than grateful for this water, since it is so blessed," Carlos replied. Before he drained the dipper, with his left forefinger he made the sign of the cross.

As he forced himself to drink slowly, Carlos saw the blacksmith's eyes warm as the hint of a smile came to his sullenly set mouth. "You are of the faith, then, *hombre?*"

"Proudly, señor."

"Praise unto Her, the blessed Mother of our Lord," the blacksmith reverently intoned as he crossed himself. "It is almost time for the noonday meal. Will you not share it with me—I do not know your name."

"But I think I know yours," Carlos said slyly. "Is it not Pedro Alazar?"

"You know me? But I have never seen you before in Coaxtil," the blacksmith replied.

"That is not strange, since I have come from Cuernavaca with a message from your brother, Tomás."

"From Tomás? What has happened to him? Is he well? I have not had word from him in nearly three years. Come inside my little house, we shall have *arroz con pollo* and the best tortillas you will find in all of Coaxtil. I cannot offer you spirits, señor, because I have taken a vow. In my youth, strong drink almost delivered me to the Evil One." Again he crossed himself.

"I am Teofilo Manos," Carlos explained as he seated himself at the table in the little room off the kitchen and watched an old, crippled woman hobble in with plates of food. When she had gone back to the kitchen, he eyed the blacksmith. "Your wife, Señor Alazar?"

"*Pero no,* Señor Manos. She is my housekeeper. My wife, may the angels guard her soul, died ten years ago. But I had lost her love long before that because I loved drink too well. In my work, you see, I try each day to make my peace with Our Lord for the sins I have committed because I did not know the right of things."

Carlos studied the blacksmith's face. It was all he could do to keep from laughing aloud. Now he knew how to convince this simple peasant to labor for him. Pedro Alazar was little more than a religious fanatic, so the smelting of the ore must be made to seem a righteous work. As he ate the nourishing, tasty food set before him and drank goat's milk, Carlos exhorted all the powers of his fertile imagination to come to his aid in fabricating a story that the blacksmith would accept without question. "You know, of course, that your brother is hearthmaster for the Banco de Cuernavaca," he began guardedly.

"Yes, that is what I last heard from him. You understand, Señor Manos, that we cannot send letters

385

from here to Cuernavaca or Mexico City. It is only when a man rides from our village to a distant one, and agrees to take a message which, in its turn, is passed on to a village beyond that one, that we have news of friends or dear ones so far away. And besides, Tomas has little to say to me. You saw his affliction? Well, he does not accept it as the will of Our Lord. Instead, he grumbles and has hate in his heart and feels that the *Nuestro Señor* has forsaken him. He does not remember what happened to Job in the Bible, Señor Manos."

"Perhaps he has come to know the story at last," Carlos interposed.

"I wish I could believe that, Señor Manos." Pedro Alazar sighed heavily and shook his head. "You spoke of a message from him—is it perhaps the promise of his abandoning his sinful ways that you bring me now after all these years?"

"In a way, yes, amigo. Let me call you this, for I have eaten food under your roof and I am in the presence of a man whose devoutness I respect. He has so seen the error of his ways that he believes a miracle befell him. You see, amigo, he has worked long and faithfully for the bank at Cuernavaca, and they gave him a small piece of land well beyond the city as a reward for his labors. He saw at last that he was not held in such low esteem as he had thought all these years, and he went to the church and made a good confession."

"Praise be unto Him who bids all sinners come to Him to confess and be redeemed!" Pedro Alazar raised his eyes to the ceiling and crossed himself.

"Exactly so. And when he came out of the church after having made this confession to the

386

good *padre*, your brother said to himself that he would till the soil of the land they had given him and live from it and be grateful."

"Ah, that is good news indeed you bring me, Señor Manos!"

"But there is much more, amigo. He began to dig so that he might plant fruits and vegetables, and he fell upon his knees when his pick struck a vein of silver ore, richer than even the mine from which the ore was sent to him to smelt for the bank."

"You see? You see?" Pedro Alazar almost rose from the table, his eyes glowing, his face enraptured. "At last my poor brother has learned that the parable of Job can come true even for a contrite sinner!"

"It has indeed, *mi amigo*. He engaged men to help him dig, and he uncovered so much ore that now he is one of the wealthiest men in all Cuernavaca. Much of this, of course, he gave to the church, asking the *padre* to distribute it to the poor and to burn candles in honor of the Blessed Virgin."

"Oh, what joyous news you bring me, Señor Manos!" the blacksmith fervently exclaimed.

"And now, *mi amigo*, I come to you not only with this news but also with the proof of your brother's redemption. Knowing how faithful you are, he asked me to bring to you a share of this rich ore, that you might smelt it into silver bars in the shape of crosses. You are to use the silver for the poor of your village, to build a more beautiful church in which all may worship, and to take for yourself what you may need to make your life more comfortable. That is why you see me here with four horses that draw a heavy wagon, *mi amigo*. It is filled with the silver ore which is your brother's gift to Coaxtil and to you."

Pedro Alazar had tears in his eyes as he seized Carlos's hands and squeezed them, his lips trembling with emotion. "Yes, silver crosses! What a glorious idea! And to think that I once feared for my brother's soul! Señor Manos, I will do it! Of course, I must spend my days serving the needs of our people as their blacksmith, but I shall work at night, with all my strength and with joy in the knowledge that Tomás has done this holy thing. Tell me, how did he look to you when you last saw him?"

"That too is part of the miracle, *mi amigo*," Carlos replied solemnly. "When I last saw him, the tic which had so long afflicted him was there no more."

CHAPTER TWENTY-NINE

On the evening of December 15, Pedro Alazar, haggard with exhaustion and dripping with sweat, halted his work at the hand-pumped bellows and turned to Carlos Macaras with a sigh of relief. "It is done, Señor Manos. I am ready to drop in my tracks. Yet the knowledge of my brother's redemption and his priceless gift to our little church has given me strength."

Carlos Macaras nodded gravely. "I shall go with you to the church in the morning and help you with the silver crosses. In that way, I shall know that my own mission has been accomplished, just as Tomás would have wished."

"How astonished the old *padre* will be when we carry these blessed symbols of the faith to him. I can imagine what great joy you must feel at being part of this wonderful undertaking."

"It is the happiest moment of my life," Carlos solemnly averred. "But now you must put out the fire, refresh yourself with food and drink, and then sleep till the morning. You have earned a good long sleep, and I know it will be filled with dreams of the happy change in your brother's life and his unselfish gift."

The blacksmith replied, "Will you not share food and drink with me, *mi amigo?* I can no longer call you Señor Manos, for you have become dear to me, almost like my own brother. Allow me to call you my good friend Teofilo."

"You are too kind. But when I see your beautiful craftsmanship as I look upon these magnificent crosses, I feel no need for food and drink, good Pedro. Let me put them into order so that they may be more easily transported in the morning. Go refresh yourself and then to your bed."

"Perhaps you are right," the blacksmith admitted, wiping his sweaty forehead with his sleeve. "My bones ache and I feel as if I have been baked to be served on the table. My furnace has seldom been so hot."

"But for such a worthy cause!" Carlos clapped him on the back and grinned.

He watched the blacksmith extinguish the fire, glancing from time to time at the pile of gleaming silver crosses. Midway through the smelting of the ore, Pedro Alazar had estimated that there was at least thirty-five thousand pesos' worth of the finest silver. After Pedro had left the smelting room, Carlos approached the crosses, his eyes blazing covetously as he bent to touch them, to savor the weight and the feel of them. When he straightened,

390

his lips were curved in a sardonic smile. Everything was in readiness. The wagon had been drawn up beside the smelting room, and the horses were in Pedro Alazar's stable just beyond. It was an hour's work at most to load the crosses into the wagon—which now would be lighter because he was carrying pure silver instead of ore—and to harness the horses.

He rolled a cigarette and lit it, his smile deepening. There were twenty-five or thirty crosses, each worth over a thousand pesos. Carlos cupped his chin in his hand while he flicked ashes from his cigarette, his eyes narrowed in thought. When he reached Nuevo Laredo, he would keep one of the crosses and hide the others in a safe place. He knew several mercenaries there who would take part in his venture. He also knew someone who sold jewelry and expensive antiques, who would give him at least five hundred pesos for the one cross he planned to keep—or, better still, trade him several of the latest rifles and plenty of ammunition. He would need not only enough men but the best possible weapons to attack the gringo stronghold effectively, to counter the repeating rifles and carbines that he knew they possessed. Such weapons were seen in Mexico only rarely, perhaps when a comanchero had to flee across the border and brought his weapon with him.

He would have to be very wary about the treasure, keeping no more than two of the crosses to show to the recruits he intended to enlist. If things went well, as he was certain they would, he could still keep most of the crosses. His men would be too excited at getting the women and the *dinero* that they would take from the gringos. After it was over, after they had glutted themselves on the spoils of the ranchhouse, he could easily disappear with the rest of the crosses and take up the life of a wealthy country gentleman in a little villa in Tampico or Vera Cruz, where he would be Teofilo Manos, with a pair of pretty girls to look after his every need.

Decisively he crushed the stub of the cigarette under his boot heel and, catlike, crept back into the house, which was connected to the smelting room by a narrow, roofed passageway.

Pedro Alazar had eaten and drunk but little, for the arduous work at the hot furnace these past nights had sapped even his dogged strength. He lay sprawled on his bed, snoring, fully clothed. Carlos sucked in his breath, slowly lifted from his neck the rosary that he usually wore, and made a noose of it as he crept forward. Very gently, so as not to wake the sleeper, he slid it under Pedro Alazar's neck, then gripped it with both hands and with all his strength began to strangle the blacksmith.

Pedro's eyes opened, alarmed, not comprehending; then he tried to lift himself, his fingers scrabbling at the beads and the rawhide thong that dug into his neck and choked off his windpipe. His eyes rolled this way and that, with horror and anger, until at last his head fell back on the pillow.

Carlos straightened, eased the rosary off the purple, swollen neck, and moved silently down the hall toward the room where the old housekeeper slept. With her it was much easier—a pillow pressed over her face and held down until her thrashing ceased, and it was done.

It was four hundred long miles to Nuevo Laredo by way of Mazapil and Ocampo, at which latter town Carlos Macaras stopped to change horses and to rest for the night. The next morning at dawn he hitched up fresh horses and drove off, skirting Monterrey and making for Monclova, in the province of Coahuila. Years before, he had met a young girl in that town, Conchita Alvarez, and they had spent a night or two together. When he came to the inn of the town he made casual inquiry and learned that Conchita and her husband had moved to San Luis Potosí. Carlos shrugged. It would have been pleasant to renew their acquaintance, but it really didn't matter. He had only to think back to his carefully planned scheme for recouping his fortune, and how each step of the way had led him safely as far as this.

Now the way was easier, and he arrived on the outskirts of Nuevo Laredo on January 10, 1868. On that day, in their little house on Windhaven Range, Mara Hernandez presented her beloved husband, Ramon, with a sturdy little son, whom they named Luke, as they had promised.

The last day of February 1868 had been unseasonably warm, and a light downpour had brought a pleasant coolness to the evening. The rain had not been hard enough to put out the cooking fires in the *Comancheria* of Sangrodo, thirty miles west of the little village of Miero. Here, on a slightly upraised plain with a series of irregular hills mark-

393

ing the boundary to the west, the Comanche chief had kept his stronghold. Here he had built a new home for his wandering people, where they could dwell in peace, trying to forget the time when an ambitious Union captain had led his men in a vicious slaughter of Indian women, children, and old men.

If Sangrodo and his braves had not been out on a hunting foray, they too might have fallen victim to the merciless attack upon their village. But when they had crossed the Rio Grande, the tall chief had promised his braves that they would try the ways of the Navaho and the Pawnee, settling upon land, farming it, and hunting for what wild game they could find. They would be safe from vengeful soldiers here, and could live out their lives without fleeing from white-eyes who hated them.

They had gone about their new land in peace, some of them visiting the nearby villages of Miero and Maxtime. They had made the sign of peace, and, because most of them spoke some words of Spanish, which their chief knew fluently, they had brought trading goods to the villagers. When at last even the children in these villages had come to accept them as friends, they had begun to court the Mexican women instead of capturing them as once had been their wont. Those raids had been retaliatory, to punish the Mexicans for having killed peaceful Comanches. Now they were learning the gentler ways of mating, and already there were many papooses in the stronghold.

Sangrodo stood in front of his tepee, arms folded across his chest. Where most Comanches were short and stocky, Sangrodo seemed to tower over all of them, for he was fully as tall as Luke Bouchard. Because his tribe was at peace, he wore neither headdress nor the traditional paint marks, except for those of his clan. He watched the braves emerge from their huts and tepees now, saw their women bustling about the fires to prepare the evening meal, and though his look was grave, his eyes lighted with satisfaction. In this land, across the border from the white-eyes soldiers, Sangrodo felt a contentment that he had not known in many years.

Out of the largest tepee now came Catayuna, who had once been the wife of Manuelo Arvilas, the *alcalde* of the village of Maxtime. Now she was known as the beloved woman, beloved not only by the chief but also by every brave of the stronghold. She wore buckskin and moccasins, and her lustrous black hair was plaited in two thick braids that fell nearly to her waist. Against the buckskin jacket her breasts rose and fell with vibrant rhythm, and there was a soft, knowing smile on her sensuous lips as she moved toward him.

"*Mi esposo, mi hombre,*" Catayuna murmured. At the soft sound of her voice, Sangrodo turned quickly. His ascetic mouth curved into a tender smile. "Catayuna. Are you content?" he asked.

"More than that, much more," was her almost-whispered answer. "We live simply here. We hunt and fish and we plant crops—that is something your people seldom did, is that not so, Sangrodo?"

"Yes, Catayuna. The Comanche has wandered over the plains from the day that he was put upon this earth by the Great Spirit. But times are chang-

395

ing and we must change with them if we mean to live. And I am proud in my life, even though it is new and strange, because I am still Comanche."

Catayuna reached out to touch his arm briefly, then drew back her hand, knowing it was unseemly for a squaw to show the least affection for her mate in public. "I too feel that I belong now to your people, Sangrodo. For now I belong to you, and it has been of my own choice. And soon, my husband, there will be living proof that I am truly your squaw."

He stared into her dark eyes and seemed to wait for her to speak, to enlighten him. She lowered her eyes before his as she murmured, "I carry your child near my heart, Sangrodo. I have known this now for two moons. It will be a son, who will be as proud and free as his father."

"May the Great Spirit let it be so," he responded gravely. Once again his eyes were gentle as he looked upon her, standing there with head bowed before him, arms at her sides.

After a moment he spoke, for only her to hear: "If you give me a son, he shall be as dear to me as Kitante, my first born. I shall name him—no, it is the right of the mother to name the child; this is our custom."

She raised her eyes to his again, and the fierceness of her dark eyes was softened by a passionate, intimate look. She answered, "Then I will name him Opinako, He Who Walks in His Father's Footsteps."

Sangrodo gripped her by her shoulders and whispered back, "Now you are truly Comanche, woman. You have given your son-to-be a name to be remembered and to guide him along the path which a chief must take one day. And I say this to you, beloved woman—I take the path which is best for our people, yet I will always walk with you and keep you from harm no matter how I choose to guide our tribe to its pride and freedom."

"Then I am content," Catayuna murmured. Then, after a moment's silence, she asked in a casual tone, "Will my husband eat at the campfire with his braves or will he permit his squaw to serve him?"

"I must hold council with my braves and with Ipiltse. He has just come back from a journey and he brings news that disturbs me. So I shall eat with them. Yet do not put away what you have cooked. When the council is over, I will join you and share what you have cooked, even if it be only a morsel."

Sangrodo strode to the center of the little village, where the stocky war chief, Ipiltse, had dismounted from his mustang and was talking animatedly to three of the older men of the tribe. As Sangrodo approached, Ipiltse saluted him and fell silent.

"Your face is as dark as the cloud which hides the moon, Ipiltse," Sangrodo said. "What have you seen that so dismays you?"

"Do you remember when that tall man whose skin is dark visited our stronghold to see his daughter who is now the squaw of Jicinte?"

"I well remember. And she is with child again. But how does that dismay you, Ipiltse?"

"Then you remember also that I told you of the younger brother of the evil *Mejicano* and how he had sworn to avenge his brother's death. This I

397

learned when I had ridden near the village of Maxtime."

"Yes, I remember. And you spoke the name of Carlos Macaras."

"That is indeed the name, Sangrodo. Now I believe that he has found the men who escaped that first raid upon the ranch of your white-eyes brother, to whom you gave the great blue talisman stone of the tribe.

"To the east lies the abandoned *Mejicano* village of Puertocare, where it is said so terrible a sickness came upon the people that no man has dared live there since."

"It is known to me. Speak on."

"But now people live in that village. They are *Mejicanos*, and they have made a kind of camp there."

"That is indeed strange. How many *Mejicanos* were there?"

"I saw at least a dozen, and I am sure there are many more. One of them hailed me as I rode near the entrance to the village and asked if I spoke his *Mejicano* tongue."

"You spoke to him?" Sangrodo gripped his war chief's arm. "What did he say to you?"

"He asked me if I were not of the Comanches, and I saw that he knew our people from the markings on my body. When I said that I was indeed of the people, he then asked me if I was at war with the white-eyes who had taken away the Comanche land."

"Ho! Tell me everything, Ipiltse. I begin to sense danger, not for us but for the family of my white-eyes brother, him whom I call Taiboo Nimi-ahkana."

"The danger is more than one feels in the heart, Sangrodo. This man, who calls himself Teofilo Manos, is an evil one. He has the marks on his face of what the white-eyes call smallpox, and his eyes are cruel as the puma's when he comes upon his prey. He said that he had need of those who hated the white-eyes as he did, and that he would pay much *dinero* and give me a *mujer gringa* if I would serve him."

"What was your answer, Ipiltse?"

"I had ridden with only my lance and my hunting knife, Sangrodo, and I could see that his *compañeros* had pistols and also some of the long guns which shoot many times quickly. I thought that if I refused him, he would kill me. So I told him that I would ask permission from my chief, and that I myself did not have reason to love the white-eyes."

Sangrodo uttered a short, barking chuckle. "So you have let him think you will join him and his followers. And what did he say to that, Ipiltse?"

"That I was to return within three suns and bring with me all other Comanches who hated the white-eyes for having stolen their land. He promised that there would be gold and women for each one of us who rode with him."

"But he did not say where?"

Ipiltse shook his head. "I knew he would not tell me if I asked, until he is sure of me."

Sangrodo turned away in deep thought, scowling at the flickering fire. Then he turned back to the war chief and declared, "Go back to this *Mejicano* when the third sun has risen, and take with you two of my young warriors. Let a third follow you at a distance, and hide himself as best he can. When it is night, give the call of the coyote three times. Then you or your two companions will find a way to go to him who hides, to tell him against whom these *Mejicanos* intend this attack. I think I know already. And this is what I think also—that Teofilo Manos is the name which Carlos Macaras has taken to deceive not only you but also those who already plan to follow him. And now, Ipiltse, we will share the food which has been cooked for us. And we will pray to the Great Spirit to watch over you and the three braves who will go without fear into that village of death. For by entering it as you will, you may save from death and worse those who are loved by my white-eyes brother who wears our sacred talisman."

Carlos Macaras had rented a little hut on the outskirts of Nuevo Laredo. He had spent his first night there digging up the dirt floor of one of the rooms to bury the silver crosses. He had buried all of them except two, which he had put into a burlap sack, and had then set out to find the jeweler whom he knew to be involved in illicit enterprises.

Heitor Favelas, the jeweler, was a little man with thick spectacles, a goatee, and an obsequious smile. After examining the silver cross that Carlos showed him, he stroked his goatee and declared, "It is excellent silver, amigo. So excellent, indeed, that it may be the property of the government. But of course you would know nothing of that. On the other hand, since I suspect it, and there are risks

400

involved, I cannot give you more than eight hundred pesos. There are more?"

"Only this other one, which I need to use in enlisting brave *compañeros* for a project I have in mind."

"I begin to understand a little. I do not wish to know your plans. I will say only that if you seek men who have courage and are not afraid to show it, you could do no better than to visit the *posada* known as the Casa del Oro."

Carlos thanked the jeweler, accepted the eight hundred pesos, and left the shop. He was not disappointed, though he knew that the jeweler would make at least three or four hundred pesos in disposing of the cross. With the eight hundred pesos and the cross that he still carried in the sack, he was certain that he could recruit enough lawless companions for the venture against Windhaven Range. As to the other crosses, they were safe enough. He had spent over an hour smoothing the ground under which they were buried, safely covered with a scrap of well-worn rug. He had paid the owner of the hut for six months' rental, and had casually explained that he would be coming and going from time to time because he was courting a señorita in Miero.

He had disposed of the wagon at a ridiculously low price and sold two of the horses, the other two being worthless by the time they had completed the journey. At the livery stable he had bought a superb horse, a chestnut gelding, quick and sure-footed and intelligent. At last he was ready to gather men and plan his attack.

At the Casa del Oro he met three rogues who

were wanted by the Mexican government for theft and suspected murder. A few bottles of tequila and his persuasive words, along with a glimpse of what was in the burlap sack, served to enlist them.

By mid-February he had enlisted twenty-five desperadoes, three of whom were part Indian, which he believed made them more ruthless when it came to torture and violation. It was one of these half-breeds, Juan Cortigo, who had told him of the village of Puertocare, which was within a week's journey of Carrizo Springs. It would be an ideal hiding place for the gang, since it was shunned by all Mexicans and Indians as well, because of the legend of the plague that had killed all its inhabitants.

Only one thing distressed him as he made his final preparations for the attack on Windhaven Range: he had not been able to procure many repeating rifles. Apart from the one that he had retrieved from the fallen soldier of the burro train, he had managed to buy two repeating-fire carbines and an old Henry rifle. The men who would accompany him in the raid against Carrizo Springs had old pistols, French or Belgian rifles, and of course knives and machetes. But one evening while Carlos and the men were discussing the method of attack, Juan Cortigo had remarked, "Have you not thought of fire, *hombre?* It is a weapon which we Indians have often used against our enemies—the fire arrow, which starts a house burning and drives out its occupants so that they can easily be killed. Wagons set afire and placed against this stockade of which you tell us would burn the posts and give us entrance into the house. It would be well for you to remember fire when you attack, Senor Manos."

Thus, when Ipiltse, Sangrodo's war chief, had ridden near the abandoned village and been accosted by Carlos Macaras, the latter had urged him to join his bandits, hoping that Ipiltse would bring others with him, since the Comanches were known to be the finest fighters, second perhaps only to the Apaches in their ferocity and cunning. After Ipiltse had left, promising to return within three days, Carlos had turned to the squat mestizo and declared, "It was a stroke of luck to find this Comanche in Mexico. I know how the Comanche hates the Texas gringo for robbing him of his hunting grounds."

Juan Cortigo slowly nodded, his ugly face twisted in a scowl. "It is strange that Comanches should come across the border and dwell here. They raid Mexican villages for horses and women, this is well known. It can only mean that somewhere they have made their stronghold. Perhaps the gringo soldiers chased them across the border."

"All the better, then, Juan," Carlos replied, chuckling. "They will have all the more reason to hate gringos."

"Sí, es posible," the mestizo agreed grudgingly. "All the same, I would like to ride out and see if I can find that warrior's Comancheria."

"Do so, then, and tell me what you learned. In three days, whether that brave returns with others or decides not to ride with us, we go to attack the gringos!"

On the day following Ipiltse's conversation with Carlos, Juan Cortigo saddled his horse and rode

403

westward, armed with his machete, his hunting knife strapped in a leather sheath around his waist, and an old Belgian rifle. His keen eyes followed the hoofmarks of Ipiltse's mustang toward Sangrodo's stronghold.

It was late afternoon on this somber, early March day, when Isobel Cortez, who had become the squaw of Menigsay, one of Sangrodo's ablest young warriors, left the stronghold to search for kindling and for juniper berries to make a poultice for her husband's wound. Last night, in a playful scuffle with Tolcamay, another of the young dissidents, Menigsay's arm had been cut slightly. Isobel planned to use wild herbs and the juice of the juniper berries to draw the poison left by Tolcamay's dulled, rusty blade.

About a mile south of the stronghold, she had broken off branches of dead wood and piled them neatly. Just beyond, on the side of a small hill, she perceived thick clusters of juniper bushes. She had noticed them first some days ago. Isobel, ripe and comely at twenty-two, wore the garments of the other Comanche squaws—jacket and skirt of buckskin, and sturdy moccasins. Her jet-black hair, like Catayuna's, had been formed into two thick plaits that dangled just above her waist. She had brought two wicker baskets to carry the wood and berries.

Juan Cortigo had spied her emerging from the village and walking south. He turned his horse due south so as to skirt the village, and dismounted near a towering clump of mesquite. Gesturing to the docile animal to remain there, he squatted behind the mesquite. As Isobel came nearer, he wolfishly grinned as he saw her set down one basket

404

and pile the broken branches into it, for her movement had hiked the hem of her skirt enough to show him fine, round, brown-sheened calves.

Juan Cortigo had been born in Guadalupe forty years ago, the bastard offspring of an Indian woman who was virtually a slave to a wealthy Mexican shopkeeper. As a boy he had been subjected to the most menial and degrading tasks in the household, and had seen his mother whipped for impertinence, while he was forced to bow his head and hold his tongue as she slumped at the post, her back bloodied by the lash. When he was eighteen, a week after his mother's death, he cut his father's throat while he lay sleeping, and did the same to his fat, middle-aged wife. Then he entered the bedroom of the sixteen-year-old daughter, whom he forced, with the threat of his uplifted knife, to serve his lust. To make certain she could not testify against him afterward, he killed her too.

Since then he had had a price on his head. At times he would lose himself in the desert to the south; because of his Indian background, he could exist on the land and adapt himself to its arduous demands. He had ridden with half a dozen guerrilla bands, narrowly escaped being hanged by a posse of *rurales* just outside Cuernavaca, and had come to Nuevo Laredo after fleeing from Monterrey, where he had killed an innkeeper over an insult to his Indian ancestry.

Now his eyes glinted at the sight of the unsuspecting young woman, for he had not enjoyed one in nearly six months. It had been Carlos's promise of white women that had made him decide to take part in the attack on Windhaven Range. Drawing

405

his knife from its sheath, he crept forward behind Isobel, who was beginning to pluck berries from the juniper bushes, suddenly clapped his left hand over her mouth, and pressed the point of the sharp blade against her back as he hissed, "*Cuidado, muchacha!* Not a sound, or you'll feel my knife to the hilt, *comprende?*" Half fainting with terror, Isobel wanly nodded, her eyes rolling in fright. "I am going to take my hand off your mouth now, *muchacha*," he continued, "but if you scream or utter a single word, I will cut off your *tetas!* Nod again if you understand me."

When the trembling young woman nodded, he chuckled viciously, seized one of her braids with his left hand, and forced her to come with him behind the juniper bushes. When she whimpered at the twinge of pain, he put the point of the knife to her throat and snarled, "Remember what I have said, *muchacha!*"

Then, kneeling beside her, the knife uplifted, he ordered her to divest her jacket and skirt, and licked his lips as the almost-hysterical young woman complied. Her eyes did not leave the gleaming knife for an instant as her fingers fumbled with the fastenings of her garments. With a lustful grunt he flung himself upon her, having already bared his swollen manhood so as to heighten her anguish and shame. Ruthlessly he possessed her, keeping the knife pressed against her naked side, commanding her to put her arms around him, to kiss him on the lips, and to thrust her tongue between them. Though retching and shuddering with revulsion, Isobel had no choice but to obey.

After he had possessed her, he forced her to use her hands and mouth to restore his virility, then gestured to her to lie on her belly. When she began to plead with him for mercy, he struck her brutally across the face, pressed the knife against the side of one full satiny breast, and promised her, in the most lewd terms, undreamed-of tortures if she did not submit. When at last she proffered herself, Juan Cortigo gripped the handle of the knife between his teeth, his talonlike fingers gripping her plump buttocks and spreading them so that he might sodomize her.

Sated, he rose at last from her sprawled, ravished body. For a moment he amused himself by running the sharp point of the knife over her naked back and buttocks and sides, giggling maniacally to see her twinges and hear her strangled plaints, which she strove to suppress in her abject terror of him. Then, tiring of the game, he lifted the knife and plunged it to the hilt into her back. Isobel lifted her head, her face twisted in agony, then sagged, lifeless. The mestizo then seized her plaits and began to scalp her. Tucking the grisly trophy through his belt, he went back to his grazing horse and rode back to Puertocare.

Two hours later, Catayuna discovered Isobel's abused, lifeless body when she herself left the stronghold to gather firewood. Ipiltse and Sangrodo followed her back to the corpse after she had returned to the stronghold with the horrid news of what she had discovered. As she turned away, covering her tear-stained face with her hands, Sangrodo said grimly to Ipiltse, "All this time Menigsay sought to walk away from my path of peace. Perhaps now he will see that if we make war at all, it is only on those who kill the innocent. Now more than ever I am convinced that this man who told you he was Teofilo Manos is indeed the brother of Diego Macaras. So you will go to Puertocare as we have planned. And the third brave you take with you will ride back to the stronghold once you learn when they plan to raid the rancho of my white-eyes brother!"

Ipiltse carried his old Sharps rifle as he rode with the warriors Ekinato and Tiskewa toward the abandoned village where the bandits had made their camp. Lagging well behind him was the young brave Kiminardo, who would hide in the bushes and signal by imitating the call of the coyote to indicate his presence.

Carlos Macaras and Juan Cortigo, idly chatting, stood at the entrance of the ruined village as the three Comanches rode up on their mustangs. Carlos held up his hand in the universal sign of peace and said, "Ipiltse, you have kept your word. But only two braves come with you. We could have used many more."

"As I said to you, Señor Manos," Ipiltse explained as he dismounted, "our chief is an old man who holds the young braves back from the paths of war. But we three do not walk in his footsteps, and we hate our white-eyes enemies as we do all who wrong the Comanche. Here are Ekinato and Tiskewa, who wish to fight beside me."

"That is good. And you have brought your

weapons—you have killed many buffalo with your Sharps gun, have you not, Ipiltse?"

"And white-eyes too, Señor Manos." Ipiltse gestured toward his two young companions and added, "They have only the old rifles which must be reloaded each time they are fired. But they have brought their lances, and they have killed as many men and buffalo as I with my Sharps. They are good fighters."

"Then all of you are welcome. Come now, we are preparing supper. You will meet the others of our band."

"That is good. I hope we shall not wait too long to attack the white-eyes enemy," Ipiltse casually declared.

Carlos stopped and smiled at the sturdy war chief. "Sooner than you think, amigo. At dawn tomorrow we ride for Carrizo Springs. A week after that, you will be counting many coups, and you will each have a white woman for your squaw, I promise this."

Ipiltse glanced significantly at his two companions as the three of them followed Carlos to the ramshackle hut that the bandit leader had made his headquarters.

CHAPTER THIRTY

The fires had gone out in the abandoned village of Puertocare, but, though it was nearly midnight and most of Carlos's bandits had wrapped themselves in their blankets and gone to sleep, some of them stayed awake with tequila and boastful stories of their valor and what they would do to the men and women of the *rancheria gringa* that they would attack within the week. Ipiltse, Ekinato, and Tiskewa had been forced to share the merriment. Traditionally, Mexicans had always dreaded Comanches, fearing them and yet respecting them for their fierce, merciless forays. Two of the men, Bernardo Villegas and Romero Suarte, seemed most eager to learn from their three new *compañeros* whether the Comanche or the Apache way of warfare was the superior, whether the deaths by torture that they meted out to their ene-

mies surpassed in inventive cruelty the methods
employed by the savage warriors from New Mexico and Arizona.

Ipiltse, his face impassive, told the story of Manuelo Arvilas and how he had been buried to his
neck in the earth, then scalped, his bleeding head
and face smeared with honey and ants set upon
him. He did not identify the victim by name, lest
one of the bandits link it to the chief who had ordered that punishment of Catayuna's former husband. Indeed, when Carlos had asked his three
newest recruits the name of the chief of their
stronghold, Ipiltse had answered, "He is called
Desmagata, and in our tongue it means He Who is
Too Old for War. This is what we who hate the
white-eyes have named him, and he sulks in his
tepee like a fearful old woman."

"Still," Romero Suarte said, his voice thickened
from tequila, "it is good to have a Comanche with
us. The *muchachas gringas* fear *los Indios* more
than a *Mejicano*. I remember two years ago in
Jalisco, there was an English señorita traveling with
her old aunt and uncle to see Mexico and to visit
her father. The señorita was very rude to me, and
this I cannot tolerate. That night, when her uncle
and aunt had gone to sleep, I crept through her
window, gagged and bound her, and carried her off
to my hut. Then I sat her in a chair, tied one hand
to the table, and left the other free for what reasons
you will soon guess. I left the gag in her mouth as I
began to cut splinters from a piece of wood I had
been whittling. Then I lit them and thrust them
under the nails of her bound hand. I tell you,

411

amigos, I have never found a more eager puta." He shrugged and winked.

"It is not only the *gringas* who are ticklish when there is pain to be felt," Juan Cortigo said, having sauntered over to the group. He pulled from his belt the still-bloody scalp of Isobel and held it up for all to see. "This is from a *Mejicana* whom I came upon not far from a *Comancheria*. Was it not yours, Ipiltse?"

The stocky war chief eyed him coldly, and with the greatest effort kept himself from betraying his feelings. "It may be. There are Mexican women who prefer the Comanche, who acts like a man and does not bray like a burro to the world about what he does, to a man who is part Mexican and only part Indian."

With an oath, Juan Cortigo thrust the scalp back under his belt and drew his knife from its sheath. "Comanche dog, I will cut out your tripes!" he snarled.

"Amigo!" Bernardo Villegas stumbled to his feet and put a conciliatory arm around the half-breed's shoulder. "We are all amigos tonight. Tomorrow we go to kill gringos and to take their women. Let us not quarrel among ourselves. We would do well, all of us, to go to our blankets."

Theobaldo Nuñez yawned, stretched, then cocked his head. "I heard a coyote howl just then."

"No, it was a *mujer* in heat who calls to you, Theobaldo," Bernardo remarked. "Sleep now and dream that you are between her legs, *hombre*. Pray also that you have something to offer her when the time comes."

"Never you mind about *mis cojones*, Bernardo, look to your own. *Buenas noches.*"

Ipiltse and his two comrades watched the men stagger off to the dilapidated huts that they had made into temporary shelters, then rose and headed for one across the way, which was not occupied. As he reached the door, Ipiltse whispered, "You, Tiskewa, go find Kiminardo. It was he who sounded the call of the coyote. Did you mark it?"

"Yes, Ipiltse. I can find him."

"Then tell him that Carlos Macaras and his men ride at dawn for Carrizo Springs. Let him go like the wind to Sangrodo with the news."

The young Comanche disappeared into the shadows of the night behind the hut. When he had skirted all the huts, he cupped his palms to his mouth and made the cry of the coyote, which was echoed from a distance to the west. A few moments later, the two young braves squatted behind a clump of mesquite. Then Kiminardo hurried to his mustang, which he had tethered far beyond, concealed by manzanita and mesquite bushes, and rode back to the stronghold of Sangrodo.

The Comanche chief had left Catayuna, drowsy and languorous with love, on the blanket of their tepee. He breathed deeply, and his thin lips curved in a smile of delight, for his Mexican squaw was the most ardent and eager woman he had ever known. Yes, even more than the mother of Kitante. Truly was she called the beloved woman. And now, that soft, satiny belly that had merged against his contained the tiny life of his unborn son, a son who might one day be chief, unless the elders voted for Kitante. By rights, of course, they should

413

and yet he felt a special tenderness for this unborn child. It had been made in love, a love born of courageous defiance and then heroic self-sacrifice. Even Amara, who had given him Kitante, could not, he thought, have taken a soldier's bullet and yet found the strength to mount a horse and ride miles over rough country to warn him as Catayuna had done.

He heard the drumming sound of Kiminardo's mustang before he saw the young Comanche gallop into the stronghold, and hurried forward to meet him. Then he listened, his face grave, and when the young brave had finished, he said, "Go waken all the fighting men of this village. Bring them here to me, with their weapons and their horses. We ride ahead of the bandidos. We shall keep here only enough to safeguard our women and children. I myself shall ride ahead of all of you, to warn the people of the ranch. It is a debt I owe to my white-eyes brother."

Half an hour later, Sangrodo and twenty of his braves rode out, armed with lances, tomahawks, knives, bows and arrows, and what old rifles they had retained in their flight across the border nearly two years ago. Among the braves who followed Sangrodo was Menigsay, the young Comanche husband of the ravished and murdered Isobel.

Catayuna stood in front of the tepee, watching the horsemen gallop out of the stronghold. Her eyes were luminous. She pressed her hands to her belly, looked up at the cloudless sky, and murmured a prayer to the Holy Mother to preserve both the father and her unborn child. She stood there watching until they disappeared into the

414

darkness, and then she turned and went back into the tepee. There she knelt down, clasped her hands, bowed her head, and prayed as she had been taught in the old church of Maxtime.

Carlos Macaras swung himself into the saddle, dressed in green tunic, riding breeches, and boots, his repeating rifle held by a cloth sling around his neck, with the rawhide-thonged rosary beneath it. The beads gleamed brightly as the sun rose, and he turned back to look at his riders, a grim smile curving his lips. *"Muerte a los gringos!"* he shouted, then spurred his horse toward the northwest.

Ipiltse, Ekinato, and Tiskewa rode at the end of the double column, their faces stolid. To have disappeared in the night would have been to rouse the suspicions of the bandit leader, who might readily turn his savage horde upon the stronghold, which Juan Cortigo had already discovered. Nor could they know what action Sangrodo would take even with the advance knowledge of the attack against Windhaven Range. They could only ride along, waiting to see what course of action to take as the moment presented itself.

But well ahead of them, the mestizo who wore that grisly scalp under his belt had his own misgivings about the three Comanches who had joined them, and he turned to mutter to Bernardo Villegas, "I do not trust those new men. They talk of a weak old chief who does nothing, and yet I myself saw that there were at least forty huts and tepees in their stronghold. Why, then, did not other young braves come to help us kill the gringos and rob

415

them of their women? I say they may have been sent here to trick us, to betray us!"

Bernardo Villegas glanced back over his shoulder, then retorted, "I too have wondered why there were not more of them to ride with us, Juan. We shall both watch them, and we shall kill them at the least sign of treachery. I will ride up to the *jefe* and tell him what we think." And with this, spurring his horse, he rode up beside Carlos Macaras and swiftly informed him of the mestizo's suspicions, then rode back to his place in the double line.

Ipiltse had not lost the significance of this maneuver, and made signs with his hand to his two companions to be on their guard. As he rode, he inspected the priming of his old Sharps buffalo gun, and kept his mustang to the pace set by the others.

It was the evening of March 10, and Maybelle was just serving supper. Tim and Connie Belcher and Carla and Hugo Bouchard were already at the table, chattering away and impatiently awaiting the special treat Maybelle had promised: her famous pecan pie. Although Celia had returned after the cattle drive to Abilene to resume her previous duties as cook and also personal maid to Sybella Bouchard, Maybelle's enthusiasm for cooking had induced Celia to agree to share mealtime preparation with her that night.

Mara and Ramon Hernandez were in the living room, seated together on the settee, the young vaquero looking adoringly at his wife as she cradled their two-month-old son, Luke, against her bosom. From time to time she sent him a long, ardent look,

416

and then blushed, seeing that Lucien Edmond Bouchard and Maxine, at the other end of the room, were watching them.

Sybella was amusing the children with stories to quell their impatience to be served, while in the bunkhouse Djamba and Lucas prepared to collect the suppers of the vaqueros. Celia was glad to have Maybelle's help, with all these riders to feed as well as what she liked to call her "own family."

Mara Bouchard looked up happily and called to Maxine, "Don't mind us, we're just new parents, that's all."

"I think it's wonderful." Maxine laughed gently, slipping her hand over her husband's and entwining her fingers with his. "The fact is, you aren't the only one, Mara."

"Maxine—you don't have to remind her that we've already got Carla and Hugo," Lucien Edmond said, laughing.

"I wasn't referring to them, darling." Maxine gave him a knowing look, then tossed her head and winked at Mara and Ramon.

Lucien Edmond started, took his wife's hands, and demanded, "Are you trying to tell me—"

"Yes, I think maybe by October."

"That's wonderful, sweetheart!" Heedless of the young couple opposite him, Lucien Edmond took Maxine in his arms and kissed her till her cheeks were flaming and she pretended to push him away in embarrassment. Then suddenly he released her.

"What's the matter? Don't tell me you're not happy about it, Lucien Edmond?" Maxine asked anxiously.

Lucien Edmond shook his head. "You know I

love Carla and Hugo, and of course I want another child. As many as you want to give me, darling. I was just thinking of something that happened on the trail drive."

"I declare," Maxine quickly recovered her aplomb, "sometimes I think you love your cattle more than you do me!"

He did not tell her that he had just remembered the prediction of the blind old Creek shaman who had said that his wife would bear a child before the next winter. And he remembered what else the shaman had foretold—that the danger he feared had already passed and that the shadow of death would be near him and yet would not touch him. And it had all come true now: the bandit attack on the ranch while he had been away on the drive and its rout by the loyal defenders of Windhaven Range; the ambush by the bushwhackers to avenge the death of the man Ramon Hernandez had been forced to kill to save his own life; and now Maxine's announcement that she was expecting. But what he said was, "It's my work, Maxine, but you're my love. And if you haven't learned the difference yet, then I'm not the smart husband you took me for."

Then he directed his words to the young vaquero: "Ramon, how are we doing with those ten Hereford bulls I had shipped from Kentucky?"

"We should have quite a few calves within the next few weeks, Lucien Edmond," he replied. "You told me that you expect to add as much as three hundred pounds to the weight of every steer when you cross the Herefords with the longhorns."

"That's what Henry Bascomb of Lexington wrote

me when I was told that he was raising prime Herefords. You know, the Herefords are sturdy, and I suspect they won't get infected with this Texas fever the people in Kansas and Missouri are so worried about. I've tried to find out something about Brahmas too. When we rode to Corpus Christi back in January to pick up our shipment from Mr. Bascomb, there was a deckhand on the steamer who'd worked on a Missouri cattle ranch before the war. He was telling me that Brahmas are about the healthiest cattle there are, and they can adapt themselves to just 'bout any kind of grazing. It's something worth looking into."

"Oh, you men!" Maxine exclaimed as she rose and held out her hand to Lucien Edmond. "Would you mind escorting your wife instead of a Brahma or a Hereford into the dining room so that we can have supper, please?"

They had just seated themselves at the table when Jubal's angry barking made them look toward the shuttered window. Lucien Edmond rose from the table and strode out to the living room, unbolted the door, and peered outside. Jubal was leaping at the gate of the stockade, and Lucien Edmond could see the figure of a man on horseback. He had left his Spencer repeating rifle leaning against the wall, and reached down to retrieve it as he called out, "Who's there?"

"It is Sangrodo of the Comanches," was the answer.

Lucien Edmond ran down the path and opened the gate. Sangrodo dismounted and, holding the reins in one hand and his feathered lance in the other, exclaimed, "My braves and I come to bring you warning and to help you. The brother of Diego Macaras and many men ride against you. They are only a few hours behind us."

"Well, this time we'll be ready for him," said Lucien Edmond. "I am grateful for your warning, Sangrodo. But I cannot ask you to take part in my battle against those bandits. You and your braves have risked your lives riding back across the border."

"Seven suns and seven moons, oh son of my white-eyes brother," Sangrodo declared. "But we have come, twenty of my strongest, youngest warriors and I, to fight beside you. We have a score to settle with those evil ones. Already Menigsay mourns his Mexican squaw, used and cruelly killed by one of the bandidos. It is our vengeance we seek here too."

"I cannot deny you that right, Sangrodo. But your men do not have weapons enough to fight the bandits. They have waited for months to attack us again; surely they must have bought the newest rifles and pistols."

"We will take them by surprise. We shall hide beyond the creek, in that grove of trees. When they come this way, as they soon will, we will fall upon them from behind. You must be ready. They will use every means they can to break down this enclosure to get to your house. Have your vaqueros arm themselves and be ready!"

"You are a loyal friend, Sangrodo. I shall not forget this. And my father shall hear of it. Now I shall go warn the men." Lucien Edmond extended his hand to the tall Comanche chief, who shook it, then touched Lucien Edmond's heart with his other palm and nodded. As Lucien Edmond ran toward the bunkhouse, Sangrodo mounted his mustang and shouted a command in his own tongue to the warriors who waited near the creek. They turned their horses, rode through the shallow creek, and disappeared among the trees on the other side.

Andy Haskins and Joe Duvray, hearing Lucien Edmond's swift explanation, assigned the thirty vaqueros to their posts. Some knelt on the south side of the stockade, their rifles and carbines aimed through the spaces Djamba had left for that purpose. Two of them stood guard over the corral, where already the horses were restless, having heard Jubal's barking. Andy and Joe dragged a ladder out of the stable, placed it against the back of the ranchhouse, and ascended to the roof, where they stretched out flat, their repeating rifles loaded and ready for action.

Meanwhile, Lucien Edmond had alerted the women, and Sybella, Maybelle, Maxine, Mara, and Celia herded the children into a large closet adjoining the master bedroom. Sybella, hugging the children, explained, "It's going to be a game, a very noisy game, and we don't want you to get hurt. Now you stay here, and if you're very good and don't make a fuss, each of you will get an extra piece of Maybelle's pecan pie. Here's your doll, Carla—and, Hugo, here's your whistle that Andy whittled for you. If you don't like the noise, you can just whistle and try to drown it out, you see?" Then, looking at Tim and Connie, she added, "You two are the oldest, so you look after Carla and Hugo. Don't let them go outside this closet. We'll

421

just close the door partway, so you'll have plenty of air to breathe. Now don't be frightened."

Henry Belcher had seized his old Whitworth and was priming and loading it, angrily muttering to himself, "Damned rascals, didn't get enough the last time? Well, we'll do a better job this time, my Whitworth and me, they'll find out!" He affectionately ran his fingers over the smooth barrel of the old sharpshooter rifle.

They were fording the Rio Grande and heading toward Carrizo Springs. Carlos Macaras, feverishly impatient now that the end of his quest was near, had begrudged his men even their sleep during this week-long ride. It would soon be dusk, and he was anxious to reach the creek beyond the Nueces River, where he would deploy his men and begin the attack. Remembering the advice of Juan Cortigo, he had taken along three wooden carts, stolen from a farmer on their way from Puertocare. Now he halted his men, dismounted, strode toward a clump of mesquite, and ordered: "Let's fill the carts. The mesquite is dry, it will go up in flames swiftly, and then we will set them rolling toward the gate."

Juan Cortigo had dismounted and was moving toward his chief when suddenly he stooped and squinted at the ground. "*Mi jefe*," he called, "come see this!"

"*Que pasa, hombre?*"

"See for yourself, Senor Manos. These are the tracks of many horses. Horses that go where we are going, I think."

"I see them," Carlos said slowly, tilting his som-

422

brero back on his head and scowling. "What do you make of those tracks, Juan?"

Lowering his voice to a whisper, the half-breed replied, "I have Indian blood in my veins, and I can scout as well as any Comanche or Apache. These are the prints of unshod horses, and only the Comanche or the Apache would have so many."

"*Por Dios y todos los santos!*" Carlos swore softly. "You think those three Comanche recruits of ours were sent to spy on us, and somehow got word to their stronghold to warn the gringos?"

"*Sí, mi jefe.*"

Carlos unslung his repeating rifle and moved toward the back of the column, a deceptive smile on his pockmarked face as he neared the three riders at the end. "Amigos," he said in an airy tone, "Juan here has found something interesting. But he is only half Indian, and you are Comanches. Perhaps you will read the signs better than he can."

Ipiltse sent a quick glance at Ekinato and Tiskewa, and as he prepared to dismount he drew the Sharps gun out of its sheath. But Carlos had seen the movement, and, dropping to one knee, brought up the repeating rifle and triggered it. Ipiltse uttered a strangled cry as he slid from the saddle, rolled over and over, and finally lay still, face down on the northern bank of the Rio Grande. Ekinato drew back his arm, ready to cast his lance, but another burst of rifle fire sent him tumbling to the ground, and then without a pause Carlos aimed at Tiskewa's head and pulled the trigger.

"There are three for the buzzards to feed on, *hombres*," Carlos said between his teeth as he went back to his horse. "Now, *adelante, mi compañeros!*

Have your weapons ready. It may be that we shall have to fight Comanches before we kill the gringos! They may be hiding, waiting for us." Lifting his rifle toward the sky, Carlos Macaras spurred his horse and rode on toward Windhaven Range.

Just before they reached the Nueces River, Juan Cortigo dismounted, having called to Carlos to halt the men, and examined the tracks. Testing them with his finger, he said, "They are only a few hours old. And they follow the same way we go. Yes, truly those Comanches were spies, and their braves will ambush us when we reach the *rancheria*."

"Then they will hide behind trees or bushes, for the land is not hilly once we cross the river. *Hombres*, the moment you see trees or bushes behind which men could hide, fire shots into it to flush them out. We shall soon be there, we shall enjoy the *dinero* and the *mujeres* as I promised you. And now, *adelante con cuidado!*"

Now they had crossed the river, taking an approach from the east that would flank the ranchhouse and come up on its southern side. Once again the mestizo called for a halt, and although it was dark he could see that the tracks had veered to the west. "Señor Manos, you have been here before—where would the Comanches hide in ambush against us?" he demanded.

"There is mesquite and trees just beyond the creek. They would be there, *hombre*. But lower your voice now. It is nearly midnight, and perhaps we can take both the Comanches and the gringos by surprise," Carlos averred in a low voice.

Then he gave orders to unharness the horses from the carts, for the clattering sound of the wheels along the ground would be a signal to ambushers. Mesquite, dead twigs, and dry branches were thickly piled, and more was added to replace what had dropped out in the jolting ride across the Rio Grande.

"Now," Carlos instructed, "tie your horses where you can, take your weapons, and you, Bernardo and Romero, push the carts up toward the stockade. It is perhaps three hundred yards from where we are now. Be careful, for the gringos are surely sleeping. Juan, have you seen any more signs of the Comanches?"

"No, *mi jefe*."

"*Bueno*. Not too much noise with those carts, you idiots!" Carlos raised his voice to an angry sotto voce as Bernardo and Romero had begun to push the carts noisily along the uneven ground. "That's a little better. You will light the fire just before you reach the stockade. Put a cart near the gate if you can, and the other one there by the side of the house. Juan, take yours still farther east. Be quick now, and as little noise as you can!"

He turned and knelt, squinting in the darkness as he looked to the west. Very dimly, at what appeared to be a good quarter mile beyond, he could see the outlines of trees and bushes. He instinctively touched the rawhide-thonged rosary at his neck; the talisman would make his victory certain. Surely if the Comanches had gone ahead, by now they would have left their ambush and attacked in full force.

Juan, Bernardo, and Romero had begun to draw

the carts slowly and as quietly as they could toward the stockade. As they neared it, the two defenders on the roof of the ranchhouse opened fire with their repeating rifles, and Bernardo spun around and fell full length, with a bullet through his brain. Romero cried out in agony as a bullet ripped through his left shoulder, dropped his hold on the cart, and ran back to where the rest of the bandits waited, a hand pressed against his bleeding shoulder. But the half-breed was more successful. At the first sound of the shots he had flung himself down on his belly and crawled under the cart. Now he made ready with his lucifer, reached overhead, and scratched it till it burst into flame. Then he very carefully crawled just beyond it, and, shifting himself onto his back to look upward, tossed the lucifer into the solidly packed mesquite and twigs. Instantly it flared up, and he grinned to himself, then began to crawl away.

Carlos Macaras smashed his fist into his palm and swore. "We have been betrayed, amigos!" he called hoarsely to several of the desperadoes crouching near him. "The Comanche braves may even now be near us, watching what we do. Attack with all strength, *fuego!*"

Five of his men leveled their guns at the shuttered windows on the south side of the house and fired. Instantly, Andy Haskins and Joe Duvray, on the roof, returned the fire with their Spencers, and two of the desperadoes slumped forward, one dead, the other mortally wounded. Juan Cortigo had crawled back to Bernardo's abandoned cart, struck another lucifer, and threw it into the cart, and the dry mesquite instantly burst into flame.

426

"Bueno, bueno, Juan!" Carlos shouted; then, taking shelter behind a live oak tree, he raised his repeating rifle and fired at the roof, where he had seen the flashes from the two young Southerners' rifles.

All the bullets whined past Andy Haskins's ear, and he chuckled as he said to his friend, "Never yet saw a bandido who could shoot for accuracy. They get panicky when they're under fire. Let's keep 'em hoppin' so they'll use up all their ammunition!"

The blazing carts had now spread their leaping tongues of flame to the tall, dry wooden posts against which they were lodged. Lucien Edmond had poked his Spencer repeating rifle through one of the wooden shutters in the living room, which faced south, and squinted through the darkness as he held his rifle trained on the conflagration, certain that some of the desperadoes would try to break through the openings made by the fire.

Sangrodo had held his warriors in check in their hiding place, waiting to see the disposition of Carlos Macaras's band. Now he beckoned to three of his youngest men, expert marksmen with the bow and arrow, to move forward, bent low to the ground and out of sight of the desperadoes, who had their backs to them. When they came within a hundred feet of the trees behind which Carlos and five of his men were crouching, sending volleys of pistol and rifle fire at the ranchhouse, they each knelt on one knee, drew back their bows to maximum, and then there was the deadly hum of arrows in flight. The man to the right of the bandit leader staggered back, dropping his Belgian rifle, reached around in an effort to tear the arrow out of his back, then pitched forward. With a cry of mingled anger and fear, Carlos slipped around the tree, knelt, and fired at the shadowy figures. One of the braves grunted as the bullet tore through his right upper arm. But another brave launched an arrow that thudded into the tree only a few inches from Carlos's head, and once again he backed away and sought new shelter.

Two of the desperadoes now ran forward, seized the tongue of Bernardo's cart, and rammed the vehicle with all their strength against the burning posts, which gave way. With cries of triumph they edged through the jagged opening, one of them instantly felled by a shot from Lucien Edmond's rifle. The other ran toward the porch like one possessed, carrying his rifle in his left hand and a machete in the other. Henry Belcher had unbolted the door and partially opened it, laid himself flat on the floor, and leveled his Whitworth. There was a sharp report, and the running desperado stumbled just as he reached the edge of the porch, then sprawled, lifeless.

Half a dozen desperadoes had crawled up to the stockade from the eastern side and were aiming at the bunkhouse and the back of the ranchhouse. The door of the bunkhouse opened, and Lucas and his father, Djamba, opened fire at the flashes of flame that betrayed the desperadoes' position. A gurgling scream rang out as one of them dropped, with a bullet in his throat, and another's hoarse shout announced a shattered arm that made him drop his gun and crawl back to the bushes and trees. Andy Haskins saw him crawling, snapped

428

off a shot from his repeating rifle, and the man shuddered, then lay still.

Now Sangrodo made a sign, and ten of his riders mounted their mustangs and, leveling their feathered lances, rode toward the bandits, uttering the terrifying war whoops of the embattled Comanche. Taken by surprise, three of the men beside Carlos Macaras turned and fired at the oncoming riders, killing one of the braves. A moment later, one of the bandits dropped his pistol and sank to his knees, the point of a lance having pierced his chest. The other two men fired again, but to no avail. They rose and began to run, but Menigsay skewered one of them in the neck, contemptuously tugged out the lance, and watched the man drop like a dead weight to the ground. The other, frantically dodging the thundering hooves approaching him, managed to elude the Comanche pursuer, but the point of the lance nicked his shoulder and made him stumble long enough for the brave to wheel his horse back and plunge the lance into his heart.

Sybella carbine in hand, crouched beside the bedroom window, saw shadowy figures drop down from the top of the stockade and fired twice. Each of the desperadoes staggered, one of them tumbling forward on his face, the other staggering, his hand clasped against his bleeding side. From the rooftop Joe Duvray finished him off with a shot through the head.

Carlos Macaras, in the confusion, had managed to lope, crouching as low as he could beyond the creek. There he found one of the horses, which had broken its tether and was idly grazing. Mounting it, he rode off to the south, mouthing vitriolic curses, hell in his heart at the downfall of his arduous and elaborate plan for vengeance. The surviving desperadoes knew their cause was lost. Half a dozen of them broke for their horses, and were shot down or speared before they could reach them. Only Juan Cortigo, who had crawled back beyond the horses, had escaped the rout of all the bandits. Mounting his horse, he rode off in the same direction that Carlos had taken.

There was silence now. The volleys of gunfire had died away and the shouts and curses of the desperadoes were stilled forever. Sangrodo emerged from the thicket behind which he had watched the attack of the braves, and lifted his feathered lance with a victorious cry, his eyes fixed on the dark, brooding sky as he thanked the Great Spirit for keeping his pledge to protect the Indian's white-eyes brother.

Warily, Lucien Edmond emerged from the house, his repeating rifle ready, and Henry Belcher joined him, having reloaded the old Whitworth. "It's over, thank God," said Lucien Edmond. "Henry, go back and tell Sybella that the children can come out now. Thank God for Sangrodo."

"Amen to that, Lucien Edmond." Henry straightened and rubbed his knee, with a grimace. "I'm not as young as I used to be, and I'm glad as hell that it's over. But if we hadn't had that warning—I don't even want to think what could have happened."

"I must go see if anyone was hurt, Henry. Go comfort Maybelle and the children." Lucien Edmond patted him on the back, then hurried around

430

to the bunkhouse. Djamba and Lucas met him, leading the exultant vaqueros, while Andy Haskins and Joe Duvray climbed down from the roof, grinning from ear to ear.

"Joe, Andy," Lucien Edmond said, "you both deserve medals. Now let's go thank Sangrodo. If it hadn't been for him, this siege could have gone on for a long time, and we might have had a lot of injuries."

The tall Comanche chief sat astride his horse, waiting beside the gate, his other braves mounted on their mustangs behind him. Lucien Edmond quickly lifted the plank to open the gate and went out to offer his hand in gratitude to the Comanche leader. "Can I send back any supplies with your braves, Sangrodo? Do you need food or weapons or anything I have to give you?"

Sangrodo proudly shook his head. "In our new stronghold we do not starve. There is much that is new for us, but we are trying to learn it with each new day. I came because of my vow to your father. That you and your family and all those who work with you are safe is payment enough for Sangrodo."

"Some things can never be repaid, except in lasting friendship, Sangrodo," Lucien Edmond solemnly answered as he gripped the chief's hand again and they eyed each other with mutual respect.

The tall Comanche leader chuckled dryly as he began to turn his mount's head toward the south. "There is a piece of news your black man and the woman who cooks at your fires will be glad of," he added casually. "Tell them that the squaw of Ji-

431

cinte is again with child. She sends greetings to her father, mother, and brother. She hopes that you will come visit her in the summer."

"Tell Prissy we certainly shall, as soon as we can, Sangrodo. And now do you go back to the stronghold?"

Sangrodo's face suddenly grew grave. "We ride swiftly back, oh son of my white-eyes brother. My braves tell me that the evil one who led these men against you has escaped, and with him at least one other. We fear they may try to take vengeance on the women and children of our village. May the Great Spirit watch over you and your family and those who work beside you on the land." Then, lifting his feathered lance in salute to Lucien Edmond, Sangrodo rode off to the south, and his braves followed, each saluting Lucien Edmond, Djamba, Lucas, and the assembled vaqueros, who returned the salutes with loud cheers.

There was black rage in Carlos Macaras's heart as he spurred his chestnut gelding back along the route whence he had come. All that was left now was the solace of those buried silver crosses, which he need share with no one. Yet how much better it could have been if he had destroyed that *rancheria gringa!*

He urged the horse to its swiftest gallop for as long as he dared, frequently glancing back over his shoulder to see if he was being pursued. Those Comanches—they would be returning to their stronghold now, but if he could get there first, he could kill a few of them to pay them back.

Suddenly he heard a shout to his left, and he

saw that it was the squat half-breed, Juan Cortigo, quickening his horse's gait to overtake him. Carlos slowed his gelding to a trot, for it was high time, and let the half-breed come up beside him.

CHAPTER THIRTY-ONE

"We came out badly, *no es verdad, mi jefe?*" Juan Cortigo exclaimed cynically as he eyed the pockmarked bandit leader.

"If it hadn't been for those *diablos rojos*, things would have been different," Carlos snapped. He glanced back over his shoulder, but the blackness of the night hardly eased his fears. He had learned years ago that many of the Comanche and Apache tribes did not subscribe to the age-old Indian tradition that attacks be perpetrated in the day lest those who were killed be denied the passage of their souls to the Great Spirit. And now that he saw that his only surviving aide was the very man who had found the Comanche stronghold and violated and killed the Mexican squaw, he began to feel fear. Somehow he must rid himself of Juan Cortigo, even if he had to kill him, because the half-breed, if left to survive, could endanger his life.

"I think we have given them the slip, *mi jefe.*" Juan's words were respectful, but his dark eyes held a sardonic glint and his lips curled contemptuously. "All the same, it would be well for us to ride as hard and as far as we can. They will be after us."

Carlos contented himself with an affirmative nod, for he was already busy planning how best to dispose of the half-breed. And his worst fears were confirmed when Juan, with a nasty little chuckle, casually remarked, "Of course, we did not come off so badly as our poor *compañeros* whom we left back there, Señor Manos. Did you not tell me long ago, when we planned this great campaign, that you had many more silver crosses like the one you showed me?"

Carlos ground his teeth in thwarted fury. Was it not enough to have failed? Would this dirty little half-breed now try to claim the only profit left to him after all the long, agonizing months of planning? If his repeating rifle had not already been back in its sheath and both his hands occupied with the reins, he would have shot Juan Cortigo down like a dog here and now. He forced himself to say in a dull tone of voice, "That's true, amigo. I'd forgotten about them. I wanted so much to kill all those gringos who murdered my poor brother— and then to find that we'd been betrayed in advance . . ."

"*Comprendo*, amigo." The half-breed nodded sympathetically, an unctuous smile on his lips, which made his beetle-browed face look even more

435

repulsive. "But we can help each other, you and I. I know very well what you are thinking, amigo. You would like to kill me now, and go back and dig up your crosses, wherever it is you buried them. Unless, of course, you only have that one, and took us all in with your fine stories."

"The crosses are there, just as I said they were," Carlos snapped, and then could have bitten off his tongue, realizing that he had been neatly tricked by the crafty mestizo.

"It is true that we did not beat the gringos," Juan continued, now glancing back over his shoulder to see whether anyone had yet picked up their trail. "But you will remember, Señor Manos, that I told you of finding the stronghold where Ipiltse and his two spying friends came from, and how I took my pleasure with that plump Mexican *paloma*."

"And what of it?"

"If the Comanches come after us, as I think they will, they would not expect us to head for their own camp." The half-breed's voice took on the patronizing tone one adopts speaking to a child whose mental capacities are limited. "It was only I, Juan Cortigo, who enjoyed the embraces of a fine *mujer* all the time we stayed in that filthy little village of Puertocare. You yourself, *mi jefe*, never brought women there, as I recall."

"Idiot, of course I didn't! What I wanted was the women of those gringos, far tastier than any *Mejicana*."

"For the sake of argument, *mi jefe*, I will grant you the difference. But suppose we were to go to the Comanche camp, which would not have many

436

braves there, since surely most of them were at the *rancheria*. What is to prevent our having our fill of their women—better still, taking the prettiest along with us to console us for our great defeat in battle?"

Carlos sharply eyed the half-breed. It was not a bad idea at all. It would certainly be dangerous, but his ego led him to think that by abducting the squaw of the chief, he might be able to salvage a victory from the defeat. He had often heard that Indian women were ferociously passionate, gifted with tricks that even a costly Mexican *puta* could not surpass. Then too, if this crafty little rogue was occupied with trying to abduct a Comanche squaw, it would be easier to use the repeating rifle on him. Then he would ride back to Nuevo Laredo, dig up the crosses, and start life all over again—this time as a wealthy gentleman.

Por Dios, the idiot's idea had a certain merit to it, if he could turn it to his own advantage. There was even an exciting bravado to it—two men riding into a Comanche camp and coming out with pretty squaws. Besides, he had enough ammunition to kill what few braves had been left to guard the stronghold.

All this flashed through his mind in an instant. He seemed to ponder, scowling at the dark terrain beyond, then glancing back once more, and finally replied, "At least this way, Juan, we can pay those red devils back a little for what they did to our brave *compañeros*."

"*Es verdad, mi jefe!* But we must keep riding or the warriors will catch up. Also, we shall need fresh horses before much longer."

"Do you remember that little village a few miles southeast of the Rio Grande? We flanked it when we rode to the *rancheria*. I saw horses there, and we shall take them."

"Agreed. Now you think like a true *jefe* of bandidos." Juan grinned and mockingly doffed his sombrero in salute.

Carlos was not deceived. He trusted Juan Cortigo no more than the half-breed trusted him. But he would go along with this amusing adventure. He would let the half-breed choose a squaw and drag her to his horse, and then he would kill the son of a *puta* take the chief's squaw, and ride back to Nuevo Laredo. She would be his slave in a villa that he would buy after he had disposed of the silver crosses. He would teach her how to obey him, to serve him on her knees, to teach him all the little tricks she knew. The first time they were alone together, he would start with a good thrashing—that was always the best way to teach a *mujer* who was the master.

After a moment he said, "How many rounds of ammunition do you have left, amigo?"

"About two dozen. But I have my machete and my knife. But you, Señor Manos, have the best weapon of all, the repeating rifle. A pity we could not get more of them."

"I am thinking that if you and the others had fired a few shots into the trees and bushes from which the Comanches attacked us, things might have been different."

"It's better this way, *mi jefe*. There are only two of us left to enjoy the money which those crosses will bring. If we had been successful and burned

438

the ranch and taken the women, you would have had to share the crosses with all the *compañeros, no es verdad?*" This time the half-breed's voice was sly and wheedling, and he sent a malicious glance at the pockmarked bandit leader.

Carlos ground his teeth again. The idiot held on to the idea of the crosses as a dog clenches an old bone between its jaws. Well, he too could play at being cunning. He turned to stare at the half-breed, and said with a sardonic smile, "Have you thought, Juan Cortigo, that if you kill me, you will never know where the crosses are hidden? You need me, amigo, as much as I need you."

"I admire your frankness, Señor Manos. Truth, they say, is good for the soul. I myself do not go to see the good *padre* as often as I should, so I cannot tell if that is really so. But since you are being frank with me, I do not mind telling you what has been on my mind for some time now. I thought of killing you when I saw that you did not move from behind your tree and did not take active part in the attack. I, you will recall, was the only one who was truly successful tonight. Was it not I who lit the cart and started the fence blazing? And I saw all my good comrades fall to the Comanches and the gringos, and I told myself that you were not a good general—that if you knew how difficult it was before, you should have taken more precautions to make sure the attack was successful this time."

"You dare—" Carlos began in a choked, furious voice.

"I dare speak my mind since you have said what was on yours, that is all, *mi jefe*. But you see, I did not kill you. And I do not think you will kill me either, since both of us must go into the Comanche camp. Besides, if the braves behind us should catch up with us, it would be better to have two guns against them than one."

"Agreed, agreed! Now, enough talk—let us ride to that village. We shall not sleep tonight, but shall change horses and go on. You will show me the shortest way to the stronghold. We must have several hours' advantage before they catch up with us."

They came to the sleeping little village just before dawn, went to one of the stables, and chose the two best horses. Quickly saddling and mounting them, they galloped on into the night. It was Juan Cortigo who proposed that they should double back on the trail, cross a little creek, then turn the horses back northward for a few hundred yards, before going through the creek again and heading south. Such dissembling would cost the pursuers an hour or two, a vital gain of time for the pursued.

On the third day they again exchanged horses, stealing two fine stallions from the stable of an elderly farmer who was the *alcalde* of a small, isolated village. Hearing the whinnying and stamping of horses' hooves in the night, he left his bed and came out to the stable. Juan Cortigo swiftly gripped the handle of his machete, lifted it, and struck, decapitating the old man. Then he glanced mockingly at Carlos Macaras as he examined the blade, after wiping off the blood. "I hope his scrawny neck did not nick this fine blade too much. No, there was no harm done, *bueno*." Meaningfully, he turned the machete over and over between his hands, eyeing the bandit leader, then thrust it back under his belt. Despite his concealed rage, Carlos could not suppress a shiver of fear.

They rode on through the night without stopping, letting the stallions water and graze only briefly at dawn. Then they continued toward Sangrodo's stronghold.

It was twilight, and Catayuna had come out of the tepee to help kindle the cooking fires. Kitante, swaggering with pride, now accepted Catayuna virtually as a Comanche. He would never forget how, long ago, she had made him saddle a horse, wounded though she was, so that she could ride to his father to tell him what the soldiers had done to the peaceful village. And the news that he might soon have a little brother puffed him up with pride, since it made him feel older and more important, truly a man now.

The older braves who had been left back at the stronghold to guard it waited in their tepees for their Mexican squaws to bring them the evening meal. Some of them sat together, telling stories of the old days in Texas, boasting of their coups. Prissy, her face radiant with the knowledge that she would bear another child soon, was the most industrious, as if to set an example for the Mexican women. Dolores Lopez, a buxom twenty-year-old Mexican who had chosen a Comanche who was twice her age, began to light a fire. Once it was going, she skillfully skinned the wild rabbit her husband had shot with his bow and arrow this very

441

morning, and began to prepare and season it the way her mother had taught her.

Kitante walked along with Catayuna, chattering about the latest gossip of the stronghold—how Mercedes Sanchez, the sulky young Mexican wife of Epikinto, had snatched the switch out of his hand when he had tried to thrash her the other night. She had actually hit Epikinto with it twice, till he forgave her. And Elena Raimondi, forever combing out her long hair and boasting about how much more beautiful it was than her neighbors', had been dragged into an empty tepee by four women who told her that if she said such a thing again, they would cut off all her hair.

Catayuna laughed and affectionately patted Kitante on the back. His eyes sparkled with pleasure at this accolade from the beloved woman of the tribe. He had his bow and his quiver of arrows strung about his shoulders, and had volunteered to help her pick a few pieces of firewood, since she had promised to make him a special corn pudding.

The two of them had reached the entry to the stronghold when Dolores Lopez hailed Catayuna and asked her to have a look at the way she was preparing the rabbit for her husband. It was at that precise moment that Juan Cortigo and Carlos Macaras rode up on their stallions. "What good luck, amigo!" Juan muttered to his companion. "They've walked right up to us, asking to ride with us. Let us oblige them at once, *mi jefe!*" With this, swiftly dismounting and drawing his machete from his belt, he lunged toward Dolores and seized her by the wrists. She uttered a shriek, but the gleam-

ing upraised blade petrified her and she did not
resist as he snarled at her in Spanish, "Get astride
my horse quickly, woman, or you die!"

Carlos Macaras had dismounted too, pulling
his repeating rifle out of the improvised sheath.
Kitante uttered a cry of warning and turned to run
back into the stronghold to summon the warriors.
With a snarl, Carlos lifted his repeating rifle, and
was about to trigger it when Catayuna flung the
basket she had been carrying for the firewood
directly at his face. Taken by surprise, the pockmarked bandit leader dropped the rifle, cursed
furiously, then stooped to retrieve it. Catayuna
drew a skinning knife from the pocket of her buckskin skirt and ran at him just as he straightened.
Savagely, still gripping the gun barrel with both
hands, he flailed at her, the heavy butt driving
against her belly. The handsome Mexican woman
uttered a cry of inexpressible agony, doubling over
for an instant, as he staggered to his feet and
prepared to level the rifle at an older warrior who
was running from one of the distant tepees at his
left, a feathered lance drawn back in his right
hand.

With a supreme effort, her face ashen pale and
contorted in agony, Catayuna lunged with her left
hand for the rawhide-thonged rosary around Carlos's neck and twisted it, pulling him toward her.
Instinctively he freed one hand from the rifle to try
to ease the sudden choking pressure, and at that
moment, with her last strength, Catayuna thrust
her skinning knife to the hilt into his belly.

He gasped hoarsely, then the rifle dropped from
his other hand as he clasped both to the haft of the

skinning knife, staggered backward, and fell, his heels digging spasmodically into the ground, his body arching in a final spasm.

There was the thunder of hooves as Sangrodo and his warriors galloped into the stronghold. Juan Cortigo had just mounted his stallion, having ordered the terrified Dolores to lock her arms around him, and galloped off to the southeast.

But Menigsay, who rode behind Sangrodo, had seen the scalp with the two long black plaits dangling from the half-breed's belt, and uttered the savage cry in Comanche: "He is mine, I claim him, Sangrodo!"

Then, leveling his feathered lance, the young warrior rode after the fleeing mestizo, while Dolores, weeping hysterically, looked back over her shoulder and began to babble prayers in Spanish.

With a swift glance over his shoulder, Juan Cortigo saw his pursuer, and with a vile oath pulled the old Belgian rifle out of its sling, took quick aim, and pulled the trigger. Menigsay responded with a derisive yell, shaking his lance above his head, then spurred his horse on. The wiry mustang, one of the swiftest horses of all the plains, began to outrun the maddened stallion, burdened as it was by the weight of two riders.

There was no time for Juan to reload the old Belgian rifle. As he saw Menigsay come steadily nearer, leveling the lance, then drawing it back at shoulder height, the mestizo clutched the reins in his left hand and reversed the rifle to his right so as to use the heavy butt as a club.

Dolores, her eyes wide with disbelief and terror,

saw Menigsay's mustang move closer to the racing stallion whose mouth was lathered with foam.

Now they were nearly side by side, and the young warrior feinted with the lance as Juan, with a defiant scream, swung the rifle toward the grim-faced Comanche. As he lunged, Menigsay countered by driving the point of the lance into his neck. Dolores shrieked, believing herself dead from the fall that would ensue, but Menigsay released the reins of his mustang and, hugging its flanks with his knees, reached for the hysterical young Mexican woman, shouting in Spanish, "Let go of him, put out your arms and lean to me, *mujer!*"

Closing her eyes and praying to the Holy Virgin, Dolores obeyed, and felt herself lifted from the back of the maddened stallion and swung over in front of Menigsay. She opened her eyes to see the stallion gallop on, as Juan Cortigo's lifeless body toppled from the saddle and fell to the ground.

Catayuna slowly opened her eyes, but she could see nothing at first. Her body throbbed with pain. Vaguely she heard the whispered words of Josefa, an old Mexican woman who served as midwife to the village. Then, more clearly, she heard the words of Sangrodo: "Josefa, will she live?"

"*Sí, mi jefe.* But the *niño*, she has lost it. I have done all I could. She must rest, and have a little food when she is able. Draw blankets over her so that the night air will not chill her, *mi jefe.*"

"It will be done, woman. Now leave us."

Catayuna blinked, forcing herself to clear her eyes, and saw her husband standing above her, his face grave with concern, his eyes dark and searching. Then he knelt down beside her. "My—my h-husband—"

"Do not talk, beloved woman. Once again you have saved our village. You have overcome the most evil enemy of all, one who would have destroyed the family of my white-eyes brother and taken you from me. I ask your pardon in coming late to the stronghold, Catayuna. They tricked us on the trail, and, like madmen, they had stopped even less than we for rest and food. Now it is done. You must sleep, beloved woman."

She swallowed, and with great effort spoke again, haltingly. "The ch—the child—"

He put his hand gently on her breast and bent to brush her forehead with his lips. "It is no more, beloved woman. But Josefa says that you will still bear many a strong son. I mourn little He Who Walks in His Father's Footsteps, but I rejoice that you were spared. You are my life—more than my woman, you are the spirit of the Comanche, Catayuna."

She wept then, as his hands stroked her cheeks, and then sleep claimed her, and the last sounds in her ears were his gentle words.

CHAPTER THIRTY-TWO

"Mornin', Mr. Parmenter, sir. Mighty fine morning for early April." Ezekiel Carruthers closed the door of the Lowndesboro General Store, and the little cowbell fixed to it jangled noisily. He made his way to the counter, behind which a short, gray-haired man in his early fifties presided, a dirty apron tied around his coarse denim trousers.

"It is that, Mr. Carruthers. Something special this morning, or the usual?"

"Jist the usual, Mr. Parmenter." The lanky, bearded farmer dug into the pocket of his overalls, took out a crumpled slip of paper, and consulted it. "Bacon, o' course, a barrel of flour, some coffee if you've got it in by now, rice, 'n hominy. Oh yes, and Maria says I'm to git some store candy for the kids."

"Coffee's high now, Mr. Carruthers. We got some

New Orleans-style in, mighty strong for some folks, and so's the price. Fifty cents a pound."

The bearded farmer whistled and shook his head. "Reckon I better tell Maria to go on makin' do the way she's been since the war."

"You're the customer, Mr. Carruthers. I'll have everything else ready in a jiffy. Got your buggy outside?"

"Like always, Mr. Parmenter. If I get a good crop this fall, I'm gonna get me a spry young gelding."

"Can't say I blame you. That mare of yours is just about ready for the boneyard." Hurley Parmenter, his graying brown hair moistly covering the right side of his forehead, reached under the counter and took out a ledger book. "I'll put it down on your account, Mr. Carruthers."

"Mighty obliged." The farmer heaved a doleful sigh and shook his head. "I dunno if we're much better off now than before the war. Seems like prices keep goin' up, but cotton prices don't hardly move up at all."

"Maybe you ought to try some other crop this spring."

"Nope. What was good enough for my daddy and granddaddy's good enough for me."

"I'll give you a hand with your order, Mr. Carruthers."

"Mighty obliged again. One thing I'll say, it's good to have a man of your sort to do business with in Lowndesboro, Mr. Parmenter. You know, I was telling Maria just last night, seems like there's more niggers around these parts than when we had plantations and slaves and everything was nice and peaceful. That's what I said to her."

"I know what you mean. What we've got now's free niggers with a little education, and that's the worst kind. And the worst of all are those uppity ones from the Freedman's Bureau. Goddamned Yankees want to teach us good old Southern boys a lesson, so they foist their sassy niggers off on us, make them officials 'n everything, and lord it over us."

"I know. The other day some big fat buck walked onto my porch as if he owned it, and said he wanted to see my farm and talk to the niggers I had working for me. He waste a good hour talking to them out in the fields and asking them all sorts of damn-fool questions, like what was their wages, were they being treated right, did they get enough food. Another year of this, Maria and me's gonna sell our land for whatever we can git, and go live with Maria's cousin in North Carolina."

Hurley Parmenter uttered a short laugh and shook his head. "You won't find things any better there. All of the Southern states are going to have niggers shoved down their throat."

Ezekiel Carruthers shrugged as he walked out to his horse and buggy, carrying a sack of rice, while the stocky proprietor brought the side of bacon. When the order was stacked in the back of the buggy, the lanky, bearded farmer touched his hand to his forehead. "Thanks for helpin' out, Mr. Parmenter. I plumb don't know what we're gonna do if things get any worse."

"Just be patient, Mr. Carruthers. Nobody likes the new way any more than you do. Maybe one

449

of these days enough people will feel that way and we can serve notice on the Yankees that we aren't going to stand for being made to feel like slaves ourselves," Hurley Parmenter predicted.

The farmer climbed into the seat and slowly started down the street, and Hurley Parmenter stared after the buggy until it receded in the distance. When he went back into the store, he went into the back room, drawing a green baize curtain that shut off the view from any customers who might come in. Seating himself at a scarred old walnut desk, he opened the top drawer and took out the letter that his helper, Matthias Parton, had delivered to him last night. He opened the envelope eagerly and plucked out the folded sheet. A bank draft for one hundred dollars fell out and he grinned. Then his watery, pale blue eyes squinted as he drew the sheet closer to him, and read with mounting satisfaction:

Parmenter:

The enclosed draft is for the cause, to let you know that you have my full support in your admirable venture. I should appreciate it if, at your earliest convenience, you would investigate one Phineas Atbury and his wife, Hannah, who presently own the castlelike domicile once known as Windhaven Plantation. It would be most helpful to my enterprise if you could be instrumental in persuading the Atburys to find a change of scenery. When this is accomplished, you will notify me, and I will appoint you as my agent to bid for the property.

Communicate with me as you have done in the past at the address at the top of this letter.

I remain, yours for the great cause of Southern freedom,

A.C.

Luke Bouchard was smiling happily as he entered the Brunton and Associate Bank this bright, warm April morning. Not only had he proved his ability as a financial administrator and thus kept his vow to restore the bank to its former illustrious reputation, but his marriage to Laure had seemingly made him young again. Now deeply devoted to each other, they shared an easygoing domesticity, which Laure spiced with liberal portions of her wit and provocative blandishments. He felt far more like twenty-five than fifty, especially this morning. For last night, as he had held her in his arms in the exquisite aftermath of their fiery lovemaking burying his face in her luxuriant yellow hair, she had whispered to him, "Would it distress you to be a father again, Luke?" And then, mercurial and whimsical as ever, she had flicked his earlobe with the tip of her tongue and added, "This time, of course, quite legally."

His answer had been to devour her with kisses, till she gasped for breath and pretended to hold him off. Then, swiftly and with the gentleness of a woman truly in love, she had drawn him to her. That second essay had been languorous and poetically tender, speaking more eloquently of their felicity than any words could.

451

As he entered the bank, Jason Barntry looked up from his desk and beckoned to him. "Might I have a word with you, Mr. Bouchard?" Luke noticed that he was frowning, and remembered that he had been intending for some time to suggest that he take some time off for a second honeymoon with his wife, Amy.

"You look especially serious, Jason. It's really too beautiful a morning to spoil with anything too serious, you know," Luke chaffed him as they walked to his private office.

"Several things I've got wind of, Mr. Bouchard, I'm not too happy with. I thought I ought to bring them to your attention."

"About Philippe Durcroit's loan?"

"No. I wish all our troubles were as easy as that one. The sugar market is going up, and M'sieu Durcroit was in yesterday afternoon to report that he expects to pay back the loan by July. His land is yielding well, and his workers are apparently responding to the wage incentive he promised them if the harvest proved profitable."

"Excellent! He's a fine old man, and I'm flattered that he took my advice about setting up a production quota and offering a financial inducement to all workers who met it. But if that isn't the problem, Jason, what is?"

"First off," the tall trust officer declared, "I've heard it from reliable sources that Governor James Madison Wells is about to be removed from office by General Sheridan. It isn't official yet, but it's supposed to happen sometime in early June."

"That's a pity, a moderate Southerner being punished for his Union sympathies and for his stand against secession."

"That, of course, but lately he's been embroiled in political quarrels that have really sealed his doom."

"A pity. Is there any rumor as to who his successor is likely to be, Jason?" Luke asked.

"From all reports, it'll probably be Benjamin Flanders, who's now city treasurer. He seems to get along with the federal military authorities, and he's kept his mouth shut about his views. Too bad Governor Wells couldn't have followed his example."

"I don't agree with you, Jason. A man's integrity depends on his ability to speak out if he has deep convictions. To go along with the tide is hypocritical. It may insure political success, but I don't see how a man can live with himself if he suppresses his feelings and participates in something that goes against his grain."

"There speaks an idealist, not a banker, Mr. Bouchard, if you'll forgive my saying so." Jason Barntry gave him a bleak smile.

"I'll admit that some of the loans I've made, and some of the speculations too, have been a bit idealistic, but so far this bank's made money, not lost it, Jason."

"True. Those pieces of land you picked up last year are going to bring in a very handsome profit. Edgar Maxton told me last week that he had a few interested buyers, very solvent ones too, I might add."

"Excellent! But now I really fail to see why you're so gloomy this morning. Everything you've told me points to an optimistic outlook for the future."

"No, Mr. Bouchard, not quite. I'll get to the point. You remember when you issued preferred stock, and four of our customers purchased the minority issue, totaling four hundred fifty shares?"

"I do. We retain a controlling majority of five hundred fifty, do we not?"

"Indeed, Mr. Bouchard. You may also recall that three of these customers bought a hundred shares each, while Armand Cournier bought one hundred fifty."

"Yes, I recall that."

"Yesterday, Mr. Bouchard, those three other clients came in and had me transfer their shares to the account of Armand Cournier. This means that he alone has a total of forty-five percent of the total issue. We still retain control, but to have all those shares concentrated in the hands of one man—and particularly a man about whom I have been hearing some disconcerting things—causes me a little concern."

"What things?" Luke queried. "His account with us is quite in order; we handle his money and make a profit for him and for ourselves. Granted, Jason, I don't approve of his business of running bordellos, any more than I condoned selling slaves, but our job isn't one of enforcing morality."

"I know, and I don't wish to sound like a prig, Mr. Bouchard. I only wish you'd talk to Arthur Traylor. He's a deputy chief in the city's civil guards, an honest, hard-working man. He also happens to be one of our customers. I had lunch with him yesterday at Moreau's. You know about

454

M'sieu Cournier's elegant houses of pleasure, Mr. Bouchard, but I doubt that you are aware that he has been entertaining known rabble-rousers and even murderers at his house on the river. That's the one he bought for a song from Mr. Amberley."

"Yes, Three Oaks. Laure told me about it. But you can't blame a man for acquiring valuable property at a reduced price when the owner simply wasn't able to maintain it. The fortunes of war, you know. And even if I had known about Mr. Amberley's financial reverses, I could not in all conscience have lent him enough money to save Three Oaks. It would have been a risk without the least bit of security, and you know it, Jason," Luke replied heatedly.

Jason Barntry nodded and looked unhappy. "Of course, Mr. Bouchard, I wasn't questioning your judgment. I myself wouldn't have advanced Mr. Amberley a penny. The property was run down, to say nothing of his bad health. But what I'm getting at is that there are rumors that M'sieu Cournier is opening his house to the worst sort of people, and that he's using them to secure land in other states that are still under the oppressive Reconstructionist rule, arranging through factors to gain control from some of the freed blacks who were able to claim title to property on which they were slaves."

"Well, I'll tell you something in confidence, Jason. If you know the history of the Bouchards, you remember Windhaven Plantation. And the former owner of this bank, John Brunton, arranged to reacquire the house and fifty acres of land through a similar factor, a certain Phineas Atbury. It is my hope that one day Laure and I will go back there and restore it. Would you say, then, that my perhaps sentimental desire to go back to where I was born indicates a corrupt use of factors?"

"Of course not, Mr. Bouchard!" Color suffused Jason Barntry's cheeks. "But if ruffians and criminals are used to scare away the black factors so that they'll sell out, then it is indeed corruption. And that, Mr. Bouchard, is what I've heard Armand Cournier is doing with his strange new companions. But you'd best talk to Mr. Traylor. In his position, he has access to dossiers on several of the men who have been seen coming and going at Three Oaks."

Luke frowned. Jason's remark about using lawless men as factors to gain control of coveted land had struck a warning note. His suspicions about the connection between Pierre Lourat and the sophisticated Creole entrepreneur Armand Cournier had been lulled for several months, but what Jason Barntry had just said set him to speculating. To date, Luke had not been able to learn anything about Cournier's past that would give him grounds for distrusting him. And yet the nagging question of just how close this collusion between the two Creoles had been, and how it affected the lives of the Bouchards, began to thrust itself into his reflections once again. He rose, still frowning, drumming his fingertips on the surface of his desk. "If it'll satisfy you, Jason," he said at last, "I'll invite this Arthur Traylor to lunch or dine with me at his convenience."

"It was most gracious of you to invite me to Antoine's for lunch, Mr. Bouchard," Arthur Traylor

456

said, neatly patting his mouth with a monogrammed napkin. "We city servants rarely have the time to spend our noon hour at elegant restaurants. Nor do we usually have friends who can afford to invite us to such a place. I confess, Mr. Bouchard, when you called at City Hall this morning and asked my clerk if I was free for luncheon, your motives intrigued me. To be honest with you, sir, that was what impelled me to accept your invitation."

Arthur Traylor was a thoroughly likable man, bluff, hearty, and of solid constitution. His eyes were shrewd, though his face was jovial, with the suspicion of a double chin, and a broad Roman nose. In his late forties, he had already won the admiration of the citizens of New Orleans for his stand against racial bigotry. Even though he was Southern-born, he believed in justice and fair play for both sides, and his candid, disarming manner enabled him to convince even the diehard ex-Confederates that he was sincere and well intentioned.

"I'll be equally frank with you, Mr. Traylor. My trust officer, Jason Barntry, mentioned a conversation that he had with you quite recently. It concerns me because my bank has dealings with a certain gentleman who apparently is well known to you in your work. Or I should say, rather, his associates."

"I follow your drift, Mr. Bouchard. Doubtless you are referring to Armand Cournier."

"Exactly. Let me be still more honest with you as to my reasons, so you do not think that I am simply trying to pump you for information which you would have every right to tell me was none of my business. Before the war, my grandfather and

457

my father founded Windhaven Plantation, near Lowndesboro, along the Alabama River. Both of them had dealings with the notorious gambler and slave dealer Pierre Lourat."

"I begin to understand a little," said Arthur Traylor.

"We were driven from the house and the land by Union troops under Major-General Wilson. My family and I went to Texas and started a cattle ranch. I kept urging John Brunton to see what he could do about regaining the house and the land on which it had been built. My feeling was that when the hate of the war died down, I could go back there and use modern methods to prime the land and make it fruitful once again. It would be in the cause of this peace, for people of this growing country constantly need food."

"I can judge from your remarks, Mr. Bouchard, that you certainly were not a fanatical Confederate, and also that you probably had no difficulty in taking the oath of amnesty."

"That is correct, sir. I did not give aid to the Confederacy, and I likewise did not lift a hand against any Union personnel or fortification."

"And now you are a banker in John Brunton's bank. I read the newspaper account of your marriage to his widow, and you seem to be beginning a new life in that regard as well."

Luke nodded. "That is also correct, Mr. Traylor. I had thought of staying here a few years more, to make certain that the bank is on a solid, even keel. But after what Jason Barntry told me of Cournier's associations, I determined to ask you for your opinion."

Arthur Traylor looked down at his plate. "Sir, have you ever heard of the Ku Klux Klan?"

"I do not think so."

"It is an organization, formed last year by General Nathaniel B. Forrest, to maintain what is known as white supremacy. Its purpose is to prevent decent, law-abiding ex-Confederates from being ruthlessly dealt with by Northern radicals and the greedy profiteers they send down upon the South, whom we now call carpetbaggers. There are indications that Congress is upset about this secret society and will soon take steps to disband it. You see, Mr. Bouchard, it is beginning to get out of hand. It is being used to terrify the Negroes away from the polls, so that the Southerners who are secessionists at heart can gain political control. If that were all, it might be quite understandable, though not pardonable. Since I am a law enforcement officer, I must declare it an illegal attempt to take the law into one's own hands."

"I follow you, Mr. Traylor."

"Now then," the deputy chief continued, "its ramifications are particularly dangerous in rural areas where there is little formal education and where Northerners have sent blacks, especially from the Freedman's Bureau. The members of this secret society use terror and the cruelest forms of physical violence to carry out their aims. In some of the states—especially Alabama and Georgia, and, to some extent, Tennessee—the members of this society are beginning to use it as a tool to satisfy their own lusts and greed. Thus, it has become a tool of vindictive punishment. That is to say, if a black happens to acquire land that some white citizen espe-

459

cially covets, the Ku Klux Klan will visit him and terrify him with threats. Once he has fled the community, the land can be cleverly transferred to the white citizen."

He paused, then added, "Why, I have even heard of an attractive white woman who refused to accept a persistent suitor who was linked to the Ku Klux Klan. A group of men in white sheets took her from her home one night, after burning a cross on her lawn. She was taken to an isolated wooded grove, stripped naked, tied to an oak tree, and cruelly flogged. When she still refused to accept the courtship of this gentleman, she was ravished, sir, by nearly every member of that white-robed group, then tarred and feathered, as an example to others."

"Horrible!" Luke said with a grimace of disgust.

"But it is typical, sir, of the kind of travesty of justice that this society proposes to mete out to those who oppose it in any way, shape, or form."

Arthur Traylor paused and began to eat his lunch and sip his wine, and after a while he resumed: "Now I shall be more specific, Mr. Bouchard, about this prominent Creole citizen. Over the last few months several of my guards have been summoned to the houses of pleasure which are now owned by Armand Cournier and were formerly the property of Pierre Lourat. My guards reported that several of the patrons of these establishments complained that the young ladies there robbed them of money and watches and other valuables during their sojourn. Of course, nothing was ever proved. Discretion had to be employed, since many of these patrons are among the most respectable and affluent citizens of the Queen

City. My men cannot arrest unless the injured parties are sufficiently aroused to prefer charges, and in every case, when they were asked point-blank, they refused. Obviously it was to keep their identities unknown to the public, or we should have had some very juicy scandals."

Luke nodded and tactfully asked, "Do you think there is an association between the men who visit Three Oaks and this sudden flare-up of petty thefts, Mr. Traylor?"

"In a sense, yes, but only indirectly. When my guards questioned not only the girls but also the clients, they had to deal with several rough-looking men who identified themselves as private guards. One of my men recognized two of the so-called guards: both were deserters from the Union Army. And it so happens, now that you have mentioned the location of your former plantation, Mr. Bouchard, that a member of my company spent his recent vacation in Montgomery, visiting a cousin. He was told that there had been appearances of the local Ku Klux Klan at houses which quarter freed slaves. These blacks were so terrorized by the Klan that they packed up and fled overnight, and now the houses are being occupied by white men who seem to be a most unsavory lot.

"This associate of mine, Lawrence Trowbridge, has the sort of mind that, once it fastens on to a puzzling fact, makes him spend a good deal of time and effort in learning what is behind it all. Well, Mr. Bouchard, since his cousin works for the recorder of deeds in Montgomery, he was able to gain access to the register of titles of property in the county. And he found that in each instance where a black had fled from a house and property, the new owner was listed as Armand Cournier."

Luke leaned forward, his face intense with interest. "That would suggest, then, that there is a definite link between Armand Cournier and this secret society of which you have told me."

"That, Mr. Bouchard, is my inference also."

CHAPTER THIRTY-THREE

In this, the third year of peace following the Civil War, there were signs of progress. George Westinghouse had just perfected the air brake, which marked the beginning of the modern railroad. Christopher L. Sholes had patented the first typewriter, and was later to sell these rights to Eliphalet Remington. The refrigerator car had just been invented by William Davis of Detroit, which would protect fresh meat being shipped between cities. In Chicago, Walter L. Newberry had died, leaving four million dollars to found a free public reference library. These were the hopeful signs of peace after what had been called Armageddon.

It was the night of May 20, 1868, the opening day of the Republican National Convention, meeting in Chicago and adopting the name of the National Republican Party. It would nominate General

Ulysses S. Grant for the presidency and Schuyler Colfax of Indiana as his running mate. The nomination of the victorious Union general could not fail to remind the conquered South of the dour, unwavering conduct of the war that had ultimately, by sheer force of numbers and persistence of high-casualty attacks, brought about the anguish and the pathos of Appomattox.

But tonight, half an hour before midnight, something very different was occurring in Alabama. A great cross had been cut with a small plowshare upon the lawn that fronted a red-brick chateau with twin towers. Kerosene had been poured along the pattern of the cross, then lighted. It blazed now, a sinister sign, for it did not bespeak the Christianity for which that symbol had been designated.

As it blazed, casting grotesque, leaping shadows upon the red brick, there stood near it a group of twenty white-hooded figures, at whose head a short, stocky man held a coiled horse whip.

"Phineas and Hannah Atbury, come forth to judgment!" he called in a hollow, booming voice that reverberated off the tall bluff that framed the house. For a moment the chirping of the night birds was stilled, and even the droning of the insects merged at last with the murmur of the gently rolling waters of the Alabama River.

The leader waited a long moment, and when there was no answer, he cupped his palms to his mouth, which, like his eyes, was revealed through slits cut in the white cotton hood, and called, "Phineas and Hannah Atbury, the Klan calls you out to judgment by your betters!"

There was a low, sullen murmuring from the hooded figures behind him, and, as if spurred by their impatience, the leader called a third and last time: "Phineas, Hannah, your punishment will be dreadful if you ignore the summons of the Klan!"

After a moment the door of the red-brick chateau was opened and a frail-looking black in his mid-forties, sparse hair graying at the temples, quavered, "Fo' God's sake, what you want of me?"

"You are Phineas Atbury, the free coon whose name is on the tax books of Lowndesboro as owner of this place and fifty acres of good land?" the leader demanded.

"Yassuh, I bought it legal, I did. I got papers to prove it."

"Coon, you and your woman have been marked by the Klan for trial and judgment. You occupy fertile soil, which takes the skill of those white men who owned it when your forebears were gibbering apes on the Guinea Coast!"

"But, mistuh, I's telling you, politelike," the frail-looking black man persisted, trembling as he clutched the doorknob, "it was up for sale, and the government man, he talked to me and said I could have it fo' a thousand dollars."

"A thousand dollars, nigger! Where would you get such wealth except by stealing from your master? You lie, nigger! Bring out your woman or we'll go in for her!"

Phineas Atbury clasped his hands in an attitude of prayer, tears trickling down his lean cheeks. "Please, mistuh, Hannah's asleep now. She didn't have nuttin' to do with my buyin' this place all legal-like, fo' God, I swears it!"

"You have one minute, Phineas Atbury, black ape, coon, low nigger, thief, to bring out your woman. If we have to go get her, nigger, you'll be sorry!"

With an agonized, pathetic cry, the frail black man turned back into the chateau and called, his voice choked with sobs, "Hannah girl, Hannah, you gotta—you gotta come out now, please, gal!"

Then, wringing his hands as he took a step toward the white-hooded men, he pleaded brokenly, "I don't care what you does with me, nossuh, but please, ah's beggin' you please not to hurt my Hannah. She didn't do nuttin' to make you mad, honest. Please don't take her, please!"

"A man's woman, nigger, has the power to influence his mind. That's why she shall have her lesson too, to convince you that we mean business. Is she coming, or do we come into the house and get her?"

"I's here. What you want?" Hannah Atbury stepped outside and defiantly faced the hooded men. She was forty, buxom, and still attractive, her skin a light brown, her face calm and dignified. She wore a cotton nightshift and an old faded blue robe over it, which was loosely belted. For a moment the leader stared at her as if nonplussed by her fearlessness, then he made a swift gesture. Two of the men behind him stepped from the ranks and seized the sobbing pleading black, while two others took his wife by the elbows, and marched them both toward the towering bluff. As he stumbled, Phineas continued to implore his captors to vent their hatred on him but to spare his wife. They did not deign to answer, but jostled him along all the more vehemently.

They came to the base of the bluff, where there was a group of live oak trees framing a little grassy knoll. The other members of the Klan carried improvised torches made of long pieces of pine wood smeared at one end with tar and linseed oil, which they had dipped in the burning cross on the lawn to ignite them. Now the conflagration of these torches lit the clearing.

The leader uncoiled the horse whip, a lash six feet long, gripped the thick handle, and cracked it in the air several times, his eyes gleaming with sadistic anticipation. Then he made an abrupt gesture, and the two men holding Phineas hustled him forward to the largest, widest tree. Each seized a wrist, looped a strong cord around it, and then moved behind the tree to fix the cords together. Thus, Phineas seemed to embrace the tree. One of the men now ripped the black's nightshirt down to mid-thigh and tore at it from the sides until it bared him from neck almost to knees. He was crying softly now, but when they had finished the preparations, he turned his contorted, tear-stained face back toward the leader, who stood at his left, holding the whip in readiness, and again supplicated, "I'll take her share, mistuh! Don' whup my Hannah!"

"Black ape from Africa, listen to the words of the Ku Klux Klan," the leader intoned solemnly. "Tonight we serve notice upon you and your woman, Hannah, that you are to quit this place by the first of August. The tax bill on this property will fall due a month earlier. You will not attempt to pay it, so that by August it will be judged delinquent. Once you leave this place forever, it can then pass into rightful and honorable hands. Do you understand that,"

"Yassuh, only I keep tellin' you, it was all done legal and proper. Mr. John Brunton of N'Awleans had me buy it fo' him. He said I was to work the land and keep in touch with him."

"That does not concern us, nigger," came the contemptuous answer. "We of the oppressed South are ready to die rather than to let a coon like you settle on rich land once owned by a true Southerner. You will let the tax bill go, and by the first of August you and your woman will be long gone. To make sure that you understand that I, Kleagle of this chapter of the Ku Klux Klan, hereby sentence you to a good whipping. Your woman will have her share next. Get ready, coon!"

With this, the stocky leader stepped back, drew the whip along the ground, then lunged forward with a grunt as the vicious lash curled around the middle of Phineas's back. He uttered a wailing shriek, jerking convulsively against the tree. A dark red welt was emblazoned on his skin, deepening and broadening by the moment. Shudders ran up and down his sides and he seemed to huddle against the tree as he waited for the next stroke.

Hannah Atbury tried vainly to wrest her elbows from the two men who held her, calling out in a voice that trembled with indignation and anger, "Cowards—he's sickly, he's never done a thing to hurt anyone—why do you do this to us?"

"You shut your mouth, you black bitch, or we might just double your count," the man at her left muttered into her ear, and with an obscene snigger passed his hand over the plump, round globes of her buttocks, then pinched one of them. Hannah jerked against the indignity, and gasped in a low, shaking voice, "Very well, mister, if it pleasures you whuppin' women, go right ahead. But you got no right to touch me like that!"

"No? How about this, you big-assed black whore?" her tormentor jeered, this time applying a pinch to the other buttock. Realizing the uselessness of any appeal, she stiffened, but closed her eyes, her jaw muscles clenched and quivering as she strove to remain impervious to the degrading manipulations of her body. By now, the other man holding her had begun to pinch her breasts, whispering lewd indecencies into her ear.

The sharp crack of the horse whip resounded twice more, and each time Phineas turned back his pain-twisted face with a wailing cry, his body grinding and twisting against the tree. Hannah bit her lips till they bled as she fought the tears of shame and despair to hear both herself and her husband so reviled.

The hooded men crowded closer to the whipping tree, and their eyes reflected the same cruel, sinister glow as the flaming torches they held. They could see the muscles crawl and knot along the victim's shoulders and back, spasmodic contractions of the lean, sinewy buttocks, the shaking of the thighs, and then the horrid stiffening of the entire body as the leather thong snaked out with its vicious hiss and clung for a dreadful moment to his writhing, naked body. His screams were inhuman now, and the tenth lash sent blood oozing down his

469

thighs. At the fifteenth stroke Phineas slumped, his head sagging to one side. The leader strode to his victim, twisted his fingers in the black's kinky hair, and yanked up his head. "The coon's passed out, boys. Reckon we'll have to give the rest of his share to his black bitch. Cut him down, and let's see how Hannah takes her whipping!"

Two men came forward and cut the cords. When Phineas's body slumped to the ground, they dragged him by the ankles to a distant tree and left him there, unconscious. Then they hurried back to see the sport of a handsome black woman stripped and flogged.

As Hannah's two guards dragged her to the tree, one of the men from the group sprang forward, seized the neck of her nightshift, and tore it from her. A mutter of lustful admiration rose from the watchers: Hannah's body was ripe, well-sculptured, with sumptuous buttocks and rounded thighs that belied her forty years. They forced her against the rough bark of the tree, her bosoms painfully flattened against it, and lashed her wrists together. One of the men who had held her during her husband's flogging muttered to her, "If you beg real nice, bitch, I might just ease you off after your whuppin' with the biggest pecker you ever saw a white man hung with. Some bitches get real hot after they've had their asses warmed with a good whuppin'."

Hannah laid one cheek against the tree, clenching her jaws in a supreme effort to obliterate the mortification she felt. Grinding her teeth, she swore to herself to give her tormentors no satisfaction.

"She's likely to be a stubborn one, Hurley," said

one of the men who had tied her wrists to the tree.

The hooded man with the whip uttered a vile oath. "By rights I ought to have you trussed up and whipped yourself, you stupid bastard! Didn't we swear the oath that nobody knows our names?" Then, moving close to the shuddering, naked woman, he whispered, "You'd best forget what you just heard, bitch, or you'll wish you'd never been born."

Hannah could not remain silent. "I already do, seein' as how the world I was born in's got scum like you in it!"

"I'll make you sing a different tune, you bitch!" the Klan leader snarled. Then, glancing back and winking at his cronies, he shifted his grip on the thick handle of the whip and, lowering it, savagely thrust it up between her buttocks. Hannah writhed, and a low, sobbing gasp was torn from her as she twisted her face around and pressed the other cheek against the whipping tree, but she could not suppress the sporadic shudders of pain and revulsion that surged through her naked body.

Laughing at his victim's suffering, the leader stepped back and measured out the distance between the quivering brown body at the tree and the long whip. Drawing it back to let it trail on the ground behind him, he lunged forward and with the full strength of his arm sent the thong cracking down in a diagonal slash from Hannah's right shoulder to her left buttock. Her head tilted back, her eyes opened, glazed with tears, and her fingernails scrabbled at the bark on the other side of the tree as she jerked madly at her bound wrists.

"Make her beg!" came a voice from the assembly of hooded men.

"I aim to, boys," the leader replied, chuckling as he drew the whip back again, prolonging the suspense between strokes to intensify his victim's terror.

Hannah endured nine strokes before she finally cried out, wordlessly, her body thrashing, her legs splaying, then stiffening and clenching under the burning torment. Blood oozed already on her buttocks and upper thighs and shoulders, but the leader continued to ply the whip with joy. His eyes narrowed pinpoints of sadistic gloating, he sent the thong out to etch new bloody streaks on her lower back and sides, sometimes flicking the double-pointed tip of the thong to nip the outer curves of her breasts.

By twenty strokes Hannah was mewling with pain, half unconscious, repeatedly turning her face from side to side, trying to summon a last vestige of courage by closing her eyes and grinding her teeth. But her gasps and shuddering sobs betokened only too well the ebbing of her heroic resistance.

"I'll make her sing out, boys, watch!" Drawing the whip along the ground again, the leader stepped forward and sent it whistling upward so that the tip disappeared between her straining thighs. Hannah arched upward, then tugged backward heedless of the chafing of her wrists, her mouth agape in a continuous, wailing shriek.

"Told you I would, boys." He chuckled, satisfied with his prowess. "Guess she's learned her lesson." Then, stepping up to his victim, he said, "Now you

472

know what it's like to cross the Klan, bitch. You just tell that coon of yours that the two of you better not be seen around here come August first. Next time, we'll burn you both. All right, boys," he turned back to his followers, "I declare the business of this Klavern finished and done with—suspended until further judgment as of August first."

One of the younger members of the Klavern, seeing the bloody streaks that crisscrossed Hannah's back and buttocks and thighs, came forward to untie her, but the leader pushed him back. "No, let Phineas loose her when he comes to. Won't do her any harm to hug that tree. If we weren't bound to a noble cause, we'd use her the way nigger bitches were born to be used, servicing her white betters! Let's get out of here now, boys!"

When the flaming torches had disappeared, there was darkness, broken only by the intermittent touches of light from the moon, filtering through trees and the foliage on the side of the towering bluff.

In the distance there was the sound of horses' hooves, gradually receding until again all was silent. Silent except for the uneven, sobbing breathing of Hannah Atbury at the whipping tree, and for the piteous, feeble moans that testified that her husband was reviving. Now slowly the nightbirds began to return, as if no longer afraid. And the gentle murmur of the river beyond merged once again with the droning of the insects. It was as if everything had been restored to a kind of primeval order.

Slowly Phineas raised his head, then painfully

began to drag himself along the ground to where his wife slumped against the tree.

Groaning and grimacing, he at last straightened, tottering in his weakness, but forced himself to pick up a pebble and rasp it back and forth against the tethering cords till at last they broke.

"Oh, my God, Hannah honey, look what they done to you!" He sobbed as he gently turned her onto her side so that the bloody welts on her back and buttocks and legs would not be pressed against the ground. "We gotta write Mistah Brunton again, 'n tell 'bout gettin' outa this place! I don' know why he don' answer—I wrote him lots of times before. Somethin's awful wrong, Hannah honey. Now you lie there 'n git your strength back. Then I'll try to git you back home."

CHAPTER THIRTY-FOUR

On May 26, 1868, the United States Senate ordered that President Andrew Johnson be acquitted of the charges for which he had been impeached. The votes on impeachment articles number two and number three stood one short of conviction. That same day, Secretary of War Stanton submitted his resignation in a letter to the president, and three days later the Senate ratified the appointment of General John M. Schofield to replace him. The very next day, Decoration Day, as it was called, was first observed in this nation.

The Brunton and Associate Bank was closed on this new holiday, but the next day Luke received three letters. The first was from Fleurette, a long, chatty letter that told how ground had been broken for the new hospital that George Hardesty was donating, with Ben Wilson to the chief of staff. She concluded with a postscript that made Luke smile at the happiness so radiantly expressed: to her great joy, she was pregnant again. She asked for news, and urged Luke to come visit them in Pittsburgh.

The second letter was from Laurette Douglas, forthright and breezy, with many a paragraph that made Luke chuckle. She detailed the horsewhipping scene at the Chicago Commercial Bank, and went on to say that she hoped there would soon be an addition to the Douglas family, and that the twins were doing splendidly. Finally, she revealed Charles's ambitious hopes to begin a chain of department stores.

The third letter was in an unfamiliar handwriting, and it was addressed to John Brunton at the Union House. It had been forwarded to Luke by the post office. Wonderingly, Luke opened it and began to read. It was from Hannah Atbury.

Dear Mr. Brunton,

My husband Phineas is still ailing, so I take pen in hand to write you this time instead of him. We are both very worried that we have not heard from you in a long time. We expected that you would send orders on what you wanted us to plant on the land, and maybe some money for seed and a plow and some other things Phineas just has to have. You see, we don't have any money to hire hands. Mostly Phineas and I do the work ourselves.

Mr. Brunton, what I have to tell you really scares us. Last night, some men in white sheets came around to the house and called

Phineas out and then had me come out, and they took us over to some trees, tied us up, and whipped us. It still hurts me even to hold this pen in my hand, but I just have to tell you about this. They said they were the Ku Klux Klan, Mr. Brunton, and that we were to get off the land for good by August first. They said we would get our tax bill in July, but we weren't supposed to pay it, so that somebody who wanted the land could.

It will be a long time before poor Phineas is up and around, and I still hurt terribly, but I had to tell you about this. Mr. Brunton, when they were getting ready to whip me, I heard one of the men call out the name of the leader. He called him Hurley. Now the awful thing is that there is a Mr. Hurley Parmenter who runs the general store in Lowndesboro. I'm thinking maybe it's the same man.

Please, Mr. Brunton, you just have to help us. We haven't enough money even to come down there and see you, and we're helpless, and we're awfully afraid. They said they'd do worse to us, and I think they mean kill us. For God's sake, please get word back to us quick as you can.

Your respectful servant,
Hannah Atbury

Luke lay down the letter and shook his head, a smoldering rage beginning to stir in him. What Arthur Traylor had told him about the machinations of the Ku Klux Klan was still vivid in his mind. And now, through the direct and earnest words of

477

this decent black woman, he clearly saw the evil that had come to haunt the South.

As he sat, pondering, Jason Barntry knocked at the door of his office and entered. "Mr. Bouchard, I hate to bother you, but there's something I want you to look at."

"Yes, Jason, what is it?"

"Well, the bookkeeper is getting statements ready for our customers, and I decided to take a look at Cournier's account. Just look at this." He laid down before Luke three bank drafts, two for one hundred dollars and one for five hundred. All three were made out to a Hurley Parmenter of Lowndesboro, Alabama.

Luke looked up at the trust officer. "What made you pick out these three drafts, Jason?"

"Wasn't Windhaven Plantation pretty near Lowndesboro?"

"It was indeed."

"I was asking myself why this fellow Cournier would send money to a storekeeper in that town. I mean, I just thought it was strange."

"Thank you, Jason." Luke's face and voice were noncommittal as he picked up the drafts, studied them, turned them over to see the endorsements, then handed them back. "It's an interesting coincidence. Is there anything else you want to bring to my attention right now?"

"No, Mr. Bouchard. Only there's something else you ought to know. I ran into Arthur Traylor yesterday, and he said that he'd had a report from the deputy who'd been scouting around some of the cities in Alabama to see if any of Cournier's nasty friends were up to any tricks there. Sure enough, he found out that a couple of them have joined that secret society they call the Ku Klux Klan to drive black families off the land that somebody else wants. And he thinks that that somebody is Cournier himself."

"That's extremely interesting, Jason. I'm grateful to you for telling me about it. Here, you can put these drafts back in the statement. We mustn't hold up the mailing of a regular monthly statement to one of our clients, no matter what we may think of him."

After Jason left, Luke sat pondering this chain of events. Though he had thus far been able to unearth nothing that really linked Armand Cournier with the dead Pierre Lourat's scheme to obtain a foothold on the land of Windhaven Plantation, Hannah Atbury's pathetic letter had opened a whole Pandora's box of troubling conjecture. Most disturbing of all was the revelation that Cournier might be in league with this obscure Lowndesboro storekeeper who was a leader in the Ku Klux Klan. It did not take much imagination to figure that if the Klan was driving Phineas Atbury and his wife from Windhaven Plantation, it would then be available for sale . . . to a buyer who could well be Armand Cournier himself. Yet, why would the Creole entrepreneur be so interested in that particular Alabama terrain?

Luke wanted more valid information and less speculation, so he took a carriage to the office of Arthur Traylor.

"Come in, Mr. Bouchard! It's good to see you, sir!" The genial deputy chief rose from his desk to offer his hand to Luke. "How can I serve you?"

"I have been remembering our conversation at lunch, Mr. Traylor. This morning my trust officer brought to my attention some bank drafts sent by Armand Cournier and made out to a Hurley Parmenter in Lowndesboro. At the same time, I received a letter from the wife of the black factor whom John Brunton commissioned to buy Windhaven Plantation. Apparently the Atburys haven't learned that John died nearly two years ago. This letter was a cry for help."

"In what way, Mr. Bouchard?"

"The two of them were taken into the woods and cruelly flogged by a group of men wearing white sheets. Then they were warned to ignore the tax bill that comes due next month and to be out of the area entirely by the first of August. But what is most significant is that Mrs. Atbury said that one of the men addressed the leader as Hurley, and she recognized it as the name of a shopkeeper in Lowndesboro. The same one, Mr. Traylor, whose name appears on those drafts sent by Armand Cournier."

"I'm glad you've come to me with this news, Mr. Bouchard. It confirms to a great extent the report I had from my deputy who was visiting in that area. Perhaps if I give you a quick rundown on what has been happening on the political scene in Alabama, it may show you why I believe Cournier is trying to extend his power and influence beyond New Orleans."

The deputy chief waved Luke to a seat, then sat down behind his desk. "Last year, sir, the Freedmen's State Convention was held in Mobile, under the direction of General Swayne. Black citizens at that convention proclaimed themselves part of the Republican Party, since that was the only party attempting to extend their privileges. They said that if they were threatened with discharge from employment because of their political independence, they would appeal for troops to protect them and for Congress to punish their oppressors, even to confiscate the property of the guilty. They declared it their undeniable right to hold office, to sit on juries, to ride on all public conveyances, and to sit at public tables and in public places of amusement. Now, Mr. Bouchard, the *New York Herald* declared that the Union element in Alabama is probably stronger than that in any other of the Southern states except North Carolina. Last summer, when a supplemental Reconstruction Act provided for revisions of registration lists, the tabulation of registered voters amounted to some seventy-four thousand whites and ninety thousand blacks. General John Pope, who is commander of the Third Military District, which includes Alabama, called for an election last October to determine whether a constitutional convention should be held and to elect delegates to it. It took place in Montgomery on the fifth of November."

"What was accomplished, Mr. Traylor?"

"Much that caused greater dissention than ever, Mr. Bouchard. A black delegate introduced a proposal to pay freedmen for their labor from the date of the Emancipation Proclamation to the end of the war. That bill was referred to a committee, where it died. The suffrage article of that convention enfranchised the blacks, but disfranchised those unable to hold office under the provisions of the proposed Fourteenth Amendment, as well as

481

those who had been convicted of treason—even though they might have applied earlier for presidential pardons. The bone of contention, Mr. Bouchard, is that men who held office before the rebellion, as the Unionists still term it, are still considered enemies of the nation unless they can take the oath prescribed by the Act of Congress for officeholders, and take it with all good faith. The effect of this was to dishearten the moderate Alabama citizens who had hoped for peace without vindictiveness."

"So, Mr. Traylor, you believe that the Ku Klux Klan works actively not only against the blacks but against those who are known to be Radical Republicans?"

"Decidedly, sir. This secret society achieves its goals by terrorist methods, like those which you've just informed me were used with that unfortunate black factor and his wife. Now, Mr. Bouchard, there was an election this February, and I understand from reliable sources that Alabama will be readmitted to the Union by the end of this month. The new governor is to be William Hugh Smith, a lawyer and a farmer who opposed secession as a Douglas elector in 1860."

"I have heard of him. From all I know, he is a decent, honorable man."

"That is what I have heard also, Mr. Bouchard. He is also for universal amnesty and the immediate removal of all political disabilities that were imposed in the controversial 1867 Constitution. But I foresee that he will be under fire from the Alabama Democrats and especially from the widespreading groups who have rallied to the banner of the Klan.

Now you see, Mr. Bouchard, how ripe the situation is for agitation and a reign of terror. In the midst of all this confusion it becomes quite possible for a scheming, powerful, and opportunistic man like Armand Cournier to gain control of property and to make himself extremely rich."

"Yes, I see very clearly. That is exactly why I came to you this morning, Mr. Traylor. I told you about Pierre Lourat's attempts to gain a foothold on Windhaven Plantation. When I learned that Cournier was his silent partner, perhaps even the power behind the throne, I began to have grave anxieties. This letter from Hannah Atbury has decided things for me. I must go back to Windhaven Plantation and see for myself what is happening. More than that, I propose to buy that chateau and land back from the Atburys, which I believe I can legally do."

"I think it is possible. You were able to prove that you gave no help to the secessionist cause, Mr. Bouchard?"

"Yes. Of course, I took the oath of loyalty because I was worth more than twenty thousand dollars, which, as you will recall, was one of the stipulations made at the end of the war for the restoration of a Southerner's rights. Obviously, since Atbury was able to buy only fifty acres, the rest of my grandfather's original six hundred acres were assigned to other freed slaves as a token payment. But if Cournier, using the Klan as a tool and Parmenter in particular, drives Atbury away, he will surely drive out the other blacks as well. Then he will be able to acquire all the Bouchard holdings."

Arthur Traylor nodded, his face somber. "If all

that can be proved, Mr. Bouchard, then, in my opinion—though, understand me, it is more personal than legal—Armand Cournier may well be guilty of treason, as one who incites rebellion against recognized authority is considered. But it will have to be proved that this Hurley Parmenter is actually the leader of the Klan in Lowndesboro and that he is in fact being paid by Cournier. These bank drafts would tend to confirm that, but we should need far stronger evidence in a court of law before we could bring charges."

Luke rose, his face taut with concern. "So much of this is speculation and conjecture, Mr. Traylor. Cournier is, as you say, shrewd. He is a businessman—polished, urbane, and wealthy. Yet, more than ever I begin to believe that he was the one who planned to take Windhaven Plantation away from the Bouchards.

"My half-brother, Mark, was never content to farm the land and to build a future for himself. We quarreled over Grandfather's legacy, and I sent him in gold what I believed to be his fair share. He hated me, even threatened to kill me if I ever crossed his path again, and went off to New Orleans to join Lourat. He died a smuggler's death, when a Union gunboat fired on his ship, which was running the blockade. But prior to that, at the age of sixteen he declared himself to be in love with a woman he knew as Louisa Voisin, who was actually Louisette Entrevois. That woman, Mr. Traylor, was nearing forty. She was the daughter of a woman whom my grandfather had loved back in Normandy, only to find that she preferred to marry his older brother, Jean, so that she could inherit

484

the title of countess once my great-grandfather died. That was why my grandfather, disillusioned in love, fearing the French Revolution, and having broken with all ties of aristocracy because he preferred to be a simple farmer, came to Alabama. Now, Mr. Traylor, it was Lourat who tried to involve Mark with that woman, so that by marrying him she could rightfully claim a large part of Grandfather's land. Eventually, of course, Lourat planned to gain control of it through her."

"A pernicious scheme indeed, Mr. Bouchard," the deputy chief commented.

"Yes, Mr. Traylor. Yet, in a way, justice prevailed. Lourat was stabbed to death, and some days later a woman's body was found in the river. I believe that it was this same Louisette Entrevois, who in some way had been bound to, or coerced by, Lourat to do his bidding, and that at last she avenged herself. Be that as it may, if Cournier was Lourat's partner, as I have been told, it is possible that he was the one who invented the notion of entrapping my half-brother, Mark."

Arthur Traylor nodded. "It would all tie in, indeed, Mr. Bouchard. Yet, as you say, it is only circumstantial evidence. Even if all that could be proved, it happened long ago and there are no witnesses, so it could not stand up in any court of law."

"But I have resolved to confront Armand Cournier and to demand of him an explanation of this alliance between himself and the man who had Phineas Atbury and his wife taken out and whipped and told to leave Windhaven Plantation."

"A risky business, sir. Cournier is an expert

swordsman and marksman, and he would demand satisfaction from you for such an insult—such he would deem it."

"I shall take that chance. If he does admit it, the very least I shall do will be to have him withdraw his business from the bank. I am certain that if John Brunton were alive today, he would feel as I do. If Cournier, to gain control of land—and I do not mean only mine, Mr. Traylor—resorts to terrorism and uses this dreadful society as a tool, then I too think him guilty of the most heinous sort of treason.

"Thank you for seeing me, Mr. Traylor, and for giving me this information."

Shaking hands with the deputy chief, Luke took his leave, hailed a carriage, and went back to the bank.

"Mr. Bouchard, sir, Armand Cournier just came into the bank and asked to see Mr. Maxton," Jason Barntry said excitedly.

"I see. Thank you, Jason. Why did he ask for Edgar instead of you?"

"I don't know, Mr. Bouchard."

"Let me go see this estimable customer of ours," Luke said, as he rose from his desk and walked slowly to Edgar Maxton's office.

Armand Cournier, fastidiously attired, was seated in the chair opposite Edgar Maxton's desk, smiling, his malacca cane indolently angling from his right hand. The door was open, and as Luke entered he exclaimed, "Good afternoon, M'sieu Cournier. I was wondering if I might assist you."

"It's a matter of indifference to me, sir," the

486

Creole replied disdainfully, glancing at Luke. "Mr. Maxton, I think, can handle this particular transaction."

"M'sieu Cournier was asking whether he might acquire more shares of the bank's stock, Mr. Bouchard," Edgar Maxton volunteered. "Also, he was inquiring whether we were ready to pay any dividends on the present issue."

"I think I can answer both questions, M'sieu Cournier," Luke interposed, stepping around to the side of Edgar Maxton's desk to look directly at Cournier. "There will be no further issue of stock. We issued a thousand shares, and quite naturally retained a majority. I believe you own the outstanding four hundred fifty shares—not quite enough to gain control of this bank."

"Sir, I resent your implication," Armand Cournier replied, leaning forward to scrutinize Luke. "It was simply a matter of good business. I happen to know the other three gentlemen who purchased what stock was offered, and for various reasons they wished to raise money, so they offered their shares to me. But you still haven't answered my question about dividends."

"It is customary to offer dividends after a full year, which term has not yet expired," Luke answered coldly.

"I see, Mr. Bouchard." The Creole shrugged. "By the way, I must congratulate you on your acumen in purchasing that small tract of land on the edge of the city. You may or may not know that I was about to bid on it. You obtained it at a slightly lower price than I was prepared to pay."

"The fortunes of war, M'sieu Cournier," Luke retorted blandly.

"War? Oh yes, I see. No doubt you mean that simply as a colorful expression. The war ended at Appomattox, I believe."

"In one sense, yes, m'sieu. In another, it still goes on, but this time under the guise of opposition to the Reconstruction program."

This time Armand Cournier's brows achieved their maximum distension. And this time he turned his chair to stare directly at Luke, his eyes narrowed, his nostrils dilating with emotion. "And what is that supposed to mean, pray tell, m'sieu?"

"Why, I meant to say that there are many Southerners who resent the North's terms of peace and wish to take matters into their own hands. For example, by baiting the blacks who have acquired property in the formerly rebellious states and driving them away by having the Ku Klux Klan call upon them," Luke answered calmly.

Armand Cournier half rose, caught himself, then resumed his seat and glared at Luke. "I do not quite see, m'sieu, what this has to do with me and why you are going out of your way to be unpleasant this afternoon."

"It is not I who am unpleasant, m'sieu, but you. Instead of asking for Mr. Barntry, who sold you your original hundred fifty shares of bank stock and who has, I believe, until now satisfactorily handled all your transactions with this bank, you select Mr. Maxton to ask about more stock and dividends. As presiding officer of this bank, I speak for the bank. Therefore, you might also have asked for me."

"Am I to infer that my account is no longer welcome here?" Armand Cournier demanded.

"I have not said that, M'sieu Cournier. I think that will depend to a large extent on your clandestine activities."

"I resent your making such an offensive statement," the Creole retorted. For emphasis, he lifted his cane and thrust the end against the carpeted floor.

"I have made no accusation—not yet, at any rate. But, for my own personal reasons, I should be very grateful to you if you would explain how it is that you do business with a man who is suspected of being the leader of the detestable Klan in Lowndesboro." Luke uttered these words in the most casual tone, but his eyes were intently fixed on the Creole.

"That, sir, is none of your business!" he said, his thin lips curving in an unpleasant smile. "Since when do bank officials examine drafts and show curiosity over the identity of the payee?"

"Rarely, M'sieu Cournier. However, the deputy chief of our city's civil guard told me that he had observed a great many unsavory characters visiting you at Three Oaks. Further, I received a letter from Hannah Atbury, the wife of Phineas Atbury, who represented John Brunton as a factor in purchasing a certain house and fifty acres of land in that vicinity. It appears that Mrs. Atbury and her husband were shamefully treated by these white-hooded vigilantes and told to leave before August first. She wrote also that she had heard the name Hurley spoken by one of these ruffians. That more or less conclusively identifies the head of the

Klan—for the man they called Hurley was the one who led the group to the door of that house and who also wielded the lash on both husband and wife."

"Why do you tell me all this? I had nothing to do with it."

"Undoubtedly, M'sieu Cournier. But it is strange that you should send this Hurley Parmenter some seven hundred dollars within a short period of time. What could you possibly have bought from him, I wonder?"

"That, sir, is my affair and none of yours or of this bank's." The Creole rose, adjusted his top hat, and tapped his cane on the floor as he disdainfully stared at Luke Bouchard. "I do not have to sit here and take veiled insults and innuendos. I shall withdraw my account from your bank, M'sieu Bouchard. I should like also to convert my shares of stock—to the amount of forty-five thousand dollars, with, of course, the addition of the interest the money has earned. You will certainly issue some kind of dividend by the end of this year, and I believe I am entitled to a representative portion, if not the full amount."

"It will take a little time to arrange all this, M'sieu Cournier. There will be no problem about giving you back the money for your stock—and I for one will be very glad to do it. You have, of course, the shares in your possession?"

The Creole uttered an angry snort. "Of course not, M'sieu! I do not go around carrying these papers, because until now I had no intention of terminating my business with this bank. Your inexplicable enmity has forced me to it."

490

"You talk to me of enmity, M'sieu Cournier? You, who were Pierre Lourat's partner and who doubtless knew more about the Bouchards than you ever cared to disclose? Otherwise, why would you have set that bullying rogue Hurley Parmenter against two decent people who had never done you any harm?"

Armand Cournier's lips twisted in fury. "And now you make a direct accusation at last, M'sieu Bouchard. Very well. I call Mr. Maxton to witness that you provoke me. Do you recall a certain Edouard Villiers, who called on Windhaven Plantation well before the war to court Miss Arabella Bouchard?"

"I do indeed. It was I who learned from John Brunton that he was an agent in league with Lourat. The first of several, I should say. Foremost among them was an unfortunate woman who passed herself off as Louisa Voisin, but who was actually Louisette Entrevois. She attempted to lure my half-brother, Mark, who was then sixteen, into marriage with her, a scheme that Lourat conceived so that he could get a foothold upon the land he believed my half-brother would inherit."

Armand Cournier smiled malevolently as he adjusted his hat again and lifted his malacca cane. "It happens, M'sieu Luke Bouchard, that Edouard Villiers was my cousin. And you are quite right. After Lourat had told me of your family and had met both your father and young Mark, we—yes, that is right—we devised the idea of sending my dashing young cousin down to Windhaven Plantation to pay suit to the very winsome Miss Arabella. We also attempted to have M'amselle Voisin—since that

491

is the name you first knew her by—ensnare Mark. It very nearly worked, I may tell you."

"But not quite. And so it comes out at last. You were the one behind Lourat and that unfortunate woman, and now, it appears also, your cousin Villiers. You coveted Windhaven Plantation—but why?"

"It goes back a long way, M'sieu Bouchard." The Creole drew himself up to his full height, his eyes heavy-lidded and menacing. "My grandfather owned a plantation in Haiti. He had lost his wife, and he met a beautiful young woman who was then married to a certain Jean Bouchard."

"My grandfather's older brother," Luke interjected.

"Just so, sir. This woman, Edmée, was distraught when she saw that the paradise her husband, Jean, had brought her to was threatened with revolution by blacks."

"She had reason to be afraid, M'sieu Cournier. My grandfather told me that they killed Jean, and would have done the same to Edmée but she managed to escape and stow herself away on a ship bound for Mobile, where my grandfather bought her indenture and then freed her."

"That is not the point at all. There was trouble in that family even before the Haitian revolution. Edmée de Bouchard was unhappy with her husband, and my grandfather promised to do what he could to get the marriage dissolved and to marry her and take her to New Orleans. She swore eternal loyalty and love to him. Then, because some house servant had spied on her and reported back to her husband, she deliberately confronted Jean and lied with such dramatic force that she convinced him that she had been forced into that adulterous liaison. And so Jean de Bouchard sought out my grandfather, struck my grandfather's face with his glove in a public place, and of course brought about a duel. My grandfather was badly wounded, but he survived. After he had recovered and sold his plantation, leaving Haiti just a few days ahead of that bloody revolution, he tried to find Edmée in New Orleans, but to no avail. He swore that he would have his revenge on her for her treachery, as well as her husband and the entire Bouchard line for the humiliation and suffering he had endured."

"But that was three generations ago, M'sieu Cournier. Why should you try to continue so old a feud? My grandfather renounced his brother because of the latter's cruelty and selfishness, and tried by his own life to set a more Christian example of how to deal with people."

"Apparently, M'sieu Bouchard, you are content to mouth specious words and platitudes instead of being concerned with your family's honor. The name Cournier is even older than Bouchard, let me tell you. My grandfather was unjustly dealt with by a Bouchard. My father heard this from his father's lips, and he in turn bade me avenge the family name. Now you have your explanation."

"All the original participants are dead, M'sieu Cournier. I am glad you have told me what you have, because it has cleared up a question that has been rankling in my mind for many years. But I do not see a need to resume so ancient a feud. I would say, however, that if it is true that you are trying to buy Windhaven Plantation from the Atburys, I shall take whatever measures I can to acquire it myself. That, sir, is why I returned to New Orleans from Texas after the death of my wife."

"Oh, to be sure," the Creole sneered, "and to become the lover of your dead friend's widow—which very likely you were while he was still alive."

Edgar Maxton rose from his desk and put out a placating hand toward the two men, but neither of them noticed it. Luke stiffened, color flaming in his cheeks, and then, mastering himself, retorted in a level voice, "I am the husband of the former Laure Brunton. And I was never her lover in the sense you imply. Now you insult her, a woman who is not here to defend herself and who has absolutely nothing to do with your family feud with the Bouchards."

"And now you call me a liar. Already I have more than one reason to wish to kill you, M'sieu Luke Bouchard." The Creole's voice was quivering with malice and his eyes were narrowed. "If you had not opened your mouth to Miss Arabella and her mother, my cousin would have been a happy man. He came back to New Orleans to work for us in the slavery trade, and died of yellow fever two days after the Battle of Bull Run. I suspect it was really because he had no wish to live."

"Come now, M'sieu Cournier, now you are fabricating pure fiction! Arabella was a young girl and could not possibly know her own mind, and your cousin was a glib dandy who thought that by whirlwind courtship he could make an impressionable young girl believe that she was his one true love. Sheer nonsense!"

494

Beside himself with fury, Armand Cournier raised his cane as if to strike Luke, then flung it down on the floor and struck him across the cheek with his open hand.

"Oh please, no, M'sieu Cournier!" Edgar Maxton cried out. "Please, gentlemen, this is dreadful—I'm sure there's been a misunderstanding—"

"You needn't try to protect me, Edgar. I am quite capable of defending myself. M'sieu Cournier, I cannot take your blow and turn the other cheek. If you wish satisfaction of me, I am at your service."

"My second will call on you tomorrow." The Creole stooped to retrieve his cane and gave Luke a look of undisguised hatred. "And I shall kill you, M'sieu Luke Bouchard, and then I shall take over Windhaven Plantation from the Atburys. Oh, I will give them a fair price for their trouble. But it will be mine. And then the name Bouchard will perish in Alabama as it should have done long ago. I bid you good afternoon, gentlemen."

CHAPTER THIRTY-FIVE

The morning after the confrontation between Luke Bouchard and Armand Cournier, a morose-looking man in his mid-thirties entered the bank and asked to see Luke. When Madelon Fortier, who still presided as official hostess of the institution, asked his name, the man stared stonily at her and responded, "I come on behalf of M'sieu Armand Cournier."

Madelon's lovely face paled; she had been present the day before, when the altercation had taken place. The Creole's voice had been so loud that she could not help overhearing it, and she had turned just in time to see Cournier slap her employer. Thus, hearing the name of the Creole pronounced by so menacing a man—though he was smartly dressed—filled her with foreboding as she hurried to Luke's office.

"By all means, Madelon, show the gentleman in," said Luke. "By the way, *ma belle,* I hear that at last you've found your Prince Charming."

The shadows of fear on Madelon Fortier's exquisite face instantly gave way to a radiant smile. "It's true, M'sieu Bouchard. You remember M'sieu Jean Robairne, who owns the pastry shop on Chartres Street?"

"Why, indeed, he's one of our customers, isn't he, my dear?"

"Yes. He asked me to do him the honor of becoming his wife, and I—I said I would. But that man's looking daggers at you, M'sieu Bouchard—I'd better show him in."

A moment later Madelon reappeared, with the man behind her. "M'sieu Bouchard, this is Peter Danziger, who has asked to see you on behalf of his principal, M'sieu Armand Cournier."

Before Luke could acknowledge the introduction, the man rudely pushed his way past Madelon and stood glowering at Luke. "I have the honor to speak for my good friend Armand Cournier," he began without preamble. "He has demanded satisfaction of you, and I am here to arrange matters."

"May I respectfully point out, Mr. Danziger, that I was the challenged, not he. It is for me, therefore, to demand satisfaction. But no matter. It is a very fine point, a nuance of the dueling code, and perhaps your principal is not entirely familiar with it."

Peter Danziger stiffened, his eyes narrowing with anger. "I do not care for your manner of speech, Mr. Bouchard. Be careful that I myself don't find it necessary to call you out—but then, my principal intends to kill you, and he has fought many duels and survived them, as you see."

"There is always a first time to lose," Luke replied, and when he saw the man's cheeks turn purple with fury, he coldly added, "I repeat, he was the one who struck the blow, before witnesses, here in this bank yesterday afternoon. Therefore, according to the strict terms of the code, I, as the challenged party of this duel, have the right to the selection of weapons. You may tell your principal that I choose pistols. At twenty paces."

"When?"

"Next Sunday at ten in the morning."

"Where?"

"Let us say the famous Allard estate, on which so many duels are fought these days. It has a towering line of oaks, I am told, and there is a trio of enormous trees, called the Three Sisters. If we duel there, your principal will be sure to draw an audience. That should gratify him enormously."

Peter Danziger clenched his fist and took a step toward Luke, then thought better of it. "Sunday at ten by the Three Sisters. Pistols at twenty paces. I shall inform my principal. I shall also inform him of your insolent attitude, Mr. Bouchard. Good day."

"I'm honored to be your second, Mr. Bouchard. But I must tell you, I'm none too happy that you forced a fight with Cournier."

"I was prepared merely to have him transfer his account to another bank, at the same time letting him know that I meant to take steps to prevent his acquisition of my grandfather's house and land.

But his insulting remarks about my wife could not pass unnoticed. Also, as I told you earlier, Mr. Traylor, he bears a resentment against the Bouchards, for something that happened to his grandfather. Cournier is determined to kill me. And of course, then he will be able to accomplish his purpose, not only of acquiring Windhaven Plantation but also whatever other lands he covets. And he will also use the Klan to disrupt the gradual understanding that the two political parties can achieve by moderation, wisdom, and levelheadedness."

"True enough, but—" Arthur Traylor began.

"I do not intend to let him kill me—unless God so wills it, Mr. Traylor. That is one reason I chose pistols. I haven't had a sword in my hands since I was a stripling and Grandfather used to practice with me in back of the chateau. How many years ago that was—and how strange it is that all through the Bouchard history, since Grandfather came to America, this sinister man has represented a dark shadow that sought to blight it."

"I do not wish to see a man of your ability brought down on the so-called field of honor, Mr. Bouchard. Besides, you've brought no pistols to the Three Sisters."

Arthur Traylor, his face gloomy, was standing beside Luke, about two hundred yards away from the appointed rendezvous. They had come an hour early, in a carriage, the deputy chief insisting that he wished to inspect the dueling ground and also too have a few words with his principal. It was a majestic, rolling lawn, covered with great oak trees, but the three tallest were seen at once as one neared the estate. And already, word of mouth having passed around the city, there were at least a hundred spectators gathered.

"But surely you should have brought weapons, Mr. Bouchard," Arthur Traylor argued again.

Luke shook his head. "I know myself to be a fair shot. I shall take my chances. Let Cournier furnish the weapons. You will inspect them, after all."

"I shall certainly do that. I wouldn't put it past that Creole to have tinkered with the pistol for you. As your second, Mr. Bouchard, I have already brought along my own. It is an old but quite serviceable German gun, which fires a heavy-caliber bullet. You are aware that the dueling code prescribes that if either party shall turn and fire before the word is given, he may be shot down?"

Before Luke could answer, Arthur Traylor exclaimed, "At last, here he comes, followed by that brute Danziger."

"You know him?"

"Decidedly. A year ago, he spent a few months in the Cabildo for beating a prostitute so badly that she nearly died. It further convinces me that Cournier's association with scoundrels and criminals makes him all the more dangerous. Well, let's go settle the details. Who is to act as judge, to count off the paces? You said twenty, I believe."

"I did. The greater distance over the usual ten paces will make it more difficult to kill. Wounding him will certainly satisfy me. As to the judge, let it be some impartial spectator who is not concerned with either of us. A man who can count loudly and slowly, to be sure."

Arthur Traylor shook his head and sighed. Then

he and Luke walked slowly toward the three giant oak trees, where Armand Cournier and Peter Danziger impatiently awaited them.

Danziger held a magnificent cherrywood case, which he opened to show, in linings of red velvet, two dueling pistols. "They are primed and ready, with a single shot in each, Mr. Bouchard. I see that you brought no weapons, but M'sieu Cournier took the precaution of offering them. You may choose whichever you wish, of course."

"Am I to understand that your principal is determined to seek satisfaction on the field of honor and will not retract his slur upon my wife?" Luke said in a loud voice, which caused a buzz among the spectators. Armand Cournier tightened his thin lips and glared furiously at Luke.

"That is not worthy of an answer, Mr. Bouchard. Have you a judge? My principal respectfully suggests that you use Mr. Frank Norrigan, who stands over there by the trees." With a nod of his head, Danziger indicated a lean, gaunt-faced man in his early forties.

"Very well. I have no objection."

Armand Cournier took off his waistcoat, doffed his silk top hat, lay down his malacca cane, and stood in ruffled shirt and flowing cravat.

"Inspect the pistols for me, if you will, Mr. Traylor," Luke said to his second as he began to take off his waistcoat. He stood in shirtsleeves and trousers and boots and around his neck was the rawhide thong with the bright turquoise stone that Sangrodo had bestowed upon him.

"You are offering me a splendid target. What a magnificent stone! If you have not stipulated a beneficiary in your will to receive it, M'sieu Bouchard, I should appreciate having it in my collection of rare stones," said the Creole.

Luke glanced down at the turquoise and affectionately touched it. "I regret, I cannot make you a gift of it, M'sieu Cournier. It is the talisman of a powerful Comanche tribe that is known for valor, honesty, and courage. It would not become you to wear it."

"*Diantre!* Let us begin! Norrigan, come line us up," Armand Cournier exclaimed furiously. Then, with an impatient gesture at Luke, he demanded, "Choose the weapon and be quick about it. I have put off my breakfast long enough."

"A wise precaution, m'sieu, since it is well known that a stomach wound after one has eaten well often proves more serious. This is the one I choose." He put his hand out to the case and chose at random one of the two beautifully polished pistols, with a long barrel and curving handle, wrought in mother of pearl and with the initial *C*, traced in garnets, set into the mother of pearl.

Arthur Traylor took the weapon from him, inspected it, nodded, and handed it back to Luke. "It is satisfactory."

"Do you impugn my honor again, Mr. Bouchard?" Armand Cournier broke out. "Did you expect to find a defective trigger or a hammer that would not cock?"

"No, not really," Luke retorted casually, "because you had no way of knowing which of those two weapons I would choose."

"*Bigre! Nom de nom*, Norrigan, I can wait no longer!" Armand Cournier exploded.

The gaunt-faced man came forward. "Gentlemen, you will stand back to back, holding your pistols lowered to the ground. I will count to twenty slowly, and when I reach that last number, I will add *Turn!*, at which you will engage. Are you ready?"

Armand Cournier snarled as he turned his back, stiffened, and stood waiting. Luke eyed Arthur Traylor, then turned and stood till he could feel the pressure of Cournier's shoulderblades against his. And then the count began.

The numbers came slowly and articulately. The crowd was hushed. At each, Luke took a long step forward, and when the count reached nineteen, he tensed himself and slowly began to raise the pistol.

"Twenty—" and then suddenly there was a gasp from the spectators, and the sound of a shot, and Luke felt a sharp tug at his left arm near the shoulder. Before he could turn, there was a louder shot, and a cry of horror from the spectators. Luke wheeled in time to see Armand Cournier stagger, drop his pistol, and fall to the ground, while Arthur Traylor lowered his own still-smoking German gun.

"He fired on you before the order to turn, Mr. Bouchard—" Arthur Traylor began, as Peter Danziger suddenly dipped his hand into his waistcoat and drew out a small derringer. But before he could aim it, Luke turned, leveled his pistol, and pulled the trigger. Danziger coughed, dropped the derringer, then staggered back against one of the huge oak trees and slid down it slowly till he was seated, his mouth lolling forward, blood pouring from his mouth.

"I call on you gentlemen to witness that my principal acquitted himself with honor," Arthur Traylor exclaimed. There were nods and murmurs of agreement.

Luke felt a spasm of trembling as he lowered the dueling pistol and let it drop to the ground. Arthur Traylor came toward him, his face pale, sweat beading his forehead. "You saved my life, Mr. Bouchard. I had only one shot in that gun. My God—he hit you—you're bleeding!"

"It's the fleshy part of the arm. He was a little wild and too much to the left. Of course, he tried to hit the heart. Please help me back to the carriage. I feel a little faint."

"No wonder! Well, sir, you've done a hero's work today. You've rid the city of a scoundrel I've wanted to see behind bars or hanged for longer than I can tell you. All right there, you people crowding onto the ground, make room for us!"

CHAPTER THIRTY-SIX

On this early June day, in Galveston, Arabella Hunter had not the slightest inkling that her half-brother, Luke Bouchard, was fighting a duel with the man who had contrived to have his cousin woo her so that he could gain control of Windhaven Plantation. Even if she had known, it would not have altered her self-pitying outlook over the duel she proposed to fight against the utter boredom of her life.

She had been nineteen, flirtatious, and extremely enamored of her own voluptuous black-haired beauty when Edouard Villiers had entered into the whirlwind courtship of her. Now, after two years in Galveston, she had reached the age of forty-four, and her tall husband's preoccupation with his work seemed to have drawn him far from her. Worst of all, though she was not yet really aware of it, her daughter was becoming a rival. Melinda was now sixteen, slim, vivacious, with glossy jet-black curls that tumbled about her neck in charming profusion. Already Melinda was beginning to notice that she found favor in male eyes, as was evidenced by adolescent callers to the Hunter house, who sat awkwardly in the parlor with her and made small talk while her mother indulgently chaperoned. Andrew, two years younger, was beginning to show his father's height and solemn manner. These signs forced Arabella to admit the inescapable fact that the exciting times of her life were over and she was now little more than a mother and homemaker.

Although there was a small orchestra as well as a theatrical company to provide cultural amusement in Galveston, Arabella's moods alternated between boredom, depression, and restlessness.

To be sure, there were social evenings when James's cousin Jeremy Danton and his dowdy wife, Jennifer, came for dinner. But Arabella was not overly fond of Jeremy, for he invariably talked about nothing but cotton production, sales, and quality, and shipping tariffs. And his wife was equally boring.

Except for having grown more buxom, Arabella retained much of the beauty she had as a young girl. Her oval face now had more fullness, but her upturned nose was still dainty and her expression was still deliciously supercilious. Her large, dark brown eyes and thin, arched black brows conveyed an intenseness and ardor when she regarded a man. And her mouth, with its full lower lip and its mercurial changes from pout to smile, retained the sensuous quality that had always made her fascinating to the opposite sex.

The frequent visits of the bachelor foreman of the cotton plant, Todd Emory, always in the company of Jeremy and his wife, might have tempted her to a mild flirtation with him. But his stolid personality and lack of education hardly appealed to her. Even if it had, he invariably talked of nothing but the cotton plant.

However, on the day when Luke was risking his life on the dueling field in New Orleans, Arabella Hunter was seated at her boudoir table, breathlessly inspecting herself, adding a bit of rice powder to her creamy cheeks and rubbing her lips with a handkerchief to make them redder and more swollen, to simulate passion. Melinda and Andrew, for a happy change, had gone to visit Cousin Jeremy and Jennifer and their two children, Ernest and Dorothy, who were eleven and thirteen, respectively. Andrew, who had always resented being Melinda's junior, enjoyed these visits because he could boss the younger boy and tease the sister without fear of retaliation. At home, Melinda, especially now that she was gaining poise and was increasingly conscious of every word and mannerism, was able to wither Andrew with a scornful, silent look or a sarcastic comment.

James had gone to Corpus Christi to confer with an official of the steamboat line there, trying to work out a more reasonable tariff for hauling the cotton that his cousin's mill processed. So, for the first time since they had come to Galveston, Arabella found herself alone, her own mistress. And she was anticipating a visit from Durwood

McCambridge, who had come to town just two weeks ago and been introduced to her at the theater.

Durwood McCambridge was as tall as James, just thirty-one, with a boyish, gregarious air and frank, regular features. His curly black hair and twinkling blue eyes had caught Arabella's notice at first meeting, and his compliments had made her cheeks color hotly and her heart pound a little more quickly than was its wont, especially during these past two years. One of James's business associates had squired McCambridge to the theater that evening, so the introduction had been perfectly proper. But, from his lone seat, the handsome Easterner had several times glanced in her direction, and when their eyes met he nodded and smiled. Arabella had not had such attention from a man other than her husband in longer than she cared to remember. Melinda's budding beauty and affectations at being a grownup young lady made Arabella feel that her own daughter was her rival, and, worst of all, that she was growing old and unattractive. Therefore, the entrance of Durwood McCambridge into her life was like a breath of fresh air.

All she knew about him was that he had come from New York to visit an old friend in Galveston, that he was a bachelor, and that he was rather well-to-do. Certainly his elegant attire bespoke that.

Yesterday afternoon, well after James had departed for Corpus Christi and Andrew and Melinda had been called for in Cousin Jeremy's carriage, she had gone out to the gazebo, seated herself on the white bench, and sighed over the thought that life was passing her by in this drowsy Texas city. And then, in the midst of her despairing ruminations, Arabella saw a tall, handsome man in a brand-new buggy coming down the street and stopping in front of her house. She hurried to the front door just in time to see Durwood McCambridge climb down from the buggy, fasten his horse's reins to the tethering post, and remove his bowler hat as he approached the door.

"Oh, Mr. McCambridge, what a pleasant surprise!" she exclaimed.

"Your servant, ma'am. I was just passing by, on a little matter of business, when I remembered our theater meeting and how taken I was by you. I know this is presumptuous, but I thought perhaps you would grant me the opportunity to talk with you, at your convenience. That is to say, if your immediate family is not in the vicinity."

Arabella hadn't dreamed that her secret hopes for a flirtatious adventure would be realized quite so soon. She stammered, "I—I don't know—why, oh, yes, perhaps you could come tomorrow afternoon. About two. That—that would be much more convenient, Mr. McCambridge."

Now, satisfied with her appearance, she rose and went to the parlor to await his coming. Her black hair, which still showed no traces of gray—the few telltale hairs were immediately plucked out before even her husband could observe them—was piled in a fetching chignon, with little curls that caressed the nape of her neck and made her look as she had in the happy days at Windhaven Plantation. She had chosen a simple blue muslin frock with puffed sleeves and high neckline, and a minimum of stays so that her figure would not seem too bulky.

She responded at once to the knock on the door, opening it and stepping back, her cheeks rosy as the tall, curly haired Easterner entered, his bowler hat held between both hands. "Good afternoon, ma'am. It was good of you to see me."

"Won't you—won't you make yourself comfortable on the couch there, Mr. McCambridge? I'll fetch some tea and some little cakes I baked last night."

"Just specially for me, ma'am? That's awfully nice of you." Durwood McCambridge had earned his living by his wits since he was a boy of fourteen. For the past year, however, he had been engaged in land speculation and, more precisely, in attempting to fleece landowners of their holdings. One of his St. Louis friends, with whom he had stayed for a few weeks, had told him about the vast territory of Texas and how, although land was sold for a pittance, many of the settlers had neglected to pay their taxes. Some valuable land could therefore be picked up virtually for a song, and Durwood McCambridge especially enjoyed work that gave him a handsome profit for very little effort.

James Hunter had already appraised Durwood McCambridge and found him more than wanting. And, despite his preoccupation with his work and his placid demeanor in domestic affairs, he had been aware of Arabella's fluctuating moods and particularly her restlessness during the last few months. He sympathized with her dislike of Galveston and the limited socializing available to her, and felt that it was high time they took a second honeymoon, away from the children, and tried to restore some romance to their marriage.

Breathless with excitement at being alone with this dashing bachelor, Arabella served refreshments, then seated herself on the couch not too far from him, and plied him with questions about the East. He had been to New York, Boston, Philadelphia, Pittsburgh, and Chicago, as well as St. Louis, New Orleans, and Memphis. Hence, he seemed to her a highly sophisticated, much-traveled knight errant. At the outset of their conversation, she made a pretense of assuring him that she would find some highly eligible, single young lady who would be worthy of him.

But Durwood McCambridge had bedded twenty times more women than Arabella had had flirtations, and he had already realized that this opulent, still very desirable matron was ripe for a last exhilarating fling before surrendering to the demands of placid, conventional domesticity. He began to edge closer to her on the couch, and before much longer his arm was around her waist and he was murmuring, "Don't try to find any single young ladies for me, my dear Bella. You are all that any man could ever desire. It's a tragedy that you're united to another, or I would court you as you deserve."

Arabella nearly swooned with delight at this. When a tiny twinge of conscience began to pick at her, she suppressed it by telling herself that James had not said such nice things to her since they had left Windhaven Plantation, and that at forty-four surely a woman's life should not be over.

Nevertheless, she remonstrated quite properly, "Oh, Mr. McCambridge, please—this is dreadfully embarrassing. I mustn't forget that I'm a married woman. Whatever would James think if he saw your arm around me?" And when he drew back his arm, she hastened to reassure him that she had not found it too offensive: "I do hope I haven't hurt your feelings, Mr. McCambridge. You're such a handsome man, I declare, if I weren't married I should have all I could do to keep from being quite helpless if I were alone with you."

"But you *are* alone with me, dear lady," he said softly, and once again circled her waist and drew her to him. Arabella sighed, then put up a hand to fend off his kiss, but an instant too late. She shivered and closed her eyes, for the sensations permeating her were intensely pleasurable, spiced as they were with the knowledge that what she was experiencing was forbidden to her.

It was well that her mother, Sybella, was far away at Windhaven Range, or she assuredly would have boxed her daughter's ears and delivered an irate lecture on the proprieties that a married woman should observe.

But, on this very day in the ranchhouse at Carrizo Springs, Sybella was mothering Felicidad Ramirez, a pretty black-haired Mexican girl, a seventeen-year-old orphan, who had been working for a tavernkeeper in Nuevo Laredo. For six months she had defended her virtue against the drunken customers of the *posada* as well as the tavernkeeper. But two weeks ago he had forced his way into her room and told her that unless she consented to be his mistress, her job was forfeit. In despair, Felicidad had run away. By chance, one of Lucien Edmond Bouchard's vaqueros, Vittorio Salancar, had gone to Nuevo Laredo for a week to visit his sister. Seeing Felicidad slumped against the side of an old, ramshackle hut, weeping bitterly, he had gently approached her and offered to help. When she told him about the tavernkeeper, he took her back with him to Windhaven Range, where he was certain she could find some kind of work.

Sybella had heartily approved of Vittorio's humane gesture, and had questioned the girl at length, in a way that readily drew out confidences. She decided to put her to work in the kitchen, helping Celia and Maybelle. Lucas, Djamba's handsome son, had quickly fallen in love with Felicidad. And as Arabella, in Galveston, was making ineffectual protests over Durwood McCambridge's advances, her mother was in the process of assuring the pretty, orphaned girl that she could find no finer man than Lucas to look after her. When Felicidad left the room and ran happily into Lucas's arms, Sybella smiled knowingly, and began a letter to her beloved stepson, Luke Bouchard.

Despite Arabella's now-earnest protests, Durwood McCambridge had advanced his courtship. One arm tightly circling her waist, his other hand caressing her bosom, he began to kiss her ears and throat. Realizing the danger, she extricated herself with considerable effort from his grip, rose to her feet, and, her cheeks fiery, reproached him: "Mr. McCambridge, you've an entirely wrong impression about me, sir! I'm a decent, married

513

woman. It was wrong of you to kiss me and hold me like that!"

He shrugged and rose, a boyish smile on his handsome face. "Never mind, Bella honey, you know you want to have fun as much as I do. There'll come a time real soon, and all you have to do is send for me."

"I—I really must ask you to leave, Mr. McCambridge. I'm terribly sorry if you thought I encouraged you. We—we can still be friends, can't we?"

"Of course we can. I intend to stay in Galveston for another two weeks. I'm at the Planter's Hotel, and you're welcome to visit me whenever you choose."

Like a proper hostess, Arabella saw him to the door. Giving her a sly wink, Durwood McCambridge suddenly drew her to him again and kissed her resoundingly on the mouth, then chuckled and strode out to his horse and buggy. Arabella promptly slammed the door to express her token outrage at this violation of her marital chastity; then she hurried to the window, stealthily drew one of the curtains, and watched his tall, lithe figure striding down the walk.

James Hunter was concluding his business in Corpus Christi the next day when Ezekiel Moncreef, the grizzled old captain of the packet that Arabella's husband was to take back to Galveston the following morning, hailed him on the street as he was walking back to his hotel. "A word with you, if you please, Mr. Hunter," he called.

"Certainly, Captain Moncreef."

"I have something private to say to you, and I hope it won't offend you. You're the only real pas-

514

senger I've got back to Galveston, or at least the only one I can trust to be a gentleman."

"That's very flattering, Captain Moncreef. What did you have in mind?"

"There's a young widow been staying in Corpus Christi for a week, trying to get her bearings. It took her about eight months to scrape together enough money to get out of Mexico City and make her way here, and now she's stone broke and doesn't have any friends at all. She was hoping to get a job as a governess or something like that around here, but you know this God-forsaken port. A few ranchers miles from here, and then just desert and swamp and plains."

"I know. Well, maybe I can help her find something in Galveston. There are quite a few families with enough children to make it worth their while to hire a governess."

"She'd be ever so grateful, sir. I'd help her if I could, but a steamboat captain doesn't have much money, and—"

"I understand, Captain. I'll do what I can."

So, the next morning, after having conversed at length Kathleen Maravedi, the redhaired, twenty-nine-year-old widow, and James Hunter sailed together to Galveston.

Before returning to his house, James installed the Irish beauty in a modestly priced room at the Foremost Hotel, and tucked some bills into her reticule, telling her to accept the money as a loan for her expenses until he could find employment for her.

He found his buxom wife strangely distraught, for she was thinking of the adventurous Durwood

515

McCambridge and half wishing that he would come back and be more forthright in declaring his affection for her. When James told her about the widow he had aided, Arabella burst into tears and fled to her room, to his utter astonishment.

At the breakfast table the next morning, even Andrew and Melinda noticed the tension between their parents. Melinda took the conversational lead by dwelling on the delightful time she had had with Cousin Jeremy's two children, and Andrew contributed some anecdotes of his experiences with his favorite playmates.

When the children had at last gone out to play, James turned to Arabella and said tartly, "May I ask why you're putting me in Coventry, my dear Bella?"

"As if you couldn't guess!"

"I confess, I can't. But the last few months you've become very irritable over just about anything, and it disturbs me, Bella."

"How do you think I feel, cooped up in this house, seeing so few people, people I haven't anything in common with, and trying to cope with the children, and then you come and tell me about playing the Good Samaritan to an attractive widow. Don't I please you anymore, James?"

"Of course you do! Stop talking nonsense!"

"Are you going to see her again today?"

"Yes, I promised her I would. Either the Barlowes or the Hardings would hire Kathleen in a flash."

"Oh, so it's Kathleen now, is it?" Arabella flared, giving him a furious look as she rose from the table and stormed into the kitchen.

James shook his head, finished his coffee, and called out, "I'll be going to the office now, Bella, but I expect to be home at the regular time for dinner tonight."

A frosty silence greeted this announcement.

Before he got to the plant, he stopped at the homes of his two friends and proposed that they consider hiring a governess, declaring that he knew of one who would be of great benefit to their children. Ardith Barlowe, a genial, plump woman in her early forties, with a brood of six children, urged him to invite Kathleen Maravedi to call upon her at her earliest convenience.

Accordingly, James went to the hotel to tell the attractive widow that a job awaited her if the interview was satisfactory.

"Oh, Mr. Hunter, you don't know how grateful I am! I'll go see that woman right away."

"I'll be glad to take you there in my carriage before I go to the office," James proffered.

"Oh, would you? You're ever so kind, Mr. Hunter. How can I ever repay you? I declare, your wife is a very fortunate woman to have a man like you, so thoughtful and helpful."

James blushed and looked down at the floor. "It's kind of you to say so, but really you owe me nothing, Mrs. Maravedi. If you're ready to go now, we should get started."

"Do you think I look presentable enough? Should I change my dress? All I had was the one case of clothes when I left Mexico City, and I do feel so shabby."

"That dress looks just fine. Come along now."

A few moments later, James helped Kathleen

Maravedi into his buggy and began to drive toward the Barlowe house. As it chanced, just as he turned to talk to her, Mrs. Ella Cantwell, a God-fearing Methodist who was a neighbor of the Hunters, was passing by the hotel and observed them driving off. She stared after them in surprise.

She lost no time in going to the Hunter house. "Mrs. Hunter, I've some news to tell you! May I come in for a minute?" By the time Ella Cantwell finished her story, Arabella was seething. She had sent Durwood McCambridge away, even though she hadn't really wanted to, but it was all right for James to traipse around town, brazenly showing off a redhaired widow in his buggy and talking to her as if they were closer than two peas in a pod.

She was at last ready for her duel, and to be sure that the stage was properly set, she sent Melinda and Andrew to play with Cousin Jeremy's children, whispering to Melinda to see if the two of them could be invited to supper because she wanted to talk to their father about some very important matters.

It was six o'clock before James got home that evening, exhausted from his intense work at the cotton plant. As he opened the door and walked in, Arabella confronted him, hands on hips, eyes narrowed, lips tight with acrimony. "I suppose you've been sparking that widow all over town, James Hunter!" she flashed at him.

"Now just a minute, Bella!"

"No, I won't 'just a minute,' James Hunter!" She stamped her foot. "You can't spare a minute to be sweet to me, you don't say nice things to me any-more, but you can drive that redhead around in your buggy for Mrs. Cantwell to see and come to tell me all about, can't you?"

"So that's what's bothering you. Well, my dear, I think I can take the wind out of your sails by telling you that I'm quite aware that that sneaky, land-grabbing Easterner, Durwood McCambridge, is a far less trustworthy character than Mrs. Maravedi."

"What do you mean by that?" Guilt as well as indignation made her voice edgy.

"Oh, come now, Arabella, do you take me for a fool? You've had these flirtations before. When he was introduced to you at the theater that night, I saw by the way he was looking at you and kissing your hand when you parted that he would visit you when you were alone. And I'm sure he did, didn't he?"

"How dare you! I hate this hot, gossipy city where everybody knows everybody else's business! I hate you too, James Hunter! I wish I could go back to New Orleans—or even Alabama!" She began to sob.

James looked up and rolled his eyes, as if seeking divine providence. Then, with an exasperated shrug, he walked toward her, his expression grim.

Arabella began to back away, a hand uplifted to fend him off. "Why are you looking at me like that, James? What is it? Talk to me, for heaven's sake! No—let go of me—what do you think you're doing?"

"Something that you may recall was done to you a few years back, Bella. Maybe this time it will drive all the nonsense out of that pretty head of yours."

Gripping her by the wrist, he pulled her into the

bedroom, seized a wooden hairbrush, and upended her over his lap as he seated himself on the edge of the bed.

"No—you shan't—you shan't ever do that to me again—stop it, James! I—I'll divorce you—I'll leave you for good—oh, stop it, stop pulling my dress up—this is dreadful—no, no, not my—I forbid you— owwwwww!"

Ignoring her plaints and threats, James pinned her wrists behind her back with his left hand as he lifted the hairbrush and brought it down smartly several times. Arabella's legs began to thrash up and down as she tried to wriggle off of his lap, wailing out as the wooden hairbrush came into crisp, noisy contact with her rapidly coloring, naked bottom.

As the heat mounted in her reddened flesh, she began to squeal and sob, then at last begged for mercy, trying to wrest her hands loose so that she could protect the all too vulnerable target of the hairbrush.

"I've put up with your antics for a long time, Bella" *Crack!* "This time I shan't stop until you promise you won't show that spiteful jealousy of yours ever again—" *Whack!* "And as long as you keep on acting like a child, Bella, you're going to get punished like one!" *Thwack!*

"Oh please—you're hurting me! Oh, James— Jimmy lover—oh no—not any more—oh, not there, *please*, not there. I'll be good—I won't ever do it again—yes—I did—I did flirt a little with—owoohhh, I can't stand it anymore, I'll tell you everything! I did flirt a little with him—but I won't ever do it again—oh please, please stop now, I'll be *so* good!"

Her body arched and twisted each time the hairbrush struck her flaming buttocks.

James was breathing hard, his eyes blazing, as he at last tossed the brush to the floor, and rolled Arabella onto her back on the bed, and swiftly mounted her.

"James—what are you—oh, James—darling—aah—oh yes, yes, love me—love me good! I won't ever be naughty again, I'll be your girl—oh, darling, harder—oh, it's so good!"

Her face radiant through her tears, her arms and legs locked furiously around him in passionate embrace, Arabella found that her life as a woman very definitely was not over at the age of forty-four.

CHAPTER THIRTY-SEVEN

Luke Bouchard's wound healed within ten days, and the afternoon on which the doctor pronounced him completely recovered, he went back to his little house and walked into the bedroom, where Laure was playing with little Lucien in his crib. Petite Mitzi effusively greeted him: "Oh, M'sieu Luke, I was so worried, and when I heard that you'd been shot, I almost died!"

"You mustn't do that, dear Mitzi, because Laure is going to need you now more than ever."

Laure turned to him, her green eyes wide and questioning. "Why do you say that, darling?"

"Because, Laure, I've decided to go back to Windhaven Plantation. And alone, except for Marius Thornton."

"Because of that letter from Hannah Atbury?"

He nodded. "Armand Cournier is dead, and that

removes for all time the real menace that threatened the Bouchards. But there is still a danger as long as the Ku Klux Klan dominates the blacks who occupy much of the land that belonged to Grandfather. I don't want you to go with me, not till after the baby is born and you've had a good long rest. Besides, there'll be much for me to do alone."

"But what do you propose to do, darling?"

"I propose to pay the taxes, and to make Phineas Atbury a reasonable offer for the chateau and the fifty acres that he now occupies. Then I shall hire him and his wife to work for me, at decent wages."

Her face softened and a radiant smile curved her red lips. "That's wonderful, darling. But once you've settled there, once you've begun to develop the land and do all the experimenting with crops and cattle, as you've told me so much about, what about me?"

"I wasn't certain how you'd feel about sharing my life back in Alabama, dearest. There's the bank to be considered. It's doing very well, and after all, it's still in John's name."

"Luke," she murmured as she came toward him, her face serious now, with none of the sauciness that he had learned to love so well, "once I told you that you were an old sobersides. I've since taken that back, and I shan't ever think of you that way again. When Arthur Traylor told me how courageously and honorably you handled yourself during that duel, I knew I could never hold back any part of my life from you. I'm your wife now, totally, for always, if you'll have me. And I'll share that life with you, no matter where you take me."

Mitzi began to sniffle and quickly reached for her lace handkerchief, overcome with emotion at this intimate scene. Luke took Laure into his arms and kissed her eyelids as he said gently, "Perhaps by the end of the year, and only if you're strong enough to travel. Mitzi, you'll come with us, won't you?"

"Oh, *oui, oui,* I should be desolate if I could not go with Madame Laure and little Lucien and the *bébé* that is to come!"

"Then it's settled. Mitzi, you'll look after my wife and our children. Laure, what would you say if I were to appoint Jason Barntry as titular head of the bank, to represent us both in our absence? Needless to say, even if we move back to Windhaven Plantation permanently, we'll still keep in close communication with the bank." Then he added, with a wry smile, and for only her to hear, "And you'll never know how glad I am that John changed the venue of the bank to the Union House, my dear one, otherwise I should never have met you."

Before Luke Bouchard and Marius Thornton took the steamboat to Mobile, Luke wrote to Sybella. He had, about a month after Carlos Macaras's attack upon Windhaven Range, received a letter from his beloved stepmother detailing the attack and praising the help of the Comanche chief Sangrodo. She had added a few bits of domestic news: Prissy had given birth to a little girl, and she and Jicinte had named it Pesumata, the Comanche word for Little Fawn. Mara Hernandez's little Luke was thriving, and Maxine Bouchard expected her child by the first week of October. And finally there was news about the orphaned Mexican girl whom Lucas had taken under his wing. Thus, Luke was assured that the affairs of the Bouchards in far-off Texas were going forward happily.

On June 20, Luke visited the Brunton and Associate Bank and bade *au revoir* to his loyal staff, appointing Jason Barntry as administrative officer in charge. Barntry would report to Laure every two weeks and give her each month a statement of the bank's financial standing, with a copy to be sent to Luke in care of general delivery at Lowndesboro. Then Luke went back to his little house and said his farewell to Laure, a long and tender meeting in which he told her his plans for the next several months. "Marius is coming along because I promised him the chance of being my foreman at Windhaven Plantation. He's still in love with Clementine, that pretty girl who has been slaving for a cranky old widow. Just before I went to the bank this morning, I visited this woman, gave her five hundred dollars in gold, and told her that I wanted to hire Clementine to go with me as a cook. She haggled a little, so I gave her an extra hundred dollars. So, Clementine is going along with Marius. They will be married once they've settled in."

"That's wonderful, dearest! Marius deserves every happiness."

"As you do, my dearest. I hope you understand, after what I've told you about Cournier's association with the Ku Klux Klan, why I don't want you there with me yet. There's likely to be trouble. The first thing I have to do is keep the Atburys from running away. Also, I want to talk to some of the other black owners on Grandfather's acreage, and perhaps work out an arrangement whereby I pay them to work for me and to cultivate the land, but pool our crops together for a good market."

"I understand. And I'll come whenever you want me. And I'll miss you dreadfully."

"I'll miss you more than I can tell you, Laure. I know I should be with you when your child is born, yet I think it's wisest to clear up all the difficulties so that when I do send for you, we can begin our new life together happily."

Laure's eyes were brimming with tears as he took her into his arms.

Luke stood at the bow of the steamer that took Marius, Clementine, and himself to Mobile, talking with the captain. But his mind was on the towering bluff that flanked the red-brick chateau, and on the grave of his beloved grandfather, whom he himself had buried in what now seemed another life.

As he stared at the churning water receding from the paddlewheel, he thought how well his grandfather had known how to confront the phantoms of injustice, bigotry, and hatred. In giving, in sharing, there was always the gift of love, a love that created a universal brotherhood that was in itself the only sure, lasting anodyne to enmity and hatred.

In Mobile they waited a day for the steamboat *Alabama Belle* to take them to the old dock in front of Windhaven. Luke was delighted to find that the old captain, Horace Tenby, had spent thirty years on the river and remembered the thriving, bustling days when Windhaven Plantation was in its glory.

"'Deed I remember that fancy red castle, Mr. Bouchard," the white-haired captain said as they stood together on the deck and watched the great Bay of Mobile dwindle behind them. "Many's the time we put into that dock to bring letters and supplies from Mobile, and when we came back from Montgomery, stopped to pick up bales of cotton—neatest, prime-quality cotton ever shipped on the *Alabama Belle*, I can tell you that, sir. And I can remember that fine woman Miz Sybella, and you too, sir. You haven't changed that much. Still straight as a ramrod, and you've got a young look to your face."

Luke found it hard to hide the well of emotion that surged within him at this link with the past, this link that brought him, as the steamboat churned its way upriver, ever closer to that red-brick chateau and all the memories it contained.

"It doesn't seem to have changed much—the scenery, I mean, Captain Tenby." He sighed. "In the old days, when my grandfather rode on a pack-horse from Alexander McGillivray's trading post to what they called Econchate—Red Ground—he always took the trail along the river. It was a guiding line as good as any compass for him."

"I'd agree that very little has changed since those old days. Of course, you don't see pack-horses anymore, but then, they didn't have steamboats like this, either."

"Tell me, Captain Tenby, when you lay over in Montgomery and Mobile, what kind of talk do you hear about Reconstruction?"

527

The stocky little steamboat captain shook his head. "It's not popular, but you know that without my telling you, Mr. Bouchard. A lot of decent people around here are worried because of this act they passed which won't let a Southerner who held office before the war serve the people again. They say that too many carpetbaggers are coming down, helped by the scalawags—that's the new term around here for folks who lived here all their lives and won't toady up to the Union."

"Captain, have you heard anything about an organization called the Ku Klux Klan?"

Captain Horace Tenby made a wry face and shrugged. "What I've heard I'd rather forget. It's a nasty thing. I can understand how a Southerner would be mighty unhappy to find a Northerner coming down here and taking everything away from him. But I don't hold with taking folks out and whipping them and tarring and feathering them and worse. Least of all niggers, because they didn't commit any crime when old Abe Lincoln set them free. It's a mess, and no two ways about it."

"Well, Captain Tenby," Luke said, trying to strike a more optimistic note, "if all goes well, your steamboat will be making regular stops at my dock to pick up cargoes for Mobile and New Orleans. But it won't be all cotton. I'm going to do some experimenting with new agricultural methods."

"I wish you luck, Mr. Bouchard. But you know, sir, it's going to be hard to get workers. Lots of these niggers—I don't mean any harm by that word, it's just that I'm used to thinking of them that way—now that they're free, don't want to work at all and figure the government ought to support them. As for white workers, well, the old-fashioned Southern gentleman wouldn't soil his hands with a hoe."

As the two men fell silent and Luke watched the scenery, it seemed to him that he could almost see his grandfather riding along on a packhorse near the river. And for a timeless moment he felt as though everything had suddenly reversed itself and he was just now returning with old Lucien after delivering their bales of cotton to the wharf in Mobile.

"Mr. Bouchard, I's sho happy to see you 'n find out that you takin' over from poor Mr. Brunton," Phineas Atbury exclaimed, wringing Luke's hand, tears welling up in his eyes. He wore a tattered shirt, blue denim trousers, and a pair of worn slippers, and supported himself with a cane, while Hannah stood beside him, an arm around his waist to support him.

"Please sit down, both of you. I'm terribly sorry to find you like this, Mr. Atbury. I received your letter, Mrs. Atbury, and I came here as soon as I could." Luke looked around nostalgically at what had once been the huge parlor of the old red-brick chateau; the walls showed faded marks left by the smoke, and there was only a dilapidated old couch and two wicker chairs. Yet, at the first sight of the smoke-scorched portico, his heart had leaped within him with a joy so strong that it was all he could do to hide his tears.

"What we gonna do, Mr. Bouchard?" Hannah Atbury asked, her eyes clouded with anxiety, as she eased her husband down onto the couch and then slowly seated herself.

"You're going to stay here—that is, if you want to work for me."

"I prayed God somebody'd come down here and help us, Mr. Bouchard, and that's no lie," Hannah exclaimed passionately. "But how can we stay here?"

"By selling the chateau and the land to me. Then I'll have the right to hire you as free workers, and I'll pay you well for your services."

"That's mighty generous of you, Mr. Bouchard. They wanted us to run away and forget all about the tax bill."

"I'll pay that, of course, and I'll give you a price that will make you a handsome profit on what you had to spend to acquire this property."

"But Mr. Brunton advanced that to us, Mr. Bouchard," Phineas Atbury interposed.

"All the same, you deserve something for your labors all this time. And certainly in compensation for the terrible treatment you had from those animals. Perhaps the Klan was founded on a noble idea, but it's degenerated into the worst kind of vigilante terrorism. I'm going to do what I can to put an end to it. Now then, what about the other blacks who purchased the rest of the acreage of this plantation, Mr. Atbury?"

"Mr. Bouchard sir, most of 'em ran away when they saw the burning cross on the lawn here. And o' course they heard what happened to Hannah and me."

"Are there any blacks still living on the land?"

"Oh yes, sir, Moses Turner, 'n Dan Munroe, 'n

Hughie Mendicott. I reckon that's all that's left right now."

"I'd like you to talk to those men for me, offer them wages to work their land but tell them I want them to pool their crops with mine. I have plans for bringing this rich but overworked soil back to its potential. I may even have a few cattle, and certainly hogs and sows and horses. Maybe one day, when the North begins to forget its hatred of the South, I can ask your friends to sell me their land at a good price."

"That's a mighty fine thing you want to do, Mr. Bouchard," Hannah Atbury volunteered, wiping her eyes with the hem of her skirt. "Poor old Phineas, he's still got the misery from that terrible whuppin' they gave him. I'll go out and talk to the men for you, Mr. Bouchard. I'm sure they'll be more 'n willing."

"If they're interested, have them come here tonight and I'll explain what I have in mind. Now, are there any horses here?"

"Oh yes, Mr. Bouchard sir, we've got two, just for pulling the plow, though, not race horses, as you might say. But Moses has a fine roan mare and Dan has three horses."

"I'd like to ride into Lowndesboro now and get some supplies. You can use some food, I'm sure."

" 'Deed we can, Mr. Bouchard," Hannah said, shaking her head.

"Is there a buggy?"

"Oh yes, Moses has one. I'll go see him right now," Hannah volunteered eagerly.

Luke walked into the general store and up to the

531

counter where the stocky man presided. "Good afternoon," he said. "I've got a buggy outside, and I'd like some supplies."

"That's what I'm here for, mister. I don't recollect seeing you here in these parts before."

"I left three years ago. My name's Luke Bouchard."

"Hey now!" The man's eyes brightened and he leaned forward across the counter, his manner at once ingratiating and confidential. "Didn't your family used to have that big red house those Yankee-loving niggers took over?"

"That's true, mister—mister—" Luke purposely paused.

"Hurley Parmenter, at your service. If that doesn't beat all, Mr. Bouchard! Are you just visiting?"

"No, Mr. Parmenter. I intend to buy back that house and Mr. Atbury's fifty acres and settle in. That's why I came for supplies."

"Well, that really does beat all! Say now, would you mind coming in the back of the shop with me? I'd like to have some private words with you, Mr. Bouchard. It does these old eyes good to see a real Southern gentleman for a change instead of these black apes we've got saddled on us by those goddamn Yankees, and that's a fact, Mr. Bouchard!"

He lifted the plank that made the top of this section of the counter and obsequiously beckoned; Luke hesitated a moment, then followed him into the back room.

"Have a seat, sir. Can I give you a prime segar? And I've got some corn whiskey aged in the barrel—came all the way from Natchez."

"No, thank you, Mr. Parmenter. I'd like to get

my supplies as quickly as possible and get back to my work."

"Surely, sir, only I'd be mighty appreciative if you'd just spare me a few minutes. Sit yourself down right there. That rocker's comfortable—I brought it from my own house just to have creature comforts, as you might say." Hurley Parmenter beamed as he seated himself on a barrel of flour and squinted intently at the man before him. Luke remained standing, arms folded, face diffident. "So you're coming back to these parts for good, are you, Mr. Bouchard?"

"As I said, I'm going to buy the house and the fifty acres from Phineas and Hannah Atbury. I'll pay the tax bill that comes due this summer, of course."

"That's great news, sir! Every true-blue Southerner will rejoice to know that the rightful owner is coming back to where he belongs, driving away all these niggers."

"But I'm not driving away the blacks, Mr. Parmenter. I intend to keep them on as workers, at a good wage. And as to the other owners of the land that my grandfather once owned, I'm going to make them a proposition of working it for me, at wages, and then pooling all our crops for the best price."

"Well, Mr. Bouchard, you've been away from these parts for some time now. Now, you don't remember me, because I was just an apprentice in this store, as you might say. When the war started, old Grantham Thorgeson, who owned the store, went back to die with his kinfolk in Illinois. I always 'spected he was a Yankee sympathizer anyhow. So he sold me the store and I've been here ever since."

"I see."

"Now, mind you, I'd have given my blood for the Confederacy. Only they didn't want me. Said I was nearsighted and my heart was acting up some, so they told me to keep on doing what I was doing. Otherwise I'd have been out there with a gun in my hand, picking off those lousy blue-bellies."

"I'm sure you're a loyal Southerner, Mr. Parmenter," Luke replied sarcastically. "If that's all you want to talk to me about, I'd appreciate your getting my supplies together."

"No need to rush off, Mr. Bouchard!" Hurley Parmenter held up a pudgy hand and gave him a fawning smile. "Now, what I've been gettin' at is, now that you're back here where you belong, you ought to join our organization. You see, Mr. Bouchard, there's people in Congress want to keep the South in slavery, make us out worse than the niggers. Well, the Klan isn't going to take that lightly. No sirree. There's a group of us patriotic citizens who want to balance things out fair and proper, and that's the size of it."

"By dressing up in white sheets to pretend that you're the ghosts of valiant Confederate dead and scaring blacks out of their wits. And if that doesn't work, whipping them and perhaps even killing them," Luke interposed angrily.

Hurley Parmenter's face twisted in outrage. "Why, no, sir, that's not it at all. Whoever told you that is a liar, begging your pardon, Mr. Bouchard. We're decent citizens, mindful of the law but also mindful of our own rights. Why should those

Yankees send these black baboons down to strut all around and stare at our women and maybe rape them and think they're the lords of creation? The Yankees said slavery was wicked, but hell, it wasn't. You just look around you now—if you hire niggers to work for wages, you'll find them the most shiftless lot in creation, take my word for it." His voice changed to a wheedling, flattering tone: "But if you was to join the Klan, I could promise you an officer's role. You see, I'm Kleagle. You could be a Grand Dragon or something fancy. After all, you've got more education and breeding than I have, I'll give you that."

"I have no intention of joining an organization of terrorists and murderers. And now, Mr. Parmenter, I'd like my supplies, without any further discussion."

"Just as you say, Mr. Bouchard."

As Luke turned his back and went back into the store, Hurley Parmenter gave him a look of undisguised hatred.

CHAPTER THIRTY-EIGHT

That evening, Luke met in what had been his grandfather's study with the three remaining black owners of the land of Windhaven Plantation, and with Phineas Atbury and his wife as well. He had invited Moses Turner, Dan Munroe, and Hughie Mendicott for supper, and he himself had helped Hannah prepare the meal. The three black owners had been hesitant at first, but when Luke had stepped forward at Hannah Atbury's introduction and shaken the hand of each man and welcomed him as a neighbor, their wariness was replaced by an attitude of almost pathetic dependency.

Moses Turner was fifty, handicapped by arthritis, but tall and sturdy, and, as he himself expressed it, "I kin still do a good day's work." He lived with his ailing wife, Mary, in a little shack at the back of what had once been an unbroken stretch of six hundred acres in the flourishing days of Windhaven Plantation. Dan Munroe, forty-one and wiry, had brought along his thirty-four-year-old wife, Katie, and their two children, Tom, twelve, and Elsie, nine. Hughie Mendicott, forty-two, was a widower with two lanky, good-natured sons, Davie, fifteen, and Louis, thirteen.

"As Hannah has told you, I'm Luke Bouchard. My grandfather, Lucien Bouchard, and my father, Henry Bouchard, built this fine house. I was a foreman here when I was a young man, and neither my grandfather nor I ever believed in slavery.

"Now, the three of you, Moses, Dan, and Hughie, got this land legally after the war. I'll be honest with you—it's my hope to get all these six hundred acres back. But right now I'm proposing that we all work together. I'll pay you wages, so you'll be working for me as free men, of course. We'll plan our crops, we'll talk things over like good neighbors, and when the time comes to market what we've produced, I'll be responsible for it—if you'll trust me."

"Sounds right good to me, Mr. Luke sir," said Hughie Mendicott, and his elder boy nodded eager agreement. "One thing worries me lots, though, just like it does Dan 'n Moses here. What happens if the Ku Klux Klan comes around here again?"

"I know who the leader of the Klan is, the man who did those shameful things to Phineas and Hannah. I'm ready for him. You can trust me. I've brought along my black foreman, Marius Thornton, and his wife, Clementine. Marius knows a good deal about land, and I'll work with him and with you to make a go of it. I'm also going to pay the tax bills for all of you. When you get them, bring them to me and I'll take care of them. It's my hope that one day you'll sell the land to me, and when that time comes, you can be sure I'll give you a very fair price and a good profit. About the other land that your friends abandoned when they ran away—I'll pay the taxbills on those properties too, and I plan to hire some workers in town, white as well as black.

"Well, that's about all I wanted to say. I'm going to buy all the new farm machinery we'll need, and also some horses, cattle, and hogs. What you men can do is to start building fences to enclose the cattle, and make a good-size pigpen. Perhaps your wives will want a flock of chickens—we could produce eggs and sell them, and also have enough for yourselves and your children and plenty of chicken to eat."

When the three men and their children had left, Luke turned to Phineas and Hannah. "I'd like you both to come to Montgomery with me tomorrow, if you will. I'm going to open a bank account for you, and, if you'll accept it, I'd like to give you five thousand dollars for this house and your fifty acres."

"Mr. Bouchard, sir," Hannah said with a gasp, "we didn't pay nuttin' like that fo' all this! No sir, that'd be cheatin'!"

"No. It's worth more, but I want to keep some of my money for improvements on the land and also for wages, or I'd offer you more. You're going to work for me, I hope. Will you stay, please?"

There were tears in Hannah Atbury's eyes as she took Luke's hand and kissed it. "God bless you, Mr.

Bouchard. God bless you and your family fo' what you done fo' us."

By the last week of July, Luke had hired ten white workers and ten freed blacks to work the fields of Windhaven Plantation. He had offered them one hundred dollars a month and stipulated that as soon as the harvest had been sold, each of them would receive a proportionate part of the profits, as an incentive. He purchased a pedigreed Hereford bull and a dozen heifers, and his workers had fenced in a hundred acres of verdant land for grazing. Nearby was a large pigpen, in which a dozen sows and three boars were quartered. Fifty acres had been plowed and planted with corn, and another fifty with beans, sweet yams, other vegetables, and fruit trees. The workers had erected temporary cabins, using logs and the sturdy red clay from the Alabama River—the same clay from which the bricks had been made to build the chateau.

Luke had sent to Chicago for one of Cyrus Hall McCormick's reaping machines, as well as the sturdiest plows that money could buy. And by now the chateau had been restored from the fire damage. New floor planing and walls were hewn from the trees that framed the plantation by six of the black workers, who had discovered that working for a Southern white man who worked side by side with them was heartening and rewarding. The *Alabama Belle* frequently dropped anchor at the dock to bring supplies, tools, and equipment.

At the beginning of August, Luke visited Governor Smith and explained his rehabilitation of land

539

and his methods for working it, as well as his incentive program for black and white workers alike, and Governor Smith declared, "As you know, Mr. Bouchard, I am being maligned in the newspapers as a Northern sympathizer, but if there were more men like you, with the vision to see ahead and to live in peace with their neighbors, I would not fear such unfounded criticism."

And, when he could spare a few moments from his work in the fields and in the chateau, Luke wrote to Sybella and Lucien Edmond in Texas, to Ben and Fleurette Wilson in Pittsburgh, to Charles and Laurette Douglas in Chicago, and to James and Arabella Hunter in Galveston, telling them of the joy he was experiencing as he saw the land of his birth grow more bountiful. To Laure he wrote impassioned letters avowing his love for her and little Lucien, telling her that his work was his substitute now for love and that their long separation would make their reunion a thousand times more rewarding. He also corresponded with Jason Barntry, advising him about new investments and contemplated loans, and urging him not to doubt his own sound judgment; he also requested that Jason visit Laure and Lucien and Mitzi and let him know how they were faring.

Marius Thornton had never been happier in his life. Luke had left to him the selection of the workers for the fields, relying on his judgment of character and his discipline as a skilled worker. It had been evident from the outset that his experience in working land when he had been a slave stood him in good stead in the restoration of Windhaven Plantation. He was also, Luke discovered, a fine trainer and judge of horses, and the remodeled stable now quartered a dozen mares, two stallions, and four geldings. Among these was Luke's own stallion, which he rode through the fields, just as his grandfather had done with his magnificent palomino so many years before.

Marius and Clementine had jumped over the broom in the traditional Negro wedding ceremony a week after they had arrived at Windhaven Plantation. The lovely young mulatto was pregnant now, and Marius's joy was great. He could be heard singing in the fields and laughing and telling jokes with the workers. Gradually, as the weeks went on, a bond of comradeship formed between the whites and the blacks who worked side by side. This bond was strengthened as they began to see the results of their labors and anticipated the profits that would accrue from their endeavors.

Thus far there had been no visit from the Ku Klux Klan. Luke had made several visits to Lowndesboro to buy supplies from the glowering storekeeper, without saying a word to him. For his part, Hurley Parmenter spoke only a grudging greeting and a sullen thank-you for Luke's patronage.

On Friday of the second week of August there was an early thunderstorm, which returned with greater fury in the late afternoon. When it was over, Marius hurried out to inspect the damage to the crops. He rode his horse to the end of the long fields and dismounted to talk to Ben Dolton, one of the white workers. He stood facing the middle-aged farmer, who had lost his own small farm during the war. Behind him was a copse of a dozen live oak trees, and suddenly Ben Dolton cried out, "Look out there, Marius, some men are hiding behind those trees—"

He had no chance to finish. Five men emerged, wearing the white robes of the Klan; four of them seized Marius and overpowered him, while the fifth brutally felled Ben Dolton by clubbing him over the head with a branch, then spat full into his face and hurried back to his comrades, who were binding and gagging Marius. Finally they dragged him into the dense foliage beyond the trees, and a few moments later the sound of horses' hooves was heard.

"Oh, Mr. Luke, they've done taken my man! They'll kill him sure!" Clementine cried. "Hughie was jist coming out of his cabin when he saw those men dressed in white come out of the woods and hit poor Mr. Ben with a stick and take my Marius off with them! Oh, what'll I do, Mr. Luke!" She burst into hysterical sobs, covering her face with shaking hands.

"Now, Clementine, try to be brave," Luke said gently. "I don't think they'll kill him. I think Hurley Parmenter wants to keep him as a hostage so he can deal with me. But if we don't hear from him in a few hours, we'll take our horses and go find the Klan. We'll get Marius back safe and sound, I give you my word."

Hannah Atbury came running in, breathless. "Mr. Luke, there's a little boy at the door with a letter for you. He said he was told to wait."

Luke tore open the envelope, unfolded the single smudged sheet of paper, and swiftly read it. "Just

542

as I thought," he declared. "It's from Parmenter. He says they've got Marius and they'll burn him unless I come to their Klavern tonight at midnight. I'm to go to the old Williamson plantation, where the slave cabins used to be."

Clementine burst into tears again, and Hannah hurried over and sat down beside her, trying to soothe her as best she could.

Luke took his watch out of his waistcoat pocket. "It's two hours till then. We'll have to ride down-river on horseback, and we'll have to start now to be on time."

"We, Mr. Luke?" Hannah looked up wonder-ingly.

"I'm going to their Klavern, Hannah. But I'm go-ing to take the men with me. I'll keep them about ten minutes behind me. They'll surround the place; that way, we can be sure of saving Marius. I'm not going to answer violence with violence, but I think that if my workers follow, armed for trouble, we can prevent what they plan to do. Maybe even teach them a lesson." He turned to Phineas Atbury. "Do you feel strong enough to go out to the cabins and tell all the workers to come here? Ask Dan to get the horses ready, and tell Hughie to bring all the rifles and distribute them to those who will go with me. I'll saddle my horse now."

Luke rode the stallion hard as he took the trail downriver, a trail he knew by heart. How many times he had gone there after first meeting gentle Lucy at the housewarming that had been given to celebrate the formal opening of the red-brick cha-teau to visitors and friends. As he neared the old

Williamson plantation he could see the glow of a fiery cross. Spurring the animal on, he came up to the old house, dismounted, tethered the horse, and strode toward the clearing in which there still stood some of the old log cabins where Edward Williamson's slaves had been quartered.

He uttered a cry of horror as he came into the clearing, for a heavy stake had been dug into the ground, and lashed to it was Marius Thornton, naked, the bloody welts of the lash on his chest and thighs and back and buttocks. On each side of the stake stood ten hooded figures, and Hurley Parmenter confronted him in front of the burning cross. Around Marius's feet were piled bushes and pieces of wood, and one of the robed figures, recognizing Luke, derisively lifted his flaming pine-tar torch as an intimation of the Klan's intent.

"I was beginning to figure you wouldn't get here, Mr. Bouchard," Hurley Parmenter said in an oily, triumphant voice. "So you finally got some sense. As I told you in my letter, we're gonna burn your nigger here unless you join up with us. Now, before you say anything, let's look at it the way a smart man like you ought to, Mr. Bouchard."

"I told you once before, Parmenter, I don't deal with terrorists and murderers. What will you gain by burning Marius Thornton?"

"There'll be one less nigger to rape our women, that's what," said one of the hooded men, and a chorus of approving shouts rose from the others.

"Be sensible, Parmenter," Luke argued. "If you kill Marius, you certainly can't expect me to be on your side. And I'll tell you something that you may not know. Armand Cournier is dead. He chal-

544

lenged me to a duel, and he tried to kill me before the word was given to turn. My second shot him down, in accordance with the dueling code. So, your backer is no longer around to give you money and direct you against decent, innocent people. I have the ear of Governor Smith—"

"That dirty Radical, that filthy scum!" Hurley Parmenter interrupted.

"Call him what you will, he's still the governor of this state. And if you continue your lawlessness, you can be sure that in good time the state as well as the federal authorities will stamp you out like the vermin you are."

"You know, Mr. Bouchard," Hurley Parmenter sneered, "me and the boys decided that you've forgotten your birthright. Here you are, a Southern aristocrat, talking down to your countrymen and neighbors like we were dirt. Our cause is noble—"

"A nobility born in hell, which no self-respecting man can stomach," Luke interrupted.

"That does it! You know what, Mr. Bouchard? We're going to truss you up and give you a taste of the whip—maybe it'll teach you to be a gentleman and know your place, just the way the niggers have to learn theirs. But first we'll burn your nigger, so you can see we mean business. Grab him, boys!"

Luke stepped back as two of the hooded men advanced toward him. Suddenly there was a rifle shot behind him, and Hurley Parmenter staggered, uttered a gurgling cry, and fell, a bullet through his lung.

"There's more where that came from!" Luke recognized Dan's voice. "We've got fifteen men here with rifles. Get out of here while you still can, or we'll give you what we gave that bastard!"

The white-hooded men broke from the clearing, rushed to their horses, mounted, and galloped off.

Luke walked to the stake, took out his clasp knife, and cut the cords. Cradling the unconscious naked body in his arms, he turned to face his men who had come out of the bushes with their rifles. "God bless you for standing by me," he said to them. "Let's get poor Marius home. They've whipped him cruelly. But I don't think we shall have to fear the Ku Klux Klan ever again."

CHAPTER THIRTY-NINE

December 18, 1868, was an unseasonably warm day in Alabama. The weather in this last month of the third year following the Civil War had its parallel in unexpected, mercurial political changes.

Last month, Ulysses S. Grant and Schulyer Colfax, on the Republican ticket, had been elected to the presidency and vice-presidency by an electoral vote of 214 to the 80 cast for Horatio Seymour and Francis P. Blair, Jr. Yet, despite that seemingly overwhelming victory, Grant's popular majority amounted to only 309,594; the South, remembering only too well Grant's bulldoglike victories on the battlefields, was almost unanimously Democratic.

It was nearly twilight, and the gently moving shadows touched the fields of Windhaven Plantation. A tall man, his blond hair streaked with gray, walked slowly through the fields toward the towering bluff. When he reached it, he searched for the once clearly visible path, now hidden by years of growth of grass and flowers. He closed his eyes a moment, as if trying to remember, and then, with assured step, ascended a path from the eastern slope.

When he reached the top, he saw what had once been a clearing in front of two massive hickory trees. The clearing was covered with plantain grass as high as a man's waist. He looked up at the sky, then he began to tear away the grass until he bared the rich red earth that had given the name Econchate to the land where once the mighty Creeks had ruled.

The years had had their way with the earth, and there was no sign of the two graves. Yet he knew where they were, and he knelt down and put his hands upon the place, and said aloud, "Grandfather, I keep my vow. Today is your birthday, and you sleep beside the beloved woman Dimarte through all eternity. Your spirit and hers hallow this place, and it is your spirit that has brought me back to pledge to you the reunion of the Bouchards, however distant some of them may be at this moment."

He bowed his head in prayer, clasping his hands, and above him there was the sound of an owl, gentle and faint, as if meant for his ears alone.

Again he pressed his palms to the earth, and he said, "Grandfather, what you dreamed of will come to pass again. This is my promise to you. Already white and black workers are upon the fields of Windhaven Plantation, in comradeship, without rancor or bigotry, as free men who work with joy at what they believe in—the earth, always responsive to considered efforts, productive for our needs, the very source of life itself. There is an escritoire in the study again, Grandfather, an exact replica of the one you had shipped from France. There is the sound of laughter and children's voices in the red-brick chateau again, for Marius's Clementine was just delivered of a fine, strong son. The children of the other workers in our fields, Grandfather, visit often and take supper with me, and I tell them stories, many of the ones you told me when I was a boy."

Again there came the sound of the owl above him, and now he rose and walked over to the place where Dimarte lay. There too he sank down upon his knees, touching the earth, his eyes filling with tears as he murmured, "Dimarte, blessed name of the beloved woman who gave my grandfather such great joy, such unwavering love in a strange new world, I pray that you are happy with him now as you once were so long ago. Know that my youngest son is named after him whom you and I so deeply loved, and that just last week my Laure gave me another son, whom she named Paul, after the son Sybella lost at Shiloh."

He bent to kiss the earth, then rose and moved to one side, again clasping his hands in prayer and bowing his head. When he had finished his prayers, he said softly, "You both still live for me, and you always will, through the children of the Bouchards. There are new names to mix with ours, and yet they bring honor, dignity, and courage to enhance our name as they do our very blood. Sweet Fleurette has had her wish and been delivered of a little girl, whom she named Sybella, after her wonderful, ageless mother. Laurette, the child born to my half-brother, who could not understand the warmth, compassion, and love that held all of us Bouchards together in the face of adversities, has had another boy, Howard, to go with her twins. And my own son has made me a grandfather for the third time, for Maxine Bouchard gave Lucien Edmond a daughter, Edwina, two months ago. Beloved woman, may your spirit touch these newly born children and imbue them with your gentle wisdom and your love for life and your sweet compassion."

He rose and turned to stare down at the surging river far below. Its murmur rose faintly to him, and there was a sudden breeze, a rustling that could have been the ghosts of the Creeks as they made their way through the ancient trails to reach their campfires by nightfall.

Then he turned back to face the stretch of ground that he had bared so that he might revere it. And he spoke again, in a low, eloquent voice that often trembled with emotion: "Grandfather, you who were blood brother to Tunkamara and then to valiant Nanakota, I rejoice unto God that you taught me so well and so unforgettably how all men can be brothers. In proof of this, I give you now the talisman of a mighty Comanche chief, Sangrodo, who repaid kindness with kindness, who helped save the Bouchards in the wilds of Texas because the Bouchards had saved his son. It is you who are worthiest of all of us to cherish this talisman, which speaks of the spirit of an unconquered, noble people. Alas, their days are numbered, as were those of the Creeks who loved you and saw your heart and mind and soul not as those of a white-eyes, but in their own honorable mold."

He took from his neck the rawhide thong and laid it beside him, and then with both hands he scooped up the red earth until the hole was large enough to hide this precious talisman. He pressed it down, covered it, and smoothed the earth with his hands until there was no sign of what he had done. Then once again he bowed his head in prayer, clasping his hands, his lips moving silently.

When at last he had finished, he rose and moved slowly away from the hallowed ground of the beloved dead. And then he said aloud, "Grandfather, Dimarte, whose spirits are with the earth and the air and the sky, may you have the God-given power to watch over the Bouchards in those distant places so far from Windhaven Plantation. Over the ranch in Carrizo Springs where my son and his courageous wife and my daughter and her heroic young Mexican husband work together to raise cattle that will feed thousands of families throughout our growing nation. Over Dr. Ben Wilson and Fleurette in Pittsburgh, where he now heads a hospital whose clinic gives aid to the poor and the needy who cannot afford to pay a doctor to cure their ills. Over Charles Douglas and Laurette, in far-away Chicago, where this imaginative and honest newcomer to the Bouchard clan dreams of building stores in many cities where people can buy the necessities and luxuries they need at prices they can afford."

He paused for a moment of silent prayer. "All of

this was your doing, Grandfather," he murmured, "for you came from France to a wilderness where you found your beloved woman, who taught you that love is eternal and defies even death. Hear my pledge that all of us will live to give of ourselves to those who rely upon us. Unstintingly, as you did, thinking not of material reward but being rewarded in the pleasure of being useful and productive. And just as Windhaven Plantation will be restored by me as you yourself would have planned it had you been alive, Grandfather, so I promise you also that the others of this dynasty that you began shall, not long from now, visit here and commune with you and your beloved woman. It is your birthday, Grandfather, a day that will be written in my heart until I draw my last breath. And when my wife, Laure, comes here next month, to mark the beginning of a new year for all of us, I shall bring her here and tell her how it all began and why I was drawn back. God bless you and Dimarte. Look down upon us and never let us forget how dear you are to all of us."

He bowed his head, then went back down the path. A last time, he heard the gentle call of the owl, and then there was a stillness, not even the rustling of the breeze. It was as if all time, all nature, stood in reverence before the graves of those who had come from two different worlds to meet and to love and to find immortality in their descendants.

The ultimate novel of
life and death.

Coming in January, 1979
from
Pinnacle Books